THE
MOMENT
OF TRUTH

THE MOM OF

ENT
TRUTH

a novel

Damian McNicholl

PEGASUS BOOKS
NEW YORK LONDON

To my siblings
Deirdre, Seamus, Siobhán, and Dermot and cousin Adrian Kealey—my
first storytelling audience when we were all supposedly fast asleep in bed.

∾

THE MOMENT OF TRUTH

Pegasus Books Ltd
148 West 37th Street, 13th Floor
New York, NY 10018

First Pegasus Books hardcover edition June 2017

Interior design by Sabrina Plomitallo-González, Pegasus Books

ISBN: 978-1-68177-426-8

10 9 8 7 6 5 4 3 2 1

Printed in the United States of America
Distributed by W. W. Norton & Company, Inc.

1

MEN AND WOMEN IN THE ARENA'S SUNNY SECTION FELL silent as I walked across the sand until a man shouted, *"¡Fuera, Espontáneo!,"* which triggered a chorus of hoarse jeers and curses. The thrumming inside my chest quickened and I broke out in a cold sweat. I peered over my shoulder to where I knew my friend Sally was seated in the first row, behind the narrow passageway packed with managers, journalists, and fighters and their teams, but I couldn't see her. The tall Mexican man who'd asked us earlier where we came from in Texas was blocking my view.

Turning back to the center of the ring, I unfolded the scarlet blanket as I shuffled toward the bull. From horn-tip to tail, he was three-quarters the length of a new 1950 Cadillac. His muscles rolled like waves along his body as he trotted toward the center of the ring, crossing two concentric circles painted on the sand, and then stopped abruptly. This was no common beef heifer from the Los Pinos stock-yard in Mexico, where I practiced cape work whenever the male students in my Rowansville school's aficionado club allowed me. This big ol' bull commanded respect and my arms wouldn't stop trembling.

A lanky banderillero in an orange silk suit with ornate black embroidery screamed at me to leave the ring. Another young man, about three inches taller than my five-five frame, stood with his long arms akimbo in front of a shield made of wooden planks, positioned before the entrance to the *callejón,* a defense to protect performers from the bull's wrath and horns. The bolero jacket of his royal blue suit was trimmed in sequins and the flowers were richly embroidered with the golden threads only matadors were allowed to wear. A constable dressed in the traditional black velvet Philip IV suit dismounted from his horse and started toward me. If I didn't act, my illegal leap into the ring would all be in vain.

"Hey, *toro, toro*," I hollered as I zigzagged, shaking my head toward the bull. It was no use fixin' to call out "Hey, bull" to a Mexican-bred animal.

My cap started to fall off, but I didn't dare risk raising my arms to stop it. A collective gasp rose from the crowd as my bun unfurled from beneath it and dark red hair tumbled down my back. Women craned their necks, some clamping hands over their mouths. The constable stopped, his bulging eyes moving from me to the bull, now pawing the sand. Even the slender matador gaped.

My plaid cotton shirt was so damp it felt like a garbage sack against my back. Holding out my shaking arms, I advanced, swaying my makeshift muleta back and forth. "*Toro, bueno toro.*" A sway to the left. Not too fast, not too slow. "Hey, *toro.*" A sway to the right.

The bull regarded me like he was a king; I fell more in love.

I'd loved fighting bulls since seeing a beautiful white-and-black spotted one with gleaming horns trot into a bullring in Mexico when I was a girl. His sleek muscles had held me spellbound—the way he moved so daintily on tiny hooves, as if he were dancing across the sand, his handsome head regally swinging back and forth as he surveyed the crowd. Our eyes had locked for a moment, but it had seemed like forever. My father always said that part was impossible, that I was seated too high up in the arena for him to see us, that bulls' eyes weren't positioned in their heads like ours.

But Daddy was wrong. An electric charge from the bull had smashed into my body, upending every cell and making the blood in my brain churn. I knew in that instant that I wanted to be a bullfighter. I just didn't know how.

The crowd recovered from its shock that I was a woman. Whistles and *olés* showered down, the cries of excitement so enthusiastic you'd have thought I was Doris Day, not just some Texan art student who'd crossed the Mexican border and made the four-hour journey to Garza that morning.

All the books and magazines about bullfighting techniques I'd read said timing the cape's movement to gear down the bull's speed was as important as keeping one's feet perfectly still and not giving ground— only cowards gave ground in the bullring. Both steps were necessary to make beautiful art.

My belly somersaulted faster than a long-tailed cat's in a room full of rocking chairs. I offered the bull my profile, planting both feet together and holding out the blanket. My leg muscles trembled more violently. Would he take the lure like a fish took bait, as one of the books said, and roar past me if I did every move correctly? Or was my belly right to want to flee? Was I about to die just short of my twentieth birthday?

This bull, as tall as I was when his head was fully raised, could kill me with the teeniest swipe of his broad head. He seemed too much for any woman, never mind one as small as me. What arrogance had possessed me to think I could tame such a huge animal?

I held the blanket away from my body and the muscled beauty launched at me like a cannonball. The ground trembled, the bull's hooves drumming up the powdery sand. When his slick black nose came within two feet of my body, I moved the cape forward and slowly twisted my upper body to the right. An acrid smell crammed my nostrils. His hair was wiry and shellacked with sweat, the rumbling breaths as loud as a train. He crowded by, the lethal tip of his ivory horn fifteen inches from my breast. There was a whining sound, not unlike that of a passing bullet. The books were right; he'd followed my lure.

After hurtling four yards ahead, he turned, swifter than a racehorse, his sleek hindquarters and butt skidding to catch up with the rest of him. The ring constable and banderillero hollered at me, demanding I move back slowly from the bull. It felt like my mind was split in two, half of me wanting to obey them and the other half hungry for the next charge. Turning a half circle, I offered the blanket again and planted my feet like real matadors do. As he approached, I realized I'd miscalculated the line of his charge, but I was not going to step back and cede the ground I'd won from him. I pulled back my chest as I swung the blanket out from my body to correct the error, then closed my eyes momentarily and felt the outer edge of his horn press against my breast as he hurtled by. People shrieked. The bull's charge continued for four feet and then his head and massive chest turned sharply, the rest of him coming around in their wake.

Before I could reposition the lure, he charged again. I still couldn't believe an animal so big could run so fast. His horn pierced the lower half of the blanket and I was dragged along like an uprooted flagpole. I tugged, trying to tear the blanket off the horn. With a single jerk of his head, he ripped the blanket from my grip and my face smashed into his muscular sides like a rag doll against a wall before I fell to the sand. The thunder roared in my ears and I saw his hoof rise and pass within a hairbreadth of my nose. A hollow groan passed through the crowd.

"Get the hell up, Kathleen," Sally shouted.

Spitting out sand, I lifted my head and saw the wooden barrier fence ten feet in front of me. I looked to my left and saw the bull standing fifteen feet from the center of the ring, shaking off the last of the shredded blanket and focusing his attention on me again. He charged for the kill, his massive neck lowering and the horns turning to glinting, ivory-colored swords as he drew closer. Every cell in my body froze in helpless anticipation. A wall of bright magenta flashed before my eyes and then disappeared, and I watched the banderillero who'd hollered at me earlier continue to distract the bull with his cape. The bull's body twisted and moved away as he followed the magenta swirls. I got up quickly.

"*¡Mujer tonta, fuera de aquí!*" the banderillero roared, calling me a stupid woman and ordering me again to leave the ring.

"The constables are coming for ya," Sally hollered, waving at me frantically with both hands as she ran toward the exit.

A grain of sand in my left eye made it sting and water. Adjusting my path to get as close to the exit at one end of the *callejón*, I ran over to the fence, sprang up on the foot rail, and vaulted over. A splinter stabbed the meat of my palm, right below the end of my thumb, but I felt no pain. Once inside the *callejón*, I sprinted toward the exit, startling a ring servant in a dusty orange shirt and blue pants, as I jumped over two bulging canvas bags.

"Stop!" The well-dressed Mexican man who'd been standing in front of Sally after I jumped into the bullring strode along the passageway toward me, one hand pressing down on the top of his Cordoban hat to keep it in place.

I leaped into a wide tunnel that stank of horseshit, tobacco, and stale urine and weaved through pockets of men on their way to the bullring. A man behind me called out, "*Oye, gringa*," and demanded I surrender. Glancing over my shoulder, I saw that one of the constables had joined the tall Mexican man chasing after me.

The passage opened into the sun-drenched *patio de caballos*, where earlier I'd watched the picadors fastening the *petos*, heavy mattresslike bibs, onto their horses to stop the bull's horns from penetrating their sides during the fights. I ran across the yard and was almost at the exit gate when someone grabbed the back of my shirt collar. I couldn't let things end this way. Just like the chickens I'd caught with both hands for fun as a child in my father's hen coop, I allowed my body to relax and soften. When the constable let go of my collar in order to seize my upper arm, I rammed my elbow into the side of his rib cage and fled out the exit gate, where I found Sally pacing back and forth.

We sprinted across the cobblestoned quadrangle and merged with the street vendors and strolling pedestrians. After passing two side streets, we turned into a narrower one three blocks from the bullring and stopped running.

"We didn't think this part through," she said, inhaling deeply. "Getting arrested in Mexico. Imagine?"

"How do you think I did back there?" I took a deep breath. "Tell me the truth. I won't be upset."

Sally looked toward the main street. "If we'd been arrested, we'd have no one—"

"Wasn't my bull beautiful?"

"*Your* bull?"

"He did everything the book said he'd do. It was so—"

"We nearly got arrested, Kathleen!"

"You can't believe the rush." I took her hands in mine. "It was like nothing I've ever felt in my life." I glanced up at the sky as I tried to find the right words to describe my feelings in the bullring. "It was like making magic. I was a magician and the blanket was my wand." I laughed until another thought cut in and made me frown. "How did my mistake look to you?"

"Like you were going to be killed." She grimaced. "I got off my seat so quickly when it happened, I nearly fainted. If the man beside me hadn't reached out and grabbed my arm, I'd have fallen like a bunch of rocks at his feet."

"I think he's part of the ring management. He shouted at me to stop running and then chased after me."

"His eyes about popped out of his head when your cap came off," said Sally. "He told me he'd seen lots of people jump into the ring, but never a woman."

"I made sure not to give ground to the bull."

"Yeah, he said that, too. All I saw was you lying on the sand and the bull's hooves."

I shuddered.

"You need to change fast," she said.

"Over there's good," I said, pointing out a narrow passageway between two houses.

I took the straw shopping bag she'd brought and darted into the passageway, its cobblestones green with lichen and slippery from lack of sun. I moved deeper inside. While Sally kept watch, I peeled off the sweaty shirt and pair of loose men's jeans I always wore when painting in art class and put on a loose cotton dress and a pair of low-heeled shoes. After I came out, Sally helped me put on a cheap black wig.

No sirens blared on the main street. But just to be sure it was safe, we walked for fifteen minutes, the delicious aromas of fried plantains and roast pork drifting from a house making me hungry. A large pecan tree lay just ahead and we sat under its shade for a bit. Children played farther along the street, watched by mothers who chatted to their neighbors and leaned over narrow overhead balconies to hang laundry on sagging clotheslines. The tree trunk's rugged bark felt good against my back. The staccato lilt of Spanish charged the hot afternoon air.

"Now you've caped a fighting bull, I guess you're done with bull-fighting," Sally said, not interrupting her drawing of a stick figure in the silky street dust with her index finger.

I studied my friend's oval face, her lively eyes and her smooth, tanned skin, which was so different from mine. My skin just reddened in the sun. Not that it was important, but Sally had always said I was pretty, too. I guess it was a different kind of prettiness than hers, me with my Anglo-Irish roots, freckled apple cheeks that make my chin line more defined, and light-colored eyes. I had a decent figure, though my curves weren't hourglass like hers. A New York modeling agency had signed Sally to their stable—that's what the scout called it—and she was set to leave for up north in two months' time. They'd promised her bookings galore, plus she'd make a ton of money and meet movie stars. Her mother wasn't sold, thinking Yankees were different in their morals to us Texas folk.

Our friendship was due to Sally. She'd spotted me reading in the dormitory common room in my freshman year and introduced herself as someone who also liked her own company. But then she'd kept visiting me in my room or joining me in the canteen when I ate there. Being an only child, I'd learned to entertain myself and enjoy my own company. My only friend back then had been a Mexican woman who worked as a cook and house cleaner for my parents and from whom I had learned to speak Spanish.

Sally played the bull when I practiced on the lawn outside the college dormitory. Though I hadn't said I'd be done with bullfighting after that day, I had let her think it. The bulls were the reason I'd enrolled at Rowansville's Rowans Institute in the first place. The Los Pinos corridas on Sunday afternoons were a short tram ride across the Rio Grande and the U.S. border, and tickets to sit in the sunny section of the bullring were cheap. I hadn't come to study at Rowans because my boyfriend, Charles, was studying there, like I'd told Mama, or because a brilliant German artist who'd fled his country during the war would teach me design. Sure, I'd wanted to paint and design things, but the bulls were my passion and traveling to Garza to jump into the bullring had been a test, to see if I really did have the guts.

"I hope you'll still act as my bull until you leave," I said, rising and dusting off the seat of my dress, "because I'm not done by a long shot."

Photographs from a Los Pinos newspaper were taped up on a wall in the room where the Rowansville bullfight aficionado club met monthly. One of them depicted me passing the bull at Garza the previous weekend, and another was of me pole-axed on the sand after I'd lost hold of the blanket. A third one showed my hair cascading down my back as I stared at the bull. The headline, in the News Gothic font whose capital A and N I'd recently mastered painting in commercial art class, inquired as to the name and whereabouts of the mysterious American woman who'd shown no fear in the bullring.

Sally's boyfriend, Jack, looked at me bug-eyed. I was just as astonished. I hadn't thought anyone would take photos of me in the ring, never mind that a reporter from Los Pinos would write about an *espontáneo* jumping into the Garza ring. Hoping to attract patrons or a matador who might help them, young men often jumped into the ring, but they never got newspaper coverage unless they were gored. The fact that I was a woman had apparently attracted the reporter's attention.

Two men and their women walked up the room to me. I'd made up my face—blue eye shadow, a little blush, and pink lipstick—and one fella smiled at me goofily, as if I were Marilyn Monroe and had just stopped by for a quick cocktail. One of the women, curvaceous in black linen capri pants and a snug blouse, regarded me like I was bad business.

"How come you never said you were fixin' to go into the ring at our last meeting?" the smiling fella's friend asked.

I would never have mentioned my plan to them. The aficionado club didn't allow women as official members and I always had to beg them to let me try caping a heifer at the stockyards whenever they got permission from the owner to practice on the cattle. The club was comprised of businessmen and students, including Sally's boyfriend. Many were accompanied by their smartly dressed wives or girlfriends, who I'd figured pretty quickly were just adornments, like the colorful ribbons on the fighting bulls' shoulders signifying which breeding ranches they came from. The men devoured *La Lidia* and other bullfight magazines, attended the corridas on Sunday afternoons in Los

Pinos, and loved meeting to drink and argue over the strengths and weaknesses of the Mexican breeding ranches and their favorite matadors. I'd first visited the club eight months ago with Jack and Sally, who'd told me soon after we'd become good friends that her boyfriend loved bullfighting, and I'd continued tagging along because the club organized interesting demonstrations on the art, as well as talks by ex-matadors and managers.

Excusing ourselves after a few minutes, Sally, Jack, and I walked deeper into the room, a twenty-by-thirty-foot windowless space lined with posters advertising past bullfights throughout Mexico. Blue tobacco smoke fogged the heavy air. The club president, a bald man who was the first divorced man I'd ever met and who always wore a traditional Mexican *charro* suit, approached as Jack was ordering drinks.

"You're Kathleen Boyd, ain't ya?" he said, in a thick drawl. His dark eyes flicked to the photographs on the wall as he offered his right hand, obliging me to slip the handles of my purse up my forearm before shaking it. "You sure was real lucky, missy. That's dangerous business for a woman."

"It's just as dangerous for men."

Sally laughed.

After a pause, the club president said, "Was ya hoping one o' them matador folks would see ya in action and sign y'up?"

His question made me think of the time my parents had seen me in action. After Daddy had taken Mama and me to a bullfight in Mexico City during a vacation with his boss, when I was just a bitty girl, my parents, who rarely walked together around their property, had come upon me out in the fields, practicing on a calf with a towel, and Mama asked what the heck I was doing. I'd been practicing on my yellow Labrador in the barn since I'd returned home from vacation, but Grouse had gotten stiff and too deaf to follow my directions, so I'd decided to work with something closer to the real thing.

"I'm bullfighting," I'd said to Mama.

She'd hated the fight in Mexico, which was why I'd always practiced on my dog out of her sight, and she was horrified to see me working the calf. Mama thought I'd forgotten all about the Mexico City bullring. That was impossible. The show had dazzled me: the slender matadors in their pigtails and blazing suits of lights; the fierce, muscular bulls winding skillfully around the flared magenta capes; the constables in their black hats atop snow-white horses; the bells tinkling on the mules and the roar and applause of the audience.

The club president's eyes widened when I didn't answer his question. "Pity ya fell on your purdy little self and burned your butt on the sand."

I shrugged.

"Ain't no womenfolk in that there game," he added.

Someone tapped a microphone on the dais at the front of the clubroom and announced that the evening's guest was ready to begin.

"Kathleen, what the hell's going on?"

An electric jolt whipped through my body. Sally's mouth slackened. I turned around to see my boyfriend standing by the door, one of the newspaper photographs half-crumpled in his fist.

2

THE PUNGENT AROMA OF BREWING COFFEE AND MELTED cheese cut through an invisible fog of women's flowery perfumes. Bursts of laughter accented the hum of conversation at the tables occupied by students and faculty staff. A male student I recognized from art history class left the serving hatch with a chocolate milkshake and toasted triple-decker sandwich, a new item on the department's café menu that cost thirty-five cents.

"I still don't get why you didn't tell me you were planning to do this before I left for New Orleans," Charles said.

The previous evening he'd had such a big burr in his saddle about seeing my photographs that he'd refused to listen to my explanation and left the aficionado club. We hadn't seen each other for a week, as he'd been out of town; and although Charles never came to the club, he'd been so keen to see me on his return, he'd turned up.

He sat across from me now, his hands clutched around a mug of tepid coffee. Thirty years old, Charles was six-one in his socks and had an oval face with a small mouth and a strong nose that bent to the left, the result of a bad tackle on the football field in high school. His hair was his best feature. It was as wavy and pitch-black as I remembered my father's being. My boyfriend used a lot of hair oil and I loved running my fingers through the cresting waves and the clean, masculine smell of it. The aroma took me back to my childhood, to those times when Daddy finished showering after a day's work as a driller in the oilfields and I'd comb his oiled hair while he sat with Mama on the sofa and listened to the radio.

Mama met Charles and his parents at a cancer charity event. His family was wealthy and, as Charles and Mama had hit it off, she'd arranged for him to meet me. She used the excuse that he'd gone to my old high school, though our attendance hadn't overlapped.

"Is that why you didn't come to New Orleans with me?" Charles asked.

"I had an assignment to finish."

"Pfft. You always hand your work in late."

Unable to meet his gaze, I started brushing cookie crumbs off the skirt of my dress, enjoying the crisp smoothness of the glazed cotton fabric beneath my finger pads.

"Why couldn't you have just told me?" he said. "That's what couples do—they talk."

"I tried to last night."

He shook his head.

"Anyway, I didn't know I was fixin' to do it."

"You and Sally took a bus for four hours to Garza. That takes planning." He reached for my hand. "'Fess up: you planned it all along."

"This all came up after you left for New Orleans. Honest."

"Hey, look at me, sweetie." When I did, his stern eyes pierced deep into mine. I felt their sting. "Did you hand your assignment in on time?"

I didn't answer.

"Just as I thought." He tsked. "Sally put you up to it, didn't she?"

He was suspicious of Sally. Charles said she was a real looker, but he didn't like her wanting to become a model. He was afraid she'd try to corrupt me. He believed "those kinds of women" were going to end up as frustrated old maids because they got big ideas in their heads and became too picky about choosing regular men to marry.

"She's got nothing to do with this." I laid my hand on his knee. "Can't you try to see this through my eyes? You know how hard I practice. I had to see what would happen when I faced a real, live fighting bull."

Charles squeezed his temples so hard his thumbnail turned white in its center. "I don't want bad things to happen to you."

"I know." I squeezed his knee gently.

"Didn't you think about how I'd feel if you'd gotten yourself injured? Heck, what if you'd gone and gotten killed?"

It felt like a pitcher of ice water had been thrown in my face. I *had* acted recklessly; I had deceived him. But he'd have tried to stop me. Charles had had his chance to experience life, to do everything he'd wanted to do when he was almost twenty. He'd joined the army a year after high school and been sent to England to help with the war. He'd loved the experience. And now he was about to graduate with an engineering degree, courtesy of the GI Bill, and spent his days interviewing for jobs in oil and gas exploration. I wanted the same opportunity to explore.

I took my hand off his knee. "I'm sorry."

His eyes softened and he smiled as he came over and put his arm around my shoulder. We'd been talking loudly and students at a nearby table watched us intently.

"Well, you've fought a bull in the ring and now you know what it feels like," Charles said. "Isn't that right?"

I nodded.

"So we'll forget this business ever happened. It's over and done."

I rose and started gathering my things.

The late October sun was fierce, the air hot as a clay oven. Everywhere I looked, the grass was scorched brown. We'd had no rain for weeks. Even a ring of Mexican fan palms in the middle of the yard looked stressed, the lower fronds limp and turning brown.

Holding both arms against the sides of her head, Sally bellowed as she charged in a straight line at my blanket. Instead of extending her arms full length, as she'd done during previous practice sessions, I'd gotten her to extend them out about a foot, approximately the length of the horns of the bull I'd encountered in the Garza ring. It helped me analyze and correct the mistake I'd made that Sunday. Unfortunately, it also resulted in the "horns" curving inward into a nearly closed circle, as Sally had to push back her shoulders severely in order to shorten the length of her arms.

"Holding my arms out this way ain't comfortable," Sally said.

"Okay, just two more charges, then," I said. "I've figured how I made the mistake in the ring and want to try something."

"*Two?*"

"Yeah."

"Why do you always need to be perfect, Kathleen?"

Mama always said I'd inherited that drive from my father. It used to frustrate her, how he hung his shirts and pants so orderly in their closet and lined up his shoes all in a straight row. He'd also required her to put his laundered underwear and socks in the dresser in a specific way, with the socks folded neatly in half. I didn't care about how I hung my clothes or folded my underwear, nor did I understand Mama's or Sally's frustration. It was just that when I enjoyed doing something, I needed to be perfect at it. It's why I'd always been at the top of my class in Spanish in high school and why I painted brilliant landscapes in fine art class at Rowans. By contrast, my soup cans in commercial art class were two dimensional and dull, because I hated that kind of art. This drive was why I wanted to make my passes with the blanket the very best I could.

A pigeon cooed near one of the dormitory entrances. Overhead, girls sat on the broad windowsills, their tanned legs swaying back and forth as they watched us, some of them filing and buffing their nails. Across the square, Betty Essop and two other girls danced to the "Tennessee Waltz," which was drifting from Betty's aquamarine-and-white transistor radio. A three-story dormitory building that housed two hundred women overlooked the courtyard and I was known for practicing there. My performances had become a welcome distraction from studying. Even our straitlaced housemother sometimes took time out to watch.

Just as Sally's fingers were about to touch the blanket, I moved it slowly forward until she'd passed my body, and then pirouetted swiftly so that the blanket flared and finally wrapped neatly around my entire body. The girls clapped. Mindy Bass even whistled, though this pass was the only one meriting such an enthusiastic response.

"My arms are hurting," said Sally, and she flopped down on the dead grass.

"Aw, just one more," I said. "Please."

From the southern entrance to the quadrangle, our housemother appeared. She walked toward me, accompanied by the tall Mexican man who'd chased me at the Garza bullring.

Sally sat up quick. "Uh-oh."

"This gentleman wants to talk to you, Kathleen," the housemother said.

The man tipped his hat. "That was a good *chicuelina* pass," he said, in perfect English. "But your friend is a very friendly bull, I think."

Sally and I exchanged glances.

"My name is Vincente Barros. I've been looking for you."

His face was wide and he stroked the ends of his waxed mustache, which stopped half an inch from the bottom of his chin. He looked to be about fifty.

I swallowed, the sound reverberating in my ears.

"You're the young woman who jumped into the bullring a month ago, aren't you?"

My body stiffened, even though I was in Texas now and there was nothing he could do to me.

"Do you have a moment to talk?" He peered around the square. "Perhaps we could sit over in the shade." He pointed to two white garden benches inside the circle of fan palms.

The housemother's eyes narrowed, but I nodded, indicating it would be okay. After we sat on the bench, Señor Barros placed his hat on his lap and looked at me.

"Do you prefer I speak to you in English or Spanish?"

"It makes no difference."

"Ah, you're like the bulls, eh?"

"What do you mean?"

"It makes no difference to them, either." When he smiled and opened his dark eyes wider, his shiny dark brows arched.

I laughed.

"What do you study here?"

"Commercial art."

"My youngest daughter is a junior at college in Dallas. Her mother's American, like you. She studies city planning." He smiled again. "My wife's not so happy with our daughter's choice. She thinks that's men's business." His eyes narrowed as if he expected me to protest. When I didn't, he continued amicably enough, "I own businesses in Los Pinos—three bars and a hotel—a hotel in Garza, and a profitable tequila distillery in Jalisco. I also follow the bulls. What you did in Garza that afternoon was very brave."

Because I was a woman, it was brave. If I'd been a man, he'd have wanted me arrested for interrupting the real performances by the matadors. Still, it was flattering to find out I'd impressed a Mexican.

"My daughter was with me and thought you very brave, too. You have talent."

"I only made two passes before I fell."

"I didn't say you're perfect. I said you've got talent—very raw, but it's even more important that you're brave." He looked me up and down. "How tall are you?"

"Five-five."

"The bull was large, yet you didn't give ground. And the way you kept your arms so straight and moved your wrists." He held out his hands to make the movements and emphasize his words. "Have you had instruction?"

A passing low cloud expunged the brilliant sunlight, darkening the orange watermarks that trailed like tears from the gutters down the building's cream-colored façade and threw the circle in which we sat into deep shadow. After explaining I'd taught myself, he inquired if I was interested in taking it further.

"I'm a woman and I'm an American."

His brow and nose wrinkled as he considered. "It's time to have a woman fighting on foot in the bullring," he said. "It would be a novel thing. Mexicans would love something new like this. And your being American would give lots of your countrymen a good reason to come to Los Pinos. When lots of Americans come to see the bulls, they spend lots of money—more money than Mexicans spend." His eyes opened very wide. "Do you know why?"

I shook my head.

"Because they earn more *dinero* than Mexicans." He rubbed his index finger and thumb together, then fished a crumpled packet of cigarettes out of the breast pocket of his linen jacket. "When Americans spend freely, everybody wins in Mexico. The bullring authorities don't understand this yet." He paused. "But they will."

"I don't know any bullfighters to ask if they'd teach me, Señor Barros."

"First, we decide if you're interested."

Although Mama and Charles's disappointed faces loomed in my mind, I nodded eagerly.

"Good. I'll become your patron. I have a few contacts in the bull-fighting business and have someone in mind to instruct you. When you're ready, you'll take part in corridas."

"What if the bullring authorities recognize me as the woman who jumped into the ring and want to arrest me?"

"I'm a well-known businessman. That won't be a problem." His cheeks dimpled. "I'll also put your likeness on the labels of my premium tequila, when the time comes. I'll pay you for that, as well. The pretty American torero—everyone will want to buy some and toast you as the conqueror of brave bulls."

I recalled how small I'd felt in the bullring when I'd faced the bull. For the first time, I'd doubted if a woman my size—if any woman—would have the strength to overcome such massive power. I pushed the thought away.

"We don't need to sign any papers," Señor Barros said. "I can tell you're a trustworthy young woman. But I should talk to your father."

"My daddy's dead. I can decide for myself."

"*Muy bueno.*" He smiled widely as his soft brown eyes regarded me. "Tell me, are you a dedicated student?"

I shifted in my seat. If I said I was, he could easily go to the Dean of Studies and discover I'd been on academic probation last year. It wasn't that I was dumb as a box of rocks. I just hated studying. I'd had to stick around Rowansville last summer to retake the History of Architecture and Theory of Color courses so I could advance to sophomore year. Staying at school had upset my mother much more than me. I'd taken the tram to Los Pinos every Sunday to attend the bullfights.

"I'm a dedicated student, Señor Barros, but exactly how is painting cereal boxes and understanding how the Romans built the roof of the Pantheon gonna help me fight the bulls?" I paused, but not so long as to let him come up with an inconvenient response. "They're different kinds of art. One's made on a page, the other's made in an open theater."

He looked at me without speaking for a long moment. From across the quadrangle, the housemother coughed to signal the meeting had gone on long enough. She was wolverine-mean, but protective of her students, always prying to make sure we ate properly and kept our rooms clean. She was constantly on patrol to ensure the brazen girls among us didn't sneak bourbon and men into the rooms after evening curfew.

When I rose, Señor Barros did, too, and offered his big paw of a hand for me to shake.

An older clientele, mostly businessmen and professionals in their thirties and forties, frequented the bar a block from the movie house. Charles and his engineering buddies preferred this dark-wooded room to the brighter ones near the Rowans Institute because the drinks weren't watered down and army reservists often came in. They'd exchange stories about the times they'd spent in Europe during the war.

We'd just seen *Sands of Iwo Jima,* but I'd actually preferred the B-movie about a gang of counterfeiters being chased by the Secret Service. Charles and his friends loved cowboy and war movies and the other men's girlfriends and I didn't mind John Wayne, but watching the same sort of movie all the time did get boring.

After his roommate, Jim, offered to buy Charles another whiskey highball and he declined, I knew we'd be leaving soon because Charles wanted to study. Like always, we'd first take a short drive to the abandoned stable north of the city for half an hour, then he'd drop me off at home. A tremor whipped through me as I reached for my purse, my mind starting to rehearse for the twentieth time how I should begin the conversation.

Outside, the oily smell of cooking French fries wafted from the open window of the bar's kitchen. We slipped our arms around each other's waists—or, more correctly, given the difference in our heights, Charles's slid across the middle of my back—as we strolled to his car. I kept our conversation focused on small talk during the short ride to the secluded spot. There were three cars already parked under the shade of a line of trees on one side of the dirt path that led to the stables, one in our usual spot.

"Would be swell if we could just go to our own place to relax," said Charles.

I froze midbreath. We'd been coming here to spend private time since the first month we'd started dating, since neither of us could entertain a member of the opposite sex at our places. But he'd never said anything like that before.

After rounding a bend, Charles parked the car under a tree and killed the engine. He pulled me gently toward him and I eased over to put my arms around his neck. We kissed. He pressed me to him and I felt his heart beating against my chest.

"They wrote yesterday to let me know I'm on the short list for that job," he said, sweeping my bangs off my forehead with his fingers. He'd been in Louisiana for a job interview with an oil company the same week I'd jumped into the Garza bullring.

"That's great, honey."

"No counting our chickens yet. Let's not jinx it."

He kissed me again, his lips turning soft as the chamois I'd used to wash my father's car as a girl.

"I need to tell you something, too," I said, stroking his baby-smooth cheek with one finger.

The springs creaked as he pushed back in the car seat.

"A man came to my dorm yesterday. He saw me in the Garza bullring and was impressed by how brave I was."

His face crinkled but he didn't speak.

"He asked, um—he asked if I was interested in . . . taking it further."

Charles's belly rippled as he laughed. "Is he Mexican?"

"Yeah."

"I guess he saw your photographs in the newspaper and is workin' a scam. Those guys are all the same. You're American an' he smells money."

"It's not a scam."

"It's crazy, is what it is."

I pulled my head back sharply "Why's it crazy?"

"We've talked this through, honey. Playing at bulls with Sally is one thing, but let's get real." He laughed. "You stick to your paintbrushes."

"I love the bulls."

"You're a woman; women don't do that."

I moved back to my part of the seat. "Who says we don't?"

"Little you and a huge bull. The guy's fixin' to start a circus." He laughed harder. "Come over here."

He sounded like my late father after I'd first told him I wanted to become a bullfighter.

Folding my arms, I stared ahead and said, "Take me home."

Charles drummed on the steering wheel for a long moment, then started the engine. We drove in silence. When we arrived at the dormitory, Betty Essop and a girl I didn't recognize were standing near the pink azalea bushes to the left of the entrance. They stopped talking and gawked.

"Now don't be sore, hon," Charles said, putting his middle finger under my chin and jiggling the skin. "I'll see you tomorrow."

I pushed his hand away. "Stop doing that. I'm not your cat."

He leaned over for a kiss, but I opened the door and climbed out. Though I wanted to, I didn't slam the car door in front of Betty. Charles didn't pull away until I'd reached her.

"Back from the stables, huh?" she said, winking at her friend. "Lucky you."

3

L EAVING LOS PINOS TO PERFORM IN CORRIDAS THROUGHOUT
Mexico during the season was something Fermin Guzmán
didn't enjoy, but the money was very good. He'd travel for
tedious hours on overcrowded buses over dirt roads and on packed
trains with passengers who stank of stale perspiration, some of them
transporting chickens, ducks, and even newborn piglets on their laps.
There were also frequent mechanical breakdowns to contend with,
and countless layovers at dusty stations.

Gone for a week or two at a stretch when the bullfights were in Tlaxcala or Aguascalientes, Fermin usually began missing the comforts of
home after the first week. He'd miss his wife Carmen's cooking, especially the delicious tortilla casserole with fried chorizo, and her mango
custard flan swimming in a lake of sweet golden caramel. He had a
sweet tooth, though he controlled it rigorously, never allowing himself
second helpings in order to keep his wiry five-nine frame in check. He'd
miss his children's high-pitched laughter as they flicked playing cards
at a target they'd selected, the leg of a coffee table or perhaps Fermin's foot. He'd also miss the cozy quiet after Carmen put ten-year-old
Emilio and seven-year-old Abril to bed, Fermin sitting in his favorite
armchair reading and sipping cold Victoria beer while his wife darned

socks or mended tears in the pants of his *traje de luces*, the embroidery adorning them now silver because he was no longer a matador.

His matador's suits moldered in a closet in one of the unused bedrooms, their flash and glitter extinguished by the darkness. No one admired them anymore but Fermin, whenever compulsion drove him to take out the blue or the white suit, lay it on top of the bed under the bright lights, and relive the glory of those times when his art had been admired in every major bullring in Mexico. Even two top Spanish matadors, whose arrogance when visiting the former colony knew no limits, had admired his prowess.

The emerald green suit of lights was also in the closet. It was the *traje* he'd worn on his last agonizing day as a matador. He despised it, but he couldn't summon the will to rid himself of it. His hungry hands sometimes sought it out. He'd lay it on the bed and watch it ignite under the lights. At first, it astonished Fermin that he could even bear to relive this ritual of intense mortification, but with the passing of time, he'd come to accept that shame, like pride, must also have an outlet.

El Cabrito's sword handler came over to the counter, sat beside Fermin, and nodded at the bartender, who brought over a bottle of tequila, glasses, salt, and a freshly sliced lime. The lime's acerbic scent pleased Fermin.

"Are you still angry at young Julio?" Patricio asked. He laid his hand cautiously on Fermin's shoulder.

Fifteen years older than Fermin, the sword handler had once been an aspiring matador but didn't have the talent. Realizing his limitations, he'd become a sword handler for a string of matadors. The father of twenty-one-year-old Julio Fernández—El Cabrito—had hired Patricio when his son had become an apprentice bullfighter.

It was now El Cabrito's second season as a full-fledged matador and his father, having known Fermin in his glory days, had hired him as a banderillero during the fights when Fermin wasn't contracted to other matadors.

"If it wasn't for the money, I'd . . ." Fermin didn't finish the complaint. He didn't have to. Patricio understood.

"These young fighters today," Patricio said, "they don't respect their elders. It isn't like when we were young. Why do you think the boy's nickname is El Cabrito?" He laughed and nudged Fermin amiably. "What do young goats do, eh? They butt heads."

"I warned him about the bull being too energetic and favoring its right side," Fermin said. "He needed us to put the second and third set of sticks in its hide to correct the defect." He poured another generous tequila. "The idiot wouldn't listen."

The matador had undermined Fermin in front of the entire team, requesting that the judge—the governor of the state, no less—allow him to move to the third act without consulting Fermin. El Cabrito had then ordered him and the other banderilleros to vacate the ring before they'd had the opportunity to complete their work. There'd been no reason to interrupt the natural order of the fight—the mounted picadors arriving in the first act to weaken the bull with their *varas*, followed by Fermin and the other banderilleros inserting the ribboned barbs in the bull's withers. This lowered the bull's head in preparation for the crowd-pleasing work by the matador with his cape, muleta, and sword in the final act.

"The lad's too quick-tempered for his own good," Patricio agreed.

Fermin jiggled his legs and his eyes flitted from Patricio's moon face to the scratched bar surface puddled with tequila. As if El Cabrito's demand to quit the ring hadn't been humiliating enough, he'd also fired Fermin in front of the other men, telling him his services would no longer be required after his contract ended the following Sunday. No longer able to perform as a matador, Fermin was a great banderillero. He consistently planted the barbed sticks into the bull's withers exactly where they needed to go, unlike other banderilleros whom El Cabrito occasionally hired when Fermin wasn't available.

Fermin poured another tequila and downed it, relishing the hellfire exploding inside his belly. "Next Sunday is Guadalajara," he said, after the flame cooled. "One more fight and then home."

"Guadalajara and *payday*," said Patricio. "Then home."

"I assume El Cabrito will pay me more for swallowing his insults during this corrida." Fermin winked at the sword handler and El Cabrito's confidential advisor, whose job, in addition to helping the young matador dress for the bullring and carrying El Cabrito's swords, was to pay the men's wages.

Patricio peered quickly over to El Cabrito, drinking with two pretty female admirers and a picador at a table near a door that led out to the courtyard, where the air was heady with the smell of Mexican orange. "It might be wise to accept Señor Barros's offer," he replied, and his right eyebrow arched rakishly. "Wanting to train a woman to fight? The man's got more money than sense. Might as well take it."

Fermin kept his face neutral and took out a packet of cigarettes. When Señor Barros had approached him through a mutual acquaintance to inquire if he'd assess whether the young American woman had talent, Fermin had thought it was a joke. He'd thought someone in the business was trying to make fun of him. After he'd realized the businessman was deadly serious, Fermin had rejected the idea as idiotic. *Loco.* An idea from someone with no respect for the art of bullfighting.

"You say the girl's American," said Patricio. "She won't last, but you'd have fun watching her hips when she swings the cape."

"I told you already, it's *loco*."

"That's so." Patricio laughed as he rose. "It's also easy money."

El Cabrito rose then and approached them. Dressed in gray slacks and a royal-blue shirt, the young matador wasn't the sequined god he was in the bullring. In fact, he looked downright ordinary, someone Fermin wouldn't give a second look to if they met on the street. El Cabrito embraced Patricio as if he was a long-lost friend. Red mist swept across Fermin's vision. The youngster shot Fermin an arrogant look as he led Patricio away, and, moments later, laughter erupted at

their table. Fermin wondered if Patricio was telling the young pea-
cock the joke Fermin had just made about getting paid more for being
insulted. He turned back to the bar, gripping his glass so hard it hurt.

A chair scraped loudly on the wood floor.

"Come and join us, Fermin," El Cabrito said.

Fermin turned again to look at him, the young man's face deeply
tanned except for a scar, a glint of a narrow diagonal stripe of pure
white skin, in the middle of his right eyebrow.

"Patricio says I was too hard on you," Julio said, extending his
hand. "I apologize for the things I said earlier. No hard feelings, eh?"

The air between them was so thick, Fermin could hardly breathe.
Tossing back the last of the tequila, he slammed the glass down on the
counter and walked out.

Fermin was not the first choice Kathleen's patron had had in mind to
mold her into a bullfighter. That person had declined because of her
sex. But then, so had Fermin, who'd been introduced to Señor Barros
by a colleague.

Thus, Señor Barros had been surprised when Fermin contacted him
two days later to say he'd reconsidered and would meet the young
woman. Señor Barros liked Fermin, who was compact and wiry with
a grave face and overly large ears. He thought his black eyes exuded
honesty, and the ex-matador's handshake was firm. The two had
also lived north of the border, albeit Fermin for much longer, as he'd
worked as a farmhand at a ranch outside Dallas for most of his youth.

The ex-matador's reputation was known to Señor Barros. He'd been
astonished to learn of Fermin's abrupt retirement from the bullring,
after eight successful years, to purchase a small bar. He'd eventually
sold it in order to return to the bullring as a banderillero. His injuries
hadn't been permanent and, like the rest of Mexico, Señor Barros had

expected Fermin to return to the ring, as all matadors who'd recovered from gorings did.

When Kathleen arrived with Señor Barros at Fermin's home, her small size astonished him. Barros hadn't mentioned how short she was and Fermin assumed it was the other, taller girl she'd brought along who wanted to be a bullfighter. At five-eight, she was the right size, the same as most male matadors. Kathleen was three inches shorter.

After Barros explained, Fermin ordered the friend to sit beneath his avocado tree, where she'd immediately picked one of the fruits and was now lobbing it from one hand to the other like she was the proprietor. Fermin wondered what it was about Americans that made them think themselves better and more knowledgeable than other people.

He sent Kathleen to stand with her back pressed against the weathered fence in his backyard and swing the cape. "One, two, three," he shouted, as she swung it rhythmically from side to side. He could tell by the way she held it that she had experience holding a cape, which surprised Fermin, because she told him she'd never had lessons. The girl gripped it like a professional, even if the actual movement was very raw. He could also tell she was tired.

"Keep swinging," he called out to Kathleen. "I didn't say you could stop."

"Why're corks sewn into it, Señor Guzmán?" she asked.

"Swing. Don't talk," he replied, but he admired her wily attempt to fool him into giving her a break by asking a question.

Woven from raw silk, the cape was heavy, with a magenta outer side, an inner side of bright yellow percale, and a stiff collar. Though tired, she didn't complain. There wasn't even the slightest hint of a breeze and she'd been practicing the same maneuver for fifteen minutes in the blazing sun, her face and the front of her dress wet with sweat.

"You grip the corks when executing different types of passes," he said. "That's what they're for."

"Thank you."

"How much longer to go?" the friend asked, holding the avocado up in her palm like she was about to offer it to him.

"Have you got somewhere to go?" Fermin asked.

"Kathleen's meeting her . . . she's meeting Charles at five and can't be late."

"Is he a boyfriend?" he asked.

The women exchanged glances.

"Bullfighters have no time for love affairs," Fermin said. "The bulls are very jealous."

Again, the pair glanced at one aother. "He's a friend of mine," said Kathleen.

"I think you're doing swell," said Sally. She looked over at Fermin and smiled broadly, exposing a set of perfect white teeth. "Don't you think so, sir?"

"She's doing good," he said, unable to stop himself from smiling back.

"I'm very glad to hear that," said Señor Barros, standing off to Fermin's right.

Next, Fermin ran in a zigzag across the yard. "Run back and forth like this, Kathleen."

"Do I still hold the cape?"

He extended his hand and she sprinted over and gave it to him. "Now run."

As before, he watched intently, splaying his hands on his narrow hips as she darted about like a hen chased by a frisky rooster. After a time, Fermin raised a hand in the air. "Okay, stop. Place your feet together." His sharp eyes slid down Kathleen's slender body to her feet. "*¡Mira!* You have large feet. What size?"

"Eight."

"They look okay to me," said Señor Barros.

"Hm. Okay, arch your back."

Kathleen leaned back.

"More," Fermin ordered. "Like a proper matador."

She arched back so far that he could hear the dull click of bones cracking.

"That's good. Now straighten up and stand on your toes." He approached and walked in a slow perfect circle around Kathleen as she obeyed. "Your hair's pretty, but it's too long. That's why your cap fell off."

"You saw me in the ring?" she asked, her expression shifting to alarm.

Fermin glanced at Señor Barros. "I heard."

"I'll have it shortened, señor," she said.

Fermin paused, and then asked, "Why do you want to fight bulls?"

"I've dreamed of it since I was a girl."

"I'm *not* interested in childish dreams. Why do you want to do it *now*?"

She lost her balance and stuck out her arms to regain it.

"Why?" he asked again.

"I *need* to do it, Señor Guzmán." She hung her head and stared at the ground. "There's nothing else I want to do."

"*Muy bien.*"

Fermin walked over to Señor Barros and the men conversed as if the women were no longer present.

4

DESPITE WORKING ON THE SOUP CAN PROJECT FOR THE past three months, I still wasn't happy with it. Neither was my teacher. The backdrop colors I'd painted on the twenty-by-thirty-inch wooden board didn't look perfect. My professor insisted that no matter how much I reduced the red value or intensified the blue of the background colors, it would never look right to the eye.

Sketching, painting, and sculpting without any pressure excited me. But working for a passing grade took the fun out of art. Since enrolling at the Rowans Institute, I'd come to understand that making commercial art had little to do with aesthetic and everything to do with budget. It wasn't the kind of true creativity where I could turn a lump of clay into Sally's head, like I'd done in my dormitory room two months ago. It had taken three nights to get her nose and eyes just right, admittedly at the cost of submitting a written assignment one week late, meaning deductions off my grade.

After class ended, I was strolling toward the Murray building, where I had an art history lecture, when a young man in scruffy jeans two sizes too big for his slender frame drew up alongside me.

"Howdy, Kathleen," he said. A copper bracelet with an etched Gemini motif on its widest part flashed as he extended his hand. "I'm

Tim Gunner and I edit *The Patrician*. We'd love to feature you in the next edition."

I had no idea the students publishing the college magazine knew my name. "Me?"

"It's not every year we get a maverick woman on campus." He smiled impishly.

My hair whisked away from my cheeks as I tossed back my head. I'd had it cut shoulder length a week ago and still wasn't used to its agile bounce. "What do you mean?"

"Your being a matador makes you a maverick, wouldn't you say?"

"I'm fixin' to be one, but I'm not there yet. Thanks, though."

I walked away and he followed, grabbing my arm when he caught up.

"Folks sure love reading about people on campus doing interesting stuff," he said, letting go of my arm. "We'd love to write an article and take photographs of you at the Los Pinos bullring." His rust-colored eyebrows lifted. "Heck, you'll be famous."

My scalp tingled like it did that afternoon in the Garza bullring. Shivers raced up and down my body.

"When would you want to do this?" I asked.

"Soon as I find you a suit of lights to wear."

"You want me to wear a *traje de luces*?"

"You're going to be a matador, aren't you? It needs to be authentic."

Though new to the real world of the bulls, I knew enough to know that only full-fledged matadors were allowed to wear the glittering suits of lights with gold threaded embroidery.

"The suit can't have gold embroidery."

"The photographs will be black and white. We can't afford color ones."

"No gold. That's the rule."

An influx of people coming to work in the oil fields during the war had boosted Dyson's population from eighteen hundred to nine thousand. As small towns go, it wasn't so different from any other in America. Its two commercial banks were squat and the stores, with the exception of the new F. W. Woolworth building on the southeast corner of Twenty-First, advertised their names in huge white lettering on the façades. The townspeople were friendly and did the same things their neighbors did every day, except on Sundays. On Sunday mornings, the town split into three groups: the Presbyterians and Southern Baptists worshipping in their respective churches at one end of Main Street and the Roman Catholics, including any Mexicans living there, flocking to their chapel, built to resemble New York's St. Patrick's, at the opposite end. Though all the women loved to dress smart, regardless of creed, the Presbyterians and Baptists preferred wide-brimmed hats, while the Catholics wore black mantillas.

Beginning when I was in third grade, Daddy had occasionally taken me to the Presbyterian services. I overwhelmingly preferred them to mass, because the congregants gathered in the church hall afterward for coffee and delicious home-baked cream cakes. After they got married in a city hall somewhere in Texas, neither of my parents converted to the other's religion. Daddy hadn't expressed any objections when, two months after my birth, Mama decided that I might as well be baptized Roman Catholic, because she understood the rules and all the sins.

Mama always insisted on attending mass for Daddy's anniversary instead of a Presbyterian service. She found the Presbyterians' altar too sparsely furnished and their services too informal, though I'd have preferred the simplicity. During the service, I'd cried every time I'd looked up at the statue of the Virgin, which Daddy and I had knelt before many times when I was a girl.

My stepfather, George; Mama; Charles; and I left the church as tiny orbs of pink and white confetti from a prior wedding whorled like crabapple blossoms over the church steps and then skittered along the sides of the flagstone path leading to the street. Halfway along the path, Mama and George stopped and peered up at a commercial airplane, tiny as a toy and backlit by the sun, tracing its way lazily across the sky. That such large airplanes could stay in the air still fascinated George.

Charles opened the door and I climbed into the spacious seat of George's new Packard, its glinting chrome fenders, unblemished dark-green paint, and white-walled tires making the other vehicles on the street appear unkempt by comparison. Only one task remained before our drive to a town twenty miles south of Dyson, where we planned to eat at a favorite diner before attending an amateur rodeo.

When we arrived at the gates of the cemetery, Mama took the grave blanket of white roses and dahlias from the trunk. She linked her arm in mine and we walked along the neatly manicured lawn, the men choosing to remain in the vehicle to smoke.

Every time Mama hugged me or reached for my hand, it still felt odd—welcome, but odd. She'd never been a person to show much affection, except with my daddy, who'd always kissed her on his return from work and was allowed to put his arm around her while we sat in the living room listening to *Fibber McGee and Molly*—though even that had stopped three months before he died. 'Round that time, she also stopped listening to the symphony concerts on the radio on Saturdays with us and, when I remarked how odd it all was, she told me I should tend to my own knitting. Daddy said he didn't know why she'd stopped either and warned me not to bug her about it.

After his death, Mama had withdrawn abruptly from me, not rising from bed until after I'd left for school and never asking how my day had gone when I returned. She still cooked franks and beans for me, and ribs smothered in her special tangy sauce, but she never sat at the table with me as I ate. Of course, I understood later that mourning was involved, but I sensed it wasn't the only reason.

When I'd asked if she wished I was dead like Daddy, after I'd had my first period and she'd discovered the bloodied underpants in the garbage bin and confronted me about it, her cheeks had gone paler than the white leather of George's brown-and-white spectator shoes. That windy afternoon, we'd gone for a long walk in the arid country- side surrounding our home and watched the ranch hands herd steers in preparation for driving them to the stockyard in town. She'd held me six times that day and five the next, on one occasion holding me so tight that it hurt. She'd told me how much she loved me and how much I resembled Daddy, which made her sad. A few days later, it had been back to normal—Mama's normal, that is.

Only when I was about to turn sixteen, after she'd married George, did she show genuine interest in what I was doing. Or rather, *anger* at what I was still doing. She'd sneaked up to the barn and caught me practicing *naturales* with a homemade muleta on my Great Dane, who really was the best fake bull I'd ever had.

"This is absolutely ridiculous at your age, Kathleen," she'd said. "You *must* learn how to fit in and stop fooling around with flags wrapped around drumsticks. Start showing interest in boys and clothes. Why don't you buy one of those Pee Wee Hunt records I hear kids playing and learn the lyrics? Then the other girls will like you and ask you to go to the diner and drink shakes."

Mama's rekindled interest had been solely panic driven. George sold encyclopedias door to door and had unknowingly interrupted a girl's sweet-sixteen party one recent afternoon, and had suggested to Mama that I have a party, too. The week before, I'd told him he'd never replace my father, so maybe the suggestion was his way of showing me that he still liked me. But Mama had panicked when she'd asked for the names of friends I'd like to invite and I'd given her only one name. Her efforts had been well meant, but she hadn't understood that fitting in simply didn't interest me. Mama had spent a lifetime not understanding.

"I can't believe it's eight years today since your daddy died," she said when we reached the grave. Mama removed a glove, touched, then kissed the center white rose on the blanket and then leaned over to place it on the grave. Her lipstick had turned its inner petals scarlet, so it looked like the rose was bleeding.

"I've remarried," she said, "so my heart's split equally now."

Lavender grew thick on Daddy's double-wide grave. It was his favorite color. Today I wore a lavender sundress with matching pumps. A year after Daddy had died, I'd taken cuttings from the wide ring of lavender surrounding our house, kept them in water until fragile roots appeared, and then planted them here. After years of tending, the plants now formed a dense, circular bed, twenty inches in diameter, in the middle of which I'd laid white marble chippings. During May, his birthday month, the grave was a riot of purple.

"I need to tell you something, Mama," I said. "I figured it best to wait until we were together again as a family."

She quit fanning herself with the limp glove.

"I'm thinking of leaving school."

Her cheeks pinked, accentuating the contrast in her strawberries-and-cream complexion. "George and I pay good money for your—"

"I appreciate that. But my grades aren't so great again this semester and I really don't want to be an art director in some boring advertising agency."

"You could do other kinds of office work. You could work as a secretary for an oil company executive. I've heard they're recruiting faster than jackrabbits breed."

"I don't want to work in an office, either." A blue grosbeak tweeted in a nearby tree, its vivid male partner responding as it flitted from headstone to headstone in the near distance. "I've been offered an interesting opportunity."

"What kind of opportunity?"

"Working with bulls."

She chuckled. "Rodeo's for cowboys."

"Not the rodeo." I took a slow breath, then let her have it. "I mean fighting bulls. Someone who knows about them believes I have a future in the ring. And he introduced me to a teacher who thinks I've got the ability to make good art with the bulls."

It looked like Mama was fixin' to keel over on top of Daddy.

"How do you know this person?" Her brow furrowed. "And more's to the point, how would he know?"

Though I'd anticipated this question, I hadn't been able to devise a response that would comfort her. I'd run a score of scenarios through my mind. I'd had Señor Barros meeting me at a ranch or even at the aficionado club. But that would have necessitated more explanations and complications.

"He's a very successful Mexican businessman," I said, truthfully enough, "and he saw me doing a demonstration recently."

Mama clutched her throat, a reflex I also had when bewildered. In her midforties, she'd given me my Irish complexion, though Mama's hair was brown, not dark red, and she wore it in an extravagant queue curl. She also dressed conservatively. She never wore pedal pushers, preferring to wear dresses with collars and epaulettes that reminded me of soldiers' uniforms.

"What kind of demonstration?"

I told her the best mostly-true lie I could come up with. "I went to a bullfight one Sunday and the ring's public relations manager asked if someone wanted to cape a calf for fun. I couldn't resist."

She released the grip on her throat and laughed shrilly. "Darling, a calf is not a bull. I thought you'd put this silliness behind you." She pulled off her other glove brusquely. "Your father told you that nasty business isn't for women. It's too dangerous." She shot a glance at Daddy's headstone, the gold inscription about "his soul resting in peace" chiseled out in such a manner that the word *his* could easily be replaced by *their* after Mama passed.

"You worked as a riveter," I said. "That was dangerous, too."

Her eyes clouded. "I did that to support the war effort. To help my country." She grimaced, her lips paring away from her upper teeth. "Going to work in a squalid country like Mexico, smelling of cattle."

"I've never lost my dream, Mama . . . and Daddy didn't say I couldn't do it."

She glanced over her shoulder toward the parking lot. "What does Charles say?"

A shiver whipped through me as I regarded the bloomless lavender. "I haven't told him yet."

"Don't." She seized my wrist. "I forbid you to leave school. You stick to making real art. Bullfighting's not art." She wagged her finger. "Don't you dare jeopardize your chances with that young man. He's perfect—good-looking, ambitious. He'll give you beautiful children. What more do you want?"

She stepped away from the grave. "This conversation never happened, young lady."

5

THE LOS PINOS BULLRING LOOKED SO DIFFERENT FROM the last time I'd been there. Then, eight thousand people had filled its seats. Now it was nearly empty. Fixing to save myself the hassle of crossing the bridge into Los Pinos twice that day, I'd arranged with Tim to conduct the magazine shoot on the same morning Señor Guzmán had scheduled my first official lesson. The thought of seeing him again made my heart thud faster.

An earsplitting squawk burst from the loudspeakers as someone tested the audio system. Two men stood on fruit crates appending a cardboard advertisement for men's shoes on an elevated, two-foot-wide wall forming a bulwark between the first row of seats and the *callejón*. Across the arena, ring servants raked the pale gold sand, while others replaced shredded planking on two of the wooden shields that offered protection to the matadors during bullfights.

"Okay, Kathleen, we're ready for you again," Tim Gunner, the student editor who'd asked me to pose for the college magazine, said. "Make sure to get the clock on top of the president's box into the background," he added to his photographer, a woman around nineteen like me but taller.

Every woman I met seemed taller than me, taller and better defined. Before facing the bull in the Garza ring and the opportunity

Señor Barros had given me, my shortness hadn't really mattered. Now it—and a growing anxiety about telling Charles I'd accepted the opportunity—was all I thought about. Concealing my decision from my boyfriend made me feel real lousy. But every time I opened my mouth to tell him, my tongue froze.

"Roger that," the photographer replied. "I think it's five minutes fast, though."

It was her watch that was running fast. Mexicans weren't governed by time like their American counterparts across the river, except when it came to the corrida. At exactly four o'clock on Sunday afternoons, a trumpet commenced the parade of the featured three matadors and their teams into the bullring. You could be late for work in Mexico. You could be late for Sunday mass. You could be late for a wedding, or even a funeral. But the main gate leading into the bullring had to swing open at four sharp. Even a minute after was unacceptable. The crowd would instantly let the authorities know their displeasure, hollering and tossing hats and coats into the ring. I'd witnessed this upheaval only once, due to the abrupt illness of a matador's picador, who fell off his horse in the passageway.

Tim instructed me to climb three-quarters of the way up a stepladder he'd set up and then twist halfway around so my upper body and the cape draping over my left shoulder would show to maximum effect. After he readjusted the nubby black montera hat I was wearing, I started climbing, but it was difficult. The breeches of the silk suit were tight, which I'd anticipated because the suits were made for men, but I hadn't expected them to be quite so oppressive. Truthfully, I couldn't have gotten into the suit after donning the traditional white shirt without the photographer's help. Her presence in the fetid lavatory under the stadium seating had added a degree of authenticity to the event, because all matadors had assistance when dressing before a corrida.

The suit was emerald green with silver embroidery. The bolero jacket was astonishingly rigid, although laces, hidden under shoulder reinforcements, connected the separate arms to ensure unimpeded movement. A gluttonous bounty of sequins caught in the sun's rays. Wearing the sparkling *traje* made my future seem closer, more real. I wondered who'd worn this banderilleros' suit and why it had been retired.

"The green really compliments your red hair," the photographer said. "It's a shame we can't afford to shoot in color."

"Let your hair fall around your shoulders for this shot," Tim directed.

Gripping the rickety stepladder's upright with my left hand, I undid a black bow securing my hair and shook my head.

"Okay, that's good," said the photographer. "Now, look at the camera in a coy way."

It took me a while to make a coy face the way she wanted. No matadors I'd ever seen in photographs had looked coy and I didn't think it was appropriate. But I decided not to say so, for fear of being thought swell-headed.

Señor Guzmán arrived at exactly eleven o'clock, but the photographer was running late. Dressed in oversize overalls, he walked into the bullring and peered around. I called out to him and waved. He stood frozen for a long time and then walked very quickly over to me.

"Howdy, Señor Guzmán," I said. "They've got a couple more shots to take of me for the college magazine and then we can start. I'm real excited."

His gaze riveted on my breeches. "Why are you wearing this suit?"

Tim and I exchanged glances.

"How dare you wear it," he continued. "Take it off and leave."

My heart stopped. The photographer was like a statue, her camera midway between her chest and face.

"I don't understand, Señor Guzmán." My voice shook. "I'll take it off right away and then we can start my lesson."

"Who do you think you are, Señorita Boyd?" A purple-red anger crept over his tanned face. "Because you're American, you think you have the right to do such a thing?"

My knees shook. "What have I done wrong?"

"You dare to wear a green *traje de luces?*" He wagged a nicotine-stained finger inches from my face. "Only matadors wear the suit of lights. Women are *never* allowed." Señor Guzmán's temples pulsed and his eyes glittered like balls of obsidian. "Not even the great Conchita Cintrón wore a *traje.*"

His reference to my idol shook me even more. During most of her career, Ms. Cintrón fought the bulls while riding a horse. She would have preferred to do it on foot, but was prevented from doing so by the Spanish ring authorities.

"But this isn't a matador's suit," I said, extending my arms for him to inspect. "The embroidery's not gold. Look, it's silver."

"And green." He shook his head. "Leave the bullring. All of you, clear off."

I didn't understand his anger. What did the color matter? Without an explanation, Señor Guzmán stared at me for a terrible moment and then strode away.

He'd rejected me. The only other rejection that came close was when my father hadn't kept a promise to return from work early one day to watch me perform in a school play when I was eleven. I'd been given five lines to say, lines I'd rehearsed a hundred times with Daddy, but he hadn't come. Only after a teacher took me home later and I found Mama weeping hysterically in the arms of one of the managers from the McElroy oil field did I understand. That afternoon killed my girlhood, as well as Daddy.

My heart bucked like a wild plug and I felt very weak. I sank slowly onto the fiery sand.

My career was over before it had begun. I lay like a fetus in my dorm room, my pillow streaked with tears and charcoal dust. Scattered on the floor and over my desk lay broken pencils, scrunched pages from a sketch pad, mangled charcoal drawings, and watercolors I loved. Even the unfinished bust of Sally that I'd intended to surprise her with before she left for New York City hadn't been spared. A dent in the wall indicated that the bust had received an especially violent demise.

"Go talk to your patron," Sally said. "Tell him he needs to find you a new instructor. Say it didn't work out with that jerk Guzmán. He'll understand."

I sat up abruptly on the bed and regarded her through blurry eyes. She was taller than me, the perfect height for a model. And a bull-fighter. Based on a portfolio she'd sent, the modeling agency had already booked her for a bra and girdle shoot as soon as she completed the agency's induction. Everything happened so easily for her.

"You don't understand," I replied. "Señor Barros *won't* listen. I messed up. It's over."

6

I BOOKED THE TABLE FOR SEVEN SHARP," CHARLES SAID, EVEN before I'd gotten fully into his car.

"Sorry. I didn't realize the time."

An old friend of Charles's from the French Quarter was visiting him at college and Charles had arranged for us to have dinner together and then go on to a new club in town that showcased blues musicians from Louisiana. He'd taken me once before, even though I didn't care much for that kind of music. Blues music is slow and the lyrics are depressing. But Charles insisted that I'd develop a taste for it, the same way I had for coffee with chicory. I felt that bitter coffee and sadness were two very different concepts. It didn't make sense that experienced people like Charles liked to develop a taste for sad music.

His eyes roamed over my red chiffon dress, its wide skirt making my waist look tiny. I'd worn it to my prom two years earlier, but it was new to Charles. He'd asked me to dress especially smart because we were dining at the top of the swanky Silverdale Hotel.

"You look swell," he said, his voice a bit high and trembling.

Gravel splattered nosily against the sides of the car as he pulled away from the curb. Three students walking along the brick path toward the dormitory building stopped and watched us speed by. Past the college theater, he turned left so sharply I gripped the edge of the dashboard to avoid crashing into his shoulder.

"I'm scared they won't hold the table," he said, by way of explanation.

"Bill will hold it."

He decelerated. "Were you playing at bulls with Sally again?" he asked. "Is that why you're late?"

"I don't want to talk about bulls."

"That suits me fine, honey."

We drove in silence into downtown, passing the building site of Rowansville's first steel skyscraper, already eleven stories high. It had taken five years for the out-of-town developer to win a lawsuit against the city council, which had insisted he build no higher than the other six-story buildings in the locality.

"The city council should have appealed the verdict to the Texas Supreme Court," Charles said, just like he did every time we drove by it. "There'll be a forest of skyscrapers here soon. It'll be like goddamned Chicago." He glanced at me. "I'm sure glad we're not going to live in this city forever."

This was the second time in two weeks he'd mentioned leaving Rowansville, but the first that he'd included me. His eyes gleamed with intensity. I knew he would leave after graduation, but hadn't considered how that would affect me. I'd been too busy trying to find a way to be with the bulls, which I'd bungled. Were Charles and I meant to be together in another city? Was he trying to let me know this?

We pulled up outside the restaurant and Charles gave the keys to the valet, then helped me out. Inside, elegantly dressed men and women my mother's age and older sat at circular tables draped in starched white tablecloths whose pointy ends flirted with the plush carpet. Candles flickered in shiny brass candelabras. Large bouquets of red and white flowers were everywhere. An old man in a dinner jacket played soft music at a grand piano.

By the time the waiter brought our margaritas, Bill still hadn't arrived. Taking my hand, Charles led me across the room and out to the balcony. The evening was warm and a gentle, southwesterly breeze caressed my cheeks. I peered out over the city. Against the darkening sky, the skyscraper was a silhouette of steel cages guarded by the booms of two huge cranes. The scene was futuristic, so full of promise.

Lights winked as a tram crossed the Rio Grande, which separated the sprawling city of Los Pinos from its American sister, Rowansville. The shanties and houses on the outskirts of Los Pinos didn't have electricity and high rises were unheard of. This detail pleased Charles, though he'd also once said he could never live in Mexico because he disliked their cities' air of dusty impoverishment. Crinkling my eyes, I focused until I could make out the bullring's exterior in the mid-distance. That had been my future and it was dead now. Beyond the bullring, the undulating crests of the mountains rose above the arid plain, their wrinkled outcrops and brush obliterated slowly by the gathering darkness.

I began tracing the main vein of a lightninglike crack on one of the multicolored tiles forming the balcony's inner wall. My finger came to a place where the vein split into many shallower cracks and hesitated.

"Ain't the city pretty at night?" Charles said.

I didn't answer.

"You want to know something?" He looked at me, an earnestness creeping across his features. "You're pretty, too." He drew me to him. "I've got something to tell you."

I arched my head back to see his face better.

"Bill's not joining us for dinner. I told a white lie. We're meeting him at the club later."

Instinctively, I took my hands away from around his neck. The whites of Charles's eyes glowed in the dusky space between us. "What's the matter?" I asked.

"That interview I had in New Orleans—they wrote to tell me I got the job. They're drilling off the Louisiana coast to a hundred feet, but new technology's gonna allow them to go much deeper." He kissed my forehead and added, "They want me to start after graduation. They're going to pay me three hundred dollars a week." His smile grew enormous. "I'll also get bonuses."

I put my arms around his neck again, stood on my toes, and kissed his lips. "I'm happy for you."

"You want to know what would make me even happier?" He fumbled in his jacket and then lowered onto his right knee. "Kathleen Boyd, you're sweet milk to me. Will you marry me?"

He *had* been trying to tell me. Everything changed to slow motion as he opened a tiny black velvet box and held it up for me to see. The facets of a large diamond solitaire gobbled up every ray of light brave enough to strike them. I looked back and forth from the ring to Charles's face.

He took my hand in his. "I want to take care of you and protect you for the rest of my life."

"But what about school . . . I have to finish—"

"You hate your classes. Now you won't have to finish them. We'll live in the French Quarter." His voice grew stronger. "There's great restaurants and music just steps away. When we have kids, we'll move to the Garden District. My new boss took me there one evening. The houses are enormous. You'll love it." He reached up and squeezed my chin the way he liked to do. "Your mother already gave me her blessing."

"You talked to her?"

"She called me."

"She did?"

"She said you'd mentioned something about finding your work difficult last time you saw her and she's been worried ever since."

I couldn't believe Mama would be so cunning. "I never said anything of the sort."

"Mothers are real protective that way. You'll find that out when you're a mama, too." He paused. "Anyways, I asked for her blessing and she gave it to me."

A million thoughts crowded my mind. Images of Charles and me dining in restaurants. Images of my father and of Mama. Of me in the Garza ring with the bull. Of Señor Guzmán angrily dismissing me. My dream of fighting the bulls was dead and it was me who'd killed it.

I looked at Charles, whose lower lip trembled despite his smile. He was handsome. I noticed the way women looked at him as we walked around campus. We'd been dating nearly a year, though it seemed like I'd known him much longer. He was intelligent. He was worldly, and I learned things from him. We seldom exchanged angry words. When we did argue, we patched up our differences in days. Was this what people meant when they said they were in love?

"Now darlin', don't keep me waiting," he said. "Make me the happiest man in Rowansville tonight."

Mama was right. Charles was my future. I was lucky to have someone like him love me. He knew where he was going. He'd never make the kind of fatal mistake I'd made with Señor Guzmán. Maybe I wasn't destined to fight in the bullring.

My eyes locked on his. "Yes. I will marry you."

Taking my limp hand, Charles opened it wider and slipped the cold ring down my finger.

I arrived at the music club feeling shocked. I didn't feel engaged, but then how was being engaged supposed to feel? Maybe exactly like this—maybe all women felt like this when they got engaged.

Charles was surprised to discover that Bill had brought a girlfriend, Amy, who sang in a jazz club on Frenchmen Street in New Orleans. She wore a thin cotton dress, the bodice of which allowed her large breasts to show. Mine were so small, I felt boyish before her.

Moments after Charles and Bill left us to chat with a saxophonist they knew from New Orleans, Amy grasped my hand. She had calluses and her palms were dry and rough, like I'd always imagined a matador's would be. She inspected the ring closer than she'd done when she first congratulated me.

"That sure is some rock," she said, then pushed my hand away.

"Thank you." Trying not to stare at her breasts, I asked politely, "How long have you been seeing Bill?"

She shot a glance at my ring. "Long enough for one of those." Amy glanced over at Bill, who was offering the saxophonist a cigarette, and said, "Bill's family is old Louisiana on both sides. His daddy's in Proteus."

"Proteus?"

"Old Mardi Gras krewe." Amy drained the rest of her bourbon. "No riffraff in the membership."

The saxophonist called over, inviting her to join his band onstage. Amy didn't even pretend to be flattered. Rising from the table quicker than a bored dinner guest, she climbed up on the stage and launched into a song called "Wedding Bells," winking exaggeratedly in my direction every time she sang the chorus.

Later, after we'd dropped Bill and Amy off at their hotel, I said to Charles, "Amy's nice."

"She's okay."

"She really likes him." I held out my hand. "I think she wants one of these."

A sleek Cadillac convertible passed us by, its shark fins cutting silently into the night air.

"Yeah, like *that's* going to happen." Charles laughed. "She's already sleeping with him."

He'd taken the long route back to the college. As we skirted southern Rowansville, I could see the border crossing and craggy mountains surrounding Los Pinos. I looked out over the sprawling Mexican city and my breath caught when I glimpsed the bullring.

7

MEN AND WOMEN CARRYING SUITCASES RUSHED BY AS Sally and I emerged from the coffee shop inside the railway station. A woman with two toddlers clutching teddy bears bumped shoulders with me. At the main entrance stood a couple, the man in a marine's uniform, tapping on the terrazzo floor with the toe of his shoe, while the woman dabbed her eyes.

"Thanks for the coffee," Sally said.

"You're welcome."

We had been reduced to platitudes, as friends are when they're about to part for a long time. We'd made promises to write frequently and tell each other everything going on in our lives, to remain friends for life, to never allow Yankee boyfriends or a future husband to come between us. When I'd told her about my engagement, she'd refused to believe me at first. And then she'd insisted I was making a mistake.

Sally's mother, an imposing woman who wore a woolen jacket despite the heat, returned from the restroom. Her eyes were puffy, their whites crisscrossed with fine red lines. Sally nodded at me discreetly to pick up one of her suitcases and we started toward the tracks.

The shrill scream of abruptly released air from the train's engine and the screech of metal against metal grated on my teeth. The sweet aroma of candied popcorn wafted from a concession stand. We stood silently in the mayhem, me watching the ticket collector punching passengers' tickets.

Sally's mother shot me a frosty look when she knew her daughter couldn't see. She undoubtedly wanted time alone with Sally, to warn her yet again about the dangers of living in a Yankee city and about meeting strange men, and to make her promise to write and call home weekly. But Sally had made me promise to stay at her side until she boarded the train to avoid just such conversations.

"Next time I see your face, it'll be staring at me from some fancy magazine," I said.

"Yeah, Sears, Roebuck." Sally laughed wickedly. "In a corset."

Her mother's lips thinned.

Sally turned to hug me and, as we embraced, she said, "Don't you dare give up on your dream to fight the bulls, especially not just 'cause some guy pitched a hissy fit over a suit you wore that wasn't even wrong."

The train's whistle shrieked. I looked down at my feet. Sally was leaving to follow her dream. She hadn't let her mama kill it, no matter how hard she'd tried to, and though I hadn't let mine, either, I'd allowed a stranger to do it. But that stranger was in the business, he was connected, and I wasn't.

"You listen to me, y'hear?" Sally said, and she put her hand under my chin and lifted my face. "You made a bitty mistake. Go eat crow even if you don't want to and he'll fix to change his mind. Heck, he's probably changed his mind already but can't bring himself to apologize. You know what men are like." She winked at me before turning to her mama and flashing a smile wider than the Rio Grande.

Scarcely able to breathe, I followed Señor Guzmán's wife down the hallway. On the walls hung branding irons from famous bull breeding ranches and signed photographs of matadors I recognized from the forties. I noticed that there were also framed posters billing Señor Guzmán's appearances at past corridas throughout Mexico.

When we reached the living room, Carmen looked back and smiled at me. I appreciated this sliver of reassurance. Plump, with a friendly face, she wasn't especially pretty by American standards, her nose being too small and her chin not clearly defined. But I'd immediately recognized her accent and learned she was from the same part of southern Mexico as the woman who'd worked for my parents and taught me Spanish, and I found that comforting.

Round, shellacked pine beams stretched across the high ceiling of the living room. Above a high adobe mantel was a full-length portrait of Señor Guzmán dressed in a green suit of lights, the same color as the one I'd worn at the bullring—except this was one trimmed in gold embroidery. Set against a dark landscape, reminiscent of Da Vinci's work, the shape of his body was correct, but his face was an abject lie, as the artist had given him normal ears. Next to the portrait was an image of the Virgin of Guadalupe, the patron saint of Mexican bull-fighters. Large French doors opened into a courtyard lush with palms, trumpet vines, and vibrant hibiscus flowers. I wondered if green was his favorite color. It would explain why my wearing a green suit at the bullring that day had set him off.

Señor Guzmán's skinny backside was the first thing I saw. He was on all fours on the clay-tiled floor, his daughter astride his back while a boy, who resembled his father, led him around the room by a silk tie fastened around his father's neck.

"You have a visitor," his wife said.

I averted my eyes from his butt to the black mouth of the fireplace. "Hi, Señor Guzmán," I said.

His daughter tumbled to the floor as he rose.

"Why are you here?" His raised voice was so cattywampus to the situation that both children froze and gawked at us open-mouthed.

"Please hear me out, sir."

"You showed me you're not serious. What's to hear?"

It had taken all my courage to come to see him and I wasn't going to leave without pleading my case. "I see you wore a green suit of lights when you were a matador. I didn't know my wearing one would insult you." The inside of my mouth felt like I'd lunched on a bale of hay; I could hear dry clicks as my tongue formed the words and pushed them out. "I'm sorry."

His wife met my eyes and smiled encouragement.

"I meant what I said to you that day you tested me," I added. "Becoming a bullfighter is the only thing I want to do with my life. It's what I've been practicing for since I was a little girl." I smiled nervously. "If my dogs were still alive, you'd only have to see how they behave when I take out a blanket to know it's true."

His jaw remained set. I considered prostrating myself like a novitiate taking her vows.

"Please, Señor Guzmán. Give me one more chance. I'll prove it to you."

"Wearing the suit showed you have no respect for the art's traditions."

"I do. That's why I wore one with silver threads."

"Leave my house."

The black, hard eyes showed not a glimmer of compassion. Both his children had the tips of their fingers inside their mouths. They reminded me of when I'd been their age and had angered my father. I didn't want to frighten them any longer, so I turned and left the room.

Outside in the blinding sunlight, Carmen caught up with me as I started along the street. She laid her soft, warm hand on my wrist. "I see this means a lot to you, chiquita." She patted my forearm, then pointed across the street. "Wait under that tree. I'll speak to my husband."

My eyes filled up. I couldn't talk. My own mother had never called me by a pet name. She'd heard Daddy call me Peanut but had never used the endearment herself.

Carmen turned and headed back toward the house. I sat on the dirty curb, the fierce sun beating down on my head. Plucking a gangly weed, I stripped off its broad, dusty leaves and began drawing aimless interlocking circles in the dust with its woody stalk. An ancient Ford lumbered by, followed a few minutes later by two laborers on bicycles, their faces half-hidden by sombreros. The sight of a redheaded, pale American sitting on a street corner amused them, their peals of gruff laughter mocking my stupidity for coming here to beg. A dog barked from an adjacent house, where the bearded canopies of two palm trees rose from the courtyard.

At the point when my emotions were moving from hopeful to defeatist, Señor Guzmán came out. I rose as fast as a pup waiting for its master and scampered across to him.

"My wife asked me to give you another chance," he said. "She says everyone is young at some point and makes mistakes."

"Thank you, Señor Guzmán."

"I didn't say I agreed." He folded his arms and the sleeves of his shirt slid up to reveal thick wrists carpeted with black hair. His big nose skewed to one side and I wondered if he'd broken it in the bull-ring. He was still young—only in his early forties—and I also wondered why he'd retired as a matador.

"You made a very ignorant mistake. Do you agree?"

I'd have agreed to ride an incensed bull up and down his street if it meant he'd take me back. No, *ten* incensed bulls. I met his steely glare.

"Yes, sir, and it won't happen again."

"If I take you back, you become an extension of me in the bull-ring," he said. "Your mistakes become my mistakes. Your reputation becomes my reputation."

"I'll never let you down." I crossed my heart.

He regarded me silently, his stern eyes tunneling deep into mine, into my brain, as if searching for insincerity. "Señor Barros knows only about making money," he said. "He knows nothing about the bulls."

I considered if this might be some kind of loyalty test. If I agreed, I was behaving disloyally to my patron. If I didn't, I was disloyal to Señor Guzmán. I said nothing and glanced down at my dusty feet.

"Do not look down like that." He waited until I met his eye. "Señor Barros informed me that your father's dead."

My mind zipped to the day of the accident and then to the hearse carrying Daddy's coffin to the church. I'd overheard a neighbor saying the casket was closed because the explosion at the oil well had created a huge fireball and Daddy had been burned to a cinder. Had he suffered, I'd always wondered, or had it been so quick he didn't even know what had happened? Why had he died so soon? If he'd been alive, he would have supported me and persuaded Mama to accept my decision, even if he didn't understand it.

"Do you believe your father always acted in your best interest?"

I bit my lip. "He was my daddy."

Señor Guzmán smiled. He actually smiled.

"Did you obey him?" he asked.

"Sure."

"Then you will also obey me, like you did your father. There are rules and, if I take you back, you must obey them completely."

"I'll obey. I promise."

"How can you agree without hearing them?" His small mouth puckered like he'd taken a drink of sour milk. "You Americans are too impatient. You never listen properly."

"Please give me the rules."

"You will address me as Maestro from now on. Not Señor Guzmán. Not Fermin. I was a great matador and nothing but Maestro will do, where you are concerned."

From listening to concerts on the radio from Radio City Music Hall with my parents, I knew maestros conducted symphony orchestras, not bulls. Nevertheless, I nodded energetically.

"Have you heard of the Plaza de Toros México?" he asked.

Of course I had. It was Mexico's greatest bullring, with space to seat over forty thousand people, and any matador worth his salt wanted to appear there in his career. Again, I nodded.

"Through me, you will get to perform there one day." He paused. "*If* you obey everything I tell you to do. You will never question my judgment. You will never complain. Do you agree to the terms?"

"Yes, Maestro."

His grin made his cheeks bulge like a chipmunk's. "Be at the bullring at ten o'clock next Monday. Bring a pair of pants and tennis shoes."

As I walked away, my heart mimicked the fluttery dance of a purple-throated hummingbird feeding in a nearby garden.

"One other thing, Kathleen," he called.

I stopped and looked back.

"I want to be certain about this. You said you have no boyfriend."

He locked eyes with me. I remembered him saying the bulls were jealous and matadors didn't have time for love affairs. An image of Charles on his knee, holding up the black velvet box containing the sparkling ring, flashed in my mind. I was a balance pan scale, both hands holding what was important in my life. But one had more weight.

Firmly, I replied, "I don't, Maestro."

A cascade of lemon, pink, pale orange and crimson roses sloped gently down to an iron pike fence that marked the park's easterly boundary. Beyond the road, the suburbs of Rowansville sprawled toward the desert and thirsty brown mountains. Narrow red-gravel paths snaked between the raised flowerbeds. The air was so thick with perfume that it felt like my nose was a drinking straw and I was sipping. Gardeners in straw hats, most of them Mexican, skillfully deadheaded the blooms, tossing what had once been vibrantly alive into their rusty wheelbarrows.

"This is something I need to do," I said, passing my free hand lightly along the cement coping of the stone wall on which Charles and I sat.

He surprised me by continuing to hold my hand, even squeezing tighter. To have this power over a man eleven years older than me, when I'd just told him I'd become Señor Guzmán's student, was equally amazing and terrifying.

"I get that you don't want to finish school, but this is madness," he said, staring at my open hand. "You promised me you were done with the bulls."

I pulled my hand from his and stood. "I didn't exactly promise that. You interpreted it that way."

"Don't feed me that crap."

"You've already done a lot with your life, Charles. I need to do things, too. Go places."

"Until our kids come along," he said, "we could go places together."

He stood now, too. At over six feet, he had to bend his head to look down at me. Somehow, that irritated me, when it had never bothered me before. Why couldn't he understand that it wasn't about traveling places and doing stuff together? Why couldn't he see that my need to fight the bulls was as important to me as eating and sleeping? As important as the army had been to him? He'd had the opportunity to work on airplanes in England, had even flown on missions over Germany and released bombs that made him feel he'd done his part to win the war. He'd proven himself. And he would prove himself again in his new job. If he loved me like he said he did, shouldn't it have been easy for him to understand that I had things to prove to myself? If he loved me, wouldn't he want me to be fulfilled?

Was this what marriage meant? Did a wife have to give up her dreams for her husband's?

A gardener stopped pruning and peered over at us, the blue smoke of the cigarette drooping from his mouth drifting languidly into the air.

"Let's sit a minute and think this through," said Charles.

I sat apart from him on the wall. He held out his hand for me to take again, like I'd done so many times before, but I needed to keep my focus. I took the ring out of my skirt pocket and placed it in his palm.

Charles's face grayed. "You don't want to marry me, either?"

"I'm too young."

"Jesus Christ, you sure know how to bring a guy to his knees."

I curled my fingers around the underside of the coping, willing myself to stay strong. We sat in silence, me looking beyond the park to the mountains, him still staring at the sparkling ring. I stole a glance and saw a tear spill over the rim of his eye.

I reached out and touched his hand. "I have to be truthful."

"How can you do this to me? Don't you love me?"

"I love the bulls, too," I said.

"You're choosing a fucking bull over me?" His eyes were hard and no longer glistened.

"I don't see it as choosing. It's something I need to do. Like breathing."

"Yeah, and it'll lead to your *not* breathing one day."

The blood rushed into my head so fast I felt dizzy.

"You're too small," he continued. "Those Mexicans encouraging you to do this should be strung up. Bullfighting's for men." He shook his head. "Uneducated men at that."

He stroked my cheek. "Don't you want to be a mother?"

I did want to be a mother—one day. Charles would make a great husband and father. He was dependable and trustworthy. He would be the same kind of man to me that Daddy had been to Mama. But he was ready to take that step. Nothing I could say would change the reality that I wasn't.

"Yes. Just not now." I rose from the wall, my eyes watering, turning the rose beds into blurry red and yellow blankets. "I didn't want to hurt you."

"I won't wait, you know."

I didn't reply.

"You can't expect me to wait until you decide you're ready," he pressed.

"I'd never ask you to wait."

"You're making a mistake."

He stood and wrapped his arms around me. I'd always loved that feeling, but it was different now. Out of his unhappiness came my happiness, and it felt oddly right. I felt guilty as hell to hurt him, but I had to be true to myself. I cared for him; I loved the bulls. The scales were right. One was heavier.

A lock of Charles's oiled hair dangled over his right eye. Before, I'd have instantly put it back in place. Everything was different; everything had changed. I wrenched myself from his embrace and started along the path toward the exit.

8

THE ROOM IN THE WOMEN'S HOME, A FORMER CONVENT now housing forty girls, had a small window overlooking a quiet side street. A friend of Señor Barros, Sister Rosemarie, was the housemother. Bullfighting interested her, as did my career plans. She'd told me that matadors were just one rung below saints in the Lord's eyes, because they attended mass regularly and venerated the Virgin of Guadalupe before every fight.

Adjacent to the switches controlling the light and a sooty overhead fan, a yellowing, handwritten sign warned occupants to restrict their electricity usage as too many appliances running simultaneously caused power outages. A black wooden crucifix hung near the window, the S-shaped body of Jesus turned from white to amber by decades of smoke and nicotine.

Single beds with matching pale pink chenille bedspreads were pushed against the room's longest walls, a mound of bras, panties, and dresses lying on top of what would become my bed. Next to a small sink with a leaky faucet was a mustard-colored armoire that I discovered was already stuffed full of dresses and blouses.

My roommate was from Los Angeles and her dyed-black hair made her pale face look as if it were made of porcelain. Enrolled for two semesters at Los Pinos University, Belinda had been surprised to find me in her room when she'd returned from class.

"Sorry there's no space in the wardrobe," she said, her black eyes flitting to a bruised rustic dresser missing all but two of its knob handles. "You're welcome to use that."

I began unpacking my sports high tops and shoes.

"The room's not great," she continued, as she took her underwear and stockings out of the dresser drawers and tossed them on her bed. "I wouldn't stay in this dump, but my father insists. He thinks nuns are the best, that they make girls like us toe the line. But they're the worst, aren't they?"

"Sister Rosemarie seems friendly."

Belinda rolled her eyes. "The woman rises at four every morning to say lauds. But she goes to bed early, thank God."

She picked her soiled clothing up off my bed, then lit a cigarette butt, took a puff, and exhaled the smoke out the window. "Will you be staying long?" she asked.

I couldn't answer that question. If things didn't work out, I didn't know what I'd do. There was no returning to the Rowans Institute.

"I'm fixin' to be here awhile," I said.

"Swell," she replied. "We're going to get along."

It crossed my mind that her opinion might be based solely on my failure to object to her smoking in the room.

"Just so you know, I have a boyfriend," she added. "He's a professor at the university."

She scoured my face for signs of admiration. It seemed strange that she'd told me this so soon after our meeting, and stranger that she was dating someone who taught at her school, especially a professor. But the latter revelation pleased me, because it undoubtedly meant I'd have the room to myself a lot.

While I unpacked, Belinda lay on her bed and read a magazine. "You need any help?" she asked, peering over the magazine.

"It's fine. Thanks, though."

I stacked my books and bullfighting magazines neatly on top of the dresser, then eased a poster out of its battered cardboard cylinder. I pinned it on the wall on my side of the room. When I stood back to check if I'd hung it even, Belinda looked over and gasped.

"Gee, you can't hang that in here."

My head snapped back to her. "Does Sister Rosemarie not like tack marks on the walls?"

"It's disturbing."

My poster depicted a matador in a royal blue and gold suit of lights, arching his back beautifully as a bull wound his muscular body around him. The poster's four corners bore rust-stained circles where I'd hung and rehung it through the years. My father had purchased it for me after we'd left the bullfight in Mexico City, a souvenir of the first corrida I'd attended.

"Did you say 'disturbing'?"

"For sure, it's disturbing."

I looked again at my beautiful poster, trying to see what she found objectionable.

"There are spears dangling from the bull's back," she pointed out. "He's being killed."

"Oh, those aren't spears. They're banderillas." I laughed. "They're like fish hooks, only larger. The bull doesn't even feel them."

A blush in the center of Belinda's milky cheeks grew and grew.

"The bull dies in the end."

The blush reached her neck.

"He doesn't always die," I said. "Sometimes the matador's injured and he dies."

"How'd you like to be killed for sport?"

"Bullfighting's not a sport. It's art. Theater."

I glanced at the poster again. From that first bullfight I'd seen as a kid, I'd recognized that the bullring was a massive stage, like no other I'd seen before, and that everyone and everything, including the horses and bulls, knew their roles instinctively. Even then, as my father put his arm around my shoulders and drew me protectively to him when the time came to kill the bull, I knew this was the kind of art I wanted to make.

"Sister Rosemarie also loves bullfighting," I added defensively.

"Yeah, she loves the crucifixion, too." Belinda sat up on the bed. "They kill the bull, drag him out of the ring, and hack him up for his meat."

This was true. If a matador was injured and had to go to the hospital, another matador appearing in the corrida was charged with killing the bull. The only exception to this rule—a rare exception—occurred if the crowd determined that the bull was very brave, and then appealed to the judge that his life should be spared.

"It's offensive," she continued. "Gross."

"You buy meat from a butcher, don't you?" I said, my cheeks heating now. "What's the difference between that and handing out the bull's meat to the poor after a bullfight?"

She held her hand out like it was shield. "I'm a vegetarian."

This explained why she looked so anemic. Her blood was weak, thin as water.

Someone knocked on the door. A flurry of activity ensued, as Belinda leaped up, grabbed a perfume bottle from under her bed, and began squeezing a tiny black pump to spritz mist around the room.

"Come in," Belinda said, after she'd replaced the perfume bottle under the bed.

A middle-aged Mexican woman, one of the nun's assistants, opened the door and inquired whether I'd had a tour of the kitchen and dining room—and if anyone had given me a schedule for cleaning the toilets.

Life in Los Pinos proved similar to life across the river. A city is a city no matter where it's located. The main difference was that I was no longer living on a student-saturated campus. Walking to the bullring took thirty-five minutes through a maze of streets, some wide and busy, others narrow, neglected, and lined with crumbling buildings and unruly vegetation. A cemetery containing weathered limestone vaults dating back to the Mexican War of Independence ran along one of the older streets I walked down. The turquoise and pink facades of the shops and dwellings, and the ranchero music swirling out from the cafés and cantinas, made me very happy as I strolled by.

On arrival at the bullring every morning, I went to a ladies' restroom, a crude space with peeling plaster walls, and changed out of my dress into a pair of men's jeans I'd worn when painting at the Rowans Institute. Señor Barros arrived at the bullring on the second day of my training, just as Maestro was walking back from berating a cocky young apprentice matador who'd wolf-whistled at me.

Smoking a Cuban cigar, my patron watched me run back and forth in the powdery sand until Maestro went over to him. The two men chatted animatedly, Maestro's slender body totally enveloped in the larger man's shadow. Finally, Señor Barros shook hands with Maestro and approached me.

"Is your accommodation at the old convent to your liking?" he asked.

Not wanting to appear ungrateful by complaining about my roommate, I told him I was comfortable. Rather than listen to Belinda ranting on about my beloved poster, I'd taken it down and replaced it with an oil portrait I'd painted of a favorite dog from my childhood.

"It seems I could become a distraction," said Señor Barros, nodding over at Maestro, who was now talking to one of the ring servants. He removed his Cordoban hat and fanned his face with it. "Fermin thinks it best I communicate directly with him. He'll report back to me on your progress on a regular basis."

"Let's get to work, Kathleen," Maestro hollered. He clapped sharply twice. "Start running again."

I grinned. "He's quite a taskmaster. Worse than one of my art professors at college."

"You'll do well with him." Señor Barros put his hat on again and made his exit.

After he'd left the arena, Maestro came up to me. "He's informed you?"

"Yes."

"I didn't tell you to stop running."

Following half an hour of running back and forth aimlessly, doing the same exercises I'd done the previous day, Maestro came up to me with a worried look on his face.

"Did I not do it right?" I asked.

"Your left leg is weaker than the right."

Given I was already short for a bullfighter, I didn't want to hear. It made me even more uncertain I could succeed in this man's world. Maestro was also leaving for Guadalajara for a few days and part of me feared that this would make him change his mind about my potential, that he'd dump me before he left.

"I'm right-handed," I said. "Isn't it normal my left side would be weaker?"

"It's more than that."

My mind raced over possible solutions. "Do they have a gymnasium here?"

"Why do you ask?"

"Don't the matadors lift weights to improve their strength?"

"There's a small room, but it's dusty and—"

"Take me there."

"Only men use it."

"Of course only men use it. I'm the first woman training here."

I thought I'd made him angry until a smile flitted slowly across his face. He beckoned me to follow him.

As we walked toward the entrance to the *callejón*, I looked up at the tiers of empty seats. No longer did I feel I was a mere spectator. Though I was far from appearing at the Plaza México, my presence here meant I was a part of this world now.

After crossing the horse patio, we went through a doorway and then walked along a hallway until we came to a windowless, twelve-by-twelve room lit by two naked bulbs. Haphazardly arranged around the floor were corroded barbells and stacks of weights, tattered work-benches, dumbbells, and skipping ropes. In one corner, a shirtless man, watched over by a companion, squatted under an enormous weight. His shoulder blades protruded like malformed wings as he strained upward. His ropy arms gleamed with sweat.

Both men regarded me, their mouths slackening slowly as their thoughts caught up with their eyes. The weightlifter dropped the bar-bell on the floor with a crash and walked over to a bench and grabbed his shirt to put it on.

"¡Hola!" one of them said.

"My apprentice needs to use this room," Maestro said.

"We heard you'd taken on an apprentice," said the man who'd been squatting. His keen eyes skimmed my body, stopping to take in my breasts twice. I folded my arms.

"Don't look at her like that," Maestro warned, his arms stiffening.

The weightlifter raised his open palms. "It's okay," he said.

"She will use this room alone," Maestro insisted.

"But you're with her," the weightlifter's friend said, a sly look on his face.

Maestro took a step toward him. "Leave."

"Why did you take on a woman as *novillero*?" the weightlifter asked instead of exiting, as if I wasn't present.

Without answering, Maestro lifted two black seven-pound disks, attached one on each side of the bar, and ordered me to lift up my arms and then raise it above my head. After I'd done what he demanded, he told me to alternately bend and raise my left leg, as if constantly genuflecting. The other men conversed in hushed voices and snickered as they crossed to the exit.

"Are those men matadors?" I asked, after the door closed. I rested the bar on my shoulders, but tiny rasps meant to assist with gripping the bar dug into my neck.

"They're apprentices, just like you," said Maestro. He met my eye. "Without the talent."

His lips curled upward. The gesture was so subtle and brief, I almost missed it. As if it had magically transformed into a sack of feathers, I lifted the barbell even higher above my head and picked up the pace.

9

HE COULD NEVER DECIDE IF THE DRY HEAT, SO FIERCE IT roasted his lungs every time he inhaled, or the clinging humidity was worse to deal with. Mopping the sweat off his neck with a handkerchief, Fermin looked ahead and figured he had about another quarter mile to walk. He trudged past shacks and tiny houses on either side of the dirt road, each with a corrugated zinc roof and an unkempt, desperate backyard. A thick layer of red dust had eviscerated the high shine on his shoes and the cuffs of his pressed gabardine pants seemed to have been seasoned with cayenne pepper. A burro in a grassless excuse for a field didn't even bother to raise her head as he passed, the cross of darker hair on her back the blackest he'd ever seen on a donkey.

The cinder blocks of Rosa's L-shaped house remained unpainted, though he'd given her extra money to paint it. The houses next to hers had been freshly painted in bright pinks, terra-cotta, and pastel greens since his last visit. Fermin noticed that Rosa's dwelling had one improvement, at least: a large oil barrel had been raised onto the roof to serve as a water tank. Two frayed garden hoses snaked around the dusty yard, where five chickens pecked the parched earth for grubs. Wet laundry hung from a precarious clothesline strung between the slender trunks of pine trees.

He gazed over downtown Guadalajara for a moment. In the far distance, the cathedral's twin spires ascended like a bull's tapering horns into the sky. Four neat plazas nestled up to its stone walls, including the Plaza de Armas, with its intricate bandstand, where bands played in the evenings. His eyes roamed Rosa's backyard again. He'd heard a massive construction project was to take place in the city, that many buildings would be razed in order to widen the streets, and he hoped some of the money would trickle into suburbs like this one.

She opened the door before he knocked. Rosa was thirty-six and her face was attractive, though not in the classic Spanish way. Her wide cheekbones bore testimony to ancient Mayan blood flowing alongside the Dutch and Basque in her veins. She wore a white cheesecloth blouse and black skirt with scarlet, royal blue, and yellow rings near its end.

Every time he saw Rosa after a long absence, Fermin's heart jolted like it was the first time he'd laid eyes on her. Blood rushed to his groin as images of her naked body whipped through his mind. Even after all these years, he still searched her face for a flirtatious look or quivering smile, like she'd used to give as encouragement. If Rosa showed even an ember of interest, he'd hand the children a few coins and send them on an errand, and then he'd kiss every inch of her neck and breasts before carrying her off to the bedroom. Once there, he'd strip her naked and position her in the way he liked, and they'd fuck and to hell with the bitter remorse that always crammed into his brain afterward.

Rosa's home was gratifyingly cool. The living room was furnished simply, years of soot from an open hearth layering the peeling white walls. His children, eleven-year-old fraternal twins, sat on a sagging couch, a light-brown-haired girl with eyes that conveyed emotions as easily as her mother's and a boy with jug ears like Fermin's, strong Mayan features, and coarse hair in need of cutting. When he'd first seen the boy, despite the ears, Fermin had found it difficult to accept he was even his child.

He hugged the children, their embraces as uncertain as his, though Fermin disguised his feelings with uncharacteristic robustness. "How's school?" he asked, addressing the boy first.

He didn't answer.

"What is your favorite subject, Ernesto?" Fermin asked.

The boy looked over at his mother for a moment. "Religion, Uncle Fermin," he said. His eyes darted to the floor.

"Learning about God and the Virgin is good." He looked at the girl. "And you?"

"Geography, Uncle." She did not look down at the floor like a servant, instead keeping her fiery eyes fixed on Fermin's. "I like to learn about different countries."

"That's good." He smiled. "Do your friends live nearby?" he asked her, at the same time realizing the idiocy of his question, because the dwellings backed up on one another.

Before she could answer, Rosa told the children to go outside and collect eggs. "Don't come back until I call you."

Unlike his legitimate children, the pair obeyed, Ernesto's black, almond eyes peeking back at Fermin before he scuttled out the door.

"They're getting so big." He winked at Rosa but she didn't smile. Fumbling in his pocket, he took out a wad of notes, earnings from the recent corridas and money he'd brought from home, and gave it to her.

Without thanking him, Rosa started counting the money. After she finished, she went to a cupboard and tugged open a drawer. Brightly colored clay cups and plates rattled as the back of the cupboard struck the cinderblock wall. She took out a shoe box, the edges of its shallow lid bound together with yellowing Scotch tape.

"They need uniforms and sports shoes," she said, as she laid the money tenderly in the box. "They start the big school next year."

Rosa worked as a seamstress in a garment factory fifteen miles from the house, catching a bus every day before dawn so she could arrive by five thirty. He admired her nobility, which refused to allow him to pay for everything the family needed. Yet thirteen years ago, it was her full breasts that had first attracted him. She'd come to his hotel with a friend of hers who'd wanted his autograph. She'd been shy, star-struck by a famous matador. He'd encouraged them to stay, then made a point of talking to Rosa and setting her at ease before asking her out.

It took three meals and two walks to persuade her to toss aside her scruples about sleeping with a man. Perhaps she'd hoped he'd fall deeply in love and marry her. Of course, that had been impossible. He'd already had Carmen and she would bear his children.

But Rosa had accompanied Fermin back to his hotel the second night and he'd sneaked her inside to protect her reputation. That night, she'd surprised him. After having dispensed of her inhibitions about nudity, she'd given all of herself to their lovemaking, pulling his buttocks to her as he thrust, moaning to inflame his passion. She'd been so unlike Carmen, who was silent and uncomfortable with the fire and stink of sex. Rosa had even ripped his back with her nails, and when he'd smarted on the bus ride home the next day, the sting had brought back her moans and her dark triangle, and made him hard again.

Their relationship fell dormant until Fermin had come back to the city and resurrected it, a relationship in which he'd never promised her marriage. He'd told her about Carmen only after his legitimate son was born. The birth had killed their affair.

"This is what I can afford right now," Fermin said, having already noticed that there was little money in the shoe box. As he had done many times before when she pouted, Fermin wished he could be like other men who'd found themselves in this situation, scoring his relationship with Rosa to a bunch of spirited rides and walking away from the confining responsibility. But he could not abandon her and the children.

"I'll get you more money," he said.

She drummed the floor with her feet. "I want them to have the same education as your other children," she said, sitting on the couch and pointing to a wooden farm chair across from her. "It's their right. I want them to grow up in a nice house closer to the city."

After sitting, he placed one foot on top of his knee. "It is their right to have nice things. I agree."

The corners of her tiny mouth quivered and then turned up in a smile. His heart beat faster. As he smiled back, Fermin wondered if all married men felt the same way when an old girlfriend smiled at them.

"Ernesto wants to be a matador," she said.

He shifted in the chair and planted both feet hard on the floor. "You will never tell him?"

"You're Uncle Fermin to them. That's how it will stay." She looked at him gravely. "When they're older, they'll want the truth, of course."

"I understand that."

Through the window, he could see his son examining an egg. It was as if the Maya in Rosa had gone to war in her womb and annihilated Fermin's Basque good looks. The boy was far too squat, nor would he ever have the good looks that people expected of a successful matador. Good looks like El Cabrito's. His son would need double—triple—the artistic ability of cocky El Cabrito in order to compensate.

"Will you stay and eat with us?" Rosa asked.

"Tell Ernesto to become a doctor," Fermin said. "Matadors always need good surgeons."

The hot, dry air smacked Fermin's face when he opened the front door of his home and started along the path. Today would be a scorcher. Still only eleven in the morning, and the air above the macadam surface farther down the street curled and trembled from the heat of the sun.

An elegantly dressed American woman walked up to him as he was about to climb into his car.

"Are you Mr. Guzmán?" she asked.

Fermin nodded. "*Sí.*"

"I'm Marie Boyd," she said, not offering her hand. "Kathleen's mother. Someone at the bullring gave me your address." She frowned. "I'm not pleased about you teaching my daughter bullfighting and it needs to stop." She waved her white gloves before her face like a fan, as her eyes roamed disapprovingly along the drab street.

From years of experience on the Texas ranch, Fermin knew never to come directly between a protective cow and her calf.

"You must fire her," Mrs. Boyd insisted.

Fermin regarded her blankly, pretending not to understand.

"What you're doing is wrong, Mr. Guzmán. My daughter's impressionable." She looked over her shoulder and pointed to a green Packard, where a man sat in the driver's side. "My husband and I want her to finish art school. So I need you to end whatever business arrangement you have with her and tell her to go home. I'll give you five dollars to do this." She nodded and smiled bizarrely at him. "That's right, five whole dollars."

Fermin's body turned hotter than the shimmering macadam. What's more, his pupil was talented and driven. He'd seen that clearly during their first training session at the bullring. And being as pretty as her mother, she'd also be a crowd-pleaser. She would earn him lots of money.

But equally as important, Fermin realized that Kathleen was his way back to the Plaza México, the pinnacle of bullfighting in Mexico. Through her, he'd win back the admiration and respect of the bullring impresarios and media. And his peers, those arrogant matadors and managers who gossiped about him being afraid of the bulls, would be crushed when they saw that he, Fermin, had taught a mere woman to do what they considered so brave.

He was not going to allow her mother to interfere. Fermin gaped now like a lunatic to exaggerate incomprehension. "No spik Engleesh," he said, shutting the car door.

Kathleen's mother stopped fanning, her gloves looking now like a bunch of wilted flowers in her hand.

"Kathleen . . . my daughter . . ." she said, as if addressing a child. "You send home." She pointed northward. "Texas." She walked a short distance up the street to demonstrate her intention. "Kathleen . . . back to America . . . understand, *¿sí?*" She walked north a little more. "No more bulls." She placed her open hands against the sides of her head so they resembled a cow's ears. "No more moo-moo. You tell Kathleen . . . go home . . . Texas." Opening her purse, she took out five one-dollar bills and held them out to Fermin. "You . . . money . . . five dollars."

Fermin walked to his front door and opened it. "No . . . spik . . . Engleeesh. Sorry." He went inside and slammed the door.

10

WHEN I ARRIVED BACK FROM THE STORE, MAMA WAS waiting in the high-ceilinged salon that had once been where the nuns entertained visiting family members. Two Gothic windows overlooking the street had stained glass and, with the sun shining through them, it looked as if sapphires and rubies had been studded into the parquet floor and threadbare armchairs. The tarnished golden haloes of the statues of Saint Joseph and the Virgin holding the infant Jesus glinted from inside their niches in the wall.

Mama rose and dusted the backside of her white dress as I walked toward her.

"Where's George?" I asked. He and Mama had married when I was a teenager. Too old to call him anything else, I'd always addressed George by his first name. He was fine with that and Mama didn't insist I call him Pops or something else as silly.

"He's fetching me a soda." Mama dabbed the base of her neck with a balled tissue. "We had to drive five hours in this nasty heat just to see you."

I stiffened.

"Why did you call off your engagement to Charles?" she demanded.

"I want to work."

"This is *not* work. I told you before."

"And I told you I needed to do it."

"I warned you to hold on to him at all costs." Her mouth tightened into a black line. "Do you know how many women would give their right arms to have a man like Charles for a husband?"

"We've been over this, Mama."

"He could provide you with an easy life. Easier than mine was."

"What do you mean by that?"

A clock in the hallway ticked in the silence. Mama walked over to the statue of the Virgin and blessed herself. A ray of sunlight struck the stained-glass window opposite where she stood and two tiny, bright-red squares burned into the back of her dress.

"Your father would be very disappointed."

Her rebuke brought a memory of him to the surface. I was standing beside Daddy; I could even smell the clean aroma of his hair oil. He was applauding two eight-year-old boys, classmates of mine, who were showing off, jumping from the roof of a low shed at our home. I ran up to the shed as Daddy shouted for me to return to his side. Ignoring him, I scaled the wall and jumped off, landing just as gracefully on the grass as the boys had done.

"Kathleen, come here now," he hollered. When I returned to him, he cuffed my ear. "Don't ever do that again, y'hear?"

"They did it," I said, pointing to the snickering boys lying on their bellies on the soft grass.

"Boys do these things. You could have broken a leg." He seized my hand and pulled me sharply back home to Mama.

"Daddy would understand me wanting to do this," I said, watching the red squares on Mama's dress blur and then disappear.

Mama turned around sharply. "He wanted you to get a steady job until you found yourself a husband."

I couldn't deny that. Once, when he and I were practicing with an old red towel on one of the dogs, I'd said to him yet again that I planned to fight real bulls one day. He'd stopped in the middle of executing a pass and looked at me, dead serious.

"No one can stop you if that's what you want to do, Peanut," he'd said, "but a woman can't fight the way men can. We're stronger. A woman's body's weaker and shaped differently."

"Then I'll work hard and make myself strong."

Daddy had tossed the towel aside. "I'd prefer you become a teacher and work at that until you find a nice man to look after you."

His words had only made me more determined to become strong—and perfect. But now that my dream had a chance to come true, Daddy wouldn't be here to see it. A vision of leaping flames and my father trapped in the dark crowded my mind.

The sound of a car passing by on the street grew louder as someone opened the front door, bringing me instantly back to the present. George came in carrying three bottles of soda.

"I figured you'd want one as well, Kathleen." He took off his hat, kissed my right cheek, and handed me a bottle.

With his round wire eyeglasses and smooth skin, which made him look thirty rather than forty-five, my stepfather was a bookish man with an aura of sincerity that people, especially mothers, responded to. He still preferred to wear his old, plain-cut suits from the war years rather than the double-breasted, more extravagant ones popular now.

"Tell your stepdaughter she needs to return to school," Mama said.

"I'm staying out of it, Marie." He rolled his eyes. Although never articulated, the boundaries of George's authority over me had been quickly established after he came to live with Mama and me. He knew I'd never allow him to replace my father.

"You haven't even graduated and you're moving on to the next thing," Mama said, turning back to me. "That's unacceptable. It shows a lack of commitment."

"You left college to marry Daddy."

"I didn't leave it for something stupid. To go live in—" Her shoulders rounded as she looked around the room. "To live in Mexico and work at something so . . . unfeminine."

"You would've let me leave college if Charles wanted to get married quick."

"Your clever arguments won't work, young lady." Mama sighed and held the balled tissue to her nose. "You lack discipline."

With the training schedule Maestro was putting me through, nothing was farther from the truth. I looked at Mama, really looked at her. Delicate lines had formed in the corners of her eyes and above her upper lip, which was smeared with the garish red lipstick she loved. Her chin had softened. Her teeth were still perfectly straight, but smoking cigarettes had turned them pale yellow. When she'd been my age, had she had a dream she'd wanted to achieve? If she had, she'd never spoken about it.

"I'd love your blessing, Mama."

"You're obstinate, just like your father was," she said. "Not willing to take advice. He wouldn't have died if he'd taken the promotion they offered him a year before the accident."

It was true that he'd been offered a desk job, but he'd loved working outdoors. The thought that he'd died loving what he did had always given me comfort. It also confirmed for me that Daddy would have supported my decision. He really would have understood.

"Please give me your support, Mama. Let me introduce you to my patron and Maestro Fermin, my trainer. You'll like them."

She drew closer to me, her eyes large and misty. "You call a man who mistreats animals for a living 'Maestro.' Anyway, I've met this so-called trainer."

"What?"

"Charles told me about him. But it was a complete waste. The man doesn't speak one word of American."

"How? Where . . . ? You shouldn't have interfered."

"Don't dare tell me what I should or shouldn't do, when you're busy throwing your life away. How did I not see this change happening in you?" She sighed and looked over at George. "How did we miss this?"

Mama tugged on a glove, her long fingers curling and extending like an eagle's talons as she forced it. "I guess a woman who plans to hurt animals has no trouble hurting her mother," she concluded.

"Don't say that."

"You're overreacting, Marie," George put in. "We all need to stay calm."

"Fighting bulls have been bred for centuries to fight," I said. "They love sparring among themselves when they're in the fields. They're not like domestic cows raised on ranches. Why can't you understand the art the bull and the matador make?"

"Sounds like hollow justification to me," Mama said. "Let's go, George."

George said, "Kathleen needs to give this a go, Marie. If it doesn't work out, she can—"

"Apologize. And maybe we'll consider paying for her to finish art school."

Mama seized George's forearm and moved him toward the door.

Mama's hissy fit only intensified my resolve. As Maestro said, bullfighting represented the ultimate battle of good and evil. Every time an artistic matador vanquished a brave bull, it represented the triumph of man over the brute force of nature, in the same way the Romans had regarded their gladiators' battles with exotic beasts. Mama loved watching films about gladiators. I couldn't understand her problem with me.

I met Maestro at the bullring that afternoon. I didn't want to meet his eye and would have preferred looking down at the sand, but he hated people doing that. If he wanted to let me go, Mama had given him one heck of a chance.

"I'm sorry about my mother," I said, deciding I should bring it up first. "She doesn't understand."

"People who aren't in our world don't understand." He smiled. "Do you have your mother's strength?"

I nodded.

"That's all you need. The rest I'll mold."

Maestro regarded Belmonte as the world's greatest matador and required me to master the three fundamentals of fighting as articulated by that great master. Belmonte's fighting style was invigorating; he stood utterly erect and extremely close to the incited bull when executing his passes, unlike his peers, who stayed far away from the razor-sharp horns. Every exercise I performed, no matter how repetitive and tedious, every swing of the cape or muleta, every posture I assumed, was intended to make certain I would keep my ground in the ring and not shrink from the bull. After I'd picked my spot to stand, every move I made was intended to make certain I would control the speed of the bull's charge and that *I*, not the bull, would direct all his actions.

One training exercise that continued daily for three months, until it became instinctive, was executing the classic *veronica* pass, named for the woman who'd given Christ a cloth to wipe his face with during the walk toward his crucifixion. The pass required me to grasp the parts of the cape where the corks were attached and bunch it up so I had a good fistful of material.

Maestro brought out a mechanical device with a fake bull's head and sharp horns mounted on a wheel. "You keep your feet planted rigid on the ground once I start the charge," he said, "and then pivot when I'm about to pass and swing the cape at the proper tempo."

Rather than doing that, I stepped back when he got within inches of me.

"Why did you move?" he said, pushing the mechanical device away from him so violently that it fell on its side.

"I panicked."

"You're useless."

The insult cut to the bone.

Next time, I held my ground, but I moved the cape too quickly. This was a dangerous habit, as doing so exposed my body to the bull, who might then see that I was the real target. I tried and failed again. I immediately believed that I really was useless, as Maestro had said, and that I should quit. But I kicked the sand angrily and struggled on.

The friendly Alfonso Ortiz, head of publicity for the Los Pinos bullring, a man who could make or break careers, encouraged me in my work. He sometimes took time out of his busy schedule to come and watch me practice ringside, and on one such occasion, he said, "You have the makings of a bullfighter. Even Fermin was once a pupil." He winked at Maestro. "Isn't that so?"

One late afternoon, when the sun was so bad-tempered it felt as if the crown of my head was on fire and I stank worse than a long dead fish, I executed the pass flawlessly. I didn't cede ground, kept my arms low and straight, and moved the cape ahead of the bull's charge at the perfect tempo. The horns passed a hairbreadth from my waist. Finally, I pivoted my body by standing on the balls of my feet, to lead the bull away and prepare for the next charge.

It happened a second time. And a third.

"Brilliant," Maestro cried, and he ran up and hugged me as tightly as my father used to do when I'd pleased him. He kissed my forehead. "You are going to be the best of them all."

Every nerve in my body vibrated. Despite the fierce heat, I suddenly felt ice-cold and shivered uncontrollably. His words were fuel for the fire roaring within me. He wanted only to make me a great fighter. His goal was also mine. He was like another father, just as he'd told me.

11

MY ROOMMATE WAS OBLIVIOUS TO HER SOILED CLOTHING, dumped across the floor and draped over the top of the dresser that she'd said was mine exclusively. Cookie crumbs and rusted apple cores littered the table and windowsill, an invitation to cockroaches, sugar ants, and other crawling Mexican critters. Half-filled mugs of coffee (laced with tequila) lay around the room for days. Belinda lay on her bed, reading a glossy women's magazine with one foot resting on her kneecap in a very unladylike way.

"I'm tired when I get home from work and the last thing I want to do is fix your mess," I said.

"Work?" Her eyes held mine for a moment, long enough to show contempt. "You're funny."

Upon learning I was a trainee bullfighter, the needle on my roommate's friendship barometer had jerked quickly from amiable to dislike. She'd told me bluntly she was a tolerant Los Angeles girl and didn't like sharing the room with a Texan with a lust for killin'. Though I thought she had more nerve than Carter's got liver pills, I'd ignored the insult. I figured the "tolerant" part of her personality would eventually emerge after she thought about the hurtful things she'd said.

But Belinda had instead stopped talking to me, except when it was essential, behaving as if I weren't even in the room. After a week, I rehung my bullfighter poster. For a while, I was scared I'd return home to find it in shreds, but a fear of Sister Rosemarie must have prevented Belinda from acting out of spite, especially since I'd mentioned that the nun attended fights at the Los Pinos bullring.

Another problem was her professor boyfriend, a tall Spaniard in his late twenties who taught history and plaited his dark hair like a Comanche brave. Despite a rule forbidding male guests anywhere but the common areas from nine in the morning until six thirty at night, Belinda entertained him in our room. Often, I found the two snuggling on her bed when I arrived home from the bullring. What got me worked up more than the breaching of the house rules was her assumption I'd accept the situation.

"I don't like your boyfriend here," I said.

"He doesn't talk to you." She tossed her magazine aside. "What's the problem?"

"*We* have to live together. But that doesn't include him."

"Room with someone else."

"There aren't any vacancies and you know that, missy."

"You're bent out of shape because he hates bullfighting, too," she spat. "Not everyone from Spain likes it, you know."

I shrugged and lay on my bed.

"Lorenzo doesn't understand men wanting to be bullfighters, never mind a woman. Women are nurturers." Belinda leaped off the bed. "He thinks you're weirder than Frida Kahlo."

"Listen up," I said. "I haven't said anything to anyone about Lorenzo, but you know the house rules."

Her anemic face went dark as a blue norther. She raised her right hand and took a step toward me. Time froze for what seemed like an eternity, until she lowered her hand, her forearm shaking as she did.

Belinda left, banging the door in her wake. A puff of dust jettisoned into a shaft of sun streaming through the window, the motes rising and falling like mosquitoes in a current.

It was my first time dining at Maestro's home and I'd been looking forward to it, because he'd told me that his wife was an excellent cook and she was preparing one of his favorite dishes, a tortilla casserole with chorizo, in my honor. I selected a full-skirted sundress with a print of bright yellow sunflowers set against a white background for the occasion. Maestro stared as I came into the living room, his surprise at my appearance no doubt caused by the fact that he saw me every day in a pair of shapeless men's jeans and an old shirt.

While waiting for Carmen to finish cooking, he served me a soda (he'd already told me drinking alcohol was forbidden) and his two children fired questions at me faster than a machine gun, including whether I had children and how many bulls I'd fought. Ten-year-old Emilio's wide, gleaming eyes dulled when I said I hadn't yet fought any live bulls. My single, spontaneous foray into the ring all those weeks ago didn't count.

Emilio wheeled around and left the salon, followed by his sister, Abril, but returned five minutes later, resplendent in a green satin matador's suit trimmed with gold sequins, a small bullfighter's nubby hat perched on his head. I couldn't believe the child's suit was green, given Maestro's reaction to mine that day in the bullring.

"Papi got this for me." He sighted my belly along the length of a wooden sword. "I'm going to be a great matador like him when I grow up."

Not to be outdone, Abril burst into the room dressed in a frothy crimson and black flamenco dress, her dark hair tied back in a bun that began unraveling as she sashayed toward me, clicking castanets.

"I'm going to marry Emilio, but only after he becomes a matador," she said, her new front teeth crisscrossed endearingly.

"Brothers and sisters can't marry," her brother said. "The priests don't allow it. I told you already."

His sister's pert little face crinkled. Before any tears came, Carmen hollered that dinner was ready and we went into a dining room fragrant with the mouthwatering aromas of cumin and freshly chopped cilantro. Carmen cut out a square of what looked like a lasagna and set it in front of me. The perfumed steam wafted up my nostrils.

"While I'm gone, I expect you to continue training at the ring every day," said Maestro, as Carmen placed a slice twice the size of my portion on his plate.

"You don't need to tell me that," I said, blushing.

I hadn't missed a day's training, arriving earlier than Maestro to use the weights and leaving at seven thirty every evening so I'd be home by eight thirty. Any later than that and townspeople, especially the older men and women, might gossip about an unaccompanied woman out in the streets. I resented that this unwritten rule in Mexico applied only to young women, but grudgingly accepted it because I was a foreigner in a different culture. Reputation was everything in the world of bullfighting, and I wasn't going to risk even the slightest reek of scandal ending my opportunities.

"Gustavo will wheel the mechanical bull when he has time off from his duties at the ring," Maestro said, referring to one of the part-time ring servants. He stabbed his fork into the casserole. "You can begin," he added, and took a gulp of beer.

"Carmen's not finished serving herself yet."

"That's okay," he said, and wiped foam off the ends of his mustache. He then blew on a forkful of food and ate. The children were also eating.

I took a small bite. It was larrupin' good, the best Mexican food I'd tasted to date. "Does this take as long to make as lasagna?" I asked Carmen. She didn't know what lasagna was and I don't think my explanation did it justice. My tryst with the bull in the arena in Garza that day was much better than my first time in the kitchen making one.

Fixin' to try my hand at making Carmen's dish when I eventually got my own apartment, I asked her if I could have the recipe. I still didn't cook often and, when I did, I liked things that were basic and quick: roast chicken, fried steak, and hot dogs. But this was too good to pass up.

Carmen looked cute as a possum when I asked, her smile taking years off her tired face. I could even see traces of the girl she'd been when she was my age. When I eventually married, would worries about raising children, looking after a husband, and running a home make me tired, too?

"Your dress is pretty, chiquita," Carmen said, in the same soft accent as the woman who'd once taught me Spanish. "Did you make it?"

"I can only sew on buttons."

Carmen laughed. I couldn't help wondering if she found my wanting to become a bullfighter strange. God knows, American women sure would.

"Do you sew?" I asked.

"I do," Carmen replied.

I looked at her dress closely for the first time, the bodice and short sleeves trimmed with cream-colored lace. The stitching was impeccable.

"Americans have beautiful clothes. I read the magazines from New York." Her liquid eyes turned dreamy. "I would love to see New York and the famous Empire State Building." She laughed again. "But I would be afraid to go inside such a high place."

"You have to go one day," I said, at the same time feeling a bit of a fraud, as I hadn't been there either.

Her gaze darted to Maestro.

"Would you like to borrow my dress and copy it?" I asked.

Light flooded her black eyes. "The pattern is different than what is for sale in the stores here."

"We can try the stores in Rowansville," I said. "Let's you and me go there soon."

"Kathleen, when will you find the time to take her?" Maestro asked, setting his beer glass down noisily on the tabletop. "You still haven't mastered the *pase de pecho*."

Though he'd once threatened that I'd spend an entire year performing only with the cape, Maestro had recently introduced the muleta into my training schedule. The *pase de pecho* was the classic chest pass to end a series of passes. It required holding the red flannel muleta in the left hand and leading the bull to raise his horns as he speeds by, just inches from the chest. Like all passes, great wrist control and flexibility were required to execute it artfully.

That Maestro allowed me to practice with the muleta at all, making sure I correctly secured the heart-shaped cloth over the two-foot dowel with the thumbscrews, meant he was pleased with my cape work. I just wished he'd acknowledge it instead of being so demanding all the time.

"Thank you for cooking such a wonderful meal, Carmen," I said, ignoring Maestro's comment.

Maestro raised his beer glass and saluted his wife.

After dinner, taking a cue from Carmen, who'd begun collecting the children's dirty plates, I rose and picked up Maestro's plate.

"Where are you going?" he asked, his forehead creasing into three hemispheres.

"It's the least I can do after such a great meal."

"Sit." He set his fists down sideways on the table and regarded me. His jaw was set hard.

"It's okay," Carmen said to me.

Maestro looked at his wife. "Put the children to bed."

Setting down the plates immediately, she told the children to follow her out of the room. Maestro was apparently the master of his home, as well as the bullring. As I took my seat, I tried to recall my father ordering Mama to do something in front of guests, but I couldn't think of a single instance.

Maestro took out a squashed packet from his shirt pocket and, with a quick flick of the wrist, shot a cigarette into his mouth. The fan creaked slowly overhead and the match exploded with a fizz when he struck it. He sat back in his chair and gazed up at the ceiling, the glowing cigarette dipping languidly from his fingers. Those same fingers had swung capes and muletas deftly, had battled and conquered ferocious bulls.

"Which are you, Kathleen?" He expelled a blast of gray smoke through his black nostrils. "Woman or bullfighter?"

I straightened up, took my hands off the table, and placed them on my lap. "I don't know what you're asking me."

"Are you a woman or a bullfighter?"

I was a woman. I was a bullfighter—though, technically, I wasn't yet. If I said I was both, would he construe it as arrogance?

"I'm a woman. I haven't fought a bull long enough, so I guess I'm not you yet."

"Let me ask another way, then." He tapped the cigarette in the ashtray. "Do I treat you as a woman or a bullfighter first?"

It took me a moment to fully consider the question.

"Like a bullfighter."

He grimaced as he leaned toward me, revealing small front teeth and grayish gums. "Then don't ask to wash dishes in my house. That is woman's work. Do you understand?"

Carmen returned and began picking up empty plates now congealed with grease and bits of food. I wondered how something that had been so beautiful could look so ugly in such a short space of time.

"Are the children safely in bed?" he asked.

"Yes, Fermin."

"Good." Maestro rose. "Bring our coffees into the salon."

12

EVERY MORNING AT THE BULLRING, I'D BEGIN AT THE GYM-
nasium, which stank like unwashed socks until my sense
of smell adjusted and I no longer noticed. I worked there
for ninety minutes, first stretching and skipping, using a frayed rope
whose wooden handles felt grubby to the touch, and then lifting
weights. Already, the left side of my body had strengthened and both
my arms were ropy and defined, though I was careful not to lift too
large of a weight. I didn't want to develop Charles Atlas muscles. I
wasn't sure if women's bodies could grow big that way and sure didn't
fix on finding out.

After skipping, I'd lie on the floor and do crunches to tighten my
belly and improve my gait. To strengthen my wrists, I squeezed and
released tennis balls until the muscles and tendons burned, and then
I'd rest for thirty seconds and begin again. Sometimes I also played
handball, batting the rubber ball back and forth against a brick wall
in an isolated section of the complex.

Out in the bullring, I worked in the shadow of the *toril* gate either
with Gustavo, the part-time ring servant Maestro hired to assist, or
alone, if Gustavo was sweeping or doing other chores.

Where I disobeyed Maestro's instructions was when I did cape work.
I was bored of performing endless *veronicas*, the workhorse of any

matador's repertoire that I now executed as beautifully as the Spaniard Antonio Ordóñez. I started experimenting with the *media-veronica*, a pass serving as the finale to a series of passes, which, when executed proficiently, caused the bull to turn quickly in on himself and come to a complete stop, thus allowing the matador to turn his back on him and walk away victoriously.

As I finished performing one of them, I heard a catcall from the nearby wooden fence. A middle-aged carpenter in dungarees mending splintered planks was gawking at me. When he saw me looking at him, he whistled again and walked toward me.

"You are a beautiful woman," he said, in a thick southern dialect. "And you move very sexy." His beady eyes fixed on my breasts and then my rear end. The greedy stare made me feel exposed.

"Please go away."

"I am just admiring—"

"Leave her alone."

Startled, I spun around to see a young man walking toward me. His chestnut skin was boyishly smooth and a narrow sandy mustache was the only proof he was old enough to shave. He cocked his head slightly, the brow high and the chin square, the eyes wide and kind. A scar ran diagonally across his right eyebrow, revealing a sliver of pure white skin.

"Go back to your work," he said to the carpenter, pointing to the barrier fence.

The man's face twitched and reddened but, surprisingly, he walked away.

"Thank you," I said.

He nodded. "You work the cape very well, Señorita Boyd."

"How do you know my name?"

"Fermin is your instructor. People talk." He smiled and held out his right hand. "I'm Julio Fernández. They call me El Cabrito."

I wasn't sure if I could speak. I'd heard of the young matador whose nickname was "The Kid." He was performing in the corrida on Sunday afternoon. I also knew Maestro occasionally worked as part of his team, performing as a banderillero, though he'd never spoken to me about him.

From across the ring, another man called out for El Cabrito to return.

"Just a second, Papá," he said, glancing over his wide shoulder at the stocky, middle-aged man. He turned back to me. "My father is strict."

His daddy watched with arms akimbo.

"You must perform the *rebolera* as your finale," Julio continued, ignoring his father. "It pleases the crowd more than a *media-veronica*." His nose crinkled. "That pass is so ordinary."

He held out his hands for the cape and proceeded to execute the flashy pass, transferring the cape from hand to hand behind his back so it blossomed around his waist. He did it a second time. His facial gestures changed as he went through the motions of the pass, the full lips pouting endearingly as he passed the cape from one hand to the other.

"Now, you try."

An urge to take out my handkerchief and wipe beads of sweat off his forehead came over me, but instead I took back the cape. It felt awkward to have his warm hands cupped around mine, his grip gentle but assured. Maestro never touched me during practice.

As Julio led me through the sequence, helping to arrange my wrist and arm positions, my awkwardness yielded to the excitement of learning something new. The cape bloomed around my waist like a huge magenta flower. I tried a second time without his help and didn't succeed. My third attempt was better.

"Julio, come back here now," his father hollered.

Julio started to leave, but stopped after walking three yards away. "Keep practicing and you'll get it." He winked. "When you perform it for the first time and the crowd roars, don't forget who taught you."

He sprinted across the ruffled sand, his sandy hair glinting in the sun.

I sat on my bed and tore open Mama's letter, her first contact since she'd come to see me months ago. Written on cream-colored paper, it smelled faintly of her rose perfume. My eyes sprinted across the lines, hunting for words showing acceptance of my decision to move to Mexico.

Her salutation—"Dearest Misguided Daughter"—was the warmest part of the letter. The rest was a rehash of the conversation we'd had when she'd visited, including her certainty that my father would be very disappointed in me if he were alive. She ended with, "Your Worried Mother."

A postscript was appended:

> *Jenny Sinclair's mother sends her regards. She bumped into me at the hairdresser's and jumped on me faster than a duck on a June bug to tell me that Jenny's getting married. Wasn't Jenny in your senior class? She left Dyson after school to go work in a fancy restaurant in Houston, where she hooked a bank director during one of the shifts. Her mother took pains to say he's an executive director, which is different than an ordinary director. Like I didn't know that. They're getting married next month and she and her mama were in Houston looking at wedding dresses. Imagine traveling to Houston to buy a wedding dress? You should also know the news made me feel sad!! Very sad.*

A trumpet cut through the surging strains of violins and a guitar as I passed by a brightly painted cantina on my way home from the bull-ring. Though I was tired, it was Thursday, which meant Belinda was entertaining her boyfriend in our room. We'd compromised on his illegal visits, she agreeing to confine them to Thursday evenings in return for my promise not to tell the nun. Not wanting to relive the awkwardness of being with them or to sit in the drab living room until he left, I decided to go into the cantina for a soda.

The interior was as colorfully decorated as its façade. Affixed to the walls were sombreros, guitars, maracas, and even an old accordion. Five men who looked so alike they could have been brothers comprised the band, all of them dressed in traditional black charro suits trimmed in silver. A bar and counter in the adobe style were at the front of the room, bottles of tequila, whiskey, and beer placed in a double row of square niches cut out of the baked clay. Only two women, who looked to be Mama's age, were present, chatting with stout, well-dressed businessmen. They wore heavy makeup, thick, black mascara clumping their exaggerated eyelashes.

Men glanced sidelong at me as I made my way to the bar, some stopping their conversations as I passed their tables. One of the bartenders, an older man wearing a white apron, approached and laid his hands on the countertop. Despite promising Maestro I wouldn't drink alcohol, I had a compulsion to order tequila.

I managed to control it. "A cola with lots of ice, please."

The bartender remained frozen. Only his thick fingers tapping the counter indicated he was alive.

"A cola with ice, please," I repeated, emphasizing the request.

He pointed to a sign next to the door: NO SE PERMITEN MUJERES. The cantina didn't allow women. I hadn't seen it when I entered.

"But there are women in here and they've been served," I said.

The barman arched his verdant eyebrows and regarded me quizzically. "Those women are different. The gentlemen bought their drinks."

"I won't stay long."

"I'm sorry." He straightened up to leave.

Blood rushed to my face. "Isn't my money good enough for you?"

Men stopped talking and looked at me.

"Please leave now," the barman said, and walked away.

I felt small as an ant as I made my way to the door. The sting of rejection remained as I walked home. Now that it was after eight thirty, fewer people were out on the streets; men made their way to the bars, couples strolled hand-in-hand to restaurants, and vendors pushed carts heavy with the aroma of ripe mangoes or bottles of luridly colored syrups for the shaved ice they sold during the day.

A street lamp flickered on Vallarta Avenue as I turned off and entered Calle Hidalgo, a street ten minutes from home. Even in daylight it smelled moldy and the cobblestones were slick where the untended bougainvillea and vines blocked out the sunlight. One side of the street was bounded by a long, crumbling brick wall, the boundary of an old cemetery containing the graves of soldiers; the other boasted both vacant and occupied houses and businesses, including a cobbler with lasts in the window, two tailors, a clock repair shop, and a bodega, all shuttered for the night.

Halfway along, I heard the metal click of footsteps behind me and looked over my shoulder to see a man walking quickly toward me. The man was in his thirties and slender as a matador. He wore dark gabardine pants and a cream-colored *guayabera* with white embroidery running up both sides.

"I saw you in the cantina, but you left before I could say anything to the bartender," he said, the words streaming out fast. His accent was curious, and one I didn't recognize. "I must apologize for my countrymen."

"Thank you," I said, "but it's fine."

I turned to leave and he grabbed my arm. He saw me staring open-mouthed at his hand and released his grip. "Would you like to come back to my hotel for a drink?"

The offer astonished me. It was as bizarre as my expulsion by the bartender.

"I'm here on business from the south," he explained. "You're American and I thought you'd like some company."

"Thanks, but I've got to get home."

He smiled thinly. "If the barman had allowed you to stay, you wouldn't be in such a hurry to go home."

His observation silenced me for a moment. "I really must go," I said, as firmly as I could, and I walked away hurriedly.

He caught up and walked alongside me, his head darting from side to side.

"What's a pretty girl like you doing alone in Mexico?"

"I live here."

"You shouldn't be out alone in Los Pinos." He glanced over his shoulder and then peered ahead.

My heart reared in my chest. I swerved to avoid a large outgrowth of bougainvillea on the cemetery wall and then, before I grasped what was happening, my back slammed into the wall. A twig from the bougainvillea stabbed my lower back. The stranger pressed his sweaty hand over my mouth. I smelled acrid tobacco as he put his face close to mine.

"I'm taking my hand away," he said. "If you scream, I'll hurt you very badly." His eyes glinted white as the blade of a matador's sword. He pushed me deeper into the shadows created by the outgrowth. "You understand?"

Though he was only four inches taller than me and despite my added strength from working out, he was much stronger and I knew I couldn't break away immediately. I let my body go limp.

He put his mouth on mine and forced his tongue between my lips. His mustache hair pricked my skin. His saliva tasted sour. He groped my breasts, moving roughly between them. He thrust against me. I could feel his hardness.

"Please," I said, "I know you're a good man. Please, don't—"

"Shut up, bitch."

His left hand grabbed a handful of my hair by the roots and he pulled fiercely, but I felt no great pain. One of my incisors accidentally punctured my lower lip. The taste of iron overwhelmed my senses, still there was no fierce pain. Cool air brushed my thighs as he pulled up my dress. I tightened my muscles and jammed my legs closed. He seized the side of my underpants, his eyes widening when he realized I wasn't wearing a girdle. After changing out of my jeans at the bullring after work every day, I never put one on, because I always went home directly and showered.

"Just as I thought," he said, his voice hoarse now. "An American woman looking for fun."

Inserting his knee between my legs, he forced them apart. He overwhelmed me. When he forced himself into me, it felt like a red-hot poker had been jammed up my belly. I closed my eyes against the reality of what was happening, pushing the lids together so tightly my ears roared.

I curled my fingers into claws and raised my hands, attempting to gouge out his eyes. I struggled, fighting hard, and he let go of my hair and right arm to get a better grip on me.

Now freer to move, I rammed my knee into his crotch faster than a camera flash. For a moment that seemed eternal, nothing happened. And then he screamed shrilly and doubled over. I broke away and fled. My shoe caught on a raised paving stone and I tripped and fell, but I got up quickly and continued, tearing along the dark street until a stitch started up in my side.

Five minutes later, I stood outside the convent and caught my breath. The man was nowhere in sight. It wasn't yet nine thirty, so the main door wasn't locked. I went into the dim salon to wait until the adrenaline stopped pumping through my system. My knees burned fiercely. Looking down, I saw they were raw and bloody.

A dreadful thought occurred: Had he been inside me long enough to make me pregnant? I was regular over every month and my period was due in a week. Was it still possible? I went to the armchair where my mother had sat and cried, sobbing until my eyes burned fiercely.

The statue of the Virgin stood in her niche, with the child in her arms and a comforting smile on her pink face. She watched me, but saw nothing. Saint Joseph watched, too. I blessed myself and uttered the Virgin's name. I dropped on my knees in front of her but the stinging grew even fiercer and I had to stand. I said the Hail Mary. It didn't help.

An ancient telephone sat on the coffee table with a cracked Carrara marble top. Going over, I picked up the receiver and gave the operator my mother's telephone number. A series of dry clicks ensued.

"Hello, Kathleen," George said, once I'd announced myself.

Two tiny chunks of Bakelite were missing from the rim of the mouthpiece, as if a mouse had bitten them off.

"Can I speak to Mama?"

"Are you all right?"

"I need to speak to Mama."

I pressed the phone to my ear until I heard the scraping sound of someone picking up the receiver.

"Why are you calling so late, Kathleen?" Mama asked.

It felt like there were a hundred hot needles in my eyes. "I just wanted to hear your voice."

"Is something wrong?"

I gripped the cord fiercely.

"Kathleen?"

It would be the end of me if I told her the truth. I would have to surrender. "Nothing's wrong, Mama." I gripped the receiver so tightly my fingers hurt. "It's been so long since we talked. I wanted to hear your voice."

"You're the one who hasn't called for ages," she said.

"I know."

"You wouldn't be lonely if you came home." A pause. "Is that why you're calling? To tell me you've decided to leave that horrible place?"

My body started quaking. The shudders were uncontrollable. I thought my insides would shake out.

"So, you haven't changed your mind?" she pressed.

"Mama, please." I was sure she'd hear me shaking. "Can't we talk about something else?"

"Did you get my letter about Jenny getting married?"

I bit into my lip hard, willed my body to stop quaking.

"Of course, you did." She sighed. "She's done really well for herself, hasn't she? And her plug ugly."

"She wasn't as bad looking as you say, Mama."

"Do you know how difficult it is for me to explain to the neighbors what you're doing with your life?" Her voice brimmed with irritation. "I can't bring myself to tell people. I tell them you're still at art school."

"I'm sorry, Mama."

"As you should be."

"I should go."

"You think about what I've said, y'hear?"

"I . . . I love you."

There was a pause, followed by a click and then the purr of the empty line. Mama was returning to her program on the television.

I looked up at the stained-glass windows. They were now just tiny lead squares and blackness. The darkness had robbed them of their jeweled brilliance. My head began to throb again. My knees stung. The pink-cheeked Virgin peered down impassively.

13

NEXT MORNING, WHEN I AWOKE AND DRESSED FOR WORK, I felt flat and my knees raged like hellfire. Before going to the bullring, I called Sally in New York, only to learn from someone at her modeling agency that she was in the Caribbean for a photo shoot and wouldn't return for a week. At the bullring, I ignored the pain and went through the motions.

Life unspooled before my eyes like a reel of film. The ring staff and apprentices working around me were of no importance in my life, nor was I of any importance to theirs. I was small. Inconsequential. I'd never felt outside my body this way before. I felt alive and dead at the same time.

I called my patron's home and his wife said he had gone to Texas on business. She didn't inquire how I was doing or ask how my training was going. I wasn't important to her. Granted, I'd met her only once. I didn't even know why I'd called Señor Barros. I never called him for anything. He dealt now with Maestro directly regarding my work.

Still, the disconnected feeling wouldn't go away and I desperately needed to tell someone. I went to Carmen and made sure she sent the children out to play, and then I began talking about the night before. After I finished, her hand remained over her mouth as if it had been glued there. She said nothing.

Then she hugged me, tears dripping from the corners of her eyes. "Chiquita, I'm so sorry. So, so sorry."

I gripped her fiercely, feeling the softness and warmth of her body beneath my hands.

"Did you meet anyone in the street who might have seen him?" she asked.

"There was no one around."

"That is not so good, chiquita. Because then you could have reported it to the police."

I couldn't help but think that if the police alerted the newspapers about the attack and they printed a story, then my career was definitely finished. "No, no police," I said. "Telling the police wouldn't help. I can't remember what he looks like."

Every time I tried to recall my attacker's features, my mind refused to dwell on it and all I got was a blur. I was also an American living in a foreign country and I had no physical proof other than my bloodied knees, which the police would think I'd gotten in the bullring.

When Maestro returned from his fights in the south, he sent Carmen to fetch me to their home that evening.

"Did you say anything to get him worked up?" he asked, after I'd explained what happened.

"He followed *me*."

"I mean, in the cantina." He crossed his legs. "Did you look at him in a sexy way?"

"I didn't see him in the cantina."

"Why did you go there?"

I didn't feel like explaining my difficulties with Belinda, whom I'd now warned could never again entertain her boyfriend in our room. "I didn't realize only men went there."

"You create trouble when you go into these places."

"Fermin, she's American," said Carmen. "Kathleen doesn't understand our culture."

Maestro stiffened. The room fell quiet, the only sound coming from a wall clock ticking in the hallway.

"You must have a chaperone," he said at last. "I should have thought of this before."

The daughters of wealthy Mexican families had chaperones. It sounded like a good solution, but I didn't like the idea that I could never go anywhere alone again. Having a chaperone during the daytime would be useless, if not unbearable. The real solution, I felt, was to overcome the horror, and the only way to do that was to focus even more on my bullfighting.

"I don't need one," I said, as firmly as possible. "I need to find a new place to live that's closer to the bullring."

"I'll find someone to meet you at your home first thing in the mornings and escort you to the bullring," said Maestro, as if he hadn't heard me object, or maybe just didn't care. "After work, someone will escort you home. You will *not* go out alone in the streets of Los Pinos at night."

"I don't need a chaperone during the day."

"I make the rules. You obey them. That's the agreement." He turned from me to his wife. "I need a beer."

She rose. "Come out to the patio with me, Fermin."

"Fetch me a beer."

"Come with me for a moment. Then I'll fetch you a cold beer." Carmen smiled at me. "Would you like juice or milk?"

"Juice."

Staring with narrowed eyes at the pitch-black hearth, Maestro drummed his fingers on the plump armrests for a moment and then sprang up and followed her. When he returned five minutes later, his features were as impassive as a bull's. I couldn't read what had transpired. He'd also rearranged his hair so the parting was rigidly delineated. Flecks of dandruff were visible in the oily waves. He returned to the armchair and crossed his legs European-style.

"Carmen says it would be better if you moved in here," he said. "We have a free room."

"I don't want to impose."

"My wife's thinking is very smart. I can take you to the bullring every day." The corners of his mouth flickered. "We can also continue our work out on the patio in the evenings."

The idea of extra practice cheered me up.

"Señor Barros pays your rent and board, doesn't he?"

I nodded.

Maestro's sharp eyes flicked to the hallway and then darted back to me. "I'll arrange for it to come to me directly from now on," he said, his voice so low it was a murmur.

"That's fine."

"We won't speak of this arrangement." He looked pointedly toward the hallway and then turned back to me. "To anyone."

Don Marcos Riviera, the elderly impresario of the Los Pinos bullring, Alfonso Ortiz, Señor Barros, and Maestro stood in the deep shadow of the entrance gate fifteen feet away from where I stood in the ring. Maestro had ordered me to practice footwork, but I couldn't concentrate. Their conversation was about me. I wanted to be over there and give them my opinion.

A group of female *toreras* was scheduled to perform in Los Pinos in two months' time. These women weren't regarded as professional bullfighters by the owners of bullrings or the paying public, but rather as an attraction, in the same way sideshow folk are billed as circus performers. I'd already seen a poster advertising the event pasted up in the plaza adjacent to the bullring's main entrance. The women had heard of me and were intrigued because I was an American, and their manager had approached Don Riviera to inquire if I'd like to perform with them during their show. Recognizing an opportunity to fill more seats, the impresario and the publicity manager contacted my patron, who was also very keen.

Maestro didn't share their enthusiasm, insisting I wasn't ready. After I'd interrupted and said I was, Maestro had ordered me out into the ring to continue practicing.

My trainer stamped his foot on the ground and Don Riviera, switching his silver-tipped walking cane to his other hand, put his arm around Maestro's shoulder and led him off to the other side of the gate's entrance. The pair conversed for a few minutes before rejoining the rest of the men. It nearly killed me not to know what they were saying. Five minutes later, all of the men glanced over at me and then shook hands. All except Maestro walked away, disappearing into the inky blackness of the tunnel.

"Why aren't you practicing?" Maestro said, as he walked up. His face was inscrutable.

"I don't think it's fair what you said to them, Maestro. I've been training for more than seven months. I *am* ready to perform."

"We shall see." A swarm of gnats danced around his protruding ears, which he tried to swat away but they kept returning as soon as his head lowered. "You'll perform with these women. And the impresario will pay us a fee. It's only a few hundred pesos, but you have to start somewhere."

The money would be my first earnings as a bullfighter. I'd be legitimate.

"You'll give the money to Señor Barros as the first step toward repaying him," said Maestro.

After dinner, Carmen and I took our coffees into the salon while Maestro spent time with the children out on the patio. It had taken a month for me to fully adjust to being part of a household full of the laughter, anger, and tears of two gregarious children. Living with these kids made me think of Charles wanting to get married and have children, and only reinforced the fact I wasn't ready for such a responsibility.

For the first week, I'd been apprehensive about going into the salon and the house's other public spaces, in case Maestro thought I was intruding on his privacy or acting too familiar with his family. But Carmen, sensing my unease, came to my bedroom at the start of the second week and insisted I join the family, watching television in the salon. The program was for children, American cartoons, but I was grateful she'd invited me.

"Do you think much about what happened to you?" she'd asked during an intermission.

I'd stiffened, gripping an arm of my chair, but then relaxed again. It was the first time she'd spoken of that horrible night, but it was normal for her to be concerned and I knew I should be grateful.

"I want to forget," I'd said, "so I try not to think about it."

"If you ever want to talk, chiquita, I'm here."

As the days passed, my relationship with Carmen developed into a friendship—but not so with Maestro. He treated me as a tenant, inquiring if I needed anything else for the room, like new bedding or additional shelves for my books. Our conversations about topics other than bullfighting were amicable but brief.

On the weekend of my third week there, Maestro left for two days to perform in a bullfight in Garza, the city where I'd jumped into the ring spontaneously. I accepted Carmen's invitation to accompany her and the children to a fun fair and skipped my usual training at the bullring, though not before asking Carmen to tell the children not to tell their father I'd gone with them.

The experience resurrected a happy memory of a day spent with Daddy at a fair years ago. I even drank lurid, blue-colored shaved ice.

"Tía Kathleen's lips are blue," said Emilio, doubling over with laughter.

He'd addressed me as "aunt." Carmen's gaze locked with mine. Before I could correct him, she said, "Isn't Tía Kathleen silly?" My head ached dully at the honor.

Carmen and Abril disliked bumper cars and refused to take a ride in them, so I went with Emilio. Waiting in line, someone tapped my shoulder from behind. I jumped, hands balled into fists, and turned around to see Gustavo with a toddler in the crook of his arm. I stared at him, speechless. He'd surely mention to Maestro that he'd seen me here.

"Are you okay, Señorita Kathleen?" he asked, still eyeing my fists as he set his daughter on the ground.

I wondered if this new instinct to defend myself when surprised would ever leave me. "You're riding the cars, too?" I asked, my voice shaky.

"It's my daughter's first time."

When the ride started, Gustavo sought us out and bumped into my car often, laughing raucously each time he sped away. Afterward, I delivered Emilio hurriedly to his mother and went looking for Gustavo. I found him at the cotton candy stall.

"Don't mention to Señor Fermin that you saw me here today," I said, and faked a laugh.

His features shifted and then firmed into a study of incomprehension.

Carmen was a voracious reader. She read Spanish and English novels and fashion magazines, including *Vogue* and *Redbook*. I'd never been interested in women's fashion, but now read them with an eye to finding out what was going on back in the States, as well as hoping to come across pictures of Sally.

"Chiquita, I'd love to have this washing machine," Carmen said, and she slid a Sears, Roebuck catalog onto my lap. "It's a woman's dream. Isn't it beautiful?"

I looked at the picture of a Lady Kenmore wringer washer. The hand-drawn black-and-white image was functional but inartistic, had probably been done by an artist bored with his job. Still, I thought about Carmen, of how she washed the laundry by hand, including mine (at her insistence), and scrupulously ironed every piece. It took her two days to complete the dreadful chore. Maestro would not allow me to help her.

"You must fill out this form," Maestro said to me, as he entered the salon, clutching a sheaf of papers. "You need an artist's passport to perform in Mexico. I sent away to the government for the application papers."

I'd never heard of such a thing, but then Maestro liked to spring information on me out of the blue. Or, as with the negotiations about my upcoming performance with the female *toreras*, he wouldn't involve me until the thing was settled.

"Fetch me your passport," he said. "Carmen, this is business. You can leave. We'll be busy for the rest of the evening."

Her eyes dimmed and her mouth turned down. "I'm interested to see how this works."

"It concerns her private business. Facts about her family and history are to be recorded on the documents."

"I've got nothing to hide," I said. "Carmen can stay."

Maestro's face darkened. "See to your children."

When she refused, Maestro thumped the arm of the chair and then sprang to his feet. Carmen rose swiftly. Their hands gesticulated wildly in the air.

"You shouldn't tell me what to do in this house," Carmen said. "I'm tired of it."

I didn't understand why Maestro treated her so dismissively. I was his pupil and grudgingly accepted when he insulted me. But she was his wife. She cooked and sewed for him and was an excellent mother to their children. Insults I'd never heard before in Spanish rained down as they moved about the room in a frenetic dance. I wanted to flee, but feared intensifying Maestro's rage if I did. I sat statuesque, for the first time in my life willing myself to be smaller.

14

AFTER LEAVING THE OUTSKIRTS OF LOS PINOS, WE DROVE south, passing peasants with deeply sun-wrinkled faces, many with sickles and rakes slung across their stooped backs. At the outskirts of villages, listless horses foraged along the sides of the roads, their ribs protruding like washboards and their atrophied buttock muscles rippling and jerking as horseflies feasted on their blood.

Maestro made no attempt to converse and I gazed out at the passing landscape, distant red hills and arid countryside pocked with mesquite, cacti, and lechugilla. The scenery reminded me of the countryside surrounding the home where I'd grown up in Texas.

Forty minutes later, the road ran parallel to a wide creek that ran to the Rio Grande. The topography began to change, becoming lush with tall sugar cane, maize, sorghum, and even fields of peanuts. We passed ranches where beef cattle sought protection from the burning sun by standing rigid under the weak shade of coreb and poplar trees, the bulls' physiques sleek, but also puny in comparison to the rippling bulk of their fighting brothers.

I was happy Maestro didn't talk. His treatment of Carmen the previous night disgusted me still. I'd been unable to fall asleep for hours, as the part of me craving success in the bullring and in need of his help to get there warred with the woman inside me. I'd tossed and turned and tried to reconcile the opposing sides of him, pitting his skills and the fragments of encouragement he doled out against the stern brute he was at home.

Late that night, someone had knocked on my bedroom door. I'd opened it to find Carmen, standing in her nightdress. She hadn't spoken as she came in and sat on my only chair, looking around the room as if appraising what bitsy decorating I'd done. The room had a high ceiling and was furnished with a bookshelf and a single bed pushed up under a window overlooking the patio. An ancient armoire contained three of Maestro's suits of lights. The only things I'd done was pin up my bullfight poster and hang the oil painting I'd done of my dog, plus five framed photographs of my parents. I'd also purchased a bright Mexican Zapotec rug.

"I didn't want you to witness us fighting," she'd said, sincerity glinting in her dark, liquid eyes. "Fermin was right. It was your business and I had no right to stay."

I'd scrutinized her face, then said, "But you're right to tell him you're tired of him talking down to you."

She'd smiled the same way the Virgin did in holy pictures. "Married people argue. They fight. It's normal. You'll find this out one day."

I had said nothing.

"My husband is a good man." She'd sighed. "He has faults and secrets, but he loves his children. Fermin provides for them—and for me." The pure whites of her eyes had gleamed. "Don't form a bad opinion of him because of what you saw tonight."

Now the car brakes shrieked as Maestro slowed and turned into a dirt road narrower than the one we'd left. Behind us, whorls of red dust turned the bright air dark as his old car rattled toward a farmhouse in the mid-distance. We pulled up next to a ring made of five-foot adobe walls, about half the size of a standard bullring.

"Get in the ring," Maestro said, and handed me a cape.

He walked around the perimeter of the arena and disappeared. No sooner was I inside the ring than I heard a scraping noise. Directly opposite me, a man pushed open a wooden gate. He looked familiar, but I didn't have time to consider if or from where I knew him, because a red-and-white bull passed through the gate and trotted into the sunlight. He stamped his right front hoof in the dirt and looked up at the blue sky. His head lowered and swiveled slowly around the ring, stopping when he saw me. Maestro and the man climbed up on the thick adobe wall and sat.

This bull wasn't large like the one I'd caped in the Garza bullring. He was around two years old and weighed about four hundred pounds, the horns short and thin but still lethally sharp. Young bulls like this had killed unskilled bullfighters. Before I had time to arrange the cape, he charged. My mind flashed back to the cemetery wall in the dark street. Racing images came of the man's hand, his face still a blur, pushing me into the bushes, and the pressure of the twig against my back. The cape was a lead blanket in my grasp. Not one of my nerves or muscles moved.

"Swing the cape," Maestro hollered.

I looked toward where the voice came from and saw the shadowy image of Maestro leaping into the ring. I turned back to see the bull lower his head, his horns aimed at my belly. My brain and muscles reconnected and I stepped back quickly from the line of charge. I'd saved myself but given ground. I'd surrendered. I'd done what no courageous bullfighter would ever do.

Swift as a boomerang, the bull turned and charged again. The cape was ripped from my hands. Maestro pushed me away and I fell flat on the hard clay. Picking myself up, I watched Maestro execute perfect *veronicas* and lead the bull toward the gate from where he'd emerged.

As he sprinted back over, Maestro said, "What the hell's wrong with you?"

Why had memories of the attack rushed into my mind without warning? It made no sense. Was I going crazy? "I just froze, Maestro," I managed.

"You're useless to me if you're afraid."

The insult was a hot slap in the face. I burst into tears.

"Stop crying. That's a woman's trick."

I wiped my eyes with the sleeve of my shirt, felt the grit in the soil graze the tender skin around the sockets.

"Because you're a woman, people will find your fear in the bullring detestable," he said. "They'll find it detestable that you are trying to emulate what brave matadors do."

Maybe he was right. Maybe my mind was trying to tell me I was too afraid to fight bulls. But I pushed the horrible thought away. I had to overcome this or I was finished.

"Let me try again, Maestro."

"We're going home."

"Please, let me. I won't fail again."

"No."

He tossed the cape over his shoulder and walked away. An unseen bird began twittering. Another responded. I longed to be one of those tiny birds. The car door slammed shut. The engine started. As I walked to the exit, Maestro signaled his festering anger by stepping on the gas.

After Maestro and I returned from the ranch, I went directly to my room, pulled down the blind, and lay fully clothed on the bed in the comforting darkness. It was hot and the creaking overhead fan didn't cool me. I tried to read one of Carmen's magazines but the disaster at the ranch and images of the assault kept returning. I kept replaying what I should have done at the ring and what I did that night on the street. Had I fought against my attacker hard enough? I had not fought the bull properly. Ceding ground to him was forbidden.

I didn't join the family for dinner. When Emilio came to fetch me, I told him I wasn't hungry. Carmen brought me a plate of food, but despite the spicy aroma of the pork and *mole* sauce, I only picked at it and tossed the rest into a bag that I intended to dispose of in secret.

An hour later, someone knocked. I picked up the plate and went to the door. Maestro regarded the plate but made no attempt to take it. He came inside.

I went to the bed and sat nervously on its edge. He turned the wooden parlor chair around so its crudely carved back faced me and straddled it as if he were mounted on a horse.

"I'm sorry I was so tough on you today," he said.

The unexpected apology turned my legs to rubber and I slid off the edge of the bed, landing on the floor. I picked myself up quickly, sat again on the bed, and folded my hands on my lap.

"It's how my old maestro treated me. He came from the Ronda school of bullfighting; he didn't like flashy passes and believed toughness during training led to greatness in the ring."

I didn't dare speak.

"I was also upset because the man at the ranch was Selveti."

Now I understood why the stranger's profile had been familiar. I'd seen an article about him in one of the bullfighting magazines.

"You need two sponsors for union membership," Maestro continued. "I'd told him I'd taken you on and I worked hard to persuade him just to come take a look at you. He wouldn't give me a guarantee he'd sponsor you, even if he liked what he saw today."

To become an official apprentice matador, I was required to join the Union of Matadors and Novilleros, which necessitated two full-fledged matadors vouching for me.

Maestro shook his head. "I've been asking around and I'm finding it impossible to find a matador willing to sign his name for you. They don't want to risk their reputations or anger the authorities."

"Why didn't you tell me about Selveti?"

A vein running from his left temple pulsed. "Why should it matter if you knew who he was? Your job is to fight well every time you're in the ring and *never* to be afraid." He looked at me earnestly. "You have a decision to make. You must decide whether to quit and return to your mother, who clearly wants you to come home, or stay."

Outside on the patio, Emilio and Abril shrieked as they played.

"Maestro, please don't send me away. I won't fail you."

His face remained grave.

"Keep looking for people to sponsor me."

He blinked. "We'll drive out to the ranch tomorrow and you'll try again."

I went over quickly and hugged him. His breath stank of stale tobacco. My mind flicked instantly again to the dark Los Pinos street, but I didn't shrink away.

Next morning at the ranch, Selveti didn't show up. I hid my disappointment and nerves while I faced the young bull. Maestro remained riveted on my every move and barked instructions on how to position myself between charges. No images of the attack came; I ceded no ground to the bull.

"Excellent, Kathleen," he said, after the seventh pass. He came over and put his arm around me. "This is what I expect from you. No more fear. Fear is unacceptable. I know this, believe me."

15

SIX *TORERAS* WERE INSIDE THE SPACIOUS HOTEL ROOM. THE women were all in their midtwenties, except two who looked almost a decade older. They were all dark-haired, slender, and wearing Andalusian suits with snug gray pants and crisp white shirts beneath bolero jackets that accentuated their shoulders. Dressed in black gabardine pants worn over a pair of cowboy boots and a frilly white blouse, I felt amateurish in comparison. I also felt superfluous. The *toreras* joked as they helped one another dress, a pair of them even engaging in a wild pillow fight until one pillow ripped and coughed feathers into the room.

After she finished braiding one woman's hair, Teresa, one of the senior *toreras* who performed in the final act with the muleta and sword, summoned me over to the dressing mirror.

"I will make your hair like ours," she said as she guided me into a chair.

Her Spanish had little dialect and I couldn't tell where she came from in Mexico. She untied my ponytail and began applying oil that she poured from a small cut-glass bottle. The delicate aroma of cinnamon and nutmeg was instantly calming.

"Your story intrigues us," she said, her husky voice suggesting controlled power. "We were excited to hear an American girl is interested in fighting the bulls. So many of your countrymen don't like bull-fighting. They shut their minds to the art."

"Texans are different to folks living up North," I said. "Many of us come to the Sunday corridas here."

Her hands worked the fragrant oil into my hair. "Today is a special day for you," she said. Our gazes locked in the mirror's reflection. "I will make you up like a proper torero."

"Don't you mean *torera*?" I asked, watching the strands of my hair turn darker in her long, graceful fingers.

Her fingernails dug into my scalp. The large, warm brown eyes in the mirror narrowed.

"We are toreros, Kathleen. We do not follow the rules of the Spanish language in this case. It's restrictive. We recognize no feminine term for 'bullfighter.' We face death in the ring just like the men. The bulls make no difference about gender. Why should we?"

While Teresa was not a matador in the proper sense, her words gave me hope. As her hands worked my hair, it felt like a sacred initiation. The anxiety concerning my inappropriate outfit and the drama about to occur in the bullring in less than twenty minutes dissipated like mist.

She created three thick ropes of hair and fashioned a plait behind my head. After she finished, she asked me to stay in the chair and took a small case from the top of the dresser. Attached to the inside of its lid were three religious pictures, the central, largest one being an image of the Virgin of Guadalupe, patron of Mexican bullfighters. To the Virgin's right was a Byzantine picture of Jesus on the cross, an arc of crimson gushing from a wound in his side. An image of a female saint was to the Virgin's left.

"Her name is Saint Teresa of Ávila," said Teresa. "My namesake."

Someone rapped hard on the door three times. Everyone fell silent.

"That's the signal we leave for the ring in five minutes," Teresa explained.

She knelt and blessed herself, the other women quickly following her example. I fell on my knees and blessed myself, too. I looked around at their bent heads and thought of how the same scene unfolded daily in cloistered convents.

"Sweet Virgin, please look after your women in the ring today," Teresa said, her invocation cutting into my thoughts. "Keep the wind away. Give us good bulls. Protect us, so we may live to honor you again."

Wind was as dangerous an enemy as the bulls to a fighter. A surprise gust could lift a muleta and expose a fighter's body to the bull. Someone behind me made a noise that sounded like a gurgle. I looked around quickly to see Anita, the other senior bullfighter, rise with her hand covering her mouth and rush toward the adjoining bathroom. Moments later, I smelled vomit.

After the prayers finished, the women rose quietly and prepared to leave. Teresa's hand dipped into the case momentarily. She took my hand and placed in my palm a gold medal bearing the image of the Virgin of Guadalupe.

"She will always be with you in your work," she said, "provided you revere and honor her."

The other women clapped. These brilliant women had already honored me by inviting me to perform alongside them. On top of that, they'd given me a gift, when it was I who should have been presenting them with something to show my gratitude.

Anita, pale and wiping her mouth, exited the bathroom. A thick flock of monarchs took flight inside my belly as my mind flew back to the ranch and I saw myself standing frozen before the charging tiny bull.

As we watched the performance from the narrow passageway reserved for bullfighters, managers, and media, I kept pestering Maestro by asking, "When?" and he kept irritating me by responding, "Soon." Though it was the women who'd invited me, it was Maestro who controlled the exact moment of my appearance. While I understood that Maestro knew better, I was a little resentful that he exercised so much control.

When the fourth bull entered the ring, I began to fear Maestro was not going to allow me to perform, that he'd been teasing me all along. The bull, just like all the fighting bulls fought by these women and a few male apprentices, was younger than four years old and weighed about seven hundred pounds. His horns were the color of spring butter in the bright sun. He trotted into the ring without any display of aggression.

With his chin resting on his hands, which in turn rested on the splintered top of the wooden barrier fence, Maestro watched intently as one of the women incited the bull to charge. He watched him charge a second time.

"It charges straight as an arrow," he said, as much to himself as to me.

A mounted picador entered the ring to pierce the bull's shoulder with his lance, helping tire him out in preparation for the final act with the matador. To my surprise, the picador was a man. He also wasn't dressed in the ornately embroidered waist jacket and chamois breeches of a traditional picador, but rather wore the pants and white shirt of a Mexican farmhand.

After the bull came to a halt by the wooden wall facing the ring, one of the toreros used her flowing cape to entice him closer and then lined him up ten feet away from the ancient bow-backed horse. The bull remained motionless. Then, without warning, he charged up to the horse and drove his horns into the thick mattress of tightly bound cotton stuffed under the waterproof canvas cover. This *peto* protected the horse's belly and thighs from the bull's horns.

"Go in now," Maestro said, after the picador drove his lance into the bull's hide.

I didn't need a second invitation. I emerged from one side of the narrow wooden protective shield positioned directly in front of the opening to the bullring. Brandishing my magenta cape, I walked across the uneven sand, focusing only on drawing the bull away from the horse.

"Hey, *toro*," I hollered, when I arrived near his right side. Remembering Maestro's lessons, I moved the cape slowly from side to side to attract his attention. "*Toro*, come here."

His muscled neck swiveled toward me. Devouring the sight of the vibrant, swaying bait, he turned and charged, his gray-black tongue dangling from the side of his mouth. Instinctively, I planted my feet firmly together, but the muscles in my thighs trembled violently. When the tips of his curved horns were a fraction of an inch from the silk cape, when he savored piercing his enemy, I flexed my wrists, arched my back, and moved the cape slowly and tantalizingly in front of him. He followed it just like I'd taught my Great Dane to do in the barn.

Maestro was right, as usual. The bull was brave. He was a matador's dream. Every charge was straight and he was beautifully predictable. I executed slow, gorgeous *veronicas* and completely dominated him. I couldn't believe this large beast had submitted to little ol' me for five complete passes. Loud approval surged from both the shady seats occupied by Texans and rich Mexicans and from the sun-scorched seats where farmhands, mechanics, and other working folk happily paid their hard-earned *pesos* to be entertained. My body shivered. This was exactly how I'd imagined the crowd's love.

"Finish now, Kathleen," Maestro hollered, his hands like protruding brackets around the sides of his mouth.

His choice to end a series of passes was the standard *media-verónica*, but I remembered the beautiful *rebolera* pass El Cabrito had taught me. The pass required me to put my hands behind my back and pass the cape from hand to hand so that the end of the cape flared out like a full skirt. If done properly, I'd transfix the bull. It had been weeks since I'd practiced it.

As the bull hurtled toward me, I summoned my nerve, but instead executed the less attractive *media-verónica* at the last minute. When the bull came to a stop, one of the toreros ran in with her cape, caught the bull's attention and led him away to position him for the second mounted picador now entering the ring. My performance was over.

As I crossed toward Maestro, I was a black-and-white feather floating above the sand. The slightest breeze would have blown me back to the bull. When I entered the passageway, he gripped my shoulders and peered into my eyes, his own moist and glittering like onyx jewels.

"You were brilliant," he said, and hugged me. "We will definitely appear in the Plaza México if this continues."

His words ricocheted inside my head. I heard nothing more of the applauding crowd.

Out on the horse patio, as we were walking away from a journalist for the *Los Pinos Gazette* whom Maestro had agreed I could interview with at a future date, Señor Barros approached. Horseshoes clinked on the cobblestones melodically as the picadors guided their mounts through the horde of visiting dignitaries, including the Spanish ambassador and his wife, who wore a beautiful black lace mantilla. Fresh horse dung cut the flowery aroma of ladies' perfume.

"Congratulations, Fermin," Señor Barros said, handing his Cordoban hat to a young assistant and shaking Maestro's hand. "I'm not an expert, but I'd say she has the makings of a bullfighter."

A pigeon flew off the red-tiled roof and landed in a vacant spot in the courtyard, where it began to stab at a crust of bread. Its iridescent breast shimmered blue and lavender.

"You've done an excellent job with her." Barros turned to me and smiled. "How does it feel to be a *torera*?"

"A *torero*, Señor Barros," I said.

His face crinkled like the skin of a withered apple.

"The bull doesn't care whether he's fighting a man or woman," I said. "He just fights. And I'm—"

"The bull's not a 'he,'" interrupted Maestro. "Bulls are things."

"He's *not* a thing. And I'm not a woman bullfighter. I'm a *torero*."

Señor Barros and Maestro exchanged glances.

"The ring authorities informed me that ticket sales surpassed their expectations," my patron said to Maestro, apparently deciding to ignore me. "And the women—sorry, I mean the *toreros* . . ." He winked at me. "They and their manager are delighted with Kathleen's performance. They want her to perform with them in Merida in two weeks. If that goes well, he'll consider offering her a permanent contract with them." He looked at me again. "Imagine yourself as part of this troupe of lovely women." He rubbed his thick thumb and index finger. "A lot of dollars for everyone."

I clapped my hands together and smiled widely at Maestro. "I'd love that."

Maestro didn't smile back. He kept his eyes on Señor Barros. "You and I will talk, Vincente."

16

CARMEN CAME INTO THE BEDROOM AFTER CHECKING ON the children one final time. Fermin suspected she loved the children more than she loved him, though he didn't feel jealous. That was the prerogative and practicality of a mother. He hadn't always been as practical as his wife. He'd been jealous for months after Emilio was born, especially as she'd constantly showered their son with attention and refused Fermin's advances.

He watched his wife pull out the tufted stool from under the well of the mahogany vanity he'd made for her many years ago. Her hips bulged over the sides of the stool like two tires gone soft. When they'd married, she'd been eighteen and slender. She'd never lost the weight she'd gained when pregnant with Emilio. During her second pregnancy, she'd added another fifteen pounds and hadn't lost that, either. When he'd spoken to Carmen about his concern after Abril's birth, she'd tried an array of diets but they'd never worked for long.

His late father, also a wiry bullfighter of moderate success who'd watched his diet carefully, had also disliked Fermin's mother's burgeoning figure. Fermin and his sister had witnessed frequent arguments about this, including one that resulted in a five-year separation. His mother had discovered that his father had a young, slender mistress and moved out, taking her children with her. Both Fermin and his sister, who'd married a picador and lived in Seville, stayed lean, his sister dropping the excess pregnancy weight within months of giving birth to each of her four children.

Fermin vowed never to make the same mistake his father had made. It had taken him a year after Abril's birth to accept that Carmen's weight gain was permanent and to stop pestering, because it made her unhappy. It had also taken that year to overcome his distaste during their lovemaking. But overcome it he had.

Carmen picked up a statue of the Virgin she'd owned since she was a child and kissed it twice, one for each child, and then set it down again. She unbraided her dark hair and brushed it until it gleamed in the moonlight streaming in from the courtyard. After she finished, Fermin raised the covers on her side of the bed and she slid inside.

He kissed her as he ran his fingers through her hair. *"Mi querida."* Fermin inserted the tip of his tongue into her ear and began to explore.

His wife jerked her head away, turned her back to him, and tugged the sheet up to her chin. Easing closer, Fermin molded his shape to her body, laid his hand on her right breast, and squeezed gently. He pressed his erection against her left buttock.

"Go to sleep," she said.

He kissed her tenderly on the neck.

"I'm tired."

Slipping his hand beneath the sheet he quickly drew up her night-dress, then slid his fingers along her thigh and into her lush pubic hair. His cock pulsated.

"Will you stop?" Carmen sat up. "I cook all day. I wash all day. I clean. Now you want sex. I'm exhausted."

"But it's your job." He pulled himself up on the bed and stared at her. "I work like a dog to provide for you and the children, and I'm also tired. But you don't hear me complaining."

"And Kathleen? I clean and cook for her, too."

"You don't want her living here anymore?"

"That's not my point. You don't want her doing women's work, but you don't see that *I'm* doing more because of it."

Her chest heaved and tears leaked from the corners of her eyes.

"She's needed," he said.

"She doesn't pay us rent."

"I mean that, if my plans work out, her appearances in the bullring will make us very rich."

"You mustn't overwork her, Fermin. She's still becoming a woman. And you mustn't forget what happened to her."

"She's over that," he said, sliding down the bed. "And she's crazy about the bulls. She doesn't see it as work."

"We live well enough on your contracts." She reached up and touched his cheek. "We have a comfortable home. The children can go to a good high school. You are saving some. There will be money for them to go to college. What more do we need?"

"A new car."

He tugged his wife gently back to the prone position on the bed and began to kiss her. Carmen sighed but didn't complain. Easing her nightdress up to her belly, he climbed on top of her and parted her legs with his knees.

As tequila distilleries in Mexico went, Fermin had neither the knowledge nor business acumen to decide if Vincente Barros's was better or more profitable than any of the others. He glanced again at the handful of finger-smudged photographs Barros had proudly pulled out of his breast pocket and given him to look at, one depicting the distillery's courtyard surrounded by pristine white buildings and a gushing, three-tiered fountain at its center. Other images showed a mule-drawn cart, a polished metal still, and a cellar stocked to the ceiling with wooden barrels.

On one occasion, in Guadalajara, Fermin had remained for two days after the corrida ended and taken Rosa on a trip to one of the established distilleries. In a mule-drawn wagon, they'd toured acres of fields of blue-leafed agave, as blue as the ocean, the pair of them holding hands like lovesick youngsters. At one stop, the *jimador* had recognized him and eagerly called upon Fermin to help him hack off the spiky leaves of an agave to reveal a large heart that would be mashed into pulp.

Tossing the photographs across the table to Barros, Fermin peered around the cantina. It was bustling with aficionados casually drinking and smoking cigars as they discussed the previous afternoon's corrida, which had again featured the female bullfighters. He recognized some of the men and knew they weren't discussing the women's bravery or their skills wielding the cape like they would have had the performers been men. The conversations were about the women's hips and breasts, and what they'd do if they had a chance to bed them.

"She's definitely ready to join the *toreras*," Señor Barros said, as he scooped up the photographs and returned them to his pocket. He picked up his beer, leaned over the small table, and raised his bushy eyebrows. "Or should I say toreros?" When he laughed, his teeth gleamed yellow from years of drinking strong black coffee and smoking.

Fermin shifted his weight to the other hip. "I don't think she has the talent, Vincente."

Señor Barros's smile vanished. He set his glass down hard. "You saw how she was yesterday."

Señor Barros was a giant, stronger than Fermin. The ex-matador knew the businessman could squash him like a water bug if he botched the execution of his plan.

"It was a fluke." Fermin tossed back his head and drank the rest of his tequila, twisting his face as it went down to show ersatz contempt for Kathleen. "That bull was good. Anyone could have worked it."

He slammed the empty shot glass on the table. "I work with her every day, Vincente. You don't see what I see. She's not easy." He snorted. "What American woman is? She's proud. Too demanding. She refuses to take direction."

"You haven't mentioned this before."

"I've tried hard to change her. I didn't want to upset you, Vincente."

"I'll speak to her. I've always found her agreeable."

Fermin glanced out the door for a moment and then stood. "Let's take a walk."

Outside, the air was thick as molasses. Fermin despised how it clung to his face.

"So tell me, Fermin," Señor Barros said, after clearing his throat. "You were a good matador. Why did you retire from the ring so young?"

Given the wretched humidity, Fermin didn't think it was possible to get any wetter, but a flash of sweat drenched his chest and back. His fists tightened, preparing to lash out at Barros. A married couple walked by whom Fermin recognized as neighbors and he stopped to greet them, while simultaneously considering how best to conclude the matter about Kathleen successfully. He figured Barros must have heard the rumors that had followed him since the end of his career as a matador and wondered if this was Barros's way to belittle him. Moreover, Barros was a businessman and understood nothing about bullfighting, only how to make money—of which he had plenty, from his hotels and bars. He didn't need to make money from the bulls. Kathleen belonged to Fermin. She was his alone to mold.

After his neighbors left, Fermin didn't speak until they were out of earshot.

"It'll do no good to talk to Kathleen," he said. "Her mind's already made up. She doesn't want to join the *toreras*. In fact, she doesn't understand why you'd want her to join them when they're not even matadors." Fermin held his breath.

"Doesn't she understand the money she can make?" Señor Barros asked.

So the inquiry about Fermin's retirement hadn't been intended as a backhanded insult. It was just a passing question, a bridge between their indoor conversation and what was to come.

Lowering his head as if it were suddenly too heavy, Fermin allowed a pause and then sighed ponderously. "It pains me to say this Vincente, but she doesn't want to see you again."

"She can't do this to me," Barros exclaimed. "I've always planned for her to join these women. I was going to put her face on the label of my best tequila when she became famous."

"If she were ever to become a great bullfighter, I'm sure that would happen. But I don't think it's possible, Vincente." Fermin paused again and squinted up at Barros. "Nothing was written on paper, was it?"

Señor Barros shook his head.

"You are a lucky man, then." Thrusting his hand into his pants, Fermin took out a fat roll of American banknotes. "She told me to give this to you."

The businessman's eyes took in the wad of money.

"When she told me she no longer wanted you as her patron, I sat her down and made her account for everything you'd given her." Fermin smiled. "I know how well you've treated her. It's the least I could do."

Taking off his hat, Señor Barros fanned his big face slowly. "She seemed so honorable. How could she change so quickly?"

"Americans." Fermin shrugged. "They can be tricky." He allowed Barros to mull over his words and then said, "She wants to be like a proper matador. Imagine, Vincente? To do that, the union must accept her. No matador's going to sponsor her to the union. She's finished."

"I knew that might be problematic." Señor Barros stroked the ends of his mustache as he gazed up the street. "That's why I thought the *toreras* a good solution."

"If I may say so, I think it's wiser you stick to growing your fortune doing what you know," Fermin said. "The bulls are difficult. The impresarios are difficult. That young woman's difficult. There are scoundrels everywhere."

Barros eyed the money again.

Fermin held it out. "The amount's nineteen hundred dollars."

Barros didn't move to take it. "Where'd she get it?"

"Her mother." Fermin sighed deeply again. "This is another very big problem. Her mother's demanding Kathleen quit the bulls."

Señor Barros took the money, removed the elastic band, and began to unroll the notes. "How much do I owe you?"

"It's okay." Fermin turned to walk away. "¡Adiós!"

He took only two steps before Barros called him back.

"I asked you to train her, Fermin. I'm grateful for all you've done and I'm a man of my word. How much?"

Fermin returned quickly and feigned thoughtfulness. "Nine hundred will cover it."

17

REVIVED BY A WARM, LIGHT RAIN THAT HAD FALLEN IN THE early afternoon, the garden looked reborn. Wrens chorused from within the cool dim of the acacia and vitex trees, and a blue-throated hummingbird darted back and forth, stealing nectar from the flaming red blooms of a flamboyan tree that Carmen had planted during the first year of their marriage. Weeks of dust had washed off the shrubbery and the lemon hibiscus blooms and orange flowers on the two trumpet trees gleamed.

The concept of rebirth appealed to Fermin. Kathleen and he sat on a garden bench directly under a palm soaring twelve feet above the house's roofline. Directly opposite where he sat, about twenty feet away, his son had drawn a series of interlocking rings in green, red, black, yellow, and blue chalk on the whitewashed wall.

Fermin figured Emilio's inspiration had been the recent news bulletin about the opening, in ten months' time, of the 1952 Summer Olympics in Helsinki. The circles were perfect. How could the boy have drawn them so well? Regardless, Emilio had a steady hand, a skill that would be crucial were he to enter the bullring when the time came.

Fermin harbored strong hopes the boy would follow in his footsteps. He thought about his other son in Guadalajara, of how he'd told Rosa to discourage the boy in his ambition to fight the bulls because of his

Mayan appearance and squat body. He remembered the chicken's egg the boy had been examining, a circle corrupted. He looked again at Emilio's perfect circles. Not everything in the world could be perfect. But was it wrong to have the highest intentions for one boy and not the other?

"Kathleen, you won't appear in the bullring with the women again," he said.

"My patron wants me to work with them. He—"

"Señor Barros is no longer your patron."

Kathleen's hand flew to her bosom. Her face and neck mottled, a red blush of confusion on her pale skin.

"The man understands only tequila," he said. "Not the bullring."

"He's been good to me. He found you to take me on." She swallowed hard. "Wouldn't joining them be a stepping stone, Maestro?"

"If you want to be a novelty act, yes." Fermin stretched his right arm along the top of the bench and twisted his torso around so he could see Kathleen fully. "Those women don't subscribe to the rules of the Union of Matadors and Novilleros. They're as professional as comic bullfighters."

Her eyes narrowed. "I can't repay Señor Barros."

He tapped the small of her back with his middle finger. "No need to worry. I calculated what he paid out for you, added some more, and gave it to him."

Kathleen's eyes widened. While it was amusing to see her gape, he controlled an urge to laugh. She was young and inexperienced in the ways of business and it was only natural she would be upset that her patron was now history.

The amount he'd paid Vincente Barros had been fair. Together with the exchange rate and fees, it had taken a chunk out of Fermin's savings, but he was confident he'd recoup the money. There was no risk.

"You told me you wanted to be a matador," he said. "Is that still true?"

"Of course, Maestro."

"Then you'll never appear with women again. It would be the kiss of death."

She thought for a moment, then asked, "Was Señor Barros angry?"

"He wishes you well." Fermin laughed. "In fact, he said he'll concentrate on making tequila from now on."

The mottling in Kathleen's neck lightened.

"Do you have any ideas who you'd like to be your manager?" he asked.

Her neck went pink again and she looked at the ground. He allowed the silence to yawn. When she eventually looked up, her eyes were nicely deflated.

"As you know, I have my own contracts with matadors," he said.

"I know."

"*But* I've given this a lot of thought, and I've decided I'll become your manager. That is, if you'd like me to be."

The sparkle returned to her eyes.

Fermin picked up the sheaf of papers he'd set on the bench beside him. "I've written up a contract that you can read later. It says I agree to be your manager and you agree to pay me twenty percent of your earnings." He shuffled through the pages, pulled one out, and pointed to a paragraph. "It also states you agree to repay me two thousand five hundred dollars that I've paid on your behalf to Señor Barros."

"You really are a father to me, Maestro," she said, and kissed him on the cheek.

Fermin's skin prickled where her lips had touched him. He followed Kathleen's eyes up to the sky, where the sun, transformed into a coppery-orange halo, had turned the fleecy clouds indigo and edged them in a thread of matador's gold.

"My father's up there looking out for me," she said. "It's why you're in my life; I know it."

"You'll continue to train hard and I'll continue to ask around until I find two matadors who'll agree to sponsor you to the union," Fermin continued, ignoring her comment. "As you know, it's no easy task—"

"Because I'm a woman." She sighed.

His children came out from the kitchen, each bearing a colorfully wrapped gift. Carmen followed them, holding a cake covered in a forest of lit candles.

"Happy Birthday, Papi," the children said in unison. Kathleen clapped.

"This is for you," said Abril. "Guess what it is?"

"I've also got a gift for you," Kathleen said. "It's in my room." She hurried inside.

Fermin went to Carmen, who held up the cake for him to blow out the candles. "I'm now Kathleen's manager and I'm going to make her into a great matador," he said, and winked. "Remember what I said about her that night in bed."

His wife nodded. "Remember what I said, too."

Fermin had known the impresario of the Colotlán bullring for years, having first met him when Fermin had performed as a matador in his ring. He'd made the man a lot of money in the past, and and still made money for him every time he appeared there as a banderillero, even if no one, not the ring authorities or spectators, seriously acknowledged the art of the banderilleros or picadors. All acclaim—and the lion's share of the fees—went to the matadors, whose names were printed in large letters on the posters pasted up around the city's plazas before a corrida.

"Juan, I've never asked a favor of you in my career." Fermin banged his fist on the impresario's carved oak desk for emphasis, but not so hard the man would take offense. "I made a point of that."

The large office on the west side of the bullring commanded a perfect view of the golden sand and ring. It was also stifling, undoubtedly,

Fermin thought, to ensure the discomfort and distraction of managers and agents arriving to negotiate contracts for their matadors. He mopped his forehead with the back of his hand.

"This is true," the impresario said. He massaged the gold rim of the whiskey glass with his thumb. "Ah, Fermin, if you'd just return as a matador to my bullring."

The two eyed each other in the ensuing silence.

"Mexico's hungry for another Conchita Cintrón," Fermin said, shifting in his chair to try to relieve a sudden, maddening itch on his buttocks.

"I think the return of Fermin Guzmán would fill seats, too."

"That's nice of you to say, Juan, but Kathleen will fill every seat in your stadium next season. She has everything: a beautiful figure; she fights artfully. Haven't you heard she wields her magenta cape as beautifully as Ordóñez?"

"She's also a gringa."

"Yes—a pretty American gringa."

"It's risk enough to book a *novillero*. But you're asking me to book a woman who's not even an official *novillera*, not until the union accepts her." The impresario's chair screeched as he pushed back in preparation for ending the meeting.

"I'll give you a discount on her fee," Fermin said.

The wheels of the chair came to an abrupt halt. Interest flickered like baby flames in the corners of the impresario's eyes.

"After five appearances, when word gets out, Kathleen will command fifty thousand pesos per corrida," Fermin added. "The same as any matador."

"You're toying with me now," the impresario said.

"Kathleen's unique. Success will happen fast for her *because* she's a woman, Juan. The public sees what the union and matadors can't. They're ready to see a woman fight on foot like a man. They'll soon adore their red-haired American bullfighting goddess." He paused. "There'll be no discounts when that happens."

Fermin's appearance at the charity corrida in the impresario's bull-ring was his last under the contract with the matador who'd hired him. Before returning home, Fermin took a two-hour bus ride from Colotlán to Guadalajara, where he'd booked a hotel room and arranged to meet Rosa. Fermin fell asleep despite the incessant chatter of two old women seated in front of him.

He woke to the breathtaking mountainous scenery on the outskirts of Guadalajara. The bus's descent into the city was precipitous, the road like a dust-covered corkscrew, and Fermin braced himself for the twists. As the bus flattened out and drove parallel with the winding river, his eyes began to sting. The water smelled like an open cesspool, but closing his window was pointless, as all the others were open.

Shortly after he arrived in town, Rosa and he drank coffee and tequila shots at a café in a plaza, near the entrance to the Plaza de Toros el Progreso bullring. Up close, the amphitheater resembled a spaceship that had landed inadvertently on top of a block of squat, drab buildings and eviscerated those at the center.

Rosa had heeded his advice and not brought the twins. When he'd met up with her and saw that she hadn't, a pang of regret took him by surprise.

As she always did, she counted the money he'd just given her, fingers flicking through the notes as expertly as a bank teller's. When she finished, she looked at him, nonplussed.

"There will be more," he said, wiping his forehead. "Much more. I've told you that already."

"We need a house closer to the city."

"I had an important debt to settle. Next year, things will be different. I'll buy you and the children a small house. With an American refrigerator . . . and a washing machine."

Her wide smile changed Rosa, transforming her instantly from a worried mother into a pretty young woman again. Fermin felt a familiar stirring in his groin. Today, she'd dressed sharply for his visit to the city center. The floral dress allowed him a tantalizing peek at the cleft between her full breasts. She wore a gold bracelet he recognized. He'd bought it for her (together with a second, thicker one for Carmen) after a highly successful corrida in Aguascalientes. He'd persuaded the jeweler, an admirer of his skills, to open his store on a Sunday.

"Why do you smile?" she asked.

"I'm happy you still wear my bracelet."

Her eyes flicked to it. "I almost had to sell it."

"I'm glad you didn't."

Her brows arched when she looked at him. "Some things should never be sold."

She slid the bracelet slowly up and down her forearm. Again, the pit of his belly stirred. His scrotum crawled.

"Will you have dinner with me?" he asked.

The strains of a happy tune playing on a hurdy-gurdy drifted over from a nearby side street. Rosa's gaze whisked to the recessed arches in the bullring's walls and then to the people sitting at the tables adjacent to them. She toyed with the gold bracelet, turning it slowly around her wrist. Finally, she looked back at him, a smile on her closed lips.

The first person he hired as part of Kathleen's cuadrilla was Patricio, the long-time colleague who had most recently been part of El Cabrito's team. Fermin knew Patricio was tired of fending off a constant stream of admirers and journalists knocking on the arrogant young matador's hotel door in the mornings before a fight. It was a delicious bonus that Patricio was El Cabrito's sword handler and would serve now as Kathleen's.

From Patricio, Fermin obtained a list of names of current banderilleros who needed steady work to feed their families and would raise no objections to appearing in the bullring with a woman. Until Kathleen was in a position to command higher fees from the impresarios, Fermin decided to act as one of her banderilleros, keeping records of all the corridas he appeared in and deducting his wages from her future earnings. The final task to round out her team was hiring two picadors, but there was no urgency to do that. Picadors were abundant. One simply had to be mindful not to hire those with reputations for wounding the bull too severely with their lances, as that left the bull with little energy for the final act, when the matador displayed his muleta skills.

18

THE DESTINATION HADN'T BEEN REVEALED TO ME. ALL Maestro said was that this would be an important day in my career. One welcome distraction from the tedious ride in Maestro's old car through the unvarying scrubland and hills surrounding Los Pinos was the stranger accompanying us on the journey. An older gentleman, his name was Patricio and it seemed important to Maestro that I like him, which was easy because he entertained me with stories about the famous matadors he'd worked with before becoming a sword handler.

"My last job was for El Cabrito," he said, peering at me over the front passenger seat. "Fermin's been in his cuadrilla, too."

El Cabrito was the handsome matador who'd taught me the *rebolera* pass more than a year ago. I'd since perfected it, but had not yet executed it in Maestro's presence. He considered that kind of pass too flashy.

"Do you know the young man, Kathleen?" Patricio asked.

"She doesn't know that conceited *maricón*," said Maestro.

Patricio guffawed. "El Cabrito's wrists are always busy, but I don't think he's a faggot."

I sat woodenly, my thoughts racing as I stared out at the sunbaked landscape pocked with stunted trees and fleshy cacti. Two vultures floated high in the air currents, their ragged-edged wings stretched wide and pitch-black against the flawless blue sky. I couldn't believe what Maestro had said about Julio, who'd been so gentlemanly to me.

Twenty minutes later, we passed through the main street of a languid town and turned into a rutted dirt lane that ended in a parking lot in front of a long, windowless building. An ancient truck with a slatted, wooden trailer was parked on one side, a ramp with two-foot-high wooden sides slanting from the end of the truck to the building's unseen entrance. From deep within the building, cows bellowed amid the high-pitched shrieks of pigs.

"Why are we here?" I asked, staring at the back of Maestro's head.

He didn't answer. The two men climbed out of the car and Patricio removed a small case from the trunk.

We entered the building via the opposite end to where the truck was parked, passing through a cluttered office in which a Mexican Indian woman in a colorful poncho and a black hat sat writing. She looked at us but didn't greet us. In the adjoining room, two Mexican Indian men in bloodied overalls sat on a crudely carved wooden bench, eating tortillas. Their forearms and shirts were stained bright red.

The stench of animal shit and blood overpowered my senses when Maestro opened the next door. I entered sandwiched between Maestro and Patricio, covering my nose and mouth with my hand. My belly roiled like a boat in a squall. The room's flaking, whitewashed walls were streaked with dried blood. Tangles of white maggot-infested entrails lay piled in a corner.

An open drain, the width of a roof's gutter, ran around the perimeter of the room and was fed by narrower, diagonal tributaries leading from two animal stalls. Dark-red blood glistened as it trickled lazily down the tributaries. I heard the black flies before seeing five of them walking over the wooly white face of an old roan bull tethered by a chain to a ring attached to the wall of its stall. Another shorter chain, secured to a second rusty metal ring bolted to the floor, had been tied around the bull's left hind foot. My stomach churned more violently. I was sure I'd vomit.

"You must learn the art of killing," Maestro said. He approached the bull and laid his hand on its thick neck. The animal's muscles quivered, but he didn't move.

"When the moment of truth comes, the bull must die," Maestro said. "Its death symbolizes complete subordination to a man's will. Complete domination." He regarded me intently, almost fiercely. "You have to use the sword accurately when you make the sign of the cross, so the killing is graceful and merciful."

"Killing must happen in a dignified and artistic manner," agreed Patricio, nodding. "A fighting bull is not a dumb beast like this one." He smiled grimly. "Fighting bulls are majestic and deserve high respect when they give up their lives." He paused. "Not all matadors kill well."

I already knew the technical aspects of making the sign of the cross, how a matador swings the muleta slowly downward in his left hand as he approaches the bull to keep the animal's attention. It also stops the bull from lowering his head, while the matador plunges the sword deep into the bull's *cruz* with the right hand and then exits swiftly over the horn to safety, before the bull knows it's dead.

"If done correctly, the sword slices easily between the shoulders and the blade's slight curve at its end will sever an artery," said Maestro. With his index finger, he drew a circle the size of a silver dollar right between the bull's shoulder blades where it joined with the base of the neck. "This is the *cruz*."

He took my hand and laid it on the bull's death-notch. The bull's hair was wiry and oily. I plunged the tips of my fingers though the hair until I felt warm, greasy skin. His shoulders rose as he took a breath.

"Few bulls die instantly by the sword," Maestro continued. "If not, the matador must perform the *descabello*. But first, you must learn to kill a living thing. Today you will use a dagger."

As if recognizing the word, the bull defecated. Dung splattered on the concrete floor. As the bull shifted position, the short chain around his leg jangled and scraped. Another bull roared next door, followed by pigs shrieking. In the background, seeping through cracks in the walls, I heard flamenco music.

Patricio stooped, clicked open the small case he'd brought, and removed an exquisitely tooled leather sheath. From that he drew a small bronze-handled dagger, its five-inch, glinting blade shaped like an arrowhead and engraved with pretty flowers.

"To perform the coup de grâce, you plunge the dagger down here," he said, resting the tip of the blade exactly where the bull's neck connected with its head. "It must sever the spine between the first vertebra and the skull. Death is swift and merciful."

I clawed back a breath only after he took the dagger away from the bull's head.

"Thank you for the lesson, Maestro." Eager to leave the slaughter room, I stepped out of the stall, nearly skidding on its slippery floor.

"Come back here." When I returned to Maestro, he placed the dagger in my hand. "Kill it."

It was strange how Maestro referred to the bull as an object, like he was a table or a chair. I didn't move. I couldn't. The dagger felt like a bar of iron in my damp palm.

"Another member of the team does that when the time comes," I said, my voice small and tight. "Why do I need to know this?"

Maestro's head snapped back. "No stalling," he said.

Until this moment, the question of killing during a performance had been academic. All I'd been required to do was swing the cape artfully and practice with a muleta and wooden sword, the kind of fake sword every matador used during his performance until the time to kill arrived. That was when his sword handler handed him the real one over the wooden barrier fence.

The concept of killing didn't concern me. Fighting bulls were bred to kill or be killed. They felt no pain from the wounds inflicted by the mounted picadors' lances and banderilleros' barbed sticks during their time in the bullring. The rules of bullfighting required the matador to kill the bull within fifteen minutes of making his first pass in the final act, during which time adrenaline floods the animal's system and mutes any sensation of pain, in the same way it does in humans who suffer broken limbs in car accidents or are knifed during a street fight.

I didn't feel sad about the bulls' deaths. Fighting bulls led far happier lives than bulls bred for beef. Fighting bulls lived in the pastures for a full year longer than beef cattle. Nor did they die in commercial slaughterhouses, driven with sticks and skidding through an ever-narrowing pathway until they arrived in the kill chamber, where their throats were cut and they were skinned alive.

"Kill it now," Maestro demanded.

Despite knowing all this, I didn't move. Nor was precious adrenaline surging through this poor beast's body.

"KILL IT," Maestro roared.

A gulf existed between the theory and practice of killing, just as it did between the admiration of and making of fine art. My hands shook as I raised the dagger, then brought it down.

But instead of hearing a thud on the concrete floor, the bull bellowed and struggled to break free of the chains. A slaughterhouse employee, one of the men who'd been eating in the lunchroom, came quickly into the stall and calmed the animal. He petted the bull's neck while repositioning him.

I tried again, with the same result. "I can't."

"What the hell kind of fighter are you?" Maestro asked. "Stop being weak."

I started trembling violently, every nerve and muscle racing up and down under my skin as if trying to break free, like the sorry old bull had just done. I vomited on the bull's back. Fiery, acidic liquid scalded the back of my throat and I choked.

"You're closing your eyes every time you strike it," Patricio said, after I stopped coughing. "You can't sever its spinal cord if you can't see what you're doing."

The bull's shoulder pressed gently against my side.

"Whether it's you or someone else at the slaughterhouse who does it, this bull dies," Maestro said. He looked over and I followed his gaze to a bloodied sledgehammer leaning against the wall. "If you won't, a worker will use that to stun it before slitting its throat. Now, keep your eyes open as Patricio told you."

Closing my eyes, I tried to think of something to help me get through this dark moment. My mind rushed through a hundred scenes and then came to an abrupt stop. I was in the dark Los Pinos street. I saw the hazy image of the rapist, felt myself pushed against the wall, felt the hot bite of the twig against my back. After raising my hand, I paused and opened my eyes, and then drove the dagger down hard on the spot that Maestro had shown me.

I heard myself shriek gutturally. Instantly, the bull fell, legs and head jerking and twitching. His body shuddered at my feet. It seemed to take an age before the animal's body went still.

Maestro applauded, the sharp cracks reverberating around the stall. Dropping the dagger, I rushed out of the room.

Maestro swapped the mechanical bull I sparred with at the Los Pinos bullring for another with cork shoulders. After my sessions with the cape and muleta ended every day, he wheeled out this new adversary. Standing four yards from the bull's head, I'd use a sword with a downward bend at the end of the blade to sight between the horns at the silver-dollar spot he'd painted in the middle of the cork shoulders. Then I'd run toward the bull and penetrate this death-notch.

As I tried to master this *volapie* method of killing, I'd often strike the cork too far to the left or right, or too far above or below the death-notch, which meant I'd struck the bull's shoulder bones and failed to penetrate and kill cleanly.

"You're careless," Maestro hollered, after yet another failure. "You're not trying."

"I just need more practice."

I tried and missed the spot again, striking too far to the right this time. Any confidence I'd gained by my small victories was seeping away with each verbal attack. Self-doubt lurked in the folds of my cape, spritzing my body every time I made a bad pass or missed the spot in the bull's shoulders. Maestro was correct; I was too afraid to make it in the business. He'd made a mistake taking me on. I was too small to be a successful matador. What was I trying to prove, wanting to fight bulls?

Maestro ran up to me, his nose and brow wrinkled as a snarling as a snarling dog's. He grabbed me by the shoulders and shook me so fiercely my teeth chattered. Instantly, I relived the horror of the attacker's grip and shrieked. Maestro let go quickly and, instinctively, I cupped my hand around my throat.

"Are you my apprentice or just a woman playing one?" he asked.

I didn't answer.

"I'm fed up with you," he said. "You're wasting my time. We're finished for the day."

Recovering from the shock, I hurled the cape on the sand and walked out of the bullring.

"Come back," he said. "You don't leave until I say you can."

I walked faster. Outside the bullring, I turned left instead of right and walked into the older section of the city, where the streets narrowed and curved. Men and women stared as I passed by. I came to a pretty café I remembered and crossed the street to it. Only when I was seated at an outside table did I remember I was still in my grubby jeans and didn't have cash with me. I rose to leave before a waiter came to take my order.

"Kathleen!"

El Cabrito and another young man were exiting the café. Dressed in a double-breasted suit and silk tie, Julio looked handsome. My cheeks passed from warm to scorching. He came over, kissed me on the cheek, and then introduced his cousin, Rafael, who couldn't take his eyes off my jeans. I'd have laughed at his astonishment in normal circumstances.

"Kathleen fights bulls, too," El Cabrito said, as if apologizing to Rafael for my attire. "I've been wondering how you're coming along. I heard you appeared with the *toreras*."

Now was not the time to point out they were *toreros*. "I did."

"Do you mind if I join you?" he asked.

"I was just leaving."

"Ah, then maybe I can escort you somewhere."

"I'm going home."

"Then I'll walk with you part of the way, if you don't mind."

His offer was unusual, but I didn't mind. "Sure."

After telling Rafael he'd meet him back at his apartment, we started down the street toward the bullring. People still stared at me and I felt embarrassed for him.

"I came right from the bullring," I said apologetically.

He shrugged. "I thought you might have."

"My trainer and I had a disagreement and I needed to get away from him for a bit," I added, feeling the need to explain more fully.

He laughed. "How is Fermin, anyway?"

"Maestro's fine."

"You call him Maestro?"

"He's a good teacher, for the most part."

"I'm sure difficult and impatient, as well." His scarred eyebrow arched endearingly. "So what did you two disagree about?"

A fragrant perfume wafted in the air as we passed a flower stand vibrant with sunflowers, Mexican orange, and enormous dahlias. On a street corner, an old woman sat before a blackened pot, spooning sizzling meat and onions onto a soft tortilla for a waiting customer. As we continued,

I explained about my trip to the slaughterhouse and how difficult it had been to kill the bull, and how I constantly missed the painted spot on the mechanical bull's shoulders, and how irritated Maestro became.

"If I'm always missing the death-notch," I said, "maybe it's a sign I'm not meant to be a bullfighter."

He said nothing. I wondered if he was just like the other men, who didn't want women doing their work. I quickened my pace.

"I'm visiting my cousin," he said, abruptly changing the subject. He explained that Rafael and he had been to boarding school together, and his cousin was now an attorney in Los Pinos.

In five minutes, we arrived at the bullring. "Thanks for walking me back," I said, and held out my hand.

"Walking? I thought we were running." He grinned. "You don't get off so lightly." He nodded toward the bullring entrance and said, "I'll show you how to strike the bull's *cruz* every time."

Thrills of delight ran up my body.

"Take me to the mechanical bull," he said.

I led him inside. Maestro hadn't put the device away and my cape and sword still lay where I'd tossed them.

"What you must do," Julio said, as he laid his hand on the metal handles of the bull, "is focus your attention only on the *cruz*. Think of nothing else but striking the mark."

Standing four feet away from the device, I bent my right knee and sighted the death-notch between the lowered horns, right in the middle of the shoulders at the base of the neck.

"Don't let anything distract you. Not the bull's horns. Not me. Nothing."

As I ran toward the bull, I grunted aloud like a matador, kept my eyes riveted on the *cruz*, and then plunged the sword precisely into it.

"You've got it. Well done."

I hugged him before I realized what I'd done. "Thank you so much, El Cabrito."

"Call me Julio."

"Thank you . . . Julio."

"Never doubt yourself as a bullfighter again, Kathleen. Because fear always follows doubt."

"What was going on here?" Maestro hollered. His face was shiny and red as a pepper.

"Fermin, it's good to see you again," Julio said, extending his hand.

Maestro ignored the gesture. "What are you doing here with him?" he asked me.

"It's okay," said Julio. "I've just been teaching her how to sight properly."

"We bumped into each other and he offered to show me, Maestro."

"She is not your business, El Cabrito," Maestro said, turning to Julio. "*I'm* her instructor."

The two men regarded each other, Maestro's chin jutting out dangerously. Julio's hands were soft fists. My heart beat so fast I thought it would explode. If they started fighting, I'd never be able to separate them.

"You're right," said Julio, and he picked his jacket up off the sand. "I meant no harm, Fermin." He smiled. "I think you've discovered a future star."

Maestro's face relaxed. He walked over to the mechanical bull and pulled the sword from its cork shoulders.

Julio came over to me. "Good luck, Kathleen," he whispered, and discreetly handed me a piece of paper. "Any time you feel like talking, call me. Even if I'm away fighting, pick up the phone."

After a quick bow, he slung his jacket over his shoulder and headed toward the exit.

"El Cabrito's an arrogant fool," said Maestro. "It'll catch up with him in the bullring one day."

A shiver whipped through me. "Don't say that."

He turned to me, eyes ablaze. "Don't ever walk out on me again."

19

A STIFF WIND BUFFETED MY BODY IN THE BULLRING AND flared the muleta, lifting up its end and leaving it as useful as a bald tire in snow. If I'd been facing a live bull, my body would've been exposed, alerting him as to what should be the real target of his wrath. To compensate for the wind gusts, I doused the bottom of the muleta with water and sprinkled sand on it, as matadors do in order to make it heavier and more resistant to the gusts.

Maestro and four men who'd been watching from the *callejón* stepped into the bullring and walked toward me. My trainer smiled sunnily as he drew up, which put me instantly on guard.

"Meet your cuadrilla, Kathleen," he said.

The men were in their forties—the two stoutest perhaps fifty—and all had neatly trimmed mustaches.

"Luís, Agustín, and I will serve as your banderilleros." He pointed at the two stout men with his thumb. "Enrique and Montes are the picadors. They are all very experienced."

A part of me was thrilled—now I had a team! But the other part was annoyed. In four weeks, it would be springtime in Mexico, the start of a new corrida season, and I was scheduled to fight in Colotlán and earn real money. Of course, I wouldn't fight as an official apprentice, like the two male *novilleros* also appearing on the billing, because

I still wasn't a member of the union. And while I was grateful to Maestro for negotiating contracts for me to perform in the states of Jalisco and Aguascalientes, I also felt I had the right to be included in any decisions about who would join *my* team.

That he hadn't conferred with me hurt, especially because Maestro and I had been getting along very well since the first—and last—time I'd walked out of the bullring. Though he'd never apologized for shaking me in anger, he hadn't tried to do it again, either. For the last four months, Maestro had taught me the two other killing methods, including the very dangerous but crowd-pleasing one in which the matador awaits the bull's charge and the bull essentially impales himself on the sword.

He'd also taught me different passes using the right and left hand, essential skills to perfect if a matador is to build a huge following of fans. In right-handed passes, the scarlet muleta's short wooden dowel is held upward at its midpoint together with the fake sword, whose aluminum blade points down. This extends the width of the fabric so it now resembles a heart. The muleta's enlarged size also means the charging bull's lethal horns pass farther away from the body, making right-handed passes far less dangerous than left-handed ones. It had taken me weeks to properly master holding the sword and dowel from its midpoint simultaneously in my right hand.

Maestro no longer belittled me when I made mistakes. I'd assumed his newfound patience meant our relationship had evolved and we were now true partners in achieving my goal of appearing at the Plaza México. But that apparently wasn't true.

The men bowed as they shook my hand and complimented me on my handling of the muleta, despite the wind. One of the picadors, as ugly as a mud fence and with a half-closed eye, kept staring at me.

"Maestro, can I talk to you?"

"Later."

"No, now."

After telling the men to wait for him back in the *callejón,* he turned back to me. The rude picador was the last to leave and I waited until he was out of earshot.

"I don't like him," I said.

"Who?"

"The last one."

"Montes?"

"He looks at me strangely."

"Montes is very skilled." Maestro laughed. "One of his eyes is lazy."

"He makes me uncomfortable. It reminds me of . . . "

"Of what?"

"Of the time I was attacked."

"Montes isn't the man who attacked you."

"I know he's not."

"Men like to admire pretty women," said Maestro, cocking his head. "That's all Montes was doing. You're too sensitive."

The men disappeared behind the wooden shield and entered the *callejón.* Not every man was a monster like the man who'd attacked me. I understood this, but Maestro didn't understand what it was like to be attacked by a man as I had. He couldn't simply dismiss my feelings.

"You shouldn't say I'm too sensitive," I said. "It's unfair. Maybe I did overreact a little, but the attack is still very fresh in my mind. I'm trying to overcome my fear, but it's hard. How would you feel if Carmen was attacked?"

Maestro whipped back his head and stared at me. "I see your point, Kathleen."

While grateful for his concession, he also needed to know he'd done wrong in appointing the cuadrilla in my absence. But I had to be careful. I was the pupil with much to learn; I needed him.

"There's something else," I said, my insides seeming to take flight like a flock of starlings.

"Oh?"

"I appreciate everything you do for me." I couldn't make the quavering in my voice stop. "I needed to be there when you hired those men."

His eyes became slits of incredulity. "What are you talking about?"

"It's my cuadrilla." I knew he could hear the trembling in my voice, but I had to continue. "I should have a say in these things, Maestro."

"You have no experience. I make all the decisions until I feel you can help me."

"Then a woman must serve as my sword handler and confidential advisor," I said, my pride unwilling to fully concede.

"Why?"

"Sword handlers help matadors to dress. That's the tradition."

"Patricio's your sword handler. I told you that already."

A bolt of white heat raced through me. "You did *not* tell me."

With a sharp flick of his wrist, he shot a cigarette out of the packet and snared it between his thin lips. He didn't respond until he'd lit it.

"Didn't I tell you that day we went to the slaughterhouse?"

I glared at him. I remembered it had seemed important I like Patricio that afternoon, but Maestro had said nothing about hiring him.

"I could swear I did," Maestro continued. "Well, it's done now."

"You'll have to tell Patricio I've changed my mind." My voice was as sturdy now as my irritation. "I need a woman."

"And I'm your confidential advisor. As you're not allowed to wear a *traje de luces,* you'll wear an Andalusian suit. You don't need help putting that on, so what does it matter?"

Spitting the cigarette on the sand and folding his arms as he coolly observed me, Maestro looked as if the sun came out just to hear him crow. It didn't help I didn't have a response to counter his remark.

"I'll bring Carmen along to help you for your first corrida," he said. "You'll be nervous and that's understandable. But Patricio is your sword handler." Maestro smiled. "Remember when you said I was like a father to you?"

An image of Daddy's coffin on the bier at the front of the church diluted my resentment. Had he had time to think of me before the fire killed him? Had he called out goodbye to Mama and me as he was trapped and knew he'd die?

"I take my role as your trainer as seriously as your father took his role in your life. My desire is for you to get to Plaza México. There's no glory in this for me."

My soul stirred at the very mention of Plaza México.

"I didn't meant to question your judgment, Maestro. I just want—"

"Don't question my judgment about these things from now on. I'm your business manager. I look after the money. I appoint the staff and set up the contracts with the impresarios." His expression changed, sunny again. "Believe me, that's a huge responsibility. You should be happy not to be involved in these matters."

I ordered two Andalusian suits to wear during the corridas. At the final fitting, as he'd done when I put the first one on, the old tailor circled me slowly, picking loose threads off the jacket and pants with his wrinkled, pale hands.

"Beautiful," he said. "You look very impressive."

The effect certainly was stunning. He was as artistic in his trade as any matador was in his.

"The crowds will fall in love the moment you enter the bullring," Carmen said, her eyes flaming with admiration.

Worn over a white blouse, this jet-black bolero jacket fitted as snugly as the gray suit. Both jackets accentuated my shoulders and made my waist appear even narrower than it was. The matching pants, held up by braces, ended midcalf and had five buttonholes sewn into each leg. By tradition, the upper two buttonholes were fastened by regular buttons, while gold or silver ornaments could be attached to the remaining three holes, in the same way men wore cufflinks in their shirts. As I admired myself in the mirror, I remembered Daddy's stash of cufflinks in a closet drawer at Mama's place, especially a pair of silver horses I'd bought him for Christmas the year before he died. I'd saved the entire year to buy them. I decided to ask Mama if I could have them to wear in the pants.

My one break with tradition related to the wide-brimmed hat and the scarf that was always tied around one's waist instead of a leather belt. These were traditionally black or gray, but I'd had them made in lavender. At first, the old man had been reluctant, but I'd held my ground and insisted.

Later, when I put on the black Andalusian suit to show Maestro, his face darkened. We were out on the patio and he leaped out of his seat as if he'd accidentally sat on burning coals.

"What is *this*?"

Abril and Emilio, who'd been playing handball, stopped instantly. The rubber ball's weakening bounces interrupted the sharp silence.

"Don't you like it?" I asked.

He looked at Carmen, who was deadheading zinnias in a nearby flowerbed. "You allowed her to buy a hat this color?"

She tossed a dead bloom into a pail by her feet. "That color has meaning for Kathleen."

"You'll make me a laughingstock," Maestro said. "Take it back and buy a traditional Cordoban hat. The scarf, too."

My leg muscles tightened in preparation to walk away, but my brain refused to order them. It was only a goddamned hat. It wasn't as if I'd disobeyed him in something crucial.

"My father will never see me fight in the bullring and lavender was his favorite color," I said.

Maestro put one foot forward like a bull about to paw the sand.

"He died when I was only a year older than Emilio," I continued, looking over at his son, who now stood beside Carmen, the pair watching us intently. "I loved him. As much as you love Carmen and your children. Wearing this hat is my way of honoring his memory when I'm fighting." My throat tightened. "I won't take it back."

Maestro's lips parted, but then shut again. He walked past me quickly and disappeared into the house.

Though Mama and I spoke on the telephone occasionally, it had been more than a year since I'd visited. Most folks think of "home" as the place where they grew up, but I didn't feel this way, and so felt no urge to return. I don't rightly know why it was like this—perhaps because Daddy died early and Mama grew distant when I was a girl, or maybe because I'd left home to attend Rowans Institute at eighteen. Her house would always have great memories, but it was no longer home.

When I arrived at her place, the first hour together was kind of stiff, since we hadn't seen each other for so long. I was sure Mama felt it, too, though she didn't say so. But over a dinner of thick steaks, greens, and her delicious fried potatoes, glistening with butter, we warmed to each other. She asked all sorts of questions about life in Los Pinos, but nothing about the bulls.

Later, in the living·room, she handed me a letter from Charles, whom I hadn't heard from, either. "You're still in touch?" I asked, as I tore the envelope open.

"I sure am," she said.

"That's nice."

"The letter came a week ago and I didn't forward it because I knew you were coming home," she said.

It was one page, describing his work in Louisiana and that he was renting a large furnished apartment in the French Quarter. Inside was also a photograph of him hugging me on the stairway at his old engineering department building. I was a study of carefree happiness on the outside. Yet when the picture had been taken, my hunger for the bulls had already unfurled like a muleta inside me. Passing my index finger along the serrated white edges of the photograph, I scrutinized the picture again. The woman looked like me, but I was someone else now. His letter finished by saying he missed me still and that he wanted us to stay in touch.

Mama scooted over on the couch, fixin' to get closer to me. "He hasn't met anyone new," she said, and patted my forearm. "You never know how things might pan out in the future, if you just keep an open mind, Kathleen."

Thankfully, George's arrival curtailed the awkward silence that followed her remark. We passed the rest of the evening watching frivolous television, something I hadn't done in months. I was always too tired from training to watch anything other than the news or the occasional cartoon with Maestro's kids.

Before I was scheduled to catch the bus next morning, I went into Mama's bedroom and found Daddy's box of jewelry in the closet. When I poured its contents out on her bed, the cufflinks and tiepins clinked as cheerfully as they'd done when I was a little girl. I examined a couple of the items, trying to remember the last time I'd seen Daddy wear the rhinestone cufflinks and a gold tiepin with a ruby garnet in its center. I picked up the tiny silver horses and impulsively kissed one.

"What are you doing, Kathleen?"

George stood on the threshold, one hand resting on the jamb.

"These were Daddy's," I said, holding up a shiny horse for him to see. "I'm taking them to wear in my suit when I fight."

"Ah, a talisman," he said.

"You're *not*," Mama said, appearing suddenly and pushing George aside as she entered. "Put those right back, y'hear?"

"I need these, Mama."

"I gave them to George. Put them back in the box."

"She can have them," he said.

"I bought Daddy these horses. You had no right to give them away without asking me."

"You're not wearing them in a bullring. I won't have it."

George put his arm around her shoulder. "Come on now, Marie. They mean something to her."

"I'm taking them, Mama." I slipped them inside my purse and snapped it shut.

"Take the damned cufflinks," she shot back. "Take all of them. You're as obstinate and selfish as he was. They'd be no lucky charm if you knew what I know."

She slid from under George's arm and rushed out of the room.

20

THE TWENTY-TWO-HOUR TRIP TO COLOTLÁN ACTUALLY took a day and a half, as we had to change buses three times and ran into a long delay near the city of Durango when the bus broke down. As Maestro had promised, Carmen, whose mother was looking after the children, had come to help me dress for my first corrida and would then travel on to spend ten days with her sister after we left for our next venue. We'd sat huddled under an acacia tree for hours in the intense heat, waiting for a mechanic to arrive. There was no drinking water and Maestro and Carmen warned me not to drink from a nearby stream, as some of our fellow passengers— ancient widows in black, housewives carrying fruit and colorful blankets to market, Mexican cowboys, and farmers with small livestock— were doing. I'd soaked my handkerchief in the cool water instead and wrapped it around my neck to keep the sweat at bay.

As it was my first time traveling into the heart of Mexico, Carmen had insisted I sit by the window to admire the view. The spectacular landscape ranged from gaping deserts pocked with Joshua trees and giant cacti to huge rocks sculpted into bizarre shapes by the wind, rivers like blue threads winding through majestic gorges, and sparkling lakes, banana plantations, and sweeping hills dense with stands of lush Mexican pine.

The poverty shocked me, though. Unpainted wooden shacks sprouted like weeds on the roadsides. Sloe-eyed children and their parents, not much older than Mama, with missing front teeth and heavily creased faces, stared out from the dim thresholds.

Situated in a densely wooded basin surrounded by low-lying hills turned coppery by a blood-red sinking sun, Colotlán had a sleepy, haphazard appearance. Many inhabitants still used horses and carts to travel around the city. Two plazas housed churches and ornate Spanish colonial municipal buildings the color of sand, while the other streets consisted of squat houses, cantinas, and mom-and-pop shops more dilapidated than those found in any small Texas town.

One block from the bullring, our hotel was small and clean, and the staff was friendly. A stream of cool air from a quick-turning fan hit my face like a splash of refreshing cold water when I opened the door to my room. After a cold bath, I went to bed and fell asleep, only to awake with a start, disturbed by a dream about the bulls waiting inside their pens at the bullring.

Though I wasn't yet an official apprentice, Maestro had determined I'd operate by the same rules as a *novillero* admitted to the union, which meant the bulls I'd fight would be under four years old. Some of these bulls might be smaller than others sent by the breeding ranches to the ring, and I prayed mine would be respectably sized and brave. No bullfighter wanted a cowardly or tricky bull, one that wouldn't charge or kept returning to his *querencia,* an area in the ring usually near the *toril* gate where he liked the smell. This kind of bull felt safest in his *querencia* and chose to defend himself there, increasing the danger to a bullfighter exponentially as he was obliged to go there to fight him.

I tried to fall asleep again, but sleep eluded me. Another anxiety soon emerged to replace the one about the quality of the bulls I'd get: that the crowd would hate me—because I was a woman, because I wasn't Mexican—and they'd look on in stony silence instead of applauding my skillful passes.

I lay awake in bed until the church bells in the adjacent plaza rang out, alerting parishioners that the first Sunday Mass was about to begin. Hurriedly, I slipped on a navy blue polka dot dress, tied my hair into a chignon, and put on a black lace mantilla and white gloves. The click of my heels striking the clay-tiled hallway was spooky in the dark silence and the lobby was quiet as a catacomb. On one wall was the head and black-tipped horns of a bull, one that had fought in the ring forty years ago and had then been gifted to the hotel owner, according to a brass sign beneath the bust. His big eyes challenged me, as if the bull somehow knew I'd be in the bullring later that day.

Carmen arrived in the lobby two minutes later, wearing a woolen cardigan. Only when we got outside and the freezing morning air brushed against my naked arms did I understand why she'd put one on. Geckos and other feral creatures, including a tiny yellow snake, scuttled and disappeared into the flowerbeds as we cut across the courtyard.

Throughout a packed Mass in the cheerfully decorated church, I recited countless Lord's Prayers and Hail Marys while staring up at the portraits of the martyrs, many of them priests, who'd died in Mexico's Cristero War more than twenty years ago. I willed one of their faces to give me the tiniest smile as a sign that all would go well for me in the bullring. When nothing happened, I directed my energy to the glassy eyes of the Virgin, and then to the cherubic baby in her arms, but with the same result. My gaze moved next to the statues of Saint Joseph and Saint John the Baptist but, again, nothing. Though I hadn't been to confession for eighteen months, a feral urge to receive Holy Eucharist came over me. When Carmen stepped into the aisle to go, I followed her.

After Mass ended, I went into a small chapel dedicated to the Virgin of Guadalupe. She was ethereal in a golden dress and a blue cloak pocked with bright stars. Taking off the delicate chain and medal bearing her image, the one the female bullfighters had given me, I gently touched her bare feet with it, then kissed the medal before rehanging it around my neck. I lit a candle and prayed that the Virgin would be with me in the ring.

Carmen and I strolled through town and breakfasted at a café we liked because its interior was so cheerfully painted.

"Where did you meet Maestro?" I asked, after we'd ordered, as much to take my mind off the corrida as out of interest.

"My father organized a meeting." She picked up the sugar bowl and spooned some into her coffee. "Fermin had seen me at a gathering and approached Papá."

"That's cute."

"Fermin's old-fashioned that way." She stirred the coffee. "We courted for six months, but I didn't see him often. He was fighting in corridas all over Mexico."

"When did you know he was the one?"

"I didn't consent the first time he asked me to marry him," she revealed. Her eyes darted to a nearby potted hibiscus plant. "He had a lot of admirers and I was younger than him. I wasn't sure I would like a husband who was away from home so much. But he kept asking and I loved him and Papá was in favor, so I eventually agreed."

We sipped our coffees and then I asked, "Do you think it's strange that I want to fight bulls?"

"At the beginning, I did. I cannot lie. But then I saw how badly you wanted it and how you work as hard as the men for success." She leaned forward and grabbed my hands. "I admire you, chiquita. You are a very strong young woman. And it's good you are this way. I could never have overcome what happened to you in the street that night."

I snatched my hands from her grasp. Blood rushed to my head and I felt instantly lightheaded. A reel of terrible images whipped through my brain.

"Oh, chiquita." Carmen rose and reached for my hands, squeezing them. "What have I done? Forgive me. I'm so stupid."

The film stopped playing and the background sound of customers talking and laughing returned. I could hear the clink of cups striking saucers once more. The image of the old bull I'd killed in the slaughterhouse came into my mind.

"It helps that he's dead," I said.

She looked at me in astonishment. "But you couldn't . . . how can you know this?"

"He's dead and I'll never see him again."

She didn't question me further.

Maestro was waiting for me in the lobby when Carmen and I returned to the hotel. Other men were also present, including a photographer and a newspaper journalist who was interviewing one of the other apprentice bullfighters scheduled to appear in the corrida with me.

"The journalist wants to talk to you next," Maestro said. "And his photographer wants a picture of you in your suit before we leave for the bullring."

"I'll make you especially beautiful for the camera," said Carmen.

"No makeup or nail polish," warned Maestro. "The bullring's no place for you to look like a woman."

Carmen rolled her eyes.

Maestro either missed it or chose to ignore her. "I've just come from the *sorteo*," he said. "I drew you two excellent bulls."

I thanked him, fully aware of the unwritten custom that the member of the cuadrilla participating in the pairing and drawing of the bulls before the fight always returned to tell the matador that the bulls were brave, regardless of their temperament. Bad bulls were also shipped to the bullring, of course. But except in those rare cases when someone of influence interfered with a drawing, a weak or cowardly bull was always paired with a brave bull, so the three bullfighters got as evenly matched pairs of bulls as possible.

Reaching behind his chair, Maestro took out a long package

wrapped in coarse brown paper. He stood and handed it to me. "This is for you."

I ripped it open to reveal an old sword case, so old the leather was soft as a baby's skin and the intricate tooling was barely visible. Inside was a sword. When I took it out of the leather scabbard, its thirty-odd-inch blade, curved down at the tip, glinted in the light of the crystal chandelier. The handle was tightly bound in scarlet wool thread, its pommel made of chamois to prevent one's hand from slipping when the blade penetrated the bull's death-notch.

"This sword was mine," Maestro said. A taut cord on his neck bulged and rolled sideways as he swallowed. "Hundreds of bulls have submitted to this sword." He paused, then added, "Patricio insisted you should have a new sword. He doesn't understand. This one is magnificent. It deserves to fight and dominate bulls, still."

"I'll treasure it," I replied. "And I won't let you down."

My head throbbed. I loved Maestro. I loved Carmen. I loved my entire cuadrilla. I loved the world.

At two o'clock, Carmen arrived to help me dress. Though I didn't need assistance, Carmen's presence helped steady my nerves. I hadn't been able to sleep during the afternoon, like Maestro had ordered me to do. As the hour of the fight had drawn closer, vivid images of the patiently waiting bulls had crowded my mind and I'd tossed and turned on the bed. Not even the sweet aroma of jasmine and roses drifting up from the courtyard could calm me.

The last thing I did was fasten Daddy's silver horse cufflinks in the buttonholes of my pants cuffs. It was comforting to know that a part of him would be in the bullring with me.

After Carmen plaited my hair and I was fully dressed, I opened a small leather case I'd bought that resembled a three-inch-thick Bible.

Inside, in the middle panel, was an image of the Virgin of Guadalupe. To her left, I'd inserted an image of the crucified Christ. Saint Francis of Assisi was in the right-hand panel. I carefully propped the case up on the top of the vanity like an open book, but it toppled over and crashed on the tiled floor. I gasped when I picked it up and saw that the pane of glass protecting the Virgin was cracked, the glass now resembling a rising sun.

"Don't worry," said Carmen. "It wasn't a mirror."

I blessed myself. "I wish it hadn't broken."

"The Virgin's not superstitious," Carmen assured me, her gaze riveted on my stricken face. "She's above such a silly thing. And you must be too, chiquita."

21

THE DARK PASSAGEWAY TO THE BULLRING STANK OF cigarettes. The scent of stale urine wafting into the air from the entrance to a men's lavatory made my eyes sting. Through the slats of the tall entrance gates that opened onto the bullring, the crowd's melodic babble flowed like water between river stones. Four banderilleros and one of the apprentices pressed their backs against the cold stone walls, each man staring at the cobblestone floor, lost in his thoughts. Another banderillero paced back and forth. These men were thinking about the bulls' sharp horns, perhaps thinking they might not see their wives, children, or girlfriends again.

I was sure they were thinking about the horns, because I was, too. I was also frightened I might freeze before the bull, like I had that afternoon in the small ring south of Los Pinos, and disgrace Maestro.

"*Buena suerte, Matadora,*" said Raymundo, the most senior apprentice, a man the same height and build as myself who looked no older than eighteen. That he was as short as me gave me some confidence.

Raymundo took his place to my left. As the least experienced fighter, tradition required I walk into the ring flanked by the two male apprentices.

"*Gracias,*" I replied, saluting him with my lavender hat. At this moment, it didn't matter that he'd addressed me as a female bullfighter. What mattered was that he'd recognized me as a fellow professional, even though he undoubtedly knew I wasn't yet a member of the union. "*Para ti, también, Matador.*"

He smiled and also doffed his hat. Like me, he was not allowed to wear the shimmering suit of lights. I pushed aside my jealousy that he would one day easily find a famous matador to sponsor him, so he could take the *alternativa* and become a full-fledged matador. Soon enough—long before me, undoubtedly—he would take part in this highly symbolic fight, and a full matador would hand his cape and sword to the novice. Then he would be a *matador de toros*. The very idea that it might happen to me gave me chills.

Esteban, the other apprentice, passed by without greeting me and took his place to my right. I nodded and smiled at him. His nostrils opened wide as he crinkled up his Roman nose.

"It's not often the passageway smells like a woman's bedroom," he said, in a thick Spanish dialect, as he adjusted the cape he had slung over his shoulder.

"Don't talk to my pupil that way," Maestro said from behind me. "Save your contempt for the bulls."

I swore never to wear perfume again.

But Esteban wouldn't let up. "Why are you here? This place isn't for you."

"Esteban, stop," said Raymundo.

"You know I'm right," Esteban insisted, leaning forward to look at him. "Why should we have to appear with a woman? It's not right."

"That's enough," said Maestro firmly.

"No woman should fight bulls," Esteban continued, his voice now low so only Raymundo and I could hear him. "It's unnatural. She'll bring us bad luck."

I looked at him. "Conchita Cintrón fought bulls."

"Pfft." Esteban adjusted his cape again. "You're not welcome here."

I tugged down my bolero jacket. What if he was right? What if I did bring these men bad luck?

A trumpet blared, the notes sharp and brief. Cigarettes were ground hurriedly into the ground. Banderilleros blessed themselves. Our cuadrillas formed hastily behind us, first the banderilleros, then the mounted picadors, then the two substitutes, in case Raymundo, Esteban, or I was badly injured in a fight and couldn't continue. Behind our teams were the ring servants, in their livery of dusty orange shirts and blue pants, carpenters, and finally a pair of mules, adorned with feathered plumes and tinkling bells, that would drag the dead bulls out of the ring.

"Keep calm, Kathleen," Maestro said. He stood directly behind me now, the edge of his nubby hat a fraction above his eyes. He wore a lavender silk suit trimmed with black embroidery. The suit was new. He'd had it made in an attempt to lessen any attention generated by my lavender Cordoban hat and scarf.

"Don't let that idiot distract you," he said. "Concentrate on what is to come."

As the wooden gates creaked slowly open, the babble of voices transformed to a roar, the noise almost drowning out the band playing a traditional Paso Doble. The snow-white flanks and silky tails of two horses reversed in perfect symmetry toward me. My eyes lifted up to take in the riders, two constables dressed in seventeenth-century Philip IV black velvet suits, frilled lace collars, and hats with silky white plumes.

Sun rays as fiery as molten lava bore down on me as I walked across the smoothly raked sand of the fifty-yard-wide arena toward the judge's box. Above the judge, the black hands of a huge clock pointed to four o'clock. The band stuck up "La Virgen de la Macarena," the perky bullfighter's anthem played during the procession at every fight. Behind the wooden fence and passageway, already inhabited by the media and managers, the tiered seating rose at a forty-five-degree angle away from the bullring. Every seat was occupied on the shady side, the less expensive half-sun and half-shade sides, and even the sunny side, where the audience was jammed tighter than beans in a can.

My blood iced up with pride and excitement. The skin on my scalp crawled as I took in this sweeping circle of humanity, all of the people smiling and applauding, the most enthusiastic cheers rushing at me from the cheapest seats. I doffed my hat, bowed to the judge and his artistic adviser, and then, with the exception of the picadors and the team of mules that went to the horse patio entrance, the cuadrillas withdrew to the shade of the passageway.

Every eye in the place cut to the red *toril* gate when the trumpet blared. A knife-edge silence descended as people waited to see what kind of bull would appear. Would he emerge like a warrior or docilely, with his head down, like he'd eat sand? The gate opened slowly to reveal an oblong of pitch-blackness. And then a black bull with wide horns burst from the darkness. He was blacker than a Texan midnight, but looked on the skinny side for a bull that was four years old. But appearances could be deceptive. Smaller bulls were swifter than a hiccup and could be as dangerous as the truck-sized bulls faced by full-fledged matadors. The animal stopped abruptly, sniffed the air, and then cantered into the *tercio*, the area between the outer and inner painted rings, where he began bellowing and pawing the sand.

"This bull's a *manso*," Maestro said, his face transforming into a mask of contempt as he watched one of the senior apprentice's banderilleros test him.

The bull refused to charge straight and returned consistently between half-charges to a favored spot near the *toril* gate. Cowardly bulls—like cowardly matadors—are not crowd-pleasers. People paid to see the three *tercios* of the fight unfold smooth as a silk stocking.

The first act consisted of three sets of three to five *faenas*, where the cuadrilla and the matador, using his vibrant cape, test the bull's aggression, speed, whether he knows how to use his horns, and what defects

he has, such as a tendency to charge to the right or left instead of predictably straight. Any deviation not found in this first act exposed the
matador in the final act to serious injury if not death.

Entering the ring toward the end of the first act were the picadors,
who gouged the bull's shoulders with their pikes to release the swelling
caused by rushing adrenaline. When the trumpet sounded, the next
tercio began and the banderilleros inserted six colorful barbed sticks to
correct any defect detected by the matador and weaken the powerful
bull. The final *tercio* began with another trumpet blare and was ideally
fought in the innermost of the two rings painted in the sand. The audience always relished this final act, as it tested the matador's courage
and dominance, as well as his ability to mesmerize, manipulate, and
tame the ferocious bull, before the bull's death by sword.

Maestro proved right. Deeming a single lancing by his picador and
one pair of bright red-and-yellow banderillas sufficient, the senior
apprentice, Raymundo, approached the judge, the city's mayor, and
obtained permission to move directly to the final act rather than having
the bull sent immediately for slaughtering, his flesh to be distributed
after death to the poor. That was the case with the brave bulls, too.
After two series of beautiful right-handed passes, when it seemed the
apprentice had cured the bull of his cowardice, Raymundo changed
the muleta to his left hand and executed *naturals*, especially dangerous
passes since the matador often stood with his back to the bull's horns
and was fully exposed when it charged. Although his were good, my
naturals were definitely more artistic, which bolstered my confidence.

While Raymundo executed a third *natural*, his body arching beautifully and left arm extending to hold the muleta low, the *novillero*
waited too long to turn in synchronization with the charging animal's
speed. The bull's left horn sliced into Raymundo's gut. I thought my
eyes had deceived me until I saw the sand turn dark.

A low groan swept through the arena. One guest in the judge's box
stuffed a piece of her mantilla in her mouth as if she were eating it.

Raymundo ran a few steps before crumpling and falling on his back, covering the gaping hole in his belly with his bare hands, his face locked in a grimace. Another groan came from the audience, most of whom were now on their feet. Men in the lowest tier of seats dangled halfway over a barrier advertising beer and Florsheim shoes.

In slow motion, I watched Raymundo's cuadrilla pour into the ring, one man swaying his magenta cape to and fro as he hollered at the bull. After he'd enticed the animal away from the stricken apprentice, the other men loaded Raymundo onto a stretcher and carried him across the sand to the bullring's infirmary, a ring servant covering the gash in his stomach with his hands to keep the intestines inside.

"Cowardly bulls are as dangerous as brave bulls," said Maestro. "This man paid the price." He turned to me. "Remember this."

"Will he be okay?" I asked.

Maestro shrugged. "It's between him and God." He blessed himself.

The arrogant Esteban walked briskly along the passageway toward us, stepping over a canvas bag containing my spare cape and muletas. As the second most senior performer, it was his duty to kill Raymundo's bull.

"You didn't bring us luck, did you, señorita?" he said as he passed. His baleful eyes penetrated mine. "Even God doesn't want women in the bullring."

The eyes of every man standing nearby seared my face. I started shaking.

"It's not her job to bring you luck," Maestro said, and he spat at the ground. "Her job's to fight the bulls, the same as you."

As I watched the second apprentice slip into the bullring, I said, "I can't go in there."

Maestro gripped my wrist in response and pulled me along the callejón. We exited into the dank passageway leading to the horse patio.

"How dare you say that?" he said

"You heard him. I brought them bad luck. Maybe I'm not meant—"

"Shut up." He gripped both my shoulders and shook me. Men passing by stared but said nothing. One laughed after he'd walked by.

"Stop shaking me," I said, my mind jumping from uncertainty to humiliation at what Maestro was doing to me in public, and finally to anger.

"You will *not* make a fool of me," he said, releasing my shoulders. "You will go out when it's your turn and fight your bull." He started back to the *callejón*.

Above the *toril* gate, a sign announcing my bull's statistics in white chalk stated his name was El Resplandor. A ribbon attached to the muscular hump at the base of his neck was red and blue, the colors of the breeding ranch where he came from. The ranch's brand resembled the mathematical *pi* and the number 13 had also been scorched into his left hindquarter. Chestnut in color and around eight hundred pounds, with enormous shoulders, the bull was every bit as splendid as his name suggested. He had a handsome face and was well-armed with long horns that glittered like virgin snow.

There was no word from the infirmary about Raymundo and the sting of the second apprentice's disapproval was still raw. Steeling myself into focus, I pushed the uncertainty and self-doubt out of my mind and scrutinized the bull's movements and speed as I watched Luís test him with preliminary passes to gauge his defects, a job that all banderilleros do for matadors during the fight.

"It's like silk," Maestro said after Luís finished. "I knew it would be a brave bull when I saw it at the *sorteo*. This is your best one of the two." He tapped my shoulder twice. "Now, show the audience what we can do."

Everyone left the ring, melting into the shadows of the sturdy wooden shields in front of the entrance to the *callejón*, the space behind the shields so narrow that an outraged bull could never enter.

The crowd fell silent as I slipped into the arena. In all the scenarios I'd envisioned about my first public appearance, I hadn't imagined such a silence. I couldn't tell if it was because I was a woman, or if the people were still thinking about Raymundo, or if it was a combination of both.

As Maestro said, the bull brimmed with courage. He had no defects I could spot. He charged straight and didn't hook with his horns to the right or left. As I executed my first pass, a *veronica*, I couldn't believe such a powerful animal could be fooled into thinking a piece of magenta silk was the target of his fury. Only a bulletlike sound and a dollop of his hot saliva on my face as he whooshed past my body told me it was true.

Raymundo's face cut through my concentration after every charge and I had to push him out of my mind to prepare for the next pass. After the mounted picadors had driven their *varas* into the bull's shoulder to tire him and the banderilleros had inserted the colorful barbed sticks in his back to further weaken him, the trumpet sounded for the final act to begin.

"You have fifteen minutes, or they'll sound the warning," Maestro reminded me, as I reentered the ring. "Five minutes to dominate and kill. Do *not* fail."

The hair on the bull's shoulder was crimson now. Blood also streaked down his front leg. As I walked across the sand toward my bull, I revisited my earlier decision about the bull's dedication. I'd thought to dedicate the first bull of my career to the audience but that was no longer appropriate. A brave man who'd been very kind to me, who'd treated me as his equal, lay on a gurney in the infirmary.

"I dedicate my bull to you, Raymundo," I murmured. "Thank you for accepting me."

Though right-hand passes were safest, they demonstrated true artistry, as the matador wound the bull like stretched toffee around her body as he chased the cape. The audience leaped to their feet after my first series of *derechazos*. I then switched to the Pass of Death, holding the extended muleta with both hands while standing rigid and perfectly still in profile, until the tips of the bull's horns touched the cloth. Slowly, I raised my arm so that he rose off his powerful forelegs in a hopeless attempt to hook and destroy the ever-elusive cloth, and the crowd began to cheer. Some even shrieked at the thrill.

I performed three of these before swapping the muleta to my left hand, in order to perform the more dangerous *natural* passes. With each left-handed pass, I brought the bull's horns closer to my body. Sweat streamed down my forehead. I smelled the iron of the bull's blood swaying like slender ropes from the gape the picadors had made in his shoulders. I smelled his acrid sweat. His gray, swollen tongue dangled from one side of his mouth. The crowd chanted *olé* and the brass band struck up dianas, the ultimate symbol of approval for a matador. Despite their feverish acceptance, I felt numb inside.

"Kill it now," Maestro shouted. "You have two minutes."

I ran up to the barrier and gave Patricio the light aluminum sword used to execute the passes, and he handed me the killing sword.

"Have you heard from the infirmary?" I asked.

"Forget Raymundo for the moment," he said, his face solemn as he handed me the sword Maestro had gifted me. "Or you'll get injured, too."

I returned to my bull and set about aligning him, working to ensure his front feet were close together so the death-notch would be fully open and the sword would penetrate completely. He wouldn't align his feet the way I needed so I had to do another set of passes with him.

"Ha-ha-ha, *toro*," I called above the sound of the music and cheers to attract the bull's attention. "Hey, *toro*, ha-ha."

"What the hell are you doing?" Maestro hollered, after my second *natural*, the best I'd given throughout the performance.

I turned the bull around my body as if he were a ribbon and then made him charge again. As I prepared to end the series with a chest pass, an image of Raymundo crashed into my mind. I heard him say my name. Raymundo was dead; I don't know how I knew this, but I knew.

The bull charged. His head lowered as if I were watching in slow motion. I tried to step away, but couldn't. People shrieked. The bull's horns ripped into the side of my bolero jacket and sliced my side, but a rush of adrenaline prevented me from experiencing pain. An explosive gasp passed through the audience. The bull's meaty shoulders crashed into me, and I careened backward. I fell on my back. I remembered the fall at Garza, only that time, I'd landed on my belly and eaten sand. As I sat up, my cuadrilla sprinted toward me, one member with his cape splayed to entice the bull. Not a muscle in his huge body twitched as he watched.

"What's wrong with you?" Maestro hollered, as I was escorted, clutching my side, from the bullring. "You disobeyed me and now look what's happened."

"I'm sorry." A sharp pain shot across my belly, causing me to clench my teeth.

His features contorted with rage. "Sorry isn't good enough. You know how difficult it's been to find two matadors to agree to sponsor you to the union, and now this."

"Raymundo's dead. I know he is." I winced.

Maestro's face softened. "Take her to the infirmary."

The men increased their pace as they walked along the callejón. When we got there, a gurney was in the middle of the brightly lit windowless room. The floor was littered with discarded bandages and fist-sized wads of cotton drenched in blood. Raymundo's body lay on the gurney, covered by a white sheet also stained crimson. I felt as if I'd come out of my body to watch myself staring at Raymundo's hidden corpse.

The doctor, a lanky, older man, asked me to follow him and we went into a part of the infirmary separated by a thin gray curtain on three sides. Another gurney covered in a white sheet and old woolen blanket occupied its center. He told me to undress down to my underwear and then left. His command made me realize there was no nurse present. Only men were here. Oddly, I didn't feel scared or anxious.

When the doctor returned, he questioned me while examining the cut. I answered without thinking, because my mind was over at the other gurney bearing Raymundo's still-warm body. After cleaning the wound, he put in six stitches, but I felt no pain.

"Rest here for half an hour and then you can go," he said.

Maestro came in and sat with me.

"I brought Raymundo bad luck, Maestro," I said.

He took my hand and cupped it in his. I felt so small and I wanted my father to be here at my bedside. I wanted him to take me in his arms, to pat the back of my head like he used to do and tell me everything would be fine.

"It's natural to feel this way, but you had nothing to do with it," Maestro said. "Raymundo made a mistake and paid the final price. I've seen it happen twice." His jug ears flattened slightly as he smiled. "This was a very tough day for you. You need to heal, so I've canceled your other appearances."

"I'm sorry you had to do that."

"After you've recovered, we'll start again. You must overcome this bad experience. We can't allow this to fester into a fear of the bulls."

Back at my hotel later that evening, Carmen came to see me. I was in bed with the curtains drawn and thinking about Raymundo. On the table was a bunch of white roses that Julio had sent me.

"How are you feeling?" she asked, hanging my bolero jacket, which she'd repaired, in the armoire.

"I'll live."

"Are you thinking about the dead man?"

I shrugged. Nothing would bring him back.

"I'm sorry death visited the bullring today." Carmen laid her hand on my shoulder. "I wish it never visited, but today especially, on your first fight."

We sat in silence.

"All matadors make mistakes in the bullring," she said presently. "Chiquita, you mustn't lose confidence because of this. My husband sees your talent."

I couldn't bring myself to tell her that it wasn't a mistake. I'd allowed myself to become distracted and then fear had taken over and rooted me to the ground.

"I appreciate you telling me this, Carmen. It means a lot, coming from you."

After she said goodbye and left—she was leaving to visit her mother for a week—I pulled out one of the white roses from the vase and held it before my nose. The petals were soft and smelled comfortingly sweet. Now that I followed Julio's schedule, I knew he was fighting in Tijuana. It took three calls to locate the hotel where he and his cuadrilla were staying. He answered on the second ring.

"I hope you don't mind me calling," I said. Every part of me trembled, the feeling far more uncomfortable than the injury I'd gotten in the bullring. "It's just, um, you said I could call anytime."

"I was hoping you would."

Men and women talked loudly in the background and I could hear a guitar playing.

"You've got company," I said.

"We fought well today and people are celebrating." I heard a woman's high-pitched laughter. "Today was your first fight. How did it go?"

"Thank you for the flowers." I sighed. "A *novillero* died today. He was kind to me and now he's dead."

"Oh God, I'm sorry."

"I was scared I'd brought him bad luck and I didn't do very well with my bull," I explained, deciding not to mention my superficial injury.

The line cracked in the silence and then more laughter erupted in the background.

"Listen to me, Kathleen. Listen very carefully. You mustn't allow what happened today to dominate you. You mustn't allow it to make you fearful of the bulls."

"That's what Maestro said."

"Fermin's right. You *must* heed what he says."

"I doubt myself."

"So do I, sometimes."

I was amazed someone as successful as El Cabrito would doubt himself.

"It's normal, I think," he added.

A woman called out his name. I bristled, though I wasn't sure why I thought I had any right to feel that way.

"I'm tired," I said abruptly. "I need to sleep now."

"We can talk some more if you like. I'm not in any hurry."

I hung up and then, despite myself, lay wondering who the woman was who'd called out his name.

22

PATRICIO ESCORTED ME BACK TO LOS PINOS THE NEXT morning as Maestro had amended his plans and was traveling to another city on personal business for two days. A day after my return, Mama called, saying she'd just heard from someone in town that I'd been injured at a corrida and insisted I spend a week at her place recuperating. No matter how I argued against it, she wouldn't back down. I eventually consented to let George pick me up on Thursday afternoon. I dreaded having to tell Maestro but, when he returned home, he was in good spirits and immediately agreed, as his wife wouldn't be at home to look after me.

"Because Raymundo died, the press were kind to you," he said, handing me a newspaper from Colotlán. "The journalist says you showed the true spirit and courage of a matador in deciding to go on with your performance, especially since you're a woman and it was your first true corrida and a man died."

I read the article hurriedly, delighted the press praised my technical skills and expressed sympathy about my injury. But I also felt conflicted, as it was Raymundo's death that had saved me from obscurity.

"We are very lucky," Maestro added. "A *noverillero* died, so bullring impresarios throughout Mexico will read about this corrida and your appearance there. They'll want to book you."

"This isn't the kind of luck I want."

He shrugged. "We take what comes."

It was as if Mama had become a different person in our months apart. Since I'd arrived nine days earlier, she'd treated me almost like an invalid. She cooked my meals, including breakfast, fluffed my pillows, and even accompanied me on walks around the property. One day, she read me an article about Laura Ingalls Wilder, my favorite girlhood author, that she'd come upon weeks ago and clipped to keep for me to read. She hadn't read to me since I was a toddler. Moreover, she hadn't rebuked me about my injury, which I'd fully expected, in addition to getting chewed out about my work and not returning to Texas.

The day before I was set to return to Los Pinos, she came out to the barn where I was practicing *veronicas* with a cape I'd brought along with me. For fun, George was acting the part of the bull. With bright red lipstick and her hair in an immaculate bun, Mama looked incongruous among the broken bales of hay, weathered flowerpots, and Daddy's rusted garden tools.

"You need to be careful of your back, George," she said. "And you as well, Kathleen. Those stitches could burst."

I nearly collapsed on the floor, I was so surprised she didn't make a scene about what I was doing.

"Someone's coming to dinner, so we're eating in the dining room tonight," she said.

I could count on two hands the times we'd sat as a family in the formal dining room, which always smelled of lemon oil polish.

"I already told you I'm going out this evening," George said.

"I know." Mama started to leave, but then paused and said, "Wear something smart tonight, Kathleen."

Her guest was the new manager of the North Valley Community Bank in town, Mama's bank. Mr. Cheves looked exactly like a banker should, with black-framed glasses, a pale, close-shaven face, and receding, mousy hair. The three of us sat at one end of the dining table, Mama and I across from each other and the banker at the head.

"Where'd you put Daddy's picture?" I asked during a lull in the conversation. His portrait had once hung in the dining room, but Mama had removed it a week after he'd died, though it had been her favorite one of him. I could still see the outline on the east wall where the frame had hung. I'd figured I'd take it back to Mexico with me if she didn't want it

Her eyes narrowed and she squinted at the rectangle of brighter wallpaper. "I don't rightly recall," Mama said, and turned right back to the banker. When their eyes met, I caught her jerking her head in my direction.

My suspicions were confirmed. Bad enough that fifteen minutes after I'd served Mr. Cheves a drink and sat chatting with him in the parlor, she'd called me into the kitchen under the pretext of making the gravy and asked what I thought of him.

"So, Kathleen, your mama mentioned you had an accident in Mexico."

"It was just a cut."

"That required six stitches, Arthur," Mama told him.

"Have you ever thought about working at a bank?" he said. "It'd be a lot safer."

I laughed at his joke. "It sure would."

"We've got an opening for a teller supervisor," he continued. "You'd be in charge of three people." His eyes flitted to Mama.

It dawned on me that she wasn't trying to set me up with him—she was fixin' to find me a job. I stopped chewing my steak and looked at Mama, real intense.

"I sure appreciate it," I said, turning back to the banker, "but I don't have the experience."

"I know, but y'all got a year of college and that sure counts for something." He smiled. "Your mama's told me all about you and I think you'd fit in mighty fine."

I set my fork down gently on the plate. "I enjoy what I'm doing now, Mr. Cheves."

"Now you hear our guest out, Kathleen. Let's not act hasty."

I thought about leaving the table. If I'd had my fake aluminum sword, I'd have poked Mama under the table with it. Heck, maybe I'd even have used the real one. Instead, I smiled and listened as Mr. Cheves went on about how well his bank was doing, the friendly staff and the changes he planned to make, and how good my prospects would be. In time, I could even become an assistant manager, if I didn't marry and get in a family way. Before he left, I told him I'd think about it seriously.

Once he'd gone and we started washing up, I said, "Mama, please don't do that ever again."

"How do you think it felt to hear you'd been injured?" she snapped. "Do you know how worried I was?"

I took her upper arms gently. They felt so soft in comparison to mine.

"It's a risk I'm willing to take."

"You're selfish. You could get killed." She backed out of my grasp. "I want grandchildren someday."

"Why?" Mama had never mentioned grandkids before. Was this another ploy to get me to quit the bulls?

"It's natural to want grandchildren. I want to be involved in their growing up. I want to play with them. Spoil them."

"Why d'you want to do that? After Daddy died, you were never involved in my life."

"How can you say that?"

"It's true."

"I fed and clothed you. I made sure you went to school . . . which was a waste of time, apparently, considering what you're doing now." She dropped a heavy pot she'd been scrubbing into the farm sink and chipped its ceramic edge. "Now just look what you've made me do."

"Let's not fight, Mama," I said gently, and tried to hug her. She wouldn't let me.

"I'll finish up here," she said. "Go to bed."

"I want to help."

"And I want to be alone."

Next morning, I arrived in the kitchen feeling drained, as I'd slept fitfully. Mama was already there, dressed immaculately in a pleated skirt and cream blouse. Her skin was paler, though, which made the scarlet lipstick she loved to wear far too brazen for seven o'clock in the morning.

"I want you to think seriously about that job," she said.

"Not now, Mama. Let me leave friendly."

"Fine."

After I sat at the table, she arrived with a skillet glistening with bacon, sunny-side-up eggs, and hash browns, but I could tell by the way she loaded them on my plate that last night's duck fit was still working her. We didn't talk anymore about the banker and I was happy to leave for Los Pinos immediately after I ate.

Carmen had returned by the time I arrived. Maestro insisted she inspect my wound, even though I was having the stitches removed the following day.

"You needn't pack away your suitcase," he said, after Carmen said I was healed.

"You've booked me for a corrida?" I said. "But I'm out of practice."

"Not a corrida." He smiled. "A famous rancher invited you to his *tienta*. You see now how lucky you were to get that good press in Colotlán?"

To be invited to test a respected rancher's young fighting bulls and future breeding heifers was a great honor. There would be matadors and other high-profile guests in attendance. There'd also be receptions and parties to attend in the evenings. The bullfighter part of me thrilled at my first invitation to a *tienta*, and the woman part ran her mind's eye over the hangers in my closet, trying to decide which dresses I should bring with me. I never traveled with pretty clothes. I didn't need them. I never went out anywhere. But this was big-time somewhere.

Everything on the ground looked so tiny and different from the air. Of course, I'd seen photographs of fields, mountains, and rivers in books—some had even been in color—but those didn't convey the bright colors, rugged beauty, and various shapes the landscape molded and unfurled and transformed itself into when one peered down from an airplane. It amazed me how I now noticed how landscapes could uncurl like muletas.

We flew over Hacienda El Ángel, which more resembled a castle. Tall palm and rubber trees grew in its huge main plaza. An enormous fountain with a life-size golden angel as the pinnacle lay at its heart. Two smaller plazas on either side of the main one had flowerbeds ablaze in red, purple, and yellow. The twin green copper spires of a church rose into the cloudless sky from its southeast corner. An old photograph of William Randolph Hearst's San Simeon castle came to mind, except the hacienda's walls were painted terra-cotta and every door and window was trimmed in mustard yellow.

The hacienda's main building formed the enormous heart of the dusty town surrounding it. A high stone wall served as the rib cage that either protected the rancher, Don Raúl de Corella, and his family when they arrived from their townhouse in Mexico City, or intimidated the indigenous townspeople from entering, except those permitted to do so on business. I wasn't sure which. A five-mile, arrow-straight dirt road led from the highway, passing through orchards and avocado groves, woods, verdant pastures studded with fighting bulls and sleek heifers, a winding creek as wide as some rivers, and, finally, the grassy air strip where I could see a car already waiting for us.

The Cessna landed bumpily. Despite folding his solid, six-foot frame into the narrow cockpit seat in a manner that looked highly uncomfortable, Don Raúl was a good pilot, as far as I could judge. The scary lurching due to turbulence hadn't agreed with my stomach and I was happy the journey was over. In two days, I would make the return trip to Aguascalientes, but at least for now, I could set aside my anxiety and relax.

Unlike Don Raúl, who was lightly tanned and blue-eyed due to his northern Spanish ancestors, whose roots went back to the conquistadors, his wife, Doña Emilia, was slender as a cattle egret. Like her husband, she was light-skinned, but she had the severe chin and thin lips of bad-tempered people. She greeted us at the massive wooden front door, then turned away from Maestro, who was midway through answering her question about the journey, and began apologizing to me. Due to the large number of guests attending the *tienta*, every room in the hacienda was occupied. She asked if I'd mind sharing a bedroom for the first night with her eldest daughter, a sophomore at New York University, who was arriving later that evening.

"Not a bit," I said, eager to please my hostess.

The room, on the same side of the main plaza as the chapel, was large and airy, with high ceilings and egg-and-dart crown molding. A majestic four-poster bed, fashioned in an ornate Spanish style and made of dark wood, stood in the middle of one wall, flanked on either side by matching nightstands. There was also a large armoire with an oval mirror in its center.

When I stepped onto the wrought-iron balcony looking out over the plaza, I had an uninterrupted view of the fountain and a riot of pink and purple bougainvillea across the square. The melodic tweets of songbirds hidden in the foliage of the trees and the intoxicating aroma of a salmon-colored oleander beneath the window made me giddy. This place was another kind of heaven. I raised my hands to the sky, tossed back my head, and let the sun wash over my face.

I figured the number of guests attending the party was the same as the student body at my old high school. There had to be three hundred people, at least. The first salon I went into after a larrupin' dinner, which had so many fixins I lost count, already buzzed with laughter and conversation. Havana fans spun from three roughly hewn beams that crossed the width of the room, drawing the blue cigarette and pipe smoke up to the clay-tiled roof above them.

"Kathleen," Don Raúl called, as he came across to me. "We've been waiting for you to join us." A pretty woman followed in his wake. Tanned the color of meadow honey and with her light-brown hair pulled back in a chignon, she was about thirty. I figured she was his daughter from New York.

"This is the young bullfighter from America I told you about, Conchita," he said as they drew up.

Stars exploded inside my head. I no longer heard the buzz of small talk. The eyes of the famous Conchita Cintrón were lighted on little ol' me. She'd retired from bullfighting two years earlier to marry her Portuguese sweetheart, a nobleman who was the nephew of her former manager. I wasn't sure whether to address her as Doña or Missus. Was Doña even the right term for a woman who was now a Portuguese aristocrat?

She extended her elegant hand. "Raúl's been singing your praises over dinner." Her tinkling laugh floated with the curling smoke up to the beams. "I'm very happy to meet you."

This small hand had dominated massive bulls. It felt surprisingly soft. I felt I was shaking the hand of the Virgin of Guadalupe herself. "Mighty pleased to make your acquaintance, ma'am."

"I'm sorry your introduction to the corrida involved someone's death," she said.

I flinched but smiled broadly.

"Do you ever ride horses to fight, or is it always by foot?" she asked, side-stepping further discussion, as if reading my mind.

"I only fight on foot."

"My preference, too."

She winked. I knew she'd caused a furor at her final fight in Spain, when she'd broken the law and dismounted to fight on foot for the third act. Women were forbidden to fight on foot in Spain and she'd been threatened with arrest by the authorities, until the crowd demanded she be pardoned.

Maestro arrived and Don Raúl introduced him, too.

"I've been training Kathleen for almost twenty months now," he said, his eyes flicking over Conchita's body when she turned to accept a flute of champagne from the waiter. "I have high hopes for her." He laughed, a self-important cackle that only I understood. "With some luck, she can be as great as you, Conchita."

"A good trainer is so important."

Maestro's smile was so wide I was sure it hurt.

She turned to me. "Though I think luck's no substitute for bravery and skill."

Another couple arrived and the conversation lapsed into generalities. Someone touched my arm lightly. It was Don Raúl's youngest daughter, a gangly, plain-faced girl of about fourteen with a shy nature.

"Mama sent me to find you," she said, her pale eyes unable to hold mine. "She'd like you to join her and the other women in the green salon."

Surprisingly, no invitation was extended to Miss Cintrón, whom I didn't want to leave. But, not wanting to appear rude in declining to join my hostess, I excused myself and followed the girl.

The salon, as large as the one I'd exited, was appropriately named. Every bit of its interior was a different but complementary shade of green: the pale green walls, the dark green, luxurious pile carpet that felt like walking on a manicured lawn, the three groupings of sage and kelly green couches and armchairs, and the mint damask curtains of the three floor-to-ceiling windows that looked out onto one of the smaller plazas. Only the grand piano and dark portraits of import-ant-looking Spanish men in tights and their women had no green. Great wealth in Mexico was expressed as brazenly as it was in the large ranches back in Texas, except this hacienda was steeped in real history and its ownership stretched back three hundred years.

"I found her with Papá and Doña Cintrón, Mamá."

"Thank you, Gabriella. Doña Conchita prefers to talk about the bulls rather than spend time with the ladies," said Doña Emilia. Her chin lifted in a proud manner and she laughed sharply.

The clutch of women seated with her in the middle grouping of couches and chairs nodded politely, glasses of sangria and champagne in their hands. The older women wore traditional skirts and dazzlingly embroidered blouses under colorful shawls. Those around my age looked immaculate in bright frocks. Dressed in an olive-green skirt and a dark green, short-sleeved blouse, I could have been a room acces-sory, except for the pink-and-white-striped sweater I'd draped over my shoulders. Thinking wealthy Mexicans would be more conservative, I hadn't packed my brightest frocks and now felt very dowdy.

Doña Emilia grilled me first about my family background and edu-cation before moving on to the reasons for my interest in fighting the bulls. When she moved the topic of conversation to current Amer-ican fashions and hairstyles, her sharp eyes scrutinized my clothes, lingering on the sweater. I was about to apologize for my attire when an old lady seated beside her on the couch, a set of double-stranded pearls barely hiding her leathery neck, leaned forward toward me.

"That garment," she said, nodding at my sweater. "May I see it?"

The sweater was a favorite of mine, but it was also eight years old and I was surprised she'd asked about it.

"Sweaters aren't common here," Doña Emilia said. "Until my daughter moved to New York, I'd seldom seen one myself."

After it had been passed around, Doña Emilia suggested we play dominoes. Having no interest in the game and fixin' as quick as I could to return to the other salon, I racked my brain to find a good excuse to leave.

"Hello, Mamá." A young, olive-skinned woman about my age walked assertively across the room with her arms open wide. "I'm sorry I'm late."

About two inches taller than my five-five, she wore flat black shoes, charcoal gray pants, and a man's tie. Her dark hair was cut short and gave her face an elfin appearance. I'd never seen a woman's hair cut so short. Doña Emilia rose so fast she knocked over the stack of dominoes on the table in front of her. The other women had transformed into gargoyles.

"Isabella, why are you not wearing a dress?" Doña Emilia's high-pitched laugh was as frantic as her tone. "This is not New York."

"I've come for the *tienta*, haven't I?"

"Go and change."

Mother and daughter traded the kind of glances I often traded with Mama. After Isabella relented and left, Doña Emilia sat again and picked up the dominoes that had fallen on the floor. "The young ladies of today," she said, as she laid two on the table. "They study in America and return like gypsies."

Scraps of laughter fluttered around the room.

When she returned, Isabella looked stunning in a lacy white dress. She'd also put on scarlet lipstick. She shook my hand firmly after her

mother introduced us and informed her I would be sharing her bedroom.

After three hands of dominoes, Isabella began talking to me,
loudly.

"If you don't want to play, why don't you show Kathleen around?"
her mother said.

Both Isabella and I rose quickly.

"Mamá, may I go with Isabella?" Gabriella asked.

"No."

Isabella and I strolled out into the main plaza. "Mother is so provin-
cial about everything," she said. "Clothes. Games. Fashion. Reading . . .
when she isn't devouring a missal."

"I know what you mean."

"You do?"

"My mother's always interfering and preachin', as well. She doesn't
know when to stop."

It felt good to vent. I pictured Mama back at her place, sitting with
George in the living room, listening to the radio.

"We have that in common," Isabella said, slipping her arm around
my waist as we continued walking.

A cool breeze carried the aroma of oleander, much stronger now
than it had been during the afternoon. In one section of the plaza,
strings of red, orange, blue, and green glass lanterns hung on the
branches of trees. The effect was magical. A ginger cat scuttled up
to Isabella and she took her arm from around me and stooped to
pet it.

We walked toward the fountain, where two men admired the sparkling jets of water. My heart jolted. One of the men was Julio. In a
white linen suit that complemented his slender figure, his face was
square and masculine, and his eyes gleamed as bright as the lanterns
in the branches. A tiny scarlet feather peeked from the black ribbon
encircling his fedora.

"Kathleen, how are you?" he said, looking as shocked as I felt.

My face blazed.

"You know Julio?" Isabella asked, her eyes brimming with curiosity.

"Isabella, you know as well as I do that the bullfighting world is small." He turned to his companion. "This is Silvario López."

I'd heard of the talented matador, a man of five-ten like Julio, with wide-set eyes and an owl-like nose. The older matador reached for my hand and brought it to his lips.

"We're on the way to the chapel," Isabella said.

"Say a prayer for me," Julio quipped, and smiled at me.

Once we were out of earshot, Isabella said, "Julio's a good man, but I think he rubs some people the wrong way. He's talented, and demands much from his team."

"You know him well?" I asked, disappointed she hadn't asked the men to accompany us.

"We fished together in the summer when we were children and rode out on our horses as teenagers." She laughed. "I think our parents hoped we'd fall in love and marry."

The smell of melting wax and furniture polish was thick inside the family chapel, a gleaming museum of marble statues and intricately carved wood comprising the altar and frames of the stations of the cross. There were eight stained-glass windows, one of which depicted a dying bull at Jesus's feet. At the altar, I genuflected and then knelt at the rails before a portrait of the Virgin of Guadalupe. Isabella didn't kneel or pray. A fat candle burned on the left side of the altar.

Isabella passed through the low wooden gates leading to the altar and ascended the three steps. The candle's tiny flame rippled as she approached. The light transformed her face, the forehead, nose, eye sockets, and swell of her cheeks now a study of light and shadow. She looked like a beautiful woman in one of Caravaggio's paintings. I followed her inside the altar and stopped one step below where she stood.

"Do you really believe the Virgin of Guadalupe will save you in the bullring, or do you pray to her out of fear and superstition?"

Images of Raymundo lying dead on the gurney and my stiff body before the charging bull crammed my mind. "I believe in her," I said.

She shrugged as she peered over at the Virgin. "I think you and I are alike," she said.

"We are?"

"Some would call us freaks."

She looked up at the writhing body of Christ on the black wooden crucifix above the altar.

"I don't know what you mean," I said.

She looked in my eyes, a hint of defiance burning in hers. "You're acting as a man in a man's world, aren't you?"

Footsteps resounded on the marble floor as Gabriella scuttled up the central aisle. "Mamá told me to go to bed, but I sneaked out." She made a hasty sign of the cross and half-genuflected before entering the altar. "Julio said you were here."

Isabella chuckled. "My kid sister's in love with him. She wants to marry him when she grows up."

Her sister blushed and hung her head.

Isabella's eyes fixed on the burning candle on the altar. "A candle burns here every time one of our bulls fights in a bullring," she said. "It's been this way for generations."

"In honor of the bull?" I asked.

She smiled. "That the matador will not die by the horns of our bull."

23

MAESTRO, SEATED INSIDE A CIRCLE OF MEN, WAS PLAYING A Spanish guitar when I came into the second salon. An attractive woman in a flamenco dress designed to look like scarlet and orange tongues of fire played the castanets and clicked her heels in spurts as she danced around him. He played the guitar well. As I watched his fingers pluck the strings, I realized there were many things I didn't know about this man who'd decided to take a chance on me.

At the end of the song, the dancer bowed and then sat on Maestro's lap, wrapping her sinewy arms around him and kissing his cheek. The men applauded. Maestro grinned like a star-struck schoolboy.

Deciding to explore the house, I walked down a wide hallway with a wall of tall windows overlooking the plaza. A full moon hung low in the sky, shining so bright between the forked branches of nearby trees that I could see ridges of navy blue mountains stretching across its golden surface. Out in the plaza, people murmured under the trees, their faces turned coppery from the light oozing from the colored glass lanterns. If I'd had a sketchbook and pencil, I'd have drawn the scene.

I passed through an open doorway and came into a large, dimly lit study. Mahogany bookcases on my left and right rose from floor to ceiling, each shelf neatly stacked with leather-bound books, most in Spanish, some in English and German. I recognized the name of one author.

"Hello," someone said, before I fully retrieved a volume of Federico García Lorca's plays.

Startled, I peered up the room and saw Don Raúl sitting at one side of a blazing hearth with a group of men, including Julio, all but one older man wearing brightly colored ponchos.

"I didn't mean to intrude," I said.

"Please, join us." Don Raúl beckoned me with a wave.

I approached, my heart beating faster than a chased hen's.

"Would you like a drink?" he asked.

"No, thank you."

"We're debating whether Ordóñez or Dominguín is the better fighter," he continued. "What do you say?"

Julio rose off his chair and slid it toward me. "Haven't you heard that Kathleen handles her cape as fluidly as Ordóñez?"

The men chuckled.

"I like both, but my favorite of all is Belmonte," I said, as I sat. "I try to copy him."

"Why's that?" a man asked.

He was the gentleman not wearing a poncho. A dinner guest seated at my table had mentioned he was an ex-king, from Italy or Romania, I couldn't remember.

"Belmonte fought hard to become a bullfighter even before he set foot in a bullring, Your Majesty. He used to sneak into the meadows and fight the seed bulls, using blankets for capes. Sometimes the guards watching over the herd shot at him, but he still risked his life because he needed to practice. That's real dedication, in my mind."

"Ah yes, we have boys sneaking onto the ranch at night to fight the bulls," said Don Raúl. He puffed on his pipe. "It's dangerous for them. And the bulls develop *sentido*, which is dangerous for the matadors.

Once a bull learns the man is the target and not the cloth, he's no longer a virgin. He'll kill."

"Don Raúl, I know young men sneaking into the meadows to cape the bulls are a curse to ranchers," I said. "I just meant that Belmonte had no contacts in bullfighting, yet he did what he needed to do to become a great matador."

"Belmonte was a great artist," agreed Julio. "No one worked closer to the bulls than him."

The conversation changed to Mexican bullfighting and then to the schedule for the *tienta* the next day. I listened to the low rumble of the men's laughter and friendly banter while admiring the two magnificent bull heads on either side of the oak mantle, one black, the other red, brass plaques beneath each animal stating their names and the dates they'd fought. Above the mantle was an oil painting of a bullfight by Édouard Manet. Executed in the Impressionist style, a bull, black as the dark under a skillet, stared at a muleta in the matador's hand. Off to his right was a picador's gored, snow-white horse. I wasn't sure if it was the original or an excellent copy, but I suspected the former.

Closing my eyes, I inhaled the nutty pipe smoke and faint aroma of cattle wafting from the men's ponchos. I was a novitiate, accepted at the altar of a hallowed priesthood dedicated to the bulls. I was one of these people.

"Kathleen, what are you doing disturbing the men?"

My eyes flew open.

"Why aren't you in bed?" Maestro asked as he strode across the room.

"It's still early," said Julio, "and she's not disturbing us, Fermin."

Maestro stopped dead. Even in the gloom, I could see how white his face had turned. "You're here as well, El Cabrito."

"In the flesh."

"It's . . . it's good to see you again," said Maestro.

"Likewise."

Recovering, Maestro continued up the room and came over to me. "Off you go to bed. You're working tomorrow."

"As am I," said Julio. "And Silvario here." He half-laughed. "We're not going to bed yet."

"Leave, Kathleen," Maestro commanded, his chin swiveling toward the door.

The others watched me. My face flashed hot. I considered refusing, but feared it would appear churlish. I rose.

"Sleep well," Julio said.

I was madder than a wet hen as I walked down the silent room, my briskness causing the naked floorboards to creak loudly.

"I don't agree with women wanting to fight bulls," one of the men said, as I crossed the transom.

"That was a bit strong, Fermin," Julio said. "You shouldn't talk to her that way."

Lingering in the shadows outside the door, I cocked my ear, hoping Maestro would get his comeuppance.

"I told you before, she's *my* concern," said Maestro. "I know what's best for her. After all, I was taught at a *proper* school of bullfighting."

"And now you're just a banderillero," retorted Julio, and laughed. "I wonder why."

"You *maricón*," Maestro shouted. A chair screeched. "You're just sequins and frills in the bullring. No substance."

"*Stop*," said Don Raúl. "I'm sorry, Your Excellency. Fermin, Julio, save your sparring for my cows."

The ensuing silence ended when someone coughed.

"I don't agree with this business," said one of the men.

"Ramiro, what don't you agree with?" Don Raúl asked.

"As I said before, a bullring's no place for a woman. Especially one as pretty as her."

"Wait 'til you see her in action," Julio said. "While we have our differences, I have to say Fermin's done a fine job. She's very good."

"She should go back to America and find a husband before she's gored and loses her womb," the man said. "Or worse."

The novel on Isabella's nightstand had no designed cover and I didn't recognize the author's name. Entitled *Spring Fire,* its first pages described a woman starting her first semester at a university in the States. I related to the author's descriptions of the Greek fraternity and sorority buildings, and soon became so engrossed I didn't hear Isabella enter from the adjoining bathroom.

"Are you prying?" she asked.

"I didn't mean to."

"Yes, you did." She regarded me with her hand on her hips.

"I didn't." I sat up in bed and held out the book for her to take. "Honest."

"I'm kidding." She tossed it on her nightstand. "That isn't published yet. An editor friend at the publishing house gave it to me. Do you like it?"

"What I read was interesting."

"So we *are* alike." She took off her robe and tossed it carelessly on the floor. "I thought so. If you give me your address, I'll mail it to you after I've finished."

"That would be swell."

She slipped between the white, cool sheets, turned toward me, and propped herself up on one elbow. "When did you find out?"

"Find out?"

She laughed. "Are you getting back at me for tricking you just now?"

"Find out what, Isabella?"

She reached out and pinched my nose playfully. "That you like women, too."

So many thoughts jammed my brain at once that it shorted. I lay stiff as post oak.

"I found out at boarding school," Isabella told me, and giggled. She opened her eyes in a wide, dramatic look. "The nuns don't know everything that goes on at night in the dorms. Okay, your turn."

"I like men . . . " My muscles reactivated. I climbed out of bed, grabbed my pillow, and looked wildly about the room.

"What are you doing?" she asked.

I took a step away from the bed as if she were contagious, then dropped the pillow on the floor and lay down. "I'm going to sleep here."

"Don't be ridiculous. You can't sleep there."

"I can and I will."

"Maybe you should sleep in the cowshed."

I gaped up at her.

"Get into bed. I'm not going to bite you."

"I'm fine."

"Get in the bed, Kathleen."

I stared up at her for a long moment, before rising and climbing into the bed, where I lay rigid.

"I thought you might like women, because you're a bullfighter," she said.

I turned my head so fast toward her, the feathers inside my pillow crackled in my ear. "What's that got to do with bullfighting?"

"Killing bulls for a living isn't exactly feminine, wouldn't you say?" She ran her fingers through her hair. "I just assumed you were different. Guess I'm as guilty of stereotyping as everyone else."

"Don't you . . . ?"

"Don't I what?"

"Don't you think it's wrong to do that with another woman?"

"Do I think it's a sin, you mean?"

"Well, yes."

"Not if you see religion as a fairy tale."

I certainly am not the type to bite the altar rails, but this kind of sacrilegious talk was a whole 'nuther thing, especially since I was fixin' to fight her father's heifers. I was sure they'd be just as fierce as the bulls, even if they got no candles burning for 'em.

"Do you know there are more than four gospels?" she asked.

I shook my head. I'd been taught that God had four people write the gospels.

"Mary Magdalene wrote a gospel and the church refuses to acknowledge it."

"Mary Magdalene was a prostitute," I pointed out. "How'd any church use one she'd write?"

She looked at me sourly. "Do you know the church treats women unfairly?"

I didn't answer.

Isabella continued, "You worship the Virgin, don't you? That's loving a woman, isn't it?"

Of course I worshipped the Virgin of Guadalupe. But I only wanted her to protect me. Isabella was twisting things, using it as justification to do what she did.

"I don't think of the Virgin *that* way."

"You believe I'm a sinner," Isabella said. "How rich is that? Don't you think it's a sin to kill bulls? If you pray and believe in wrong and right, how can you do that?"

Now in familiar territory, the tightness left my chest. I sat up in the bed.

"You eat meat, don't you?" I countered, asking the question that always ended this kind of argument.

"Yes, and I'm a hypocrite because of it. So are you."

This girl was smarter than a Texas politician.

"The bulls aren't killed like cattle are in the slaughterhouses," I said. "Believe me, I know that." A shiver rippled through me unexpectedly as I remembered killing the old bull in the stall. "Fighting bulls live like kings in the pastures until it's time for them to fight in the ring."

"Bullfighting's immoral."

"You're wrong, Isabella. It's above moral judgment. Bullfighting's an ancient drama."

"It's butchery."

"It's wrong to hunt foxes and deer in the woods. It's wrong to hunt elephants. They're not bred to fight; that's why the poor things are terrified. It's a massacre. But the bulls are bred to be brave. They're bred to fight. You should know this—you've grown up around the bulls. Look how they charge, how they paw the ground and roar and stay in their favorite spots to protect their territory."

"That's false," she argued. "Don't you know why they paw the ground and bellow in the ring? Why they shit all over the sand? Why they seek out a favorite spot in front of the roaring crowd?" Her eyes sparkled. "It's fear. Bulls and cows are docile by nature. They seek protection in numbers. When they're separated from their herd, like they are in the bullring, bulls paw the sand and bellow because they're afraid. They're terrified because of what butchers like you are going to do to them."

Isabella tossed back the blanket and got out of bed. "You matadors call a bull brave when he charges straight and often. You call him a brave bull because he's predictable. That's a misnomer. What you really mean when you say the bull's 'predictable' is that he's easy to butcher." Balls of saliva burst from her mouth. "You call an unpredictable bull a coward because he doesn't play your game. He doesn't charge straight, he doesn't move his horns the way *you* want." She laughed scornfully. "It's the cowardly bull that's brave and makes the fight with you matadors fair."

I was torn between reminding her I wasn't yet a matador and responding to her ignorance. She was the daughter of a rancher, yet didn't understand one thing about the nature of bulls. She'd been living away from home too long. Learning alongside Yankees had turned her dumber than dirt. I stretched out my arms until they cracked and yawned.

"Get back into bed," I said, acutely aware of the irony that our roles were now reversed. "I need to sleep." I couldn't resist one last shot. "I've got work to do tomorrow."

The large breakfast room smelled of warm tortillas and fresh coffee. A long table decked in fresh linen tablecloths ran down the middle of the room. As I took a seat beside a friendly general in the Mexican army and his wife, whom I'd met the night before, Maestro arrived. Julio and Silvario sat across from me, their plates as loaded as mine with warm tortas (mine stuffed with scrambled eggs and red salsa), spicy chorizos, and slices of baked ham. Maestro glanced at my plate as he passed by on the way to the row of silver chafing dishes on a wide sideboard at the head of the room.

"So much food," he said. "There will be a lunch."

"I'm hungry."

"Serious matadors don't eat so much before a testing," he said.

I looked pointedly at Julio's and Silvario's overstuffed plates. The general and his wife regarded their own laden plates, then mine, and exchanged baffled glances.

"Eat the torta and one slice of ham," he said. "No chorizo. And as much coffee as you wish."

"Look at ours, Fermin," Julio said, and he glanced sidelong at Silvario. "We're serious matadors and we're eating well." He smiled at me briefly, then looked back at Maestro. "Why do you tell her how much she can eat anyway?"

"You know as well as I do she's testing the heifers soon. Her body isn't the same as a man's." His lips upturned into a sneer. "Maybe you don't know what a woman's body is like?"

Julio sighed and rolled his eyes.

"That's enough now, Fermin," Silvario said.

"Silvario and I are testing before her," Julio said then. "Let her eat."

"If you eat like that every day," replied Maestro, his gaze sliding to Julio's plate, "you'll soon look like a picador and need to ride a horse into the ring."

After Maestro left, Julio told me to eat everything on my plate if I was hungry. "He's no doctor," he said.

I didn't eat anymore, though. Maestro was probably right. A woman's body was not dense like a man's. The food was heavy and would lie hard on my belly.

Half an hour later, I stood in the testing area, a ring twenty-five yards in diameter, exactly one-half the diameter of a standard bullring. A five-foot-high stone wall encircled its perimeter. On one side stood a red-roofed viewing stand with wings capable of holding sixty guests on either side. Beyond the viewing stand, the undulating mountains in the far distance served as both the hacienda's eastern boundary and a scenic backdrop.

Julio stood across from me, his shirt dark with sweat and a folded magenta cape resting on his forearm. He'd just tested a two-year-old cow that had not been brave, her future as the mother of fighting bulls now extinguished—a bull inherited his courage from the mother. Like many of the other tested young bulls and cows, she'd fatten in the pastures for another year and then be sent off to a slaughterhouse.

Don Raúl and his foreman, who held the large ranch book containing the names and lineages of the animals to be tested, sat side by side in the gallery. Men and women, including the ex-king, two actors from Hollywood, and European and American diplomats and their wives sat in the wings observing the activities.

"Quiet," Don Raúl hollered.

Silence was essential during the testing. Being in the arena, even though it wasn't a real bullring, brought back memories of

Raymundo and the crimson gash in his belly. Instinctively, I touched my side, now fully healed. I pushed the unpleasant thoughts aside and unfurled my cape.

Possessed of smaller-than-normal horns, the young heifer's freckled pink nostrils widened as she sniffed the warm air before she walked back to the gate from where she'd just emerged. She stood looking at me in an indifferent manner. Nothing I called out or did with my cape enticed her to charge. Don Raúl's eyes fixed on me. He expected me to draw her out so he could judge her. I walked into her *querencia* before the gate, where, in theory, she would feel most threatened and do something to protect her space. I waved the cape close to her face. She half-charged and then sniffed the air again. Her face creased as if I disgusted her and then she walked nonchalantly back to her favorite spot in the shadow of the gate. Twice more I went to her and twice more she half-charged.

As I turned away for the third time, Maestro, accompanied by the flamenco dancer, entered the right wing of the viewing stand. I stood for a moment watching them. A second later, I was rising inexplicably toward the sky. I fell on my backside as Julio rushed toward me, swaying his cape back and forth.

"I've got her," he said.

My cheeks were as fiery as the burning sand. The heifer had seen an opportunity to make a fool of me, rushing in and butting me into the air. I walked as nonchalantly as I could with a throbbing tailbone and watched Julio work her.

She transformed into a different animal for him. It was as if she knew I was also a female and had determined I wasn't worth expending her energy on. Time and time again she charged, allowing him to execute two series of perfect *veronicas* and ending with a beautiful *rebolera*. Occasionally, Don Raúl called out to him to try a particular type of pass with the cow and she'd follow Julio's lead as if they'd been rehearsing for months.

"Breeding stock," Don Raúl called, and the gate creaked open to allow the vengeful female to exit the ring.

My next heifer was kinder and I willed myself to forget the earlier mortification. I executed some decent passes, though nerves caused me to trip on the end of the cape when Isabella arrived, accompanied by her mother and sister. It felt strange to test an animal's bravery when I knew someone in the audience despised what I was doing. Isabella didn't applaud when I finished, as her mother did.

"You did well," said Julio.

"Better than with my first cow," I said, wiping sweat off my forehead. "That one made a fool of me."

"You followed her into her *querencia*." He laid his hand lightly on my right shoulder. "That demonstrated courage, especially given what you experienced in the bullring recently."

His words refreshed me like a sea breeze and I tested several more heifers successfully.

"Are you finished testing?" he asked, as I came out of the arena. When I nodded, he said, "Let's go back to the hacienda and shoot at tin cans. The plaza's cooler."

"I can't shoot."

"And you're from Texas?"

"I never learned."

"I'll teach you."

The shooting area occupied one corner of a smaller plaza and was completely tiled in large white and black marble pavers. Diagonally across from the main entrance was a twelve-foot *stela* that Don Raúl's grandfather, an eccentric amateur archaeologist, had shipped from a Mayan ruin in the Guatemalan jungle.

As Julio had said, the plaza was cooler than the bullring. He was a patient instructor, laying his steady hand on mine after I'd selected the target I wanted to shoot, the center can of five perched on top of a pink stucco wall pocked with tiny holes. His hot, sweet breath tingled the skin on the back of my neck and earlobe when he pressed close and helped me aim the BB gun. It took six tries, six pressings together of our bodies, before I successfully shot the can off the wall.

He plucked an enormous lemon hibiscus bloom from a nearby tree and placed it in my hair, just above the right ear. "It's not a bull's ear, but you deserve some kind of a trophy," he said.

His eyes locked on mine and then his face started moving toward me, as if in slow motion. My heart thrummed so loud I thought he'd hear it. I took a breath, but it didn't feel as if I'd taken in any air.

As soon as his lips touched mine, I jerked my head away, pressed my hands against his chest, and pushed. I couldn't stop myself. I thought I'd murdered him when I'd killed the old bull at the slaughterhouse, but the monster was alive still.

"What's the matter?" he asked.

"I don't know . . . I'm sorry."

"Don't you want me to kiss you?"

"I do, but . . . I'm being stupid."

"What is it, Kathleen?" He touched the side of my head, his warm hand covering one of my ears.

I looked down at the marble floor. "Nothing's the matter."

"Tell me."

I stared at the tiles so long my eyes began stinging. "Someone . . . a man . . . he attacked me. That's why I pushed you away. I couldn't stop myself."

His eyes overflowed with compassion and he took my hand in his, rubbing the fingers gently.

"I'm okay," I said.

"Did they arrest him?"

I shook my head, then lifted my face and met his eyes. "Please kiss me now."

He looked very uncertain. But, tilting back my head, I offered my mouth to him. His lips, when they met mine, were soft. They reminded me of a fuzzy peach. After the kiss ended, he took his face away slowly, as if doing it quickly would distress me again. His hazel eyes focused on mine. I heard nothing from real life anymore, no sound of voices, no birds singing, no rattle of pots in a nearby kitchen. There was only a soft roar inside my ears as if I'd held a seashell to them.

"Was it okay?" I asked.

He took me in his arms and cupped the back of my head. We stood pressed against each other for what seemed like a lifetime. I could hear his heart beating next to me.

"I'd kill the bastard who did that to you, if I knew who he was," he said, stroking my back slowly. "Nobody will touch you again while I'm around."

I pressed my hands against his sides, unable to find words to reply.

"I want to ask you something," he continued. "I know it's not my business." He smiled shyly and swiped wisps of my damp hair from in front of my eyes with his fingers. "I know Fermin's been having trouble finding someone to sponsor you into the Union of Matadors. Would you like me to sponsor you?"

I reared back immediately. I didn't want his pity. "Are you offering because you feel sorry for me?"

"I'm offering because you have a future in the business." His gaze was firm, the white scar crossing his right eyebrow adding to its severity. "If you didn't, I wouldn't offer."

A shadow passed over us. We both glanced automatically toward the sky to see a golden eagle gliding overhead, its wingspan nearly seven feet tip to tip.

"Aren't you afraid other matadors won't like you for doing this?" I asked.

"Many of them don't want women fighting bulls," he said. "The others are afraid you'll show them up if you take the *alternativa* to become a full-fledged matador and fight alongside them in the ring." He squeezed my chin playfully. "When the time comes for you to take the *alternativa*, I'll act as godfather and welcome you to the rank of matador de toros. I'll also find a second matador willing to act as the witness."

"I don't know how to thank you."

He laughed. "Another kiss will do."

"I must tell Maestro."

"Of course."

I took his hand and tugged him toward the plaza's exit.

Julio seemed bemused. "Now?"

When we returned to the bullring, Maestro was in the ring testing a heifer. I watched him impatiently, willing Don Raúl to make his decision about the cow's future. Silvario came up to us.

"I've told Kathleen I'll sponsor her to the union," Julio said. "She needs another matador. Will you second her?"

The bridge of Silvario's beak nose crinkled. "Kathleen, I respect you, but this is a dangerous business for a woman."

"Are you afraid I'll be better than you?"

My audacity shocked me. His mouth slackened, then tightened into a grim line.

"I don't think any such a thing," he said.

"What is it, then?"

"Don't you want to be a mother one day?"

"Sure, I do."

"What if you're injured by a bull and can't bear children? Think of your future husband. You're young now, but try to imagine his great sadness when you tell him."

I felt Julio's eyes burn into my face and didn't dare look at him. Don Raúl called out that the heifer was a coward and dismissed her. The flamenco dancer sashayed across the sand toward Maestro, accompanied by two other women. She kissed him on both cheeks and looked as happy as a dead pig in the sunshine. You'd have thought it was she who'd just tested the heifer. How easy it was for men like Maestro and Silvario and Julio to win the fawning adulation of women like her.

"Are you a father?" I asked, turning back to Silvario.

"Not yet."

"Do you want to be one day?"

"Of course I do."

"Don't you think a man runs the same risk as me?" Silvario looked at Julio, nonplussed. "The bulls don't discriminate," I continued. "What if a horn stopped you from becoming a father?"

There was a long silence and then Silvario guffawed. I took that as acceptance.

To my astonishment, Maestro wasn't happy when I gave him the news. He stood with his back pressed against the wall of the bullring, his arms folded and staring at the dirt. His sweaty face had a purplish hue. I didn't understand Maestro's distaste for Julio. People said he was young and cocky. But Maestro was old and cocky. And Maestro had worked for him once. Didn't that count for something? Apart from Julio's kindness, they were more alike than they realized.

"I appreciate your offer, El Cabrito," he said, "but it's not necessary."

"Maestro, please let him." I laid my hand on the wall to steady my trembling. "No one else has offered."

"Fermin, we've had our differences, and I know you think I'm all show and no substance." He paused and smiled at Maestro. "Maybe I am a bit arrogant in the bullring. But it's my way." The severe look I'd seen back in the patio came into his eyes again. "But we're gentlemen, you and I. And gentlemen do the right thing. This isn't about us. This is about your protégée."

Maestro's chest heaved at the emphasized word.

"She needs Silvario and me to sponsor her," Julio continued. "Let us help you to help her."

Maestro looked at Silvario and then Julio, the purple hue draining from his face.

24

MAESTRO, PATRICIO, LUÍS, AGUSTÍN, AND I SET OUT A WEEK after Don Raúl's *tienta* to take part in bullfights that Maestro had contracted for me after my recovery. Knowing I'd successfully tested heifers at the *tienta* boosted my confidence, but I knew fighting a bull in the ring would be the true test of my abilities.

The cuadrilla depended on me and I hid my anxiety about fighting again in a real corrida, especially from Maestro. I'd confided my anxiety to Julio, who'd said it was normal to feel fear, especially since I'd been injured, and he'd offered to cancel his appearance in Aguascalientes to come and support me. I wouldn't hear of it. We'd also decided to keep the change in our relationship a secret from Maestro and the others. Though it would be difficult with our schedules throughout the season, we promised to meet whenever we could.

Zacatecas was the first city on the itinerary. It lay two hours from Colotlán, the city where I'd made my disastrous appearance. The city had grown wealthy from mining silver and gold, as it sat high in the mineral-rich mountains. It was a romantic and stunning place, the ghosts of conquistadors seeming to reside in every one of its ancient nooks. It most resembled the photographs of Mexican towns I'd seen in books during my childhood. Fiercely hot during the day, the streets turned frigid after the sun dipped below the horizon and invisible trains of brisk wind hurtled down from the rugged sierras.

We arrived on Saturday morning and, seeing my enthusiasm to explore the city, which he knew very well, Patricio offered to take me sightseeing. We spent an easy afternoon visiting the cathedral in the Plaza de Armas, whose walls were built of beautiful, pale pink stone. Mindful of my test in the bullring the following day, I prayed to the Virgin of Guadalupe that the fight would go smoothly.

As a surprise, Patricio arranged for a miner friend of his to take me on a tour of a silver mine located just a twenty-minute walk from the city center. When I entered, a breeze as crisp as air-conditioning dried the sweat on my bare arms. Deeper underground, the air turned musty, different from what I knew from the bullring's passageways, a mustiness tinged with dust and seeping water full of minerals. It also felt as claustrophobic as the jerky elevator ride to the floor of the mine, my fear heightened by the din of men shouting above the clang of grinding machinery whose monstrous form I couldn't even begin to imagine.

A rumbling commenced, either underfoot or in some dark corner, the sound so close and so distant all at the same time that I thought the mine would collapse. But the quakes silenced as quickly as they'd begun, and my fear was quickly forgotten when I saw the precious metal glinting within the dull seams of rock. Still, I was happy to return to the fierce heat of the city when Patricio said we should leave, as I needed to rest for the corrida.

The Virgin of Guadalupe ignored my request for good bulls, because my first one was a red-and-white sorry sack of bones.

"A pathetic roach," Maestro said to me, after he'd tested him with the preliminary passes to determine the defects I'd need to cure before the final act. The bull even tried to jump over the wooden barrier fence, so great was his cowardice. If I hadn't been so nervous about failing again, I'd have found Maestro's contempt amusing. After the sorting of the bulls at midday, he'd returned to the hotel and told me I'd drawn the finest pair of bulls of the six.

"Hey, *TORO*," I hollered, trying to provoke him into action. "Ahhhaa, *toooro*."

The bull flicked his ears and looked at me blankly, as the clever heifer had done at Don Raúl's *tienta*. Remembering the apprentice Raymundo's fate with a cowardly bull, I approached the animal gingerly, gripping the collar of my cape tightly and swaying it back and down as Maestro had advised. I shimmied toward the bull, standing before the *toril* gate. Bullfighters worth their salt dominate the cowardly bulls as well as the brave ones, working skillfully to cure the defect and encourage the bull to leave his favorite spot and perform for the crowd.

But no matter how many tricks I used to lure the bull with my cape, he refused to charge two times out of every three attempts. On one occasion, he even laid down on the sand and stretched out, as if he'd just finished grazing in a sunny meadow. I muttered to myself and even said prayers to steady my nerves. Finally, after three decent charges, when I was able to show off my *veronicas* and one chest pass, he lapsed into half-charges again and had to be constantly coaxed from his *querencia*.

Fearing the crowd would become disappointed in me (especially since they were already silent), I approached the judge's stand smartly. Removing my hat, I bowed to him, thus requesting his permission to go directly to the kill. He consulted with his veterinarian adviser and then, to my horror, waved a green handkerchief, signaling the animal was to be retired.

As I waited for my turn with the second bull, my shirt was wet with nervous perspiration. Thankfully, no one could see it because of my bolero jacket. Since I'd begun bullfighting, I'd made mistakes, stood frozen with fear, and drawn bad bulls. I was beginning to think the Virgin, like many male apprentices, was sending messages that she didn't want a female matador in the ring, either. It was impossible to talk to Maestro about any of this, because self-doubt and fear were like poison to him. I wanted Julio with me, which was selfish, as he had his own corrida that afternoon. My head felt as if it were in the grip of a vice.

"A big fight for you," Patricio said, as he walked over to where I stood in the passageway. My sword handler, now in his early fifties, had once been a matador but had never been good enough to reach the top tier like Maestro had. He set down the canvas bag bulging with my capes and the case containing the real sword. "This bull is much better. Good luck."

"Do you think I need luck?"

He looked at me intently. "Shake your arms," he said. "Tilt back your head and move it slowly to the right and then the left."

I did as he instructed.

"All matadors are nervous at this time," he said. "You're no different."

"Patricio, what if I don't perform well?"

He held up his hand like a policeman. "Don't think this way. Think only of the bull. Watch his every move. Don't give Fermin or me or anyone a second thought when you enter the bullring."

I hugged him, feeling his bony back stiffen under my touch. This was probably the first time a bullfighter had embraced him before entering the ring. If I'd been a man, he'd probably have pole-axed me.

Smaller but swifter of foot than the bull I'd faced in Colotlán, I saw within minutes in the first *tercio* that my second bull was brave. He charged straight as an airplane runway and had an instinctive knowledge of how to brandish his horns. With him, I was able to employ every pass I knew. The crowd, at last, began to applaud. Caught up by a ravenous need to move them more so they'd roar in unison at the judge to award me an ear as a trophy, I remembered the *rebolera* that Julio taught me eighteen months ago. Though I'd never done it in public, I felt Julio beside me as I moved the cape around my waist like a flouncy skirt, executing it perfectly. I did three series of passes and ended each with a *rebolera*.

The crowd screamed and applauded. The band played dianas, the shrill notes lifting into the superheated air. My head felt like I'd drank wine too fast and, though I didn't want the first act to end, I led the bull over to my first picador, Montes, to lance his neck muscle so he wouldn't hold his head dangerously high during the final act. After the banderilleros inserted the six barbed sticks to weaken him further, the *tercio de varas* ended and it was then my turn to work the bull with the muleta.

By the middle of the final act, the crowd began hollering, "*La diosa Tejana.*" Their adulation sent my confidence high as an airplane. I worked flawlessly, bringing the people to their feet as I brought the horns closer and closer until the bull was passing a hairbreadth from my chest.

And then it was time to kill my brave bull. After requesting permission from the judge, he assented with a wave of his white handkerchief. Laying my lavender hat on the sand as a mark of respect for the bull, I began shuffling, one foot forward at a time, toward him. He made no attempt to charge. When I was five feet away from him, I extended the muleta slowly with my left hand and, just as slowly, wrapped the bulk of it around the dowel, taking care to do so clockwise so the bull would think to charge to the right. I checked to ensure his front hoofs were squared and close together, which meant the death-notch where his shoulders and neck met was fully open.

An arctic shiver passed through me. "Please, dear Virgin, don't let me hit bone and make this an ugly death for my lovely bull," I muttered. Sighting with the sword between his horns to the *cruz*, I shook the muleta to tempt him.

The bull charged and I ran toward him with my heart beating violently and my right elbow raised high. When the point of the sword entered the invisible death-notch between his shoulders, I experienced a jarring sensation in my right arm. I made sure to complete the sign of the cross by swinging the muleta low in front of the bull's face, so his head would move to the right and the left horn would miss my legs.

The arena erupted. The band struck up dianas again. Everywhere I looked, there was a wall of dancing white handkerchiefs. People screamed that I should be awarded an ear. The bull turned and began to stagger as if drunk. I approached and held up my hand, moving the palm downward at the exact moment he surrendered completely to me and sank to the sand.

I looked up at the ecstatic crowd. A tangle of emotions warred inside me: sadness for the bull's death, which in turn made me think of my father's death and my sadness about that; sadness that Mama didn't accept my new way of making art and wasn't here to witness my triumph; utter respect for the bull; respect for Maestro, for bringing me to this beautiful time in my life. I looked down at my brave, lovely bull for a moment, and then compulsively knelt, touched a curved horn, and finally kissed his massive forehead. His heat warmed my face. I kissed him twice, his course damp hair pressing against my lips.

The band grew discordant in its fervor as the trumpet players battled the French horns and the flutes. The spectators were delirious, hanging over the balconies, waving hats and flowers, *olé*-ing and applauding.

"Thank you, brave *toro*," I said.

Maestro drew up as I was getting on my feet.

"What do I do now?" I asked.

"We walk around the ring and accept their respect."

As I walked around the perimeter of the ring, a man approached and placed something hairy and firm in my hand. I looked at the bull's chestnut colored ear in disbelief. My first kill, and the judge had awarded me a trophy.

"The second ear," the crowd roared at the judge. "Give La Diosa Tejana the second ear, too."

I led my cuadrilla around the ring, waving my hat slowly in the air, stooping now and again to pick up shoes, hats, ladies' fans, watches, and even fat wallets thrown down by the enthralled aficionados, which I then tossed back to their delighted owners, as was customary.

Halfway around the ring, the person who'd given me the first ear returned. He waited until I'd put on my hat and then gave me the bull's second ear. My body tingled so much I thought my skin would bust. I focused on tossing a beautiful mother-of-pearl fan back to its owner, a dignified middle-aged woman who was laughing like a child, worshipping me as if I were a famous matador. I bowed my head to her.

25

FERMIN WALKED AROUND THE BULLRING WITH KATHLEEN, tossing wallets, ladies' fans, and even shoes back to their enthusiastic owners. He'd taught her the *media-verónica* as the pass to end a series, a pass he'd always done in the bullring when he was a matador, and had been astonished when she'd executed a *rebolera*. She'd never attempted the pass during their practice sessions.

He watched as she stooped and picked up a fat Havana cigar off the sand and then raised her arm to toss it back to the man who'd thrown it. He seized her wrist and squeezed deliberately hard.

"Maestro, you're hurting me."

"You never throw back cigars," he said. "Or money. Those things we keep."

Another young man in the front tier blew kisses at her and Kathleen kissed her palm and then sent the kiss his way, laughing when he plucked it from the air and pressed it on top of his heart affectedly.

"Where did you learn to do *reboleras*?" Fermin asked now, ignoring the crowd.

"At the Los Pinos bullring . . . a long time ago. I think you were away fighting in Guadalajara and, um . . . somebody showed me."

Fermin waved at a young woman who'd tossed down a bunch of banknotes. "Who taught you?"

She didn't answer and stooped to pick up the money.

He stared at her. "Who taught you?"

She didn't meet his eye as she rose. "El Cabrito."

Blood surged to Fermin's head. He didn't see a Cordoban hat lying on the ground in front of him until it was too late. He stepped on it and squashed the crown. Picking it up, he inspected it and then turned it over and started punching out the inside with his fist. The hat's shape returned but it now had permanent wrinkles. With a curt flick of his wrist, he sent it spinning fast as a spear back to its owner.

"Why didn't you tell me?" he asked.

"I forgot."

"Why did you do those passes today?"

"Everything was going so good, Maestro. It seemed right to do something extra special."

He grabbed her by the shoulders, but kept his smile. "You will never again take lessons from anyone but me," he said. "I'm your instructor. Do you understand?"

Kathleen nodded, her face now pale. They continued on in silence, tossing articles back to the adoring crowd.

"Marry me," a man hollered.

"The people loved it when I did the *rebolera*, Maestro."

He stopped again and gripped Kathleen's shoulders even tighter than he had before. She winced, but he kept the pressure on. "I don't like El Cabrito's style of fighting. It's too showy. You'll do only the *media-verónica*, like I taught you."

Since her excellent performance that afternoon, Fermin had been mulling over how best to manage Kathleen's emerging confidence. The quality was essential for a bullfighter with ambition, which his protégée had in spades, but it angered him that she'd hidden El

Cabrito's lesson on the *rebolera* from him. He didn't really despise the pass and had done it in his time, as many matadors had. But it was something Fermin associated with El Cabrito—it was flashy like him.

After dinner that evening, he suggested the cuadrilla go to a well-known cantina frequented by aficionados that was only two blocks from the hotel.

"Where are you going, Kathleen?" he asked, when she came out of the hotel with the other men. His gaze darted over the sundress that his wife had made for her, an attractive print of toucan heads with rainbow beaks against a white background.

"To the cantina, with you and the other men."

"We're leaving early tomorrow. You need to sleep."

"The men are leaving tomorrow, too," she said, nodding toward Luís and Agustín, who were already twenty yards down the street.

Hollering that he'd meet the men later, Fermin ordered Kathleen to follow him. They walked in silence in the opposite direction, until they came to the bullring, where he stopped at a quiet spot under its loggia.

"I planned to discuss this with you on the bus tomorrow," he began.

"Discuss what, Maestro?"

"We're now in a new stage of your career. There will be much travel and staying at hotels. So it's important we talk about propriety and expectations." He paused and studied the curved wall of the bullring. "In the ring, you're the same as any man in the cuadrilla. But outside of it, you're a woman. A pretty woman." He fell silent again, waiting for her to acknowledge the compliment. She said nothing, her expression remaining blank.

"The bulls are a world of men who are easily tempted by pretty women. The rest of Mexico is no different. That's why decent, young Mexican women are always chaperoned in public, Kathleen. They don't go out in the streets alone. They don't go to restaurants or cantinas alone. They certainly don't go to aficionado cantinas. Those are for men only."

"I'm an American." Kathleen tapped the point of her shoe against a loose cobblestone, ballast from conquistadors' ships that the ancient fathers of the city had purchased from seaports and used to construct the streets. "We don't have those rules."

"Not true," Fermin said, anticipating this rebuttal. "There are places where American women are not welcome in your country. I lived there too, remember."

"Women are free to go out alone at night in American cities," she argued. "You lived there and know that as well as I do."

"If you should be in Rome, live in the Roman manner," he said, keeping his tone as calm as a concerned high school teacher. "If you should be elsewhere, live as the citizens do there. Those are Saint Ambrose's words." Fermin's lips turned up in a bright smile. "You live in Mexico now."

He watched a man paste up a poster for a forthcoming corrida on the bullring wall, laying it over the one that had included Kathleen's name.

"That's very restricting, Maestro," she said uncertainly.

"I know you haven't forgotten what happened when you went out alone once in Los Pinos."

Kathleen slapped her right hand over her heart like a shield. Her face turned white as a bedsheet.

"Don't you think it's enough you're doing a man's work in Mexico?" he continued. "You can't do that in Texas."

Kathleen looked toward the bullring entrance for a long moment and then turned back to Fermin. "I don't think there are rules in America stopping women from doing men's work. Most women *want* to become secretaries and teachers until they marry and become homemakers. That wasn't what I wanted to do and I shouldn't be punished for it."

"Punished?" Fermin's eyes widened and he affected anger. "Is that how you see what I'm doing here?"

She winced. "I just mean that having a chaperone is too much."

"My decision isn't negotiable," said Fermin. "When we're performing in the *fiesta bravas*, you're to remain in your hotel room until I call you to eat or practice, or when it's time to leave for the bullring. You won't accept invitations to parties or any other social or charitable events before you talk to me and get my consent. Neither will you go out alone at night, unless a member of our cuadrilla agrees to accompany you." He laid a hand on her shoulder and squeezed firmly, a deliberate reminder of his grip on her at the bullring earlier. "My rules are for your protection. And propriety."

The man who'd hung the new poster took a step back to admire his work, his paste bucket and glistening brush in his hands.

"Do you agree?" Fermin pressed. He watched Kathleen unblinkingly.

She met his stare with her own. "I won't be chaperoned in Los Pinos, or in Texas or anywhere else in the States," she said, a steeliness in her tone that he hadn't heard before. "Only when I'm on the road." She straightened her posture. "That's not negotiable, either."

While it wasn't exactly what he wanted, Fermin decided he'd won enough. She was rising toward fame and he didn't want to push. She could find another manager, if she asked enough people in the business.

26

THE NEXT FOUR CORRIDAS WENT EXTREMELY WELL AND WE arrived in the city of Reynosa for the final bullfight of the tour. My first bull was a bit cowardly, but I buckled down and drew what mileage I could out of him, the crowd, judging by the warm applause, seeming to understand that I was working with a misfit and doing my best. The second bull was brave and dignified, and we worked as if one for the first two acts.

Partway through my work with the muleta in the third act, I noticed Maestro hadn't been hollering his usual orders to me. I looked quickly over at the *callejón* to see if he was watching me. He stood behind the barrier fence talking to a man I recognized, though I didn't know where I'd seen him before. I turned back to the bull, who was just emerging from the hypnotic state the bulls enter at the end of a series of passes.

A violent surge of energy raced through me. The hairs on the back of my neck stood on end and I could hardly breathe. I looked over again at Maestro and the stranger. Since that frightening night, I'd been unable to recall anything about my attacker. The only thing I remembered with clarity was the pressure of the twig stabbing my back as he'd slammed me into the wall. I wasn't certain that this stranger was the man who'd attacked me, but I was having such a visceral reaction, it was impossible to ignore. Was it just my subconscious working overtime, reacting to the new rules Maestro had given me and his mention of the attack to justify their imposition?

Someone in the audience screamed. I turned back to see the bull lower his head as he charged toward me, his creamy horns aimed at my belly. There was nothing I could do—I had to cede ground. I took a step back, but was too slow. The bull's right horn shredded my jacket and shirt. The tip of the horn grazed my flesh, but I felt no pain.

Luís raced toward me swaying his cape to distract the bull.

"What are you doing?" Maestro shouted. "Wake up!"

I held up my hand to Luís. "Leave me."

He stopped abruptly, looking at me and then over at Maestro. The stranger was no longer at Maestro's side.

"Leave, Luís," I repeated. "It's just a scratch."

He nodded and walked away.

I still felt no pain. Approaching my bull, I squared him for the kill. Instead of the sword entering the death-notch smoothly, I struck bone and had to line the bull up again for a second attempt. I failed once more, striking the shoulder blade again.

"Sweet Virgin, please don't let him bleed from the mouth," I begged, twice. The audience despised seeing bulls bleeding this way, because it meant the matador had inexcusably blundered.

"Kill your bull cleanly," Maestro hollered.

The third time worked like a charm and the bull dropped at my feet. But I took no pleasure in his submission.

"Are you hurt?" Maestro asked, when I stepped into the *callejón*. "Is that why you made such a mess?"

"It's a scratch. I was lucky."

"Luckier than your bull. *That* was a disgrace. A fiasco."

"Who was that man you were talking to earlier?" I asked.

His face screwed up in a mask of incredulity. "You're asking me this after what you've just done."

"Who is he?"

"Bernardo and I worked together before he went to live in Spain. He's one of the best banderilleros around."

My body relaxed at the news the stranger lived in Spain. He could not have been my attacker. My wound began to hurt, but it was slight, no more intense than a sting from a bee.

"The Texan Goddess," Patricio said, his liquid brown eyes regarding me slyly. "Do you like the nickname the aficionados have given you?"

He'd just shown me a newspaper that bore the headline, MEXICO'S LA DIOSA TEJANA ENDS HER TOUR IN REYNOSA. We were on our way home to Los Pinos on a bumpy, overcrowded train, the erect, wooden seats hurting the small of my back. Our luggage was stacked in the aisle, because the overhead bins were already crammed full. The air smelled of sweat and smoke. A squat woman holding a cage containing three plump pigeons shuffled by, obliging Patricio to invade my personal space until she'd passed.

"I'm not sure I like nicknames," I said.

"It's good you have one now," he said. "People will remember you easily. All the great matadors have nicknames. Think of Calisero. El Gallo."

I peered out the window as I thought about this. "Do you think El Cabrito is a great matador?" I asked, glancing back at him.

His eyes darted to Maestro, who sat with Agustín in the seat diagonally across from us.

Though my employee, Patricio's loyalty was naturally to Maestro. All the men's loyalties were to him. When Maestro had talked to me about the chaperone issue, I'd felt like one of the mustangs I'd watched cowboys in Texas breaking in, how they'd try to slip a bridle on them and the horses would rear up and lash at them with their whirling legs. I'd wanted to lash out at Maestro, but hadn't, because he could easily leave me, fire my cuadrilla, and walk away, and the cuadrilla would follow his lead.

"El Cabrito's making a name for himself, but he's still very young," Patricio said in a low voice. He flicked the end of his cigarette and cold ash fell on his knee.

Curiosity made me bolder. "Maestro worked for him in the past many times."

He didn't take the bait.

"Why doesn't he work with him anymore?" I asked.

"That's Fermin's business." Patricio shifted in his seat.

"Why did Maestro retire so young?"

The cigarette drooped and threatened to fall as Patricio's lips slackened. He reached up quickly and took it out. "He was gored. You know that already."

"But he recovered fully."

He picked up the newspaper and resumed reading.

My new name and news of my successes in the bullring reached Los Pinos before I did. Shortly after arriving home, Carmen handed me a stack of telegrams and letters from admirers and three journalists who wished to interview me. Like a kid on Christmas morning, I went to my room, stretched out on the bed, and read and reread them. One made me especially happy. A radio station in Dyson, the town where I'd grown up, congratulated me for "becoming a matador" and requested an interview.

"I want to do these interviews, Maestro," I said, over dinner the next evening. I'd deliberately waited until he and I were both rested, hoping he'd be in good spirits and more easily persuaded. "Especially the one from my hometown."

During my training, Maestro had discouraged me from doing interviews. He didn't like the media treating me like a novelty. Plus, he thought it too distracting. Setting my fork down, I braced myself to put up a fight.

"Yes," he said, stabbing a piece of steak with his knife. "An interview in your hometown will increase the Americans' interest in you. We'd be foolish to ignore the station's request." He set down the knife with the meat still attached and took out a crinkled envelope from his pocket. "This is for you."

I figured it must be my wages, though the envelope seemed very thin. One Sunday evening, I'd come down to the hotel lobby after the corrida and seen Maestro giving Luís and one of the picadors fat envelopes, the same color as this one. The bullring's impresario paid Maestro for our performance and he, in turn, paid the members of my cuadrilla their wages in cash. When he hadn't paid me that night, I'd assumed he didn't want me carrying money on my person, and so hadn't asked him for it.

"We'll open a bank account for you tomorrow," he said.

My hands trembled as I took out a check, my name written out clearly in blue ink in Maestro's spidery handwriting. It was drawn in the amount of twenty-two thousand pesos—a little over sixteen hundred dollars. I wasn't even an official apprentice, but my career successes already allowed me to hire a manager and five men when I performed at festivals. I felt rich as an oilman.

"I earned *this* amount," I said, the corners of my eyes stretching tighter as I looked at him.

"Don't forget I had to pay your cuadrilla . . . and you also had a lot of expenses." He didn't hold my eye. He pinched the base of his reddening neck, right under his chin, with his thumb and index finger. Beads of sweat glistened on his forehead. "Your name is known now, so I'll be able to demand higher fees very soon."

27

MAMA HAD GOTTEN RID OF HER OLD HAIRSTYLE, CIRCA 1945, since I'd last seen her. Now she wore her hair in a short, sleek style that ended in a wave at the earlobes, with bangs halfway down her forehead. It made her look younger than a woman in her late forties.

I'd thought real hard about whether I should contact her to let her know I was coming to town to do the radio interview. We hadn't talked much since she'd tried to fix me up with the job at the bank, just a couple of minutes on the telephone every couple of weeks. I'd asked Carmen to accompany me for my overnight stay, selfishly planning to use her first as an icebreaker and then as a pacifier if Mama got argumentative. She'd been excited to come, but Maestro had forbidden it.

Since last seeing Mama, I'd traveled throughout Mexico on three additional tours. To my surprise, Mama admitted she'd heard about my successes from a neighbor who attended corridas in the border towns. She'd also read articles about me, though she wouldn't say whether she was proud or displeased. I figured displeased and fixed not to overreact if she said anything to inflame me.

George was gone on business the first night of my visit and Mama and I spent it like old times, sitting in the living room, listening to the radio or watching television. We didn't talk much, just about who'd

died and who'd gotten married and about a fire at my old high school
that had destroyed the gymnasium. She'd even bought a bottle of Jack,
remembering I liked to drink it occasionally, but I told her I was off
alcohol now.

"That manager of yours stopped you drinking whiskey, huh?" she
asked, as she poured herself a double.

"For as long as my career lasts." I fidgeted with the doily on the
chair's arm, straightening and restraightening it.

"Uh-huh."

I went over to where she sat on the settee and sat on the arm next to
her. "I wish you'd give me your blessing, Mama. It'd mean so much."

The gray glare and flicker from the television screen had turned
Mama's face pale and not a muscle in her folded hands twitched. A
harsh buzz started up from behind the bureau across the room, like a
housefly or some other bug was caught in a web or in a life struggle
with a bigger adversary.

The phone in the hallway rang and Mama went out to answer it.
Moments later, she returned to say it was a Mexican man calling for
me. I knew it was Julio and nearly tripped over the leg of the coffee
table in my haste to take the call.

"How's it going with your mother?" he asked.

"Much better than I thought it would."

"So, can I visit?"

Julio had a free week and was keen to see where I'd grown up, but
I'd said I needed to test the waters first. We hadn't seen each other
since Don Raúl's *tienta*. As a successful matador, he was booked for
corridas throughout the season and was unable to visit his cousin
Rafael in Los Pinos when I was there, and I couldn't go visit him
wherever he was because of my schedule. Such was the situation
for all bullfighters and their cuadrilla members, and we were no
different.

"I need to see you," I said. "Come quickly."

After we made the arrangements, I returned to the living room. Mama lowered the volume on the *I Love Lucy* show before I even sat down.

"Was that your boss?" she asked.

"No, it was Julio."

"Who's he?"

"A matador friend."

"They all sound alike on the telephone, don't you think?"

I watched the moving figures on the television, but didn't take in what was happening.

"He wants to come visit while I'm here," I said, in the most casual tone I could muster.

"Why?"

"He's interested in this part of Texas."

"He's a friend, you say?"

"Yeah, he loves driving and offered to take me back home after my radio interview."

"You calling Mexico 'home' now?"

When I didn't answer, she turned up the volume. But she lowered it again seconds later. "By the way, do you ever hear from Charles?"

"Not for a long time."

Out of the corner of my eye, I could see her watching me intently. It surprised me she'd asked about him. I hadn't thought about my old boyfriend in an age. I marveled now how different I felt about Julio, how I missed him so much when we spoke to each other on the telephone from the hotels where we were staying, and the butterfly feeling I'd gotten in my belly just now when I'd talked to him. I'd never felt this way about Charles, not even at the beginning of our relationship.

"He writes every few months to tell me how he's doing." Mama laughed casually, but it was anything but. "His job's going very well." Another short laugh. "He's making very good money now. I always knew Charles would go places."

"I'm happy for him."

"He still asks about you and tells me to pass on his regards . . . not that you and I see each other very much." She paused. "Now Mexico's called home."

When I didn't respond, she turned back to Lucy and Desi.

We sat on the edge of a large, circular tank on the northwest boundary of her place, Mama feeding stale bread and cake crumbs to a family of ducks and I nibbling on an apple. Nearby was a jetty Daddy had built to launch his rowing boat, its north-facing pilings half-rotted and planks loose where the nails had rusted through. I tried to recall if Mama had ever been in the boat with him and me, but couldn't. Tossing the apple core into the black water, I went over to the jetty, eased down on my knees, and passed my hand over the weathered planks. Dipping my pinkie into a circular hole on a silver-gray board, I rummaged around until I could feel the rusted nail head beneath. The last fingers touching that nail head had been my father's and now, years later, it was a conduit to him.

"Don't walk on the jetty," Mama hollered. "It's not safe."

The old jetty was rotting to oblivion. In ten more years, it would be gone—like Daddy. Another piece of his legacy would be gone forever, even if he'd have scoffed at the idea of me thinking of the puny jetty as a part of his legacy. But not everyone who'd lived could leave a legacy as big as Roosevelt's. As I passed my hand over the weathered planks once more, I wondered if I was part of Daddy's legacy. Could a child be a legacy? Had he ever thought of me that way?

"We ought to fix it, Mama."

"No one uses it anymore." A fish leaped from the surface of the inky water to catch a hovering fly. Mama watched the dissipating ripples. "I never liked this water. It's so black. And scary."

"I'll send you the money to fix it. Will you get someone to do it?" A splinter pierced my finger and a tiny dome of bright blood formed over the top of my skin.

"You can afford that?" Mama asked.

She was shocked when I told her how much I'd earned from my first fights.

"So, will you have it fixed?" I asked.

"It's a waste of money."

I let the subject drop for the moment, moving over to sit beside her. "Do you miss Daddy?" I asked.

"I've got George. He's reliable and steady."

It was an answer, and not. But I didn't push that, either.

"Mama, what was it like when you worked in the aircraft factory?"

Her gaze turned inward. The look lasted a moment, and then she peered out again at the black water. "Why are you asking this now?"

"I never thought much about what you did during the war. Now that I'm working, I'm interested."

Her shoulders relaxed. "I worked with a woman called Roberta. My God, Kathleen, she was big enough to hunt bear with just a switch. I'd shoot rivets into the metal and Roberta would use a bucking bar to make them seamless." The faraway look returned to her eyes. "I wonder what she's doing now."

I remembered what Maestro had said about my doing men's work in Mexico, how he'd asked if that wasn't enough.

"After the war ended, did you want to stay on at the factory?"

"The men needed jobs." A breeze tousled her bangs. "We did our duty and it was time to turn it back to our menfolk. Some of the women wanted to stay on. They liked the work. But the government and the bosses didn't need them anymore." She shook her head. "Told them it was their duty to return home and look after their husbands and children, or else go back to teaching or being a secretary—proper women's jobs."

She looked pointedly at me. It seemed that what Maestro had said about women not being allowed to do men's work in America was true, after all.

"You were tossed out," I said, averting my eyes from hers. "That was unfair. Why should y'all have had to go back to homemaking if y'all loved your jobs?"

Mama's eyes crinkled. She looked much older with the puffs and wrinkles.

"I hope living in Mexico isn't filling your head with strange ideas, Kathleen. Because I have no truck with that kind of thinking. There's work for men and there's work for women. Men are the breadwinners and we women are the homemakers. Those're the rules."

"Those rules are all backward," I said, watching a red-winged blackbird skim over the calm surface of the dark water. "Who made them?"

She shrugged. "I guess it goes back as far as the Bible. Maybe before that. It's how it's always been."

"It seems women gave up more than men with these rules."

"Why do you say that?"

"When it suited, the government brought women into the factories to do men's work. Then they were told to leave when they weren't needed anymore."

"Are you turning the conversation to suit yourself?" she asked. "Because of what you do down in Mexico? Your being different is not going to change anyone."

I didn't answer.

"Think of it as men and women doing their part for their country," Mama said, "and then things returning to normal once the threat was over. We're living now in normal times. Which is why I don't understand you." She gripped my forearm. "When you're older, you'll want a husband and a comfortable home to raise your children in."

"Why can't I have that *and* do my work?"

"Raising children's a full-time job. You won't have time for that terrible bull business." She sighed. "I just hope Charles'll still want you when you decide."

My eyes flitted to my father's decaying jetty. Where its shadow should have extended out into the water, there was nothing. The silent, black water had devoured it.

"Mama, why didn't you talk to me about Daddy after he died?"

Her grimace thawed. A deep blush started in her neck and moved rapidly up her cheeks and forehead.

"I tried to get you to talk about him but you never would," I continued. Tears crawled down the sides of my cheeks. "It was like every memory of him went into his casket. It was like he never existed."

Mama rose and began brushing stalks of dry grass and seeds off her dress, brushing so hard it looked like she was beating herself. She stopped as abruptly as she'd begun and looked at me. Her eyes were moist.

"I was grieving," she said. "I had no time to talk. And what was there to say? Your daddy was dead. I couldn't bring him back for you, even if I'd wanted to."

I gaped at her.

"Now, listen here, missy, I'm concerned with your thinking," she continued. "You've formed mighty strange ideas since you went to Mexico. Is that how women down there think?"

"Why do you always try to distract me when I want to talk about Daddy? Why can't you and I remember him like other families who've lost their people do?"

She walked away, tying the thin scarlet ribbons of her straw hat under her chin. I watched as she strode across the low brush, puffs of coffee-colored dust rising up from her heels.

Behind the glass window of the cramped studio, I could see Mama watching intently, even nodding in agreement as I leaned toward the silver microphone and told the interviewer that the countryside around Los Pinos was as dusty as around Dyson and the similarity had helped me adapt quickly to living in Mexico. I was speaking to Kitty Bell, a woman in her late sixties with a deeply wrinkled face. Not knowing what to expect from the interview, I'd been very nervous beforehand, but she'd quickly set me at ease, asking questions about my childhood, my time at Rowans Institute, and my reasons for wanting to become a bullfighter, all of which I answered without getting tongue-tied.

"Now tell me," Kitty said, "when you're fixin' to kill, do ya feel sorry for the bull?"

Mama was as rigid as a swing frame.

"If he's a brave bull, I feel happy, because he and I have given the people joy from our performance," I said. "I thank him and tell him it was an honor to fight him before I kill him."

"Y'all hear, folks," said Kitty Bell. "She tells the bull it was an honor."

I hoped this wasn't some kind of segue into a discussion about morals and cruelty, and was relieved when she asked me instead for the name of my favorite pop singer. I didn't have time to listen to popular music in Mexico, so I said Rosemary Clooney, the first name that came into my mind, whereupon Kitty played "Come on-a My House" and then urged the listeners to travel to Garza to see me perform in a few weeks.

On the drive home, Mama said, "I was proud of you back there. I couldn't do a live interview. I would be so nervous, they'd think I was a jabbering idiot."

The velvety hairs on my arms stirred. My brain fizzed.

"You're like your daddy in that regard," she continued. "Nothing fazed him when he spoke in public, either."

Her refernce to Daddy surprised me. She hadn't once mentioned my bringing him up that day when we'd sat at the tank. I'd returned to the house an hour after she'd stomped off back to the house to find it was as if nothing awkward had occurred between us.

"When did Daddy speak in public?"

"He discussed life as an oil driller on the radio. You'd have been two or three at the time." Her eyes remained focused on the road as she negotiated a sharp turn. "He was interesting . . . and funny." She sighed. "Those were the good days."

When I peeked over, two tears were slowly rolling down her cheeks. I reached over and wiped the nearest one away with my finger.

"What's wrong, Mama?"

She sniffed and shook her head. "I don't want to talk anymore."

While Mama prepared supper, I offered to take Julio, who'd just arrived, outside, under the pretext of showing him the outbuildings and tank.

"George, you go along with them," said Mama from her place at the stove. "You can answer any questions he might have."

"I lived here, too," I said, a bit too quickly. "George wants to read the paper. Let him be."

"The air will do him good," she said.

"If it's all the same to you, honey, I'd like to read," said George, and he winked at me.

I grabbed Julio's wrist and tugged him to the door before Mama could come up with another obstacle. Figuring she'd persuade George to follow us outside, anyway, I skipped taking Julio for a stroll around the tank and headed toward the nearby hill, instead. After passing into a copse of medium-sized trees at the foot of the hill, he took me tightly in his arms and kissed me. His lips were as soft as I remembered.

"I'm glad you came," I said.

"Me, too." He ran his fingers through my hair and stood taking in the scenery. "This is so quiet and beautiful. You must have loved living here."

"I never saw it that way growing up. Only when I visit now do I see it."

"One day you'll come with me to my parents' home near Aguascalientes," Julio said.

"I'd like that."

We kissed again. Something rustled in the dry underbrush nearby. A moment later, a possum came out of the thicket and ran toward us, foam spewing from its mouth.

"It's rabid," I shrieked. "Run."

We raced from the woods and sprinted all the way back to the tank, recovering our breaths by the jetty. As the dusk gathered, frogs hiding in the reeds began singing. We started walking around the pond and when we got halfway around, Mama called out that dinner was ready.

George and Mama were seated at the kitchen table when we arrived inside. A steaming jug of fragrant tomato gravy stood beside bowls of sliced carrots and peas.

"What do you do in Mexico?" Mama asked Julio as she handed him a plate containing a thick slice of meatloaf.

"I already told you he's a matador, Mama."

"It slipped my mind," she said regally, and turned to Julio again. "How did you meet my daughter?"

Julio glanced across the table at me.

"He taught me how to do a very tricky pass at the bullring," I said, "and then we became friends." I laughed. "The bullfighting world is small."

Mama ignored me. "Don't you find it strange my daughter wants to do this for a living?"

"Not so much." Julio lifted his beer glass. "Kathleen is dedicated."

"This sure is good meatloaf, honey," George cut in. "Do they eat this in Mexico, Julio?"

The conversation turned to Mexican and Texan food, and I made sure to keep it there for the rest of the meal. Later, as we sat in the living room while Mama cleared the table, George offered Julio a cigar and he accepted. We sat in an easy silence that was broken only by the men's lips clicking on the shafts of their cigars.

"I was just thinking how well you speak American," Mama said as she came in and sat on the sofa beside George. She set her bib apron on her lap. "Where'd you learn it?"

"I studied English at school," Julio replied.

"It's very good. I'm really surprised."

"Your daughter speaks excellent Spanish, ma'am, so why shouldn't my English be just as competent?"

Mama frowned. "I didn't think Mexican schools were so good."

"I attended a private school."

She jerked her head back and fidgeted with her apron strings.

"Did Kathleen tell you she's engaged?" she asked.

Julio's head turned to me faster than a hot knife through butter.

"Mama!"

"She *was* engaged, I mean." Mama chuckled. "I always forget. But we're hoping things might work themselves out down the line. Isn't that right, George?"

My stepfather's eyes locked on mine. "Kathleen's old enough to decide for herself, Marie."

"Of course, she is," Mama agreed, in a tone that implied she didn't believe it.

So much sweat trickled down my underarms you'd have thought it was my third act in the bullring. "My God, it's nine o'clock, already," I exclaimed, checking the clock on the fieldstone mantel for the thirtieth time that evening. I rose. "I'm ready for bed. We've got to leave early in the morning for Los Pinos."

Julio rose, too.

"We'll say our goodbyes now," I said. "No need for you to get up to see us off in the morning, Mama."

"What about breakfast?"

"I'll make coffee and toast." I looked at her gravely. "You just rest up in bed."

Julio's new Mercedes was yellow and beautiful, but after I'd told him that, we didn't talk. The road was empty of traffic and we drove through the desert landscape in silence. I tried to put it down to his having had to get up so early; maybe he wasn't a morning person. But the tension soon became unbearable.

I cleared my throat. "I know what Mama said last night surprised you," I said.

"Why did you not tell me you were once engaged?"

I didn't immediately respond. "It was a difficult time for me," I managed. "I ended the relationship only a week after I told him I'd marry him."

The car swerved a bit as he looked over at me. "Did you love him?"

"He was much older, and I thought I did," I said. "Charles was smart and knew a lot about life, and he'd done so many interesting things. But he didn't want me to fight the bulls and I had to choose."

"Are you happy with us?"

I laid my hand on his knee and squeezed gently.

"Your mama doesn't like me," he said, cracking his window open and spitting outside. "She thinks I'm a bad influence."

"It doesn't matter what she thinks."

We drove again in silence for two or three miles, and then he slid his arm across the seat and began stroking the back of my head. To the east, the blood-red sun slid up into the gray sky, turning the craggy face of the mountain, the shinnery oak and other shrubs, and the road a deep reddish-gold. I closed my eyes and listened to the smooth hum of the Mercedes's powerful engine and the sizzle of tires on the raw macadam. I didn't want the journey to end.

28

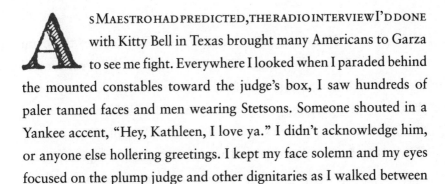

A S MAESTRO HAD PREDICTED, THE RADIO INTERVIEW I'D DONE with Kitty Bell in Texas brought many Americans to Garza to see me fight. Everywhere I looked when I paraded behind the mounted constables toward the judge's box, I saw hundreds of paler tanned faces and men wearing Stetsons. Someone shouted in a Yankee accent, "Hey, Kathleen, I love ya." I didn't acknowledge him, or anyone else hollering greetings. I kept my face solemn and my eyes focused on the plump judge and other dignitaries as I walked between the two male apprentices.

A slew of *fiesta bravas* ensued, some deep into the fecund central interior of the state of Jalisco and others in towns bordering Arizona and California. I gave all my energy to each performance, whether I drew brave or weak bulls. I surrendered my entire being, physically and emotionally, to dominating them, as Maestro demanded. He supervised every detail of the performances, even insisting I kill the bull exactly when he told me to. Soon, I'd made enough appearances with picadors to satisfy the rules of the Union of Matadors and Novilleros and Maestro submitted a formal application for admission as an apprentice, together with Julio's and Silvario's signatures as my matador-sponsors, shortly before we left for a corrida in Aguascalientes.

What I disliked about touring was traveling long distances in baking heat in hard-seated buses, often leaving the smooth paved roads to travel along bumpy dirt roads for miles on end. To my American sensibilities, the haphazard, back-and-forth nature of the itineraries was also absurd, traveling north then south, and then north again, often doubling back on routes we'd already taken. But I didn't complain. Maestro worked hard to secure me contracts and I was fully aware that both he and the other men had to leave their families for weeks at a time to perform alongside me.

When I walked into the private dining room adjacent to the main restaurant, Maestro was busy. The men of my cuadrilla sat around the table with him. Before Maestro, on top of the rustic table, was a sheaf of pages, an uncapped fountain pen, and sealed envelopes that I figured contained the men's wages. It was the cuadrilla's last evening dining together on this tour and we were going our separate ways in the morning. I was looking forward to seeing Carmen and Julio, who'd called to say he would be in Los Pinos for three days to see me before leaving for a corrida in Baja California.

"I told you to come at nine o'clock," Maestro said, glancing at his watch. "It's only eight fifty-four."

Checking my wristwatch, I saw it was running fast.

"I'll come back," I said, as I took off the watch to reset it. "I've still got some packing to do, anyway."

"No, wait in the lobby." As I walked away, he added, "By the way, we're not going home tomorrow."

I spun around. "Why not?"

"You and I are leaving for a *tienta* outside Aguascalientes. We check out of here at five sharp tomorrow morning."

He'd said nothing about this to me. We'd already agreed a long time ago that he'd tell me about invitations to *tientas* and other events taking place while we were on the road, so I'd know to pack suitable clothes. A larger problem was the meeting I'd arranged with Julio in Los Pinos.

"Maestro, I need to speak to you. Can you come to the lobby with me?"

"I'm busy."

"Come now."

He slid a page across the table to Enrique, the older and plumpest of the two picadors, and held out the pen for him to sign something. "Tell me here," he said, not looking at me.

"When did we get this invitation?" I asked.

He looked at me, puzzled. "Before we left Los Pinos."

"So why are you just telling me?"

"What does it matter?" He shrugged. "This is a very important rancher who wants you to test his heifers."

"I haven't brought a proper dress to wear."

"Pfft. The rancher wants to see your skill with his heifers, not how you look in a dress."

The other men laughed.

"I'll need money to buy a dress," I insisted.

"There aren't any stores open. It's Sunday." He held his palms out. "Anyway, I pay you by check."

A dense bank of red, as intense as a Martian desert, rose up and eviscerated the yellow-green rings expanding and contracting behind my lids when I closed my eyes tightly.

"I'm going home tomorrow," I said, through clenched teeth.

"You're coming with me."

He knew I was a professional and I wouldn't risk insulting an important rancher by not accepting his invitation. Already, I was thinking about what to tell Julio when I called him with the news. I wanted to punch Maestro, I felt so powerless.

"The invitation might have come to you," I said, "but it came because of *me*. The next time you do this to me, I will go home."

He laughed and peered around the table. "She sounds like our wives, eh?"

"I mean it. I'm to be told everything related to my work from now on."

"Okay, okay." He held up his hands in fake surrender. "I'll tell you about the *tientas* in time. Now leave me in peace. I need to finish my work. The men want to eat."

His agreement to share information seemed weak. I considered reemphasizing that I was to be informed about *everything* connected to my work, but, as I opened my mouth to speak, I decided against it. I was like a lawyer picking through the bones of his words. Maestro and the cuadrilla would think me petty. They'd think I was an insecure woman, worried about her appearance and unable to work as men do in these situations. I left them to it, fixin' to do the best I could with the skirts and blouses I'd brought along with me.

Julio had left for Baja when I arrived in Los Pinos three days later. Though he'd also thought Maestro extremely inconsiderate, he'd calmed my resurgent anger by reminding me that the *tienta* would be an opportunity for further exposure to important people in the bullfighting world. He and I had chosen a life of unpredictability, after all, and we'd consequently accepted that we wouldn't see each other for long periods of time. Still, I was sad he wasn't there to welcome me back, and my spirits lifted only when I opened a waiting envelope from the Union of Matadors and Novilleros and found a letter of acceptance inside.

I framed the letter and hung it on my bedroom wall. Every time I came into the room after a hard day's practice at the bullring, the first thing I did was go over to check that my name was still there. After three weeks, the novelty of belonging officially to the union still wasn't old.

A month later, I was booked to perform in a *fiesta brava* in the Los Pinos Plaza de Toros. Maestro and Alfonso Ortiz, the bullring's publicity manager, had agreed early on in my career that I'd appear in my home city only when I was an official apprentice and known well enough to fill seventy-five percent of the twelve-thousand-seat arena. Though this made sense financially, I'd feared it would never happen. Selling nine thousand tickets had seemed as elusive as becoming a union member. But my nickname—the Texan Goddess—was now so well known in Texas border towns that the corrida was nearly fully booked and scalpers were already selling tickets on the black market at prices much higher than their face values.

My appearance also presented a swell opportunity to make the kind of art I used to make. Aware I'd studied art and design, Señor Ortiz asked me if I'd like to create the official poster for my fight, and, after I eagerly agreed, he contracted me at a healthy discount, though I'd have done it for free. Stealing hours from my sleep every night for two weeks, I designed and hand-painted an original poster of myself performing a flaring *rebolera* pass on a huge spotted black-and-white bull. Predictably, when he saw it, Maestro demanded I destroy it, but I wouldn't back down. In this kind of art, I was no apprentice. Señor Ortiz arranged to have the poster reproduced and then had it pasted on telegraph poles and buildings around Los Pinos and Rowansville. He also ran it in advertisements in the newspapers of both cities.

On Wednesday evening, knowing I was anxious to see the bulls I would fight, Carmen came to my bedroom and told me the bullring impresario had just called Maestro to say the bulls had arrived and were now in the pens. After dinner, I told Maestro that Carmen and I were fixin' to take a walk. We rushed the six blocks to the bullring, our faces and necks shellacked with sweat by the time we reached the pens.

Creeping up, I peeked through a teeny hole in the wooden slats. The eight bulls munched contentedly on hay. Two were sorry half-bulls and not worth fighting. I wondered why the ranch had even sent them. But when I clapped eyes on the black-and-white bull, I fell in love. He nudged one of the half-bulls aside with his straight, bone-white horns to get a better feeding spot. It could not be a coincidence he'd been sent to the bullring. I'd painted a black-and-white bull for my poster and here he was in the magnificent flesh below me, the muscles in his haunches quivering like he was already itching to perform. I didn't care about the *sorteo* taking place at noon on Sunday, where Maestro and the other apprentice's representatives would draw lots for the pairs of bulls. This bull was mine. Every hair and eyelash on him was mine.

"I must have the black-and-white bull, Maestro," I said, as soon as we got home.

"What are you talking about?" He set his pipe and newspaper down on the coffee table.

"I saw the bulls. I must have him."

"When did you see them?"

"She's been waiting all week to see the bulls," Carmen said. "I couldn't keep the news of their arrival from her."

"You've been eavesdropping on my business, Carmen." Maestro went over to the children who were watching television. "Emilio, take your sister to bed."

"But, Papi, it's still early."

"*Now.*"

The children gathered their toys in a flash. After they left, Maestro caught my eye and nodded to the door. "Leave us."

"It's my fault," I said. "Don't blame Carmen."

"This is between her and me."

"Chiquita, you can go. It's okay."

I picked up a magazine and left, but stopped just beyond the door.

"Why do you disobey me?" he asked her.

"So I took her to see the bulls. Why are you making such a big deal of it?"

"You made me look like a fool in front of her. In my own house!"

There was a silence, and then I heard what sounded like a quick crack.

"Don't ever cross me again," Maestro said, his voice rising.

A brief struggle broke out. Everything went silent again for a moment, and then Carmen shrieked as if she was in great pain.

"Fermin, no," she cried out.

My arm and leg muscles flexed in preparation to rush into the room. Instead, I edged slowly to the threshold and peered inside. He had her by the hair. He sat on the sofa and dragged her down, her hands clutching his as she tried to lessen the pain. His breathing as labored now as a charging bull, he pulled her roughly across his lap and raised her skirt with his free hand.

"Please, Fermin. Kathleen will hear us."

I saw her pink underwear and naked coffee-colored thighs. I saw them and couldn't believe I was seeing them. But it was very real.

"I'm master of this house," he said.

He hit her, hard, three times. I bit down hard on my knuckles as the sharp cracks reverberated around the room. Carmen lay inert.

"You obey me," he said, "and don't you ever fucking forget it."

I knew I should run inside and try to stop it, but instead I ran to my room and threw myself on the bed. A moment later, I rose and paced the room. I remembered the afternoon he'd lost his temper and shook me hard. I closed my ears with my hands and continued pacing. What was happening out there was none of my business. They were a married couple. It was private. It was their business.

You're a hypocrite, my mind screamed. *She's your friend. Go out and stop it.*

But if I went to the living room, my debut in the Los Pinos ring, my career, everything I'd worked so hard for, would be over. I needed him. He was going to get me to the Plaza México. He'd reject me for interfering in his private business, and I'd be seen as damaged goods. No other trainer would take me on as an apprentice.

I went back to my bed and lay down. I waited, scarcely breathing, until I heard the front door slam shut. I waited for five more minutes and then went out to find Carmen sitting on the couch, darning a pair of socks. It was like I'd dreamed the whole dreadful scene.

"Are you okay?" I asked.

When she looked up, there were telltale streaks of dried tears on her coppery cheeks. She held a sock up to the fading light streaming in the window. "Fermin wears holes in his socks like they're made of paper." She laughed.

"I heard him hit you."

She didn't reply.

"Did he hurt you?"

"He didn't hit me like you think," she said. "He spanked me. Married people have disagreements. I told you this before."

The children came silently as cats into the room. They sat wide-eyed beside her on the sofa. She leaned over and kissed them on the tops of their heads.

I went to pick up a new shirt and bolero jacket I'd ordered to wear in the bullring on Sunday. When I returned from the tailor, Julio was waiting for me in the living room. I couldn't believe he'd come to Maestro's home to see me.

"Why aren't you in Nuevo Laredo?" I asked.

"I broke three fingers during practice." He held up his hand to show his fingers bound together with a splint. "Only one and I could have gone on. But three? Impossible."

Carmen rose and walked to the door. She looked at me and smiled before leaving.

"You shouldn't have come here," I said.

"I couldn't stop myself. I had to see you." He blew me a kiss. "I'm one of your union sponsors. It's normal I'd want to wish you luck."

"Do you think Carmen suspects?" I asked. "Maybe I should ask her not to say anything to Maestro."

"I brought you a gift," Julio said, ignoring the question.

He handed me a sword case. The aroma of new leather wafted up as I opened it. A beautiful sword gleamed inside. Like Maestro's sword, its pommel was made of chamois. The letters KB were initialed halfway along the curving silver blade.

"I can't accept this, Julio."

"Your professional career begins officially on Sunday. It's only right you should have a virgin sword." We sneaked a kiss. "A sword only you will ever use."

He invited me to join him for an early dinner and I agreed, then spirited him from the house in case Maestro came home. Later on, seated in the spotless Mercedes as we drove through the city, I felt like Mrs. Truman being whisked away from the White House to attend an official function. At the restaurant, too excited to fell hungry, I asked him to choose what we'd eat and declined his invitation to break my no-alcohol rule and order tequila. Like me, and despite his Spanish heritage, Julio loved simple Mexican fare and chose rice and red beans, pork chops with onions, and slices of fresh avocado drenched in lemon juice.

"I really want you to meet my family," he said, his scarred eyebrow lifting impishly. Julio was the eldest of two siblings. His sister was a surgeon (and also married to one) and lived in Mexico City. His father, Oscar, was second generation Mexican and his mother, Juanna, was

Spanish; he'd grown up on a breeding ranch ten miles outside Aguas-calientes.

"I'll meet them soon," I said.

"When is this 'soon'?"

"We have time," I replied. "Maybe when the season ends."

He regarded his splinted fingers. "I plan to cut my *coleta* off on my twenty-ninth birthday," he told me. It was tradition for matadors to cut off their pigtails immediately after their last appearance in the bullring.

"Why retire so young?" I asked.

"I want to buy some land and breed fighting bulls like my father." A smile slowly formed on his wide lips. "What do you plan to do when you cut off your *coleta*?"

"My ponytail, you mean?" We laughed, and then I admitted, "I haven't thought that far ahead."

"Life's so short," he said, sounding much older than his twenty-three years. From the kitchen came the piercing sound of breaking glass. "I don't have time to waste."

"Do you like being called El Cabrito?" I asked.

"I am a kid," he said, grinning. "Just not a young goat."

"I'm serious, Julio."

"I don't mind it." He cocked his head. "Do you like your name?"

"Well, I'm a foreigner, after all."

"A beautiful foreigner with thick red hair." He touched a rope of it. "What a pity the people never see your hair this way in the bullring."

My belly flipped like a hotcake and then my entire body started tingling. When I'd been with Charles, I'd never felt electricity flow through me like this when he'd complimented me. Why was it so different?

"Some matadors say I'm cocky," Julio continued. "They think I'm arrogant. But it's not true." His eyes narrowed. "I give everything when I perform and I expect the same from my team."

His earnestness penetrated my every cell. I wanted to reach out, cup my hands around his face, and kiss him. My nerve failed me and I sat rigid and aflame instead.

"Did Maestro give everything when he worked for you?"

"Why do you ask?"

"There must be a reason you don't have him in your cuadrilla anymore."

He set his fork down on the plate. "Fermin was once a great matador."

"That's not what I asked."

"He doesn't like me, which you already know."

"Do you like him?"

"I neither like nor dislike him." After taking a slow sip of tequila, he set the glass down carefully. "I fired Fermin."

My heart stopped beating. Firing Maestro felt the same to me as firing God.

"He didn't respect me," Julio continued. "Papa hired him when I was seventeen, but Fermin and I never saw eye to eye. He's too conservative." He paused, then shivered. "I've never liked that Fermin's terrified of the bulls. I didn't want someone like that around me when I'm fighting."

"Stop." I laughed. "Maestro's *not* scared."

"He is."

"But he works with them in the bullring."

"Sure, as a banderillero. He runs toward the bull, plants the sticks any which way, and flees. Courageous banderilleros stretch over the horns to plant the set of banderillas in the bull's shoulders at the same time. He *never* does that."

It was true Maestro didn't plant the colorful barbs in the normal fashion, but some other banderilleros didn't either. Maestro's calling had been as a matador, not a banderillero, so it was normal to expect he might not be as good a banderillero as he had been a matador. It seemed more a case of inelegance than fear.

"And you and me, we stand still before the angry bull and work with a muleta and sword. Fermin can do that only with a mechanical bull now—well, maybe a small bull, as well. But with the large bulls I fight, he'd give ground. Run, even."

"You're making fun of me now, because I'm just an apprentice and not allowed to fight the massive bulls you do."

He didn't laugh. "Fermin's turned you into a brave fighter and I respect him for that. But I feel it's time you know the truth about him." His expression turned lighter. "Mind you, he will get you to the Plaza México one day. Of that, I'm certain."

29

I WILL NOT ACCEPT THEM, MAESTRO," I said.

The midday drawing of the bulls was over and Maestro had just returned to the stockyard and told me I'd drawn the two weak bulls that I'd seen the day Carmen and I went to the pen. I'd never attended the sorting of the bulls and the drawing of the pairs before, content to leave it to Maestro. I'd done so that day only because it was my first professional appearance as a union apprentice in Los Pinos and I wanted to be involved soup to nuts.

Before he'd gone to draw my bulls, Maestro had insisted I wait for him in the stockyard. He felt a woman's presence at the *sorteo* would be unacceptable to the men. While I waited, the air was thick with the stink of bull feces. Musty hay lay in heaps in a corner by the barn. Not a blade of grass was visible in the two paddocks, their red earth tramped into hard clay. Tiny clumps of coarse red, black, and white bull's hair adorned the rasped surfaces of the split-rail fence.

Maestro seized my wrist and led me away from the entrance to the pens, which the ring servants were cleaning out. I flinched and pulled my hand from his grasp. Since Julio had told me about Maestro's fear, I hadn't known what to think. At first, I'd refused to believe it. But Julio had been very serious when he'd told me and he was not the sort of man to exaggerate such a thing. If it was true, one part of me believed it didn't matter, because Maestro had risked his name in the business to take me on and I was confident he'd win me a contract to appear in Plaza México—Julio had promised as much, too. But the other part of me was shocked that he could be so hypocritical, when I recalled how unkind he'd been when he'd witnessed my own fear of the bulls. There was also his despicable treatment of Carmen, unrelated to the bullring, but unforgettable, nonetheless.

"Today's a vital day for us," Maestro said. "Nothing must go wrong."

I folded my arms and regarded him coldly.

"It's excellent news you drew these bulls. There will be many journalists here today. Your fights will go easy. They'll write beautiful things." His teeth gleamed like a swamp alligator's. "I'll be able to arrange many important contracts based on your great performance."

"Those bulls are like two-year-old calves and I want to get to the Plaza México honestly."

"What if you perform badly?" he asked. "What if you'd drawn a difficult bull and your performance was weak? They'd say you have no talent. Or worse, they'd write you're an incapable woman. They'll lose interest and no press will attend your corridas again."

As I considered this, I couldn't help seeing his skinny butt fleeing from a charging bull. "Who drew my black-and-white?" I asked.

"No one. It's a substitute bull."

"Those half bulls shouldn't have been put in the same pairing," I said. "A strong bull's always paired with a weak one. Something's not right, Maestro."

He shrugged.

"How can you *accept* this?"

His eyes darted to the empty holding pens. "Hush, Kathleen."

One of the ring servants was looking over at us. I wondered now if my lot had been fixed. Sometimes a famous matador would use his fame to demand weaker bulls so he'd look good in the ring. Sometimes up-and-coming matadors were allocated dangerous animals because a top-billed matador, through his confidential advisor, let it be known he wouldn't accept them. It occurred to me that maybe the ring impresario had been involved in the drawing of my bulls. Money was king in bullfighting. I wondered about Maestro, too. He'd just said he believed I was real lucky.

I shrugged off the idea about Maestro quickly. Despite his overbearing ways, he was honest and wouldn't get involved in that kind of trickery. "Do you think the impresario arranged for me to get those weak bulls?" I asked.

His head snapped back. "Jesus, do you hear what you're saying?"

"I'm going to have the same quality of bull the other two matadors alongside me are fighting today. I'm in the union now. I'm their equal."

"You are *not* a matador yet," Maestro said, the words forced out through tightened lips.

This was true. Officially, I was a *matador de novilleros*, acknowledged throughout Mexico as having the right to fight bulls up to four years old. I wasn't a full-fledged *matador de toros*. Still, his words cut to the quick.

"Well, I'm sure as hell not making my professional debut fighting calves. I *won't* be seen as weak or second-rate." Hoping the breeding rancher and the bullring officials were still assembled at the corrals by the *toril* gate, I started toward the entrance leading to them.

Maestro ran after me and grabbed my forearm. "What are you going to do?"

"I'm going to get me my bull. Don't you worry, I won't be a smartass. I'll be polite and say there's been some kind of an oversight and my lot isn't properly balanced."

"You *can't* do that."

"Watch me."

I wrenched free of his grip. He gave chase and stopped me again just before I entered the building.

"Stay here," he said. His face blazed even deeper red than I'd seen it the time he and Julio had had words at Don Raúl's hacienda. "Maybe there was an error. If you go in there, you'll upset the breeding ranch's foreman and the officials. They'll throw both of us out. Let me see if I can persuade them to give you that damned substitute bull."

Wanting all the members of my cuadrilla to leave together for the bullring at the same time, Maestro had booked rooms for us in an old hotel near the Los Pinos bullring. When I returned to the hotel from the *sorteo*, in addition to newspaper reporters and aficionados wanting to talk to me, I was overjoyed to see Sally in the lobby.

I'd written to tell her about my official debut and invite her to come, but I hadn't heard back from her. We hadn't seen each other since she'd gone to live in New York, but we'd kept in touch with brief letters about what was happening in our careers and personal lives. We hugged so tightly anybody watching us might have thought we were trying to merge into a single body.

"I can't believe you came," I said.

"I was in Garza with you when you started this thing," she replied, her hair tumbling off her back when she leaned back her head to look at me. "You think I'd miss your confirmation?"

"My debut," I said. "It's not some kind of religious service, you know?"

"Whatever it's called, I wouldn't miss it."

I squeezed her tightly, still unable to believe she was standing before me.

"But I can't stay long after the show."

Sally explained she had to get back to New York, because the agency was flying her and two colleagues to Paris for an assignment. It was her first contract with a foreign fashion house. I'd come across photographs of her in fashion catalogs and twice with groups of models in Redbook and Harper's. Like cream in a can of milk, she was clearly rising up her employer's stable of models. Dressed now in a double-breasted suit with padded shoulders that showed off her hourglass figure, I saw that Sally had lost weight. It showed in her face, the lines of her high cheekbones even more pronounced by makeup that I figured was just as expensive as the suit she had on.

"Next time, I'll stay longer," she promised. "Or better yet, you come to New York and I'll show you the city."

A young man approached then with a curly walnut pipe drooping from his mouth. Setting it on the lip of a nearby ashtray, he said he was Miguel from *La Lidia*, a bullfighting magazine, and his photographer wanted to take pictures of me. They wanted me first in the dress I was wearing with my hair loose and falling over my shoulders and then, later, after my nap, in my Andalusian suit. In the hotel lobby, the photographer posed me pretending to smell a vase of silk flowers on top of the reception desk.

"Do you think you'll fight better now you're officially in the union?" the reporter asked, taking a notepad and pencil from his breast pocket.

Sally peered over at me. I felt guilty because we hadn't much time to spend together.

"We'll do the interview later," I said, and started walking away.

Like an apparition, Maestro appeared at my side as I hooked my arm into Sally's and headed toward the elevator.

"Where are you going?" he asked.

After I introduced him to Sally, he bowed courteously, then turned back to me. "I arranged this interview," he said. "Do you know how hard it is for even some matadors to get featured in *La Lidia* magazine?"

"You didn't tell me about it."

"Just like you didn't inform me your fashion friend was coming to the corrida," he shot back.

"The difference is, I didn't know she was coming."

Maestro glanced toward the exit. "Miguel's leaving."

Scoring a point over Maestro was going to cost me dearly if I didn't do the interview. In any case, I'd scored a victory over him at the *sorteo* earlier.

"Get him back here," I said.

Maestro inserted two fingertips inside his mouth and whistled shrilly. The noisy lobby fell silent. People gawked. Even the exiting journalist stopped and glanced back.

Once in my room, Sally and I lay on the bed and talked. She was about to move into an apartment she'd bought in a place called the East Village, which seemed like a strange name for a place, when it was a huge city she lived in.

"I've also got a boyfriend," she said. "Did you ever think I'd go out with a Yankee?"

"How's your mama feel about that?"

"Happy he's Episcopalian, but pitching a hissy fit with a tail on it because of the apartment." She sat up on the bed. "But what about you? Am I going to meet your man this trip?"

"He and Maestro don't get along so good. We're still keeping it quiet."

The sound of a guitar drifted up from the plaza below, its notes winding around the curtain ballooning out in the breeze. Moments later, a man started singing "Solamente una vez," a Mexican love song. His voice was soft and melodic.

After the first verse and chorus, the singer called up, "*¿Dónde estás encantadora*, Kathleen?"

Sally looked puzzled. "What's he saying?"

"He wants to know where I am."

The second verse and chorus ensued and then the singer stopped again. "*Sal al balcón, querida.*"

"He wants me to come out on the balcony."

"Seems you have an eager admirer," she said, her eyes glinting with mischief. "I feel like I'm on a movie set." She went over to the window and peeked down. "I can't see him."

Crossing back to me, she pulled me up off the bed and embraced me tightly. When she let go, her eyes sparkled with tears.

"What's wrong?" I asked.

"I'm so glad everything's working out."

"Why wouldn't it?"

"When you told me what that monster did, I wanted so badly to be with you, but the agency wouldn't let me leave New York. I still feel so guilty about that."

The walls crowded in and an image of myself struggling with the faceless man flashed before my eyes, his hand grabbing my throat, the twig biting into my back. The room began to spin. Sally's face loomed toward me.

Someone moaned, a long, guttural sound. I realized it was coming from inside me just seconds before enormous quakes rocked my body.

My nerves vanished when the trumpet sounded and the gate leading into the bullring swung open. If four hours ago someone had said I'd parade into the bullring after my meltdown, I'd have said they didn't have the sense of a goose. I'd cried in Sally's lap for a good half-hour and she'd just sat there, stroking my hair and listening. I hadn't known how much of that terrible night I'd still kept inside me; I'd thought it was entirely behind me. The whole black nightmare streamed out in words, snot, and sobs, and I felt beaten as a rented mule afterward. I hadn't known if I could do the corrida, even if it was my official debut,

but Sally had pulled me right off the bed and said I was a professional and that's what professionals like she and I did.

"There'll be good times and bad times in our work, Kathleen, and we ain't going to get to pick when they happen," she'd said.

Then, just as I was about to dress and he knew Maestro wouldn't be there, Julio had arrived at my room, wearing a pair of pitch-black sunglasses so no one in the hotel would recognize him and cause a fuss.

"These are for you," he'd said, handing me an extravagant bouquet of white zinnias and plump red roses.

I'd already been nervous as a gnat in a hailstorm about the bulls, and now feared Maestro might come unexpectedly to my room. After hastily introducing Sally, I'd kissed him quickly on the lips and said, "You need to leave."

"It's only bad luck to see you before the ceremony if we're getting married." He'd laughed as he crossed to the door to leave, but I hadn't found it funny at all.

The mounted constables looked mighty fine in their velvet suits and feathery plumes. They gently kicked the sides of their mounts and started forward toward the judge's box. Shivers scurried along my body, knowing both Sally and Julio were watching me. Sandwiched between the two male apprentices, I led my cuadrilla into the bullring to a traditional Paso Doble. Although I knew every hole and crack in the painted red barrier fence surrounding the bullring, both it and the smooth golden sand seemed utterly transformed. I knew now what a newly minted Roman gladiator had felt when he made his first appearance in the Colosseum.

I scoured the faces of the people seated in the front two rows of the shady area. Seated in the middle of the first row, Sally wore a bright silken headscarf and pure white gloves. Julio sat on her left, looking sharp in a camel-colored jacket and matching fedora. When he caught my eye, he stood and waved, his smile as full as the sun overhead.

The most senior apprentice commenced his fight after the parade ended. Later, when my turn came, spectators began cheering and whistling, and then the band struck up dianas after I finished a series of perfect *veronica* passes. They understood that their Diosa Tejana intended to put on a show.

My bull was a looker, with shoulders and buttocks as white as Sally's gloves, a glowing white star on his pitch-black forehead, and four black socks that ended at his knees. His only physical defect was his right horn, slightly shorter than the left, though both were lethally sharp. As his name—El Torrente—suggested, he was a torrent of speed and raw power. He charged straight and kept his head higher than was normal after the picadors had worked him with their lances and my banderilleros had inserted the colorfully ribboned barbed sticks.

Aware I had the dreadful half-bull as my second opponent, I overlooked no opportunity to dazzle Julio and Sally with my muleta work with the first. I brought El Torrente, whom I now adored, closer and closer to my chest as I executed *pase de pecho*s to end a series of *naturals*. The smell of sweaty domination energized me. The horns were so close, women screamed. My jacket and pants were splashed with blood and bull saliva. Every time the bull passed by and bumped against my thighs, I got a whiff of iron from the fresh blood spurting from his shoulder.

I wanted the performance to go on, but I could see my beautiful El Torrente was tiring. I got permission from the judge to kill him. Removing my lavendar hat, I raised my hands high and slowly pivoted to the crowd to let them know I was dedicating my bull to them. Then I tossed my hat over my shoulder, as matadors do when not dedicating the kill to an individual. When I turned to retrieve it, to my horror, it had landed upside down, as if it were a goblet ready to accept my blood. Quickly, I stooped and retrieved it, raised my hands to the crowd once more, and then set it back on my head. I went to the barrier fence to exchange my fake aluminum sword for the brand-new sword Julio had given me.

Patricio held out my old sword, the one Maestro had gifted me.

"I told you I'm using my new sword today, Patricio."

His eyes darted past a journalist to where Maestro was standing, drinking a glass of water.

"I can't give it to you," he said, his face turning pale.

Maestro came up to him. "You will use the sword I gave you for all official corridas."

"Is this yet another rule?" I asked.

"It is."

"How come you didn't say so when you gave it to me?"

"Why do you question your Maestro?"

I thought about what Julio had told me, but bit my lip. I was still an apprentice. "Because these rules are mighty one-sided."

His mouth opened wider than a catfish's out of water, but he recovered quickly. "You kill using my sword." He glanced at the judge's stand. "Go kill the bull or they'll sound the trumpet and you'll get timed out."

I snatched Maestro's sword from Patricio and went out again to the bull. I checked the clock on top of the judge's box, its hands slightly blurry as my eyes watered with anger. There were still five minutes to go before I defaulted and got a warning. I had to square El Torrente in that time, getting him to place his front hoofs close enough together so the death-notch between his shoulder blades would be fully open. His head was also too high. I decided to do one more series of passes. He charged perfectly, but wheeled around much faster than I'd anticipated and charged again. I stumbled as I pivoted around to meet him. The crowd squeezed out a low groan. The band stopped playing. Children and women shrieked.

Before I grasped what was happening, the bull's head lowered and veered to the left. An intense sting, like a bee's sting, radiated from my upper thigh. The next moment, I experienced what I can only describe as vertigo and fell hard on my back. The bull's body thundered past me. I couldn't see him anymore. He snorted loudly and I knew at once he was turning again, in preparation to charge and finish me off.

Instead of feeling his horn penetrate my chest or rip my belly apart, hands seized my body and I was carried toward the barrier. I felt no pain. Isabella's face came into my mind. It was true what I'd told her at her father's *tienta*—the bull felt no pain when he was lanced and barbed, as adrenaline overwhelmed the sensory system, just as it did mine now.

I let my head loll back so I could see into the ring. Luís was caping my beloved El Torrente. Soon, he would die at another's hands. Someone who didn't love him.

Men, including some from another apprentice's cuadrilla, hustled me through the passageway. Newspaper reporters, the rancher and his foreman, and ring servants pressed their bodies tight against the wooden fence to give them space to carry me by. We turned right into a wide tunnel that I knew led to the gymnasium where I'd practiced. A thin thread of scarlet stained the cobblestones behind me. Halfway along, they turned sharply left into a corridor, passing the tiny chapel where earlier I'd prayed to the Virgin, and then we entered the cool infirmary.

Its partly bulged walls were constrcuted of exposed red brick, an ascending crack like a ten-step staircase running along one wall. Where the walls met the plaster ceiling, the bricks were furred with desiccated lime from centuries of water seepage. An operating light blazed over the metallic gurney, its gleaming coldness surpassed only by the glint of the scalpels, knives, and scissors neatly laid out on a cart at one side. The doctor, dressed in a spotless white coat, was already waiting.

The men laid me on the gurney and the reek of antiseptic made me nauseous. The doctor examined my wound, applied antiseptic, and began to wipe it with cotton wool.

"I need her pants off so I can get a better look at the wound," he said.

The men exchanged uncertain glances.

"No," I said. My voice sounded disembodied. "My bull's out there." I pushed the men away, sat up, and swung my legs over the edge of the gurney just as Maestro ran in. He came over to me.

"Are you badly hurt?" he asked, his eyes almost as wide as his jug ears.

"No one can finish El Torrente except me, Maestro."

"But señorita," the doctor said, "I must examine your injury. You could have torn an artery."

I laid my hand on Maestro's arm and climbed down off the gurney.

"Señor Guzmán, please tell her she is mad," the doctor said. "She must allow me to do my work."

Maestro held up a hand in front of the doctor's face. "Kathleen, are you sure?"

"Yes." I stared at him and he scrutinized me intently. "My bull's waiting for *me*."

Maestro nodded.

I walked quickly out of the infirmary. I still felt no pain; even the sting was gone. Camera bulbs flashed electric blue as I walked through the *callejón*. Patricio handed me Maestro's sword and my muleta when I reached the narrow entrance that led into the ring. I cursed myself for allowing my earlier anger to make me so careless.

A gasp rippled throughout the arena as I walked out. I saw the crooked line of my dried blood on the sand. I could see Julio and Sally, both standing and watching me. A silence arose as I walked toward the bull. Then an enormous cheer erupted from the audience as the people rose to their feet, applauding when they realized what I intended to do. Bouquets of flowers usually reserved for the end of the fight were tossed onto the tufted sand.

"¡*Viva La Diosa Tejana. Te amamos!*" they hollered, men, women, and children alike.

"Leave," I shouted at the substitute, the most senior apprentice, who'd squared my bull in preparation to kill him. "Go."

"Señorita, you're injured."

"*Leave.*"

I sighted the silver-dollar-sized *cruz* between the bull's shoulders along the length of my sword. My exhausted, beautiful bull looked at me. I shook the muleta to distract him from my body and ensure I had his full attention. When his amber eyes fixed on it, I sprinted toward him, praying I would make the sign of the cross perfectly, that I'd find the tiny entry hole and my sword would sink easily to the haft, that I wouldn't hit bone like I'd done in Reynosa and cause him to bleed from the mouth. He deserved to die with dignity and honor.

The sword entered with the same resistance as slicing into a potato and then its bent tip plunged downward. El Torrente tottered, took two steps, and then fell over on his side. I knelt to kiss him. My head spun. I felt very dizzy. Everything was cloudy. Then dark, dark gray. Then black.

30

MY VISION WAS SLIGHTLY BLURRY WHEN I AWOKE, A SIDE EFFECT OF the ether. Julio sat at my bedside. I looked around and realized I was still in the bullring's infirmary. The doctor came over, checked my vitals, and said I'd been lucky, if a goring can be considered lucky. The horn had made only one, three-inch gash, and no arteries had been pierced. It had penetrated my groin, entering a muscle between the great saphenous vein and femoral vein, and had perforated two minor veins that required seven stitches. I didn't feel any acute pain, just discomfort where the wound was located.

"Sally's gone back to New York," Julio said, after the doctor left. He interlocked his fingers in mine.

"Where's Maestro?" I asked.

"Gone. You're also free to leave after you . . ." His face reddened. "After you pee. They want to make sure everything's working. I told Fermin I'd stay and take you home."

"He agreed to leave?"

Julio grinned mischievously. "I insisted."

A twinge of white-hot pain shot across my lower belly when I laughed.

Twenty minutes later, I left the infirmary with the aid of crutches. When I arrived at Maestro's house, Carmen made a great fuss about making sure I was comfortable. Maestro was in my bedroom, installing a television I'd bought a month ago. He'd promised to connect the antenna but never gotten 'round to it. As I watched him pull the thick antenna wire down from the ceiling, I thought about how I probably had enough money to rent my own place, perhaps even buy one. But the truth was, I enjoyed Carmen and the children's company. Living alone, I figured, would be too lonely.

Three days later, though the aspirin I took hadn't fully extinguished the pain I'd begun experiencing since leaving the infirmary, I felt comfortable enough to take a short drive with Julio into the mountains. He insisted the mountain air would do me good. As usual, he was right. I felt almost giddy as we drove along the winding dirt roads, stopping now and again to take in the views of Los Pinos beneath us. I even dipped my toes in the icy water of a secluded pond surrounded by soaring pines, its mirrored water so clear in comparison to the black water at Mama's place.

That evening, Julio was leaving for Mexico City to meet up with his cuadrilla and prepare for a bullfight at the Plaza México on Sunday afternoon. If it had been any bullfighter other than Julio getting to fight there instead of me, I'd have been as jealous as the first runner-up at a beauty pageant.

"You need a vacation before returning to work," Julio said later, as we pulled up in front of Maestro's house.

I loved that he used the word "work." What he and I did was theater, but it was also work, honorable work that allowed matadors to purchase homes, raise families, and pay their taxes, just like company men. Because of the injury, I couldn't work for six weeks. Maestro had had to cancel two bullfights, one in Tlaxcala and another in Merida. He'd also postponed an invitation to appear on a television show in Los Angeles that, again ignoring our agreement that he tell me everything relating to my career, he'd known about for several weeks.

"I'll go see my mama after they remove the stitches," I said.

Julio took my hand and kissed my fingers. "I don't mean that sort of vacation. I want you to come to my parent's ranch. In three weeks, I have some free time. We can be together."

"Maestro insists that I have a chaperone when I travel in Mexico and Carmen has the children to look after."

"Fermin knows about us," he said.

I squeezed the door handle tightly.

"He's not stupid," he continued. "When you were gored, I was beside myself with panic. It was fairly obvious why, so I told him."

"What'd he say?"

"Nothing." Julio shrugged. "Anyway, there's no need for a chaperone, because my mother will be at home." He laughed as he blessed himself exaggeratedly. "She's stricter than a priest."

Later, after dinner, when I told Maestro that I planned to travel to Aguascalientes to stay with Julio's family, he leaped off the couch as if cattle-prodded.

"We need to talk about this."

"What do you need to talk about?"

Julio had only been gone two hours and already I missed him. I wanted to feel the weight of his arm around my shoulders. I wanted him to run his fingers through my hair. Nothing Maestro said could stop me from traveling to see him.

"When I took you on, you made a promise there'd be no distractions."

"You're not so good about promises, either. And Julio's not a distraction."

"What is he, then?"

"Fermin, can't you see our chiquita's in love with him?" Carmen broke in.

Her words jolted me and silenced Maestro. He wheeled around to Carmen. "This is none of your business. Stop encouraging her in this foolishness." He turned back to me. "*You* have a career to consider. There's no time for El Cabrito."

"Many matadors have girlfriends," I argued. "Didn't you meet Carmen when you were a matador?"

"Kathleen's just like you in this," said Carmen. "She's no fool. She won't destroy one thing by having another."

Maestro peered at her. "Leave us a minute," he said, a peculiar tremble now in his voice.

Carmen sighed, but rose. "I'll bring you some cold mango juice later, Kathleen." She nodded at Maestro. "You, too. It'll sweeten you up."

"You mustn't listen to my wife," he said once she'd gone. "She thinks only of silly love stories." His mouth twisted in disdain. "She reads them in those magazines of hers."

"I read them, too."

"It was a woman got Manolete killed. He was thinking about her rather than the bull when he made his mistake and was gored. Women have caused the deaths of many matadors."

I shuddered when I thought back to my own fight, but said, "I'm not Manolete."

"No, you've got a long way to go before you're as skilled as he was."

He sat on the sofa beside me. "There's no time in your life for him. El Cabrito's not good for you, Kathleen."

In the silence that followed, I could hear tinkling glasses as Carmen prepared the drinks in the kitchen. A fluttering started deep inside my chest. It grew stronger and stronger. My brain told me to keep quiet, to say nothing, not to upset him.

"I'm visiting Julio and his parents," I said, my voice quivering.

He sat back heavily on the couch. He gaped at me, but didn't speak.

"You will disobey me?" he asked finally, and stood. "You choose *him* over me?"

"I'm not disobeying you. You're my trainer; he's my boyfriend. There's no choice being made."

"I can finish you, just as I started you."

My career would end in this living room, where I'd once begged him to take me back as his pupil. I waited for the order to leave. The silence grew.

Maestro walked to the door leading to the hallway and back. "Go to El Cabrito. I don't give a shit," he said. He pointed a curled finger at me. "Just remember, the bulls are jealous. You'll pay a high price for this choice."

I couldn't form words to reply. All I knew was I'd ceded no ground and he hadn't quit on me.

Equally as vast as Hacienda El Ángel, which lay ten miles southwest, Julio's parent's estate stretched for fifteen square miles over green countryside and rolling hills. It incorporated three dusty villages, where their managers and farm laborers lived. With an entrance influenced by ancient Rome, the portico was a long row of Corinthian columns that ran the length of the main dwelling. The center plaza was a peristyle with climbing jasmine vines forming the perfumed roof of the stone gazebo at its center.

The smallest of the three original plazas had been converted into an indoor swimming pool, its chlorine-infused humidity overwhelming my senses temporarily when I entered. The walls and ceiling were a geometric riot of exotic Moorish patterns, created from cobalt, saffron, ivory, and emerald tiles. A coat of arms had been painted on the floor of the swimming pool.

When I asked Julio about it, he said it was his family's coat of arms.

"Mama's of Spanish nobility," he said. "I didn't want to tell you until you arrived, because I was afraid you'd be too intimidated to meet her and change your mind about coming."

His reasoning was half-right—I'd have been worried, but I still would've come.

"I'll inherit the title marquis when she dies," he added, "but, the Virgin willing, that won't be for a long, long time. She's only forty-six."

"What do I call her when we meet?" I asked.

"Juanna. She only uses her title when she goes back to Spain. She prefers people not know in Mexico. It creates a barrier that she feels takes too much energy to break down."

When I met her, his mother was the antithesis of what I'd pictured. I'd expected a dainty, regal woman, but she was big-boned with square shoulders, and her nose and mouth were too wide to consider pretty. Of course, I felt guilty even thinking that, because she was Julio's mother. She was not unattractive and her face definitely had character. Julio had her beautiful hazel eyes, but his strong jawline and chin came from his father.

The man in question sat across from me in the drawing room, in a thronelike chair done in a fabric covered with dragons and crowns.

"We're pleased to meet you," Oscar, his daddy, said as he approached. He had a slight limp and a strong handshake. "I've heard good things about you."

As Julio had said, his mother was informal and insisted I call her Juanna. She was surprised I didn't drink wine, but, given the occasion, I was eventually persuaded to try a glass of cava that she served specially for me. I'd never tried it before. Its pleasant coldness warmed the roof of my mouth and the bubbles burst like sherbet on my tongue. No one would ever need to persuade me to drink sparkling wine again.

"I'm intrigued by your choice of profession," Juanna said, when we were sitting alone in a cozy drawing room after dinner. "Your being a matador tells me things. It tells me you're strong and determined."

"I'm not a matador yet," I said, and took a sip of cava.

"You know what I mean." Her lighted cigarette was stuck into a long ebony holder. It was so sophisticated. I could see myself smoking like that, too. "My son's taken with you," she added, and the corners of her wide mouth licked upward in an unreadable smile. "There have been many girlfriends, but you are the only one he's invited to my home."

I didn't know if this was a question or remark, so kept my mouth shut.

"Do you also like him?" she asked.

I answered immediately. "Yes."

"He likes independent women," she continued, seeming satisfied with my response. "The women in this household are this way. His sister is a surgeon."

"He told me."

She hooked one foot behind the other and leaned forward in the chair. "I must alert you that Julio has serious family obligations." She paused. "If this relationship proceeds, would you give up the bullring to become a mother?"

Her frankness killed the buzz inside my head.

"One day, I'll marry and have children."

"Very good. He will also live in Spain for part of the year, too. He goes presently for two months every winter. Would that trouble you?"

Before I could answer the question, two ranchers she'd invited to dinner, middle-aged, bachelor brothers who were like uncles to Julio, came into the room with Julio and his father.

The ten days spent at the ranch passed quickly, and were exactly what I'd needed. Other than dressing up for dinner every evening, I lazed away the days. Juanna invited Don Raúl and his wife and a posse of Spanish expatriates, local writers, artists, and dignitaries, including the family priest and his visiting bishop, to our evening meals. But during the day, I read, swam, and practiced cape passes, with Julio acting as my bull. On the day before my return to Los Pinos, Julio asked if I felt strong enough to ride, because he wanted to show me something very special.

It had been three years since I'd been in the saddle and I was nervous, given my injury, but he promised the ride would be a gentle one through flat pastures. Experiencing a little discomfort when I cantered, due to the horse's choppy gait, we either galloped or walked. After twenty minutes, we rode up to a copse of linden and oak trees and dismounted.

Warning me not to speak loudly, he took my hand and we walked through the trees. Shafts of sunlight filtered down from the canopy, splattering the dry underbrush with shards of gold and highlighting pollen floating in the air. When we emerged from the copse, we climbed a tall grass bank and then he whispered to me to lie down on my belly. Beneath us, eight massive bulls grazed and drank from a sparkling pond, the sound of their relaxed chomping drifting up to us. Clouds of tiny black flies jiggled about their broad heads and kept their sleek tails busier than a moth in a wool mitten.

"You see the gray bull standing over by the water?" he said in a low voice, pointing to one of the largest bulls among the herd.

The animal was magnificent, about sixteen hundred pounds of muscle and armed with fierce horns nearly as big as a female elephant's tusks.

"My father's donating two bulls for a charity corrida in the new year, to benefit the family of a matador who was killed last year," Julio explained. "I'm going to fight that one."

This was Julio's special surprise. I felt cheated. He was a full-fledged matador and allowed to fight such massive beasts. As an apprentice, I was restricted to four-year-olds that never weighed more than eight hundred and fifty pounds. Jealousy rattled through my brain; I couldn't stop it.

But he wasn't finished. "I want you to pick one now. Do you like any of the black ones?"

"Why should I pick a bull?"

"Because I want you to fight in the corrida, too."

"Are you playing with me?"

"I'm not. The corrida's four months away. Make sure Fermin doesn't set up any corridas for you in the last week of February. You and I will fight *mano a mano*. The union rules don't apply to charity events. You can fight any size bull alongside a *matador de toros* if he's willing to appear with you." He laughed. "So, which do you pick?"

Ecstatically, I looked over the herd and selected a roan with black-tipped, ivory horns.

Julio kissed me. His warm tongue pushed against my lips and I opened my mouth to accept him. He began unbuttoning my blouse but, after the first button, I seized his hand.

"I want you," he said, his voice trembling.

"I . . . I can't."

"I'll be gentle. It won't be . . . " He didn't finish the sentence. He didn't have to—we both knew what he meant. He kissed my neck tenderly. "We do this together." He kissed me again on the lips. "Together . . . at your pace."

My heart knocked hard against my chest. What if I couldn't go through with it? I wanted to be fully with him, but part of me recoiled. His eyes locked on mine.

"I'm with you every step," he said, and took me in his arms until I stopped trembling. "It's only you and me. There's no one else here."

The smell of the sweet grass and the bulls' languid chomping and contented snorts filled me with peace. I wrapped my hands tightly around his neck and we kissed as he unbuttoned my blouse and began to unfasten my bra. But he was all thumbs and couldn't undo the clips. His clumsy inexperience calmed me and gave me courage. I helped him.

When he entered me, I first remembered the faceless monster driving inside me. But I closed my eyes tighter and forced the devil out of my mind. I was with Julio and he was my boyfriend and I was doing something I wanted to do with him, because I loved him and he loved me. He was gentle and loving and everything I wanted in this beautiful place that was exclusively ours and the bulls'.

Afterward, we lay on our backs, gazing up at the cloudless sky. A dragonfly zigzagged into view, its shiny cobalt head and gauzy wings exquisite as it regarded us before flying over the lip of the bank and down to the bulls.

"Kathleen?" Julio tickled my nose with a blade of grass.

"Hmm."

"Do you love me?"

"Very much."

He propped himself up on his right elbow. "Then will you marry me?"

I sat up quickly, reaching for my bra and blouse.

"I love you," he said. "We have very dangerous lives and things can happen. Why should we wait?"

"I can't, Julio."

"Why not?"

"I was engaged before and I shouldn't have agreed."

"Because you wanted to work with the bulls and he couldn't accept that. But you and I, we're the same kind of people. We respect our careers."

I thought about this for a moment. "Does your mother know you want to marry me?" I asked, finally.

"I think so."

"She says you'll spend part of every year in Spain."

"We have an estate there that produces wine. The cava you drank comes from there. But right now, I'm a matador, not a winemaker."

"You're allowed to fight bulls in Spain. I'm not."

"Maybe the rules will change. Anyway, I don't want to fight the bulls in Spain. And we'll want to have a child." He smiled impishly. "Or many children. These things can all be worked out in time. Right now, all that matters is that we love each other."

I rose quickly and started back to the horses.

31

THE HOUSE THAT FERMIN AND THE MOTHER OF HIS TWO illegitimate children stood in front of was narrow but deceptively deep, and lay one mile from the Guadalajara city center. Situated halfway down a long street lined with old cars parked on the sidewalk and stunted jacaranda trees, its façade had once been canary yellow, but, over the decades, had faded to cream where the sun struck it during the hottest hours of the day.

Fermin had asked a friend living in Guadalajara to look out for a suitable property and had wired him the money when it came on the market, its former owner having died suddenly and her relatives wanting to sell quickly.

"It's all mine?" Rosa asked, her surprise giving way to a wide smile.

"And the children's," he said. "There's a bedroom for each of you." He smiled like an eager puppy and added casually, "My friend will deliver a refrigerator on Wednesday . . . as well as a television."

Her dark eyes glowed with an appealing combination of joy and disbelief. She pressed her hand flat against the front door before inserting the key into the lock and opening it.

A desiccated mouse lay inside the tiled fireplace and the husks of black houseflies were scattered around spiderwebs in the corners of the room. Their footsteps sounded hollow as they walked across the living room and passed down a narrow hall leading to the kitchen. There was no furniture in the house and every room needed painting, but Fermin was content to leave such things to Rosa.

He'd earned a decent wage before Kathleen's arrival, but life had become extremely comfortable for Fermin since taking her on. Indeed, he planned to retire very soon from working as a banderillero in other matadors' cuadrillas so he could manage his protégée's career more closely. She required more supervision. Despite her great skill and a natural ability that was the equal of any man, Kathleen, at her core, was a woman and had to be managed as such.

One troubling wrinkle was her affair with El Cabrito. When Kathleen had refused to give him up, it had taken every ounce of self-control to step back. He'd have lost the battle if he'd given her an ultimatum to choose El Cabrito or him. Women were stupid about love, and though she was a talented bullfighter, she was still subject to this weakness.

The crowds attending the bullfights and the reporters loved Kathleen, their Diosa Tejana. She was special, so different from the aimless novelty of the female bullfighters with whom she'd once appeared in the ring. The American and Mexican audiences loved her so passionately that even the impresario from Plaza México had now heard of her and had contacted Fermin to arrange for her to perform in his arena.

It wasn't squabbles over the fee that hindered a contract with the plaza. Like all the other bullring impresarios, the owner understood that interest in Kathleen was translating into filled seats and Fermin, as he'd shrewdly predicted and despite her being still only an apprentice, was now able to command a sum just below the fee payable to a full *matador de toros*. She was a woman. She had Titian hair. She was beautiful. She was American. Once, these traits had been hindrances, but they now worked in their favor.

For Kathleen to be seen and celebrated as the equal of any full-fledged matador, it was important to Fermin that she fight a bull nearly as large as those fought by a matador. Knowing he could finagle this at the noon drawing of the bulls on the day of the fight, like he'd done before, Fermin demanded from the Plaza México impresario that one of the bulls to be shipped for Kathleen's corrida would be older than four years old. The bullring owner had no problem with this demand.

The remaining obstacle to finalizing a contract was that he and his public relations man were nervous about Fermin's other demand: that Kathleen enter the bullring on a pure white stallion. They understood that such a spectacular entrance would instantly link Kathleen to the infamous Conchita Cintrón in the audience's mind, but, as far as the impresario recalled, Ms. Cintrón had walked in her entrance parades into the bullring. She rode only during the fight. So why should the American woman be any different? Audiences were fickle. They could turn quickly on their heroes. The impresario feared that they would take this entrance as an attempt to surpass their retired heroine and then react with fury.

Fermin knew it was only a matter of time until he won the concession. So he refused to yield to the impresario, who didn't understand that Kathleen's performance in Plaza México was as much about Fermin as it was about her. This would be his shining moment, too. Everyone who mattered—the impresarios, the matadors, and their cuadrilla members, who gossiped like washerwomen and snickered behind his back—would see he'd returned to Plaza México with his protégée. All of Mexico's eyes would be on a fighter that he, Fermin, had trained, a woman whose skill and bravery he had molded. She was a woman and now their equal, and Fermin dominated everything she did in the bullring. He commanded how she controlled the bull. He commanded when she could kill. And when she did, she used her Maestro's sword.

"How did you buy this?" Rosa asked.

"What do you mean?"

"This house cost a lot of money. Does Carmen know about us now?" She sneezed twice. "This house is very dusty."

Carmen's name on Rosa's lips brought them perilously close to traversing a barrier he'd erected that would brook no trespass. "Don't ever mention my wife's name again," he said, wagging his index finger. "And never ask if she knows about you and the children. How I've paid for the house is not your concern. Your concern is that I provide for our children."

Her crestfallen face made him immediately sorry. He'd been too defensive, too harsh. She still had the ability to soften him and make him feel guilty after all these years.

"This house is not the end of my providing for Ernesto and his sister." He placed two fingers underneath her chin and raised it until her eyes caught his. "All you need to understand is that I earn very well now. I'll also pay for them to attend a private school in Guadalajara. It's important they attend a good school. The boy, especially."

She swatted at a fly circling her nose. "Thank you, Fermin. The other schools are so bad. Not all the children have books."

Her smile was a crescent moon. Laying his hands on her narrow shoulders, he kissed her cheek. She didn't pull away.

"¡Más rápido, mi matador!" she said, her voice thick with desire. "Ahhh. ¡Cogeme duro, matador! Aaah. Aaaah."

Fermin fucked Honoria even harder from behind. He smacked her taut buttocks as he penetrated her, the high-pitched cracks reverberating around the room in synchronization with the creaking bedsprings. Yet she screamed for more. Another of Fermin's women, she was insatiable. He was at full capacity and she wanted more.

"Who am I?" he asked breathlessly.

"Mi matador."

He slapped her buttocks even harder. "Who am I, *Carda*?"

"*Mi matador*. Aaaahhhh."

After he came, Fermin climbed out of bed and started dressing.

"Why don't you lie with me for a little while?" she asked. "It's been so long since we've seen each other. We could have supper together."

Fermin paused in putting on a sock and looked over at Honoria. To this woman, he was still a virile matador. They both ignored reality every time they met, and they fucked as if he were master of the bullring. Their relationship had never developed beyond pure sex. They'd been meeting since she was twenty-one, after he'd picked her up in an aficionado bar after a bullfight at the Tampico bullring. Now she looked older than her thirty-five years, despite a voluptuous body. Fifteen years of servicing sailors, matadors, and bull aficionados had given her deep wrinkles around the eyes. Her skin was also too pale. She still looked pretty enough; she had two or three years yet to get out and make something of her life. He hoped she'd been saving money over the years, but he didn't want to ask and get himself involved in another complicated situation.

Having supper with Honoria was not what he needed to do. He needed to get back to the hotel and repent to the Virgin for his sin. Fermin finished dressing and left.

When he got back to the hotel, the other banderilleros and the young matador who'd hired him for that afternoon's *fiesta brava* were in the lobby. They asked him to join them for dinner at a cantina frequented by bullfighters and aficionados, but Fermin quickly declined, pretending he had to pack, as he was setting out for Los Pinos first thing in the morning.

In his room, he took three long swigs of tequila from the bottle he kept in the drawer of his bedside table. Across from him, in the small leather case he'd propped open on a small table against the wall, the Virgin of Guadalupe stared accusingly at him. To her right was a picture of the Sacred Heart, streaks of blood dripping down his cheek. A photograph of Carmen was on the Virgin's left side.

"Why must I do this?" he said aloud in the silent room. He tossed the liquor bottle on the bed, went over to the open case, and knelt. "Forgive me, sweetest Virgin. Forgive me, Jesus. Forgive me, Carmen." He reached out and touched his wife's face.

It was this way every time Fermin returned from having sex with his women. Remorse was as essential a part of the ritual as the sex itself. It cast away his demons and brought his life back into balance.

"Dear Jesus, why do you not stop me?" Fermin said, and he kissed Jesus's blood-streaked face. "Why do you allow me to betray Carmen? You know what a good wife she is. Why, Jesus? Why?"

These questions were another necessary part of the ritual, though Fermin already knew the answer. He lusted for the rough sex he could not ask gentle Carmen for, for the rough sex an experienced, much older widow had taught him to crave when he was a young teenager living in Texas.

"Holy Virgin, don't let me desire this again. Give me strength to remain faithful to my wife from this moment. Oh, my God, I am heartily sorry for having offended thee . . ."

After he finished the Act of Contrition, Fermin blessed himself and put the smaller case into his suitcase. He climbed on the bed, unscrewed the top of the tequila bottle, and drank greedily.

When he arrived home, his son was playing ball in the street with a skinny neighborhood boy. Emilio's eyes bulged when he saw it was his father driving the blue Cadillac Fleetwood. He abandoned the game and raced into the house. Moments later, as Fermin was parking it on the street, Emilio came out with Carmen, Abril, and Kathleen. Fermin was disappointed Kathleen had returned from her vacation in

Aguascalientes. He'd wanted to take the family on a drive before he spoke to her about the Cadillac.

"Has something happened to our car?" Carmen asked, both hands resting on her hips in the way she did when she thought he'd done something stupid.

"I bought this one in Guadalajara," he said. His eyes darted from Carmen to Kathleen. "I wanted to surprise you."

"It's beautiful," Kathleen said, and pushed Carmen gently toward the car. "But it's your wife who should be pleasantly surprised, not me."

"I bought it for your use, Kathleen," he said. "We're tired of taking buses and trains to the bullfights. This way, you, Patricio, and I can travel in comfort."

Her face turned ashen. "This is an expensive car. Shouldn't we have discussed it first?"

"You can afford it."

"I should have had a say, Maestro." Kathleen's face pinked and tightened. She folded her arms. "You used my earnings to buy it."

No one spoke. The throaty coo of a pigeon shattered the prickly silence.

"Papi, I love the smell of our new car," said Abril, who'd climbed into the backseat.

"See Kathleen, Abril likes it," said Fermin, hoping to use his daughter's nine-year-old innocence to diffuse her anger.

"We could have looked for a car together in Los Pinos," Kathleen said.

"Remember, you're a foreigner," Fermin said. "You can't sign contracts in Mexico. I'd still have to represent you."

"Even to buy my own car?" Kathleen asked, stricken.

He smiled and nodded. "Anyway, car salesmen won't deal with a woman. They negotiate with men."

32

THE JOURNEY IN THE NEW CAR FROM LOS PINOS TO LOS ANGELES for my first TV appearance took just over fourteen hours. It was comfortable, except when the sun got particularly fierce as we drove through the wind-sculpted, russet landscape between Tucson and Phoenix. I'd read that Chrysler was about to introduce air-conditioning in one of their models and told Maestro, who shrugged it off, and insisted that the gulf between driving a Cadillac and that sort of car was like the gulf between caping a mature bull and a half-bull. That he could draw comparisons between cars and half-bulls only one month after the upsetting Los Pinos *sorteo* didn't make me feel better about his not having involved me in the purchase decision.

Coffee and snacks were provided for guests in the television studio's air-conditioned green room, including a refrigerated cabinet stocked with fresh, juicy peaches. I gorged myself on three of them before an assistant producer called my name and escorted me to a dressing room. She sat me before a large, round mirror studded with fourteen naked lightbulbs. Though interviewed often on the radio, I was unused to having makeup applied by gushy Valley girls eager to find out what foods from home I missed—they were shocked when I said I loved eating rice and beans every day and didn't only eat avocados in salads—and if I had ever dated a Mexican.

I was surprised by how small the studio was in comparison to what I'd always imagined when watching the news anchors behind their desks on television, and I marveled at the camera operators negotiating the bulky cameras around chairs and thick electric leads snaking over the white-tiled floor. Despite the brisk air-conditioning, it soon became very hot in my Andalusian suit. The producer had asked me to wear it, and my face sweated under the layer of pancake makeup.

The starter questions from the genial, middle-aged host about my decision to fight bulls were easy, mostly because I was used to responding to them by now. I also got the usual question about animal cruelty and gave my standard response that most people enjoyed steaks and the animals providing them were butchered cruelly in slaughterhouses.

"And you, Mr. Guzmán," the host said, turning to Maestro, who sat next to me. "How did you have the good fortune to fall in with such a pretty young gal?" The interviewer chuckled and glanced at the camera.

"Good fortune had nothing to do with it," Maestro said. "I was a top matador and chose to retire."

"Ah," the host said.

"After successfully ending that part of my career, I was looking out for someone to mold." Maestro leaned forward in his seat and stared at the camera as easily as a movie star. "The idea of molding a woman to fight as well as the best matadors challenged me. True, Kathleen was rough and immature, but I saw she had a natural ability and decided to take her on."

"Was her small size a problem?"

"It concerned me a little at the beginning."

"Did she learn fast?"

Maestro's dark eyes shot to me. "There were a few hiccups."

"What kind of hiccups?"

"She had to overcome an early fear of facing a bull. She froze the first time and I had to save her." He laughed. "But I will take her to the very top of the business in a short while."

"How do you mean, sir?"

"In three months, I've contracted for her to appear in the Plaza México, where only the greatest matadors perform."

I nearly slid off my chair. "You have?"

"You didn't know, Kathleen?" the interviewer asked, as the huge camera rolled toward me.

"I wanted to surprise my protégée with the news on your show," said Maestro, grinning like a possum eating peach seeds. He leaned toward the camera again. "Though she's only an apprentice, I've arranged this fight and hope you Americans will travel there to see her. I've made her the equal of any male matador alive today and she'll demonstrate that in the great plaza."

Everything Maestro had said was true and I was delighted with the news. But I didn't like that he'd highlighted my initial fear of the bulls. His invitation to the viewers to come to the plaza had also been as self-serving as an invite from the devil to take a tour of hell. I looked at Maestro, bathed in the studio lights. Even behind the makeup, his face glowed with arrogance and self-importance.

After the interview ended, as we drove along Sunset Boulevard on our way to the bus station downtown, I mulled over the interview, trying to decide if I should let go of what he'd said or tell him I was annoyed.

Maestro was in good spirits, the show's producer having agreed to his request to air the interview before my bullfight in Tijuana in two weeks' time. "Would you like to eat?" he asked.

"I'll grab a sandwich at the station."

My catching a bus to Monterey had caused a rift between us. Maestro had to return to Mexico for a bullfight and had wanted me to hire a chaperone to accompany me, but I'd refused, based on our prior understanding.

He pulled to a stop just outside the busy Greyhound terminal, climbed out of the car, and opened the door for me. "I hope you and Sally enjoy that pretend bullfight you're going to see," he said, his tone reflecting the contempt with which he viewed the bloodless corrida I planned to see, the only kind legally permitted in the United States.

I'd also lied to him about meeting Sally there. In fact, I was meeting Julio, who was participating in the corrida.

I merely hummed in response.

"What's wrong with you?" he asked. "You've been moody the whole way here."

"I didn't appreciate your saying in the interview that I was scared of the bulls."

He laughed.

"It didn't need sharing," I said. A bus honked before emerging from the terminal and signaling to merge into the traffic. I decided to go for it. "Haven't you ever been afraid of the bulls?"

He hesitated, then slammed the door shut.

"Have you?"

"Never." His shoulder bumped against mine as he passed by to wrench the trunk open. "Not one time have I been afraid."

His answer was certainly definite. "You might as well know I'm appearing with Julio in a charity corrida after the new year," I said, not satisfied I'd put him in his place. "So don't go arranging any contracts for the last week of February."

"We have rules." He set the suitcase down hard on the sidewalk. His face was apple red. "You need my consent for charity events."

"It's a *mano a mano* with Julio and I'm doing it," I said, as calmly as I could. I smiled so wide, the sides of my face started aching.

His high color retreated and he looked away to the terminal. His chest slowly expanded and contracted twice before he turned back to me.

"It seems you're serious about El Cabrito," he said.

"What if I am?"

He shrugged. "I'm pleased you're happy." A slow smile formed. "Your mama must be pleased."

"They're such docile little things, aren't they?"

Standing at the pens with Julio watching the bulls, I peered over my shoulder to see a white-haired woman approaching. She was expensively dressed and wore black horn-rimmed glasses, which, together with deep brackets around her thin mouth, made her look very severe. She introduced herself as Nancy, the wife of a film executive, and informed us that she'd been dispatched from Los Angeles by the Humane Society to ensure the animals weren't mistreated.

"It's kinda a shame what they do to these poor animals at these"—her nose furrowed like she'd stepped in manure—"at these festivals." She sighed. "I know it's bloodless, but these precious babies are still scared as heck."

Julio nudged me in the ribs and I nearly burst out laughing. Fighting bulls, especially the two fifteen-hundred-pound black ones inside the pen, were neither docile nor little. Earlier, I'd watched Julio execute passes with the muleta, which he'd done as skillfully as in a regular bullfight. When it had been time to kill the bull, he'd sighted with a scarlet rose instead of a sword and then placed it on the exact spot between the bull's shoulders where a sword would have penetrated.

"Mommy knows you're terrified, little ones." Nancy smiled at one of the bulls as he approached, attracted by her white-gloved hand. She held her hand out, beckoning him to come closer like one would a tame horse in a pasture. "Mommy feels the same way you do, sweetie. I don't like nasty matadors, either."

Julio nudged me again and this time I giggled, which I quickly disguised by pretending to sneeze.

"I get hay fever in these nasty sheds, too," she said to me, sympathetic. "But somebody's gotta make sure these people obey the law."

Placing her left foot on the lowest rung of the fence, she hopped up as the bull approached. Nancy and the bull regarded each other. A gold bracelet over her glove tinkled as she extended her hand toward the bull's forehead.

"I ask you, how could anybody wanna mistreat such a cute face?" The bull's dark chocolate eye focused on her hand.

"Take your hand away," Julio said.

Just as she was easing it back, the bull's head turned quickly and his horn rammed into the fence where her hand had been. Nancy shrieked and fell backward into the dirt. After Julio helped her to her feet, she stammered her thanks and walked quickly away.

"Serves her right," said Julio, as we started back to the hotel two blocks from the exhibition hall. He slung his arm around my waist. "People like her think they know better than us."

When I arrived at the hotel, I went in first and requested my room key. A few minutes later, Julio came in and fetched his. While he would sleep over in my room, I felt it very important that we keep up appearances.

My room was painted brilliant white and the bedcover and sheets were soft gray. A French door opened out onto a beach with sand as pale gold as the sand at the Los Pinos bullring. The crisp aroma of the sea wafted inside on a gentle breeze. Sleek gulls scolded one another as they wheeled high in the air, their angular, snow-white wings as wide as a buzzard's.

We stripped and lay down on the double bed. It didn't feel strange, though it was only my second time nude in his presence. We made slow, tender love. A bond had formed between us since our time in the bull meadow and Julio made me feel very safe. He was my safe place, my *querencia*.

"So, what's your answer?" he asked, as I snuggled up to him afterward.

I exhaled gently. I'd wanted him to ask this question, was in fact afraid he might have changed his mind since he'd first asked and I walked away. Before I'd left his home in Aguascalientes, I'd told Julio I needed time.

I looked over at him. "Does anybody ever refuse El Cabrito?"

His expression turned serious. "Sure, people refuse El Cabrito. But the question is, are you going to refuse Julio?"

I rolled on top of him. "I want to marry you."

I'd been home from California only two days and planned to do some cape work with Maestro in the courtyard, when Mama called saying she needed me to come home quickly.

"I had an accident," she said.

"What happened?"

"I smashed the car into a tree." She sniffed.

"Were you hurt?"

"Oh, no need to worry." She sniffed again. "I'm not planning to die from it."

The last time I'd seen her, she'd been rude to Julio and I'd been angry, but time had passed and there was no point holding grudges. Still, I couldn't up and leave whenever she called. "Mama, I'm just back from a trip and Maestro won't let me."

"I'm your mother." She let out a couple of strangled sobs. "It was so scary."

"Maybe he'll let me come see you next week, if I work hard."

"Please ask Fermin . . . your Maestro, whatever you call him."

After we hung up, I went to see Maestro, who was pruning bushes in the courtyard. He was horrified when I told him about the accident.

"Of course, you can go and see your mother," he said after I asked if I could visit her for a few days. "There will still be two weeks to practice for the corrida in Tijuana when you get back. Take a cape in case you can squeeze in some practice while you're there."

Feeling guilty about my churlish behavior at the bus terminal, as well as the lie I'd told him, I gave him a hug as I thanked him.

"Do you remember I said I'd be like a father to you?" he asked. "That I would always look after you like your own father did?"

I nodded.

"That's what I'm doing now." He smiled. "Your mother needs you and you must be with her."

When I arrived at her home five hours later, Mama was in the kitchen, baking a cake. She had a bandage around her left ankle and limped across the floor to hug me.

"It's my fault," she said. "It was raining so hard, I just didn't see the fallen tree on the road." She pulled out a chair from under the table. "Sit." She groaned and held out her wrist for me to inspect. "My wrist hurts, too. Not that you'd think it, mind you. There's no bruise, thankfully."

She excused herself and hobbled off to her bedroom to take some aspirin.

When the kitchen door next opened, George came in, accompanied by my ex-fiancé. The place started revolving and a dozen tuning forks rang in my ears.

"Hello, Kathleen," Charles said. "What the heck are you doing here?"

Mama must have heard his voice, because she padded back into the kitchen mighty fast. This time, she had the aid of a walking cane that I badly wanted to use on her.

Charles looked shocked to the exact degree that Mama looked guilty. George glanced at me sheepishly and left under the pretext that he needed to take the dog outside.

Charles, affecting casualness, broke the silence. "How's my favorite Mexican wanderer?" he asked, though I had no doubt his brain was spinning like mine.

Even though we hadn't spoken in two years, I remembered every nuance in his voice. He'd grown thick around the waist, due, I was sure, to Louisiana gumbo and fried catfish.

"I'm surprised to see you, too," I said, and kissed him on the cheek.

"I met Charles's mother in town and she told me he was coming home this week," Mama said in a tremulous voice. "You're like family to us, Charles, despite you two not seeing each other anymore."

I wanted to laugh and scream all at once.

"Would you go outside and tell George we'll have lunch in town?" I said to Charles.

After he left, I turned to face Mama. "What the hell were you thinking?"

"Don't be angry," she said, her eyes moistening as she sat at the table. "That Mexican you brought here. There's something going on between you, I just know it."

"You're insane, Mama."

She reached out a hand for me to take, but I ignored her. "You met Julio months ago. Why are you thinking about this now?"

George's dog barked outside.

"It's been working on me a while now," she said. "It all came to a head when I had the accident."

"Did Maestro call you?"

"Why would he call me?" She looked at me almost fiercely now. If she was lying, she was darned good.

I took a deep breath and squared my shoulders. "You might as well know," I said slowly, "I'm engaged to Julio."

She rose and came over to me, leaning her cane against the leg of the table. "You can't. It's a mistake."

"You done stopped preaching and gone to interfering, Mama."

She gasped. "Don't think badly of me because I want to protect you. Don't marry that man. I don't want you making a mistake like I did."

The outside door creaked open. Charles and George came in, followed by the dog, panting heavily, as Mama ran sobbing from the kitchen.

Charles and I stood at the tank, he staring at the black water and I looking directly across at the woods where Julio had kissed me for the first time.

"I'm sorry Mama did this to you," I said. "She meant well, but it wasn't right."

"If I'm honest, I was hoping something might happen and we'd meet again," he said. "I think about you in Mexico, you know? I wonder what you're doing, where you're fighting." He laughed. "We don't get much news about bullfighting in Louisiana."

A purple finch tweeted shrilly and then took flight, rising off the crumbling jetty and moving away until it became a black speck against the vast blue sky.

"I've had girlfriends, but..." He waited until I caught his eye. I felt nothing. When Julio looked at me this way, I was ensnared. "I've never met anyone like you, Kathleen."

"Charles, don't do this."

"I admire what you've done, even if I've never agreed with it." He laid his hand tenuously on my forearm. I could feel him trembling. It was strange to see he was nervous to touch me now. "Don't you ever think about me . . . what I'm doing . . . if I'm happy?"

"Let's not talk about this anymore."

"You've proven you can fight bulls." He gripped my wrist firmly. "Why don't you settle down with me now?"

It felt like a spear had pierced my chest. I realized that he didn't know yet.

"I'm engaged to Julio," I said, as gently as I could. "He's a matador I met in Mexico."

His eyes fixed on his hand curled around my wrist for what seemed an eternity. Finally, he took his hand off and looked away, his chin thrust out, but quivering.

He laughed scornfully. "Do you know how many women chase after these men? He'll be unfaithful."

"He's *not* like that."

"What happens when his career's over and the public's no longer interested in him? What happens if a bull kills him? You'll end up in a back street in some dirty village. Your kids will have nothing."

Every muscle in my body stiffened. It would be easy to destroy his arguments, but what purpose would it serve, other than to pile more hurt on a man who still loved me?

"I need to go now," I said, and held out my hand. "Goodbye, Charles."

Mama looked at me grimly when I went into her bedroom. The week after Daddy was buried, she'd tossed out their bedroom furniture and bought a new blond-wood headboard and matching nightstands that she'd had shipped from Neiman Marcus in Dallas. She still had the set and I still resented how quickly she'd made a big change like that.

"I need to say something, Kathleen." Her voice was raspy as a pond toad's croak. "You're only twenty-one. That's too young to marry. You've still got lots of things to do with those bulls of yours."

I stopped dead and stared at her. "If I agreed to marry Charles right now, you'd have me in a wedding dress before I could even brush my teeth."

"Charles is a decent American. Mexican men are different. He'll promise you the sun and hand you a corn tortilla."

"Julio's Spanish."

"Is there any difference?"

The room smelled of the oversweet rose perfume she liked and made me slightly nauseated.

"Mama, I don't want us to stop talking like we've done in the past," I said, barely containing my frustration. Life's too short for that."

"I don't want it, either."

A silence followed, which ended with the springs creaking as Mama slid her legs over the edge of the bed and sat up. She regarded me real strange, her eyes blazing.

"You get that independent streak from your father."

"You're always telling me that."

"I've been jealous of you, Kathleen."

"Jealous of *me?*"

"You wanted to fight bulls and didn't allow anything to stop you. Me, I caved into your daddy's demand." She nibbled her lower lip. "At the tank that day, you asked me if I'd wanted to continue working at the aircraft factory when the men came back from the war, and I said I didn't. I lied. I enjoyed doing my part to make those airplanes fly." She looked up at the ceiling as if it were the sky. "I would've liked to stay on."

Mama passed her hand over the tufted bedspread. Her hands were small and slender, and she'd painted her manicured nails in an opalescent pink. Those beautiful hands had once been as tough as mine were now.

"The factory boss wouldn't rehire us," she said. "The men needed work and we were tossed into the trash. Oh, the owner thanked us for our service, very gentlemanly. But we were tossed away like wallered out tires."

Picking up bits of chenille fluff, she rolled them into a ball and pitched it on the floor. "Some of the women were glad. They wanted to return to baking and laundering. Your father demanded I stop working altogether. He said I'd done my bit for the country and he didn't want his wife doing men's work anymore."

"Daddy was a man of his time. He wanted to look after you."

"Look after me?" Her laugh was a bark. She rose and went over to the window. "It's time you know the truth."

I knew everything about my father. I remembered him vividly. There was nothing else to know.

Mama wiped her brow with the back of her hand. "When we were at the pond that day, you asked why I never talked about your daddy after he died."

A vein in her neck pulsed, something that happened when bad news was coming. I recalled her queer comment that afternoon, how she couldn't bring him back from the dead for me, even if she'd wanted to. She'd also said earlier today that she didn't want me making the same mistake by marrying Julio that she'd made in marrying Daddy.

"I told you I was grieving for him," Mama continued. "That was another lie."

She walked over to me quickly and took my hand. It felt strange to feel the warmth of her touch. The last time we'd touched like this had been the day we visited Daddy's grave at the cemetery, when she'd linked arms with me.

"You need to know I was very angry at him," she said. "I was furious. It took me two years to come to terms with what he'd done." She squeezed my fingers. "Your daddy was having an affair when he died. It had been going on for six months. The tramp worked in the oil company's secretarial pool and I found out about it a week before the accident."

"Mama, stop." Blood colder than river water rushed from my heart to my face. As I tugged my hand to free it, she gripped more tightly. Her gaze penetrated mine.

"You want me to stop with the bulls and give up Julio," I said. "I get that. But lying like—"

"It's all true, Kathleen. Your daddy never looked after me like he promised he would. But what could I do? I couldn't leave him because I had you to think about. I was trapped."

I tore my hand free and pressed both of them over my ears.

"It wasn't your daddy's first affair," she continued. "He had one shortly after you were born."

Her mouth wouldn't stop.

"I even blamed myself for his straying. I was a bad wife. Working outside our home had made me too independent, too much like a man. Pregnancy isn't beautiful. My body was flabby. I had permanent stretch marks. I didn't want to make love when he wanted to." She grabbed both my hands and pried them off my ears. "Don't think I didn't love you. I was young and upset and very angry when he died. I loved your father and he'd betrayed me. And then he was dead. I had to grieve for my marriage and grieve for him at the same time. I didn't know what to do, so I buried his memory."

I regarded the blond wood footboard. "You're *lying*. You lied about your injury to get me here and you're lying about Daddy." I wrenched my hands from her grip. "I *hate* you."

I ran out of the room and ascended the stairs two at a time to my bedroom. Flinging open the doors of the armoire, I began stripping blouses off their hangers and tossing them into my suitcase.

33

THE PRODUCER OF THE TELEVISION SHOW I'D DONE IN LOS Angeles kept his word to Maestro and the interview aired a week before my performance in Tijuana. As a result, every seat in the bullring was filled. I'd never seen so many American faces in the crowd.

As I walked toward the judge's box in my lavender Cordoban hat and Daddy's silver horse cufflinks, I felt my father's presence in a way I'd never felt before any other bullfight. He was everywhere, beside me as I walked across the sand, inside the judge's box, and watching from the first row of seats in the shady area. I would deliver a brilliant performance and it would be for him only.

"I knew this day would come, Kathleen," Maestro said, as we walked around the bullring after my second fight, after which I'd been awarded two ears. He bent down to pick up a gentleman's fedora, which he then passed to me to kiss and toss back to its delirious owner. "You and I have single-handedly woken the Americans to the art of bullfighting." He laughed. "They'll go home and demand changes to their laws to allow real bullfights."

Maestro didn't understand Americans like he thought he did. It would take more than a woman like me to change the country's psyche. But I let him have his moment.

From Tijuana in Baja California, we traveled inland during the cool of the evening to our next *fiesta brava* in Nogales, Senora. A real frogwash of a rain and very strong wind, the kind that could lift even a soaked muleta and expose a matador's body to the bull, began on the day before the bullfight and didn't let up. The governor of the state of Senora canceled the corrida at ten on Sunday morning. An aide came to my hotel to invite me to dinner that evening with the governor and I accepted. But when Maestro learned the invite was extended only to me, he called him back and declined, saying we had a long trip ahead of us for our next appearance in Monterrey, Nuevo León. Though furious he'd snatched such an honor from me, I kept my cool. We were on tour and I didn't want any tension between Maestro and me to adversely affect the performance of the other members of my cuadrilla. That would only expose us all to danger in the ring. I was a union professional now and bore all the attendant responsibilities.

In Monterrey, at around eight on Sunday evening, someone knocked lightly on my door. An hour earlier, I'd dined with Maestro and two other members of my team. We'd been in good spirits, as the bullfight that afternoon had gone especially well.

Patricio stood in the hallway. "I'm sorry to disturb you."

I invited him inside. Taking a seat near the window, he laid his hat on one knee and started pinching the skin under his lower lip.

"How do you like the new car?" he asked.

I'd had the Cadillac nearly two months and wondered why he was asking now. "You already know I like it."

His right leg jiggled. "It's a very expensive car, yes?"

It clearly wasn't the car that was on his mind. "What are you trying to say, Patricio?"

"I hate to speak about the business side with you, but some of the men are very unhappy." Patricio's hat slipped off his knee as he leaned toward me. "Fermin doesn't treat them right."

He explained that, instead of paying the men the union rate as required now that I was a member, Maestro paid them fifteen percent less and demanded they sign a receipt stating they'd been paid the legal amount. I recalled the day I'd walked into the restaurant and come across Maestro paying the cuadrilla members, how he'd had a disorganized sheaf of pages before him, and how he'd demanded I leave the room.

"Are you sure?" I asked.

"I am."

"Why haven't they said something to me before?"

"This kind of thing happens in the business. Fermin warned them they'd never work in a bullring again if they complained to you. He knows a lot of people." Patricio picked up his hat. "But the Cadillac has upset them. They're saying they own part of it. They're also saying you must know what Fermin's doing."

"I don't." I crossed my heart. "Please believe me."

"I believe you. He doesn't even allow you to drive the car."

Though men always drove in Mexico, I was nevertheless shocked that Patricio knew about the prohibition. Maestro had obviously told him. Moreover, it was one thing to be angry at Maestro for canceling the governor's invitation, but this was another, graver matter. I would not tolerate him cheating my men, corrida tour or no.

Patricio took me to Montes, the most religious of my team. While he had no tangible evidence, because Maestro paid his wages in cash, I saw he was short after he counted out his wages in my presence. Moreover, because he'd incurred a debt with a loan shark that he needed urgently to repay, I could tell by his agitation he was speaking the truth. After assuring him I had known nothing of the error, I promised I'd see both he and the other picador were paid correctly for that afternoon's corrida—and all the other fights since I'd joined the union.

An adolescent iguana lay outside Maestro's bedroom door, but it scuttled off when I approached. I knocked, but Maestro wasn't there, despite his having announced he was going directly to his room after our return from the restaurant. I tried three more times throughout the evening.

At ten o'clock, just as I was about to leave his door after a fourth attempt, I heard movement inside.

"Maestro, I need to see you," I called.

"Go away."

I knocked louder.

Moments later, the door opened halfway. His eyes were red, as if he had an allergy. I pushed the door open sharply and walked inside, and he looked at me with eyes as big as a horse's. I'd never been in his room, never mind marching into it without an invitation.

The room was larger than mine and had two pictures of the Sierra Madre mountains. A bottle of tequila lay on his double bed. A small case like mine, containing a picture of the Virgin, the Sacred Heart, and his wife, was open and propped up on the vanity.

"What the hell do you want?" he said, putting the bottle of alcohol inside the drawer of his nightstand.

His rudeness killed the little anxiety I felt about confronting him. "Patricio told me you've been making mistakes with the men's wages."

Maestro's mouth fell open, but quickly shut again. "I always pay them correctly. If that's all—"

"They're accusing you of shortchanging them. Is that true?"

"Give me names. I'm going to fire them."

I was about to add I knew he'd gotten the men to sign false receipts but thought better of it. I didn't want the situation to spin out of control. "One of the picadors counted out his money in front of me and it's not right," I told him. "Was it a mistake?"

He smirked. "Not a mistake—but not a crime, either. This happens all the time in bullfighting circles, Kathleen. The men demand a certain wage knowing they're not going to get it." He shrugged.

"Why is it done this way?"

"You don't need to worry about it. I take care of these things, remember?"

While I understood he was looking out for my interests, this was crooked as a barrel of snakes. The men had families to support. "This isn't how I was raised, Maestro," I said, and laid my hands on my hips. "This might be how business gets done in Mexico, but I want things done the way they're done in Texas. You'll pay the men what they're due."

"But you—"

"I want my cuadrilla paid the union rate. You go right back to the day I was accepted and correct it."

He glowered at me, his jug ears red as beets. Going to the door, he wrenched it open and stood like a prison guard.

"Something else," I said, as I was about to step out into the hallway. "From now on, you and I meet once a month and go through the contracts and financial records so I can see everything I've earned and what the expenses are. And you will not cancel invitations to dinner without getting my consent."

I put out my hand and jiggled my fingers.

He regarded my hand for a moment and then looked at me. "What do you want?"

"The keys to *my* Cadillac. I'm driving home tomorrow."

Motherhood had always been something I wanted in the future. But my definition of the future was after I'd ended a successful bullfighting career, was married two years, and my husband and I were living on a ranch and breeding quality fighting bulls. I was now eight days late. My cycle was exactly thirty days, had been that way for years, and the fact that I might be pregnant terrified me.

No impresario would book me for corridas. I would never be regarded as the equal of Conchita Cintrón, who'd conquered the bullring and then retired to marry and become a mother. I would be viewed as a failure, a woman who'd had the nerve to break into and dominate exclusively male terrain, but, in the end, had given ground, subordinated by the laws of nature. If I was pregnant, the best I could hope for now was inclusion as a footnote in the history of Mexican bullfighting, a talented American woman who might have made it in a man's world had she not done what women are born to do. Even worse, if I didn't marry before I started showing, the public who'd previously loved me would regard me as nothing but a common whore.

Crippled by indecision, I called Sally two days later. First, I reminded her I was engaged, so she wouldn't think as badly about me getting pregnant. My strategy didn't work. There was dead air.

"I know you're disappointed in me," I said.

"Don't even think that," she said. "I'm not a virgin anymore, either." She laughed. "Mind you, I live in the decadent Big Apple."

I took a deep breath, unsure how to respond.

"Didn't you use protection?" she asked.

"Julio and I didn't talk about . . . I couldn't ask him that."

"You need to tell him immediately," she said. "Get married. It's the only way."

When I called Julio at his hotel in Saltillo, there was such silence after I told him, I thought we'd been disconnected. Then he asked if I was sure.

"I just don't know—but I think so, yes."

"I'll stand by you," he said.

"I'm scared."

"It's going to work out, *mi amor.*" He paused, then added, "Now that the shock's passed, I really hope you are pregnant."

"Why do you say that?"

"We'll be the best parents in the world."

"I'm not ready to be a mother, Julio. There's so much I want to do before—"

"A part of us is growing inside you. Doesn't that feel right to you?"

That stopped me for a moment. I loved Julio and the idea of sharing an experience so sacred with him was special. I just didn't feel ready. Getting pregnant needed much discussion, didn't it? Isn't that what couples did?

"Even if we wanted a baby, we have no idea how to look after one. We're both too young."

He laughed. "If we can both handle a bull, we can handle a baby. Do you want a girl or a boy?"

I hadn't thought about the baby's sex. Whatever was maybe growing inside me was still an "it" to me, in the same way a bull was an "it'" to Maestro.

"If it's a boy, I'll teach him to be a great matador," Julio said.

His remark stung. "Would you not do the same if it's a girl?"

"Of course, *mi amor*." He chuckled. "But then you'll want to teach her, and I'll be left out in the cold."

There was little to do but accept I was going to have a baby. I insisted upon a small wedding and he agreed, though he told me his mother would wish to have several close relatives attend from Spain. I agreed to marry in his family's chapel at the hacienda, as was his family's tradition. Sally would be my bridesmaid and Julio planned to ask his cousin in Los Pinos to be his best man. As we talked, I couldn't ignore the stirring of excitement in my belly.

When we discussed possible wedding dates, it became clear nothing would happen until after my appearance at Plaza México at the end of January, because our contracts until then required us to be in different parts of the country. We settled on the first Saturday after my Mexico City appearance—I wouldn't yet be showing—and after the wedding, I'd live at the hacienda with his mother and father until our baby was born.

"I'll return to bullfighting soon after that and nobody will know anything," I said. "I'll still be able to become a full matador."

"Do you really want to become a *matador de toros* now?" he asked. "Is it so important?"

"Are you saying you won't keep your promise? Because that's not negotiable, Julio."

"Having a baby changes a woman. If you decide to retire and stay at home, that would be fine with me. I make enough money."

His argument sounded far too similar to Charles's for my liking.

"Don't you want me to have my dream?" I asked.

He didn't answer.

My body stiffened. I wished I could be in his hotel room and see his face, have this argument in person. "Don't you, Julio?"

"I want our baby to have a good mother." He sighed. "I want the child to have the best parents."

"So do I."

"Then if you say you can be a matador and a good mother, I'll sponsor your *alternativa*," he said. "I'll be the one to hand you the sword to take your first bull as a new-minted *matador de toros*."

My heart burst with happiness. I was certain he could hear it.

34

ON OUR RETURN FROM MONTERREY, MAESTRO PAID ALL THE members of my cuadrilla what they were owed and gave me a full accounting of my earnings and expenses. The books seemed in order (I'd never envisioned having so much money in a business account in my name) and I was happy to put the unpleasant business behind us.

Any regrets he had about his shoddy treatment of the men didn't translate into treating me more leniently during our practice sessions at the Los Pinos ring. As the date for my appearance in the Plaza México drew ever closer, he became obsessed with every detail. I hadn't told him I thought I was pregnant, figuring it wouldn't yet interfere with my training or appearances.

He insisted I add an extra half-hour to my workouts in the gymnasium—ironic, considering I'd initiated the workouts in the first place. I could never satisfy his need for perfection in my cape passes, which were perfect in my judgment. Something was always wrong: a wrist flicked too slowly or too sharply, an unacceptable bend of the arm resulted in a lack of artistry. My muleta work fared no better. I didn't arch my back elegantly enough or I moved my feet when I shouldn't have. Once, he even accused me of dancing. No matador wanted to hear that kind of insult, and I was already thinking of myself as a full-fledged matador. When I practiced with the sword and missed the silver dollar–sized *cruz* on the mechanical bull's cork shoulders, he went berserk, his outburst unnerving me. I missed again. And then again.

"You will do everything I say in Plaza México," he said one afternoon. "It will be flawless."

I nodded.

"You'll dominate the bull in the exact way I say."

"Aha."

"And you'll kill it precisely when I tell you it's time."

"Yeah, yeah."

"Are you listening?"

"You're my confidential adviser, aren't you?"

"I've made you into what you are."

"I know, Maestro." I laughed. "If I make mistakes, my shame is your shame. I get it."

"Are you making fun of me?" He wagged his finger in my face. "This is not funny. Anything less than perfect and you will shame me. When you walk across the sands of the Plaza México, every eye will be on *me* as much as you."

The public didn't care what a matador's manager or trainer said or did. The glory and trophies went only to the bullfighter. Of course, I didn't dare say this aloud. As my confidential adviser during a performance, I listened to Maestro's suggestions all the time. But every matador did this with their advisor. Maestro and my decisions rarely diverged, now that I was experienced, and if he thought this was because I obeyed his every command, then that was fine by me. Ultimately, I was the matador and all the decisions during the performance were mine to make. It would be no different at the Plaza México.

Though situated on the warm waters of the Gulf of Mexico and close to the Pacific Ocean, Nuevo Laredo had a semi-arid climate, because the Sierra Madre Oriental and the city's proximity to the desert prevented sufficient moisture from reaching it. Weeks of hot, dry heat often ended abruptly in violent thunderstorms, just like the one I was now viewing from the comfort of my hotel bedroom. Enormous flickering branches of moon-colored lightning darted across the black sky, followed swiftly by terrifying thunder booms that made the walls shake.

Maestro knocked on my door and came inside, his gaze focuing immediately on the book I had in my hand.

"What's that you're reading?"

"A novel," I said. "Reading calms me before a performance."

"You should be reading books on technique, not that housewife rubbish Carmen reads. Mexico City is coming."

Maestro mentioned Plaza México's approach more often than a Buddhist monk chants mantras.

"I've just been told the other two apprentices won't be coming," he continued. "They're traveling from the south and all the major roads have been washed out."

I'd heard of corridas where only one fighter arrived to perform. It was a dream come true—I'd have all six bulls to myself. After Maestro left, I lay back in bed and visualized myself strolling around the arena time after time, lapping up the praise showering down on me from the dignitaries and spectators in attendance.

My vision of perfect happiness didn't last very long. Maestro interrupted my nap two hours later to inform me the governor of Tamaulipas had canceled the corrida on account of the weather. He closed by telling me, "I won't be dining with you and the cuadrilla this evening. I'm tired and ordered some food to be sent to my room."

The thunderstorm ended after four thirty and the sun came out. Not having fought in the bullring and bored with sitting in my room,

I disobeyed Maestro's rule about having a chaperone and went for a stroll. The streets hummed with folks taking advantage of the sharpness in the city air that lasts for only a brief time after a violent storm. People stared at me, mostly because my dark-red hair was still exotic to most, and, though it was still daylight and I wasn't nervous, I made sure not to make eye contact with any men I passed. I walked confidently, holding my head high and my shoulders squared.

Even the countless stray cats and dogs found in every Mexican city had emerged from the nooks and holes where they'd sought refuge from the storm. Cleansed of the grime and city dust, the flowers were so vibrant, they looked artificial. Street vendors had set up their carts and I purchased a peeled mango on a stick, its flesh so succulent the juice streamed down my chin as I ate.

In Plaza Miguel Hidalgo, a man inflated colorful balloons that he sold to the parents of excited children, which made me think of the baby growing quietly within me. I felt my belly, though there wasn't much to feel just yet. In three years, Julio and I would buy balloons for our child in a park like this. The thought didn't excite me and I felt a twinge of guilt that I still wanted to reach the top of my profession instead of simply being content to become a mother, like I supposed every other pregnant woman felt. Despite Julio's assurances that we'd be good parents, I also felt scared. What if I became like Mama, who had been distant since Daddy's death?

Cheerful music rose into the air from behind a row of mesquite and oaks. It came from an ornate bandstand across from a tall clock tower and I started toward it. As I left the line of trees to move closer to the brass band, I spotted Maestro and stopped dead. He sat on a park bench off to one side of the elevated bandstand, his arm slung around the shoulders of the flamenco dancer I'd seen at Don Raúl's *tienta*. As I watched, she turned to look at him and he kissed her. The act was so unexpected, so bizarre, I squeezed my eyes shut and then opened them quickly again, to make sure my mind wasn't playing tricks. Their mouths remained pressed together. I couldn't move. It was as if my feet were as deeply rooted in the earth as the trees I stood underneath.

I watched them cuddle, laugh, kiss, and whisper in each other's ears. I knew I should leave, but was a prisoner of my own morbid curiosity, in the way a passing driver stops to see the flashing lights of an ambulance at a roadside accident. You know how the story ends, but you're still compelled to watch. After they left the plaza, I followed automatically. Out on the street, Maestro walked faster. They went inside a hotel two blocks from the park.

As I stood staring at the lemon yellow entrance door, a memory rushed unexpectedly into my mind. I was eight and Daddy had taken me to visit the oilfield where he worked. I'd been fascinated by the orange-yellow flames shooting out one of the vents. On the way home, he'd stopped at a house I didn't know and told me to wait in the car. I'd watched him climb three steps to the porch and knock on the front door. A woman had answered and they'd talked, then she'd stooped and peered down at me sitting in the car. Her hair was long and the exact same color as Mama's. Daddy had stayed inside long enough for me to read two comics and color in three drawings in my sketchbook. When he'd finally returned, I'd folded my arms across my chest and asked why he'd been so long.

"I mended a broken water pipe for a man who works with me," he'd said.

"Is that his wife?"

"She is, Peanut."

"Her hair's like Mama's."

Daddy's hands had been on the steering wheel and his elbows had cracked like a whip as he'd straightened his arms. He'd kept them stiff as fence posts as he drove, and we hadn't talked anymore on the ride out of town.

The roof of our house and the soft brown slopes of the hills had appeared as Daddy turned the last bend. "We don't need to tell your mama about me stopping to fix that water pipe," he'd said as he'd pulled up to the door.

"Why not?"

"She'll pitch a hissy fit because I kept you late for your dinner," he'd said. "Let's keep it a secret." He'd winked.

I turned away from the hotel. I was dizzy and I felt sick. I was sure I'd faint. Mama's words ricocheted inside my head: *"I was trapped."*

A million other thoughts spun around my mind like a hurricane as I started back slowly to my own hotel: Mama trying to make life normal for me while she raged against my father; Mama cooking for me, but never joining me at the kitchen table, and fixing my hair when I didn't want her fussing; her horror on discovering I had only one friend to invite to my sixteenth birthday party, which turned into a frantic attempt to make me do things other girls liked so I'd fit in.

"But what could I do? I couldn't leave him because I had you to think about. I was trapped."

Daddy's image replaced her words. I saw us fishing at the tank, and me helping him pluck a turkey he'd reared for Thanksgiving. I was back in Mexico City with him, standing in line to get into my first bullfight and, later, taking the poster he got me as a souvenir. I heard his voice after I told him I wanted to be a bullfighter. After each of these moments spent with him, my father had left our home to go and have sex with another woman.

The same lips that kissed me had also kissed women who were not my mother. The arms that had held me had also held these women. All the years I'd looked up to him, that I'd thought him a perfect man, he'd betrayed Mama. Were the feelings he'd felt for me even genuine? Had he truly loved me, or was I an obligation? On the nights we'd discussed my dreams of fighting bulls, had he sat on my bed with half his brain thinking about me and the other half thinking about a woman he'd see later?

I thought about Carmen, content at home with her children, unaware. I thought about my father again, and how I'd thought

I'd known him one hundred percent, but I'd known nothing. Then Mama's face loomed again. When she'd discovered what he'd done, how dead had she felt inside? I'd behaved so badly when she'd tried to tell me the truth. We hadn't spoken since.

I rubbed my belly tenderly, then checked my watch. It was still only nine o'clock in Texas. I sprinted back to the hotel.

The raps on my door were insistent. I pulled myself up in bed and checked the clock on the nightstand. It was quarter after twelve.

"Señorita Boyd, are you awake?" a man said, and rapped again.

I leaped out of bed, put on my robe, and opened the door to find the night manager standing there.

"There's an urgent call for you in the lobby," he said.

We scuttled along the silent hallway. The old-fashioned phone lay on top of the reception desk, its worn handset beside the base. My blood curdled when I heard Julio's father's voice.

"Julio's been injured badly," Oscar said, his voice cracking. "He's in the hospital."

My face blazed. Beads of sweat burst from the pores. "Will he be okay?"

"He's asking for you."

The heavy rains had washed out the roads to the south of Nuevo Laredo. I could travel north to first cross the bridge into Texas and head south from there, but the journey would take twenty-four hours by car.

Oscar had apparently thought of that and nixed the idea. "Don Raúl's plane is already on its way for you," he said.

After telling me the whereabouts of a landing strip inside the city boundary, where the airplane would arrive in five hours, he hung up. I hurried back upstairs and found it much easier to face Maestro than

I'd anticipated. I informed him what had happened and that I needed him to drive me to the airfield. He smelled of liquor and attempted to hug me, but I pushed him roughly away and told him not to disturb me until it was time for us to leave.

35

ALTHOUGH THE HOSPITAL HAD ALLOCATED JULIO A PRIVATE room, I could still hear the nurses, dressed in starched blue and white uniforms, assisting patients in the general wards. Tethered to a drip, Julio looked so fragile, lying on the polished brass bed made up with crisp white linens.

His face seemed to have shrunken, the beautiful tanned skin turned ash-gray and his sparkling hazel eyes now dull and deeply sunken. The white scar on his eyebrow, a souvenir of the bullring and so endearing to me, appeared sinister now. When I pressed my lips to his, Julio's felt cracked and uncomfortably dry. His hands were clammy to the touch. His parents and an old priest I'd met when I'd stayed at the hacienda, his black suit so worn the fabric gleamed in the overhead lights, sat on the other side of the bed. Juanna wheeled a pair of jade rosary beads in her pale hands.

"Thank God, you've come," she said. She stood and hugged me fiercely. "I've been so afraid."

"He'll make a full recovery now," Oscar said, black raccoon rings encircling his eyes.

The priest acknowledged my arrival with a languid wave. He'd baptized both Julio and his sister, who, Juanna informed me, had gone to find a hotel and book rooms for the family and me.

Juanna pulled me gently aside. In a hushed voice, she explained there'd been two horn trajectories, in addition to the original puncture, because the bull had tossed him into the air. The horn had perforated Julio's intestine and a bacterial infection had set in that was being treated with penicillin. He'd also had blood transfusions, as an external artery had been nicked. The surgeon, inexperienced in treating such complex injuries, had managed to stanch the flow of blood, but my fiancé wasn't yet stabilized. This mystified the doctor, as he couldn't detect any other injuries. The hospital authorities were urgently trying to track down an experienced surgeon from Guadalajara, who was hiking with colleagues in the mountains.

"Mama." Julio took a little breath. "Mama."

His mother rushed back to Julio's side and cocked her ear to his parched lips.

"I want to speak to Kathleen alone," he said, his voice faint but audible.

"Of course, darling."

Juanna shepherded the priest and her husband out of the room. After they'd left, Julio stared at the ceiling without speaking. Thinking he'd drifted off, I checked to see if his eyes were shut. He grimaced as he turned his head toward me.

"I'm happy you're here."

I took his clammy hand. "No one could keep me away."

"I was a fool. This shouldn't have happened."

"The bulls are unpredictable."

"I didn't place the bull right." He grimaced. "I was between him and the fence."

He'd broken a cardinal rule, a rule all bullfighters learn in the first days of training. You never place yourself between the fence and the bull, as you then have no escape route should the bull lower its head and charge.

"I was too cocky," he said. "I believed El Cabrito could break the rules, like Belmonte, and get away with it." He grimaced again. "Now I'm going to pay the ultimate price."

My heart slammed against my rib cage. "Hush, Julio."

"The crowd at Plaza México will be so amazed at you, they'll cheer 'til your eardrums split. You'll win four ears and a tail . . . maybe even a hoof." He smiled wanly. "I'd cancel all my contracts for an entire year to be able to come and see you."

"A brilliant surgeon's coming to save you."

A sparkle came into his dull eyes, but his lips turned up in a ghostly smile. A terrifying smile.

"I want us to marry," he said.

"We will. After Plaza México, like—"

"Now." The hazel eyes dimmed and grew dull again. His voice grew fainter, the breathing labored. "I want you to be my wife. I want our child to know it had a mother and father who were married." The muscles on both sides of his mouth flickered. "I also want to call you my wife." His eyes slid to mine. "Please. I've waited for you to come."

My head felt too heavy to hold up. "Don't talk like this."

"Please, *mi amor*. You'll make me the happiest man in the world." He nodded toward the bedside table. "I had Mama bring my great-grandmother's wedding ring here. It came to me in her will."

I took the ring from the drawer. It was beautiful, with the family's crest etched in the center. But it was a size too big.

"It can be resized," he said, and smiled.

The priest returned and heard my confession. He'd already heard Julio's. His parents acted as our witnesses, while a pink-faced nun watched from the doorway, the white wimple and robes making her look like a hovering angel. There wasn't a full mass, only the exchange of vows and communion. We sealed our union with a kiss and everyone clapped softly, so as not to disturb the other patients.

I didn't feel any different after the ceremony. I'd always thought that a new me would emerge, that there was a sacred, invisible boundary the couple traversed during the marriage oath, that they emerged on the other side with some sort of unified knowledge and understanding of each other that only they could know. I'd thought unseen bonds would extend between Julio and me, locking us together permanently and making us truly one. That's what the church taught, that marriage made the man and woman one. I'd heard it since my Catholic elementary school. But after the priest's questions and our *I do*s, we were still separate. My health hadn't flowed into his body; he was still seriously ill in bed.

They gave us half an hour alone. We kissed, joined hands, and kissed again. His skin was still gray. New blood trickled into him from the glass container hanging over the bed.

"I love you," he whispered, his muscles still energetic enough to allow his eyes to roam my face.

"I love you, too. And I need you to get better. I need my husband."

He squeezed my hand feebly. I looked down at his fingers and wrist. Those same fingers and wrist just hours ago had wielded a cape and made it bloom like a great magenta flower, as he'd executed his beloved *reboleras*.

Early the next morning, while I was snatching an hour's sleep at the hotel, Julio died. The surgeon from Guadalajara arrived ninety minutes too late. A small artery deep inside Julio's groin had also been nicked, and his life and dreams trickled out of it.

His beautiful face was so peaceful when I arrived at the hospital, my hair mussed and dress heavily wrinkled from sleeping in it. His lips were still warm. I pressed mine against them for a long time and could not take in the reality that my husband could no longer feel me. Julio had fought the fiercest bulls. He had loved me and I had loved him, in every way lovers can. He was my husband. Now he no longer existed. He was dead, like the hundreds of bulls he'd killed.

I sat in the family chapel between Juanna, wearing a high comb and long mantilla, and Mama. My husband's casket lay on its mahogany bier, adjacent to the place on the altar where we'd have taken our vows, had he lived. The Virgins of Guadalupe and Macarena peered down at me from their plinths. I was a widow, but death had taught me quickly how to feel like a wife. I felt Julio's breath caress my cheek like a warm breeze. His laughter echoed inside my head. I heard the deepness of his voice when he teased me and felt desolate at the thought that I'd never experience it in this life again. I felt the touch of his assured hands on mine as he'd taught me the *rebolera* in the Los Pinos bullring. I saw him naked beside me after we'd made love in the meadow, the sun's rays turning the sparse silky hairs on his forearms to gold while our world grazed contentedly below us.

Mama patted me gently on the back when I pressed my damp hand-kerchief to my nose. I was grateful for her presence. Initially, the haci-enda's dignified opulence had shocked her. Momentarily forgetting I was grief-stricken, she'd gripped my arm and looked at me with her mouth as wide open as a *toril* gate. The news I was married had also shocked her, but she'd said nothing. I hadn't told her I was pregnant— it was not the time to talk about new life.

Only the blood family and I were present in the crypt beneath the chapel, including five of Juanna's relatives who'd arrived from Spain that morning and looked as if they needed sleep. Mama hadn't been invited and that was okay. She had never accepted the world of the bulls. The priest blessed the casket with holy water one final time and then it was slid into the vault. Like the three other vaults beside his, Julio's would be sealed with a slab of red-veined Spanish marble. The head of a fighting bull would be carved into it, to forever memorialize the matador he'd been. Later, his full name would be etched in gold leaf. I wondered if the vault beneath his would hold me one day. I wanted that very much.

Outside in the stark sunlight, Juanna asked me to join her and we went to the gazebo in the main plaza. The scent of climbing jasmine was cloying. I was tired and I didn't want to be in this place, where I'd been with Julio when I was happy.

Juanna raised her mantilla with both gloved hands and peeled it over her head. She looked gaunt.

"I was extremely angry with you and my son when I found out you'd had relations under my roof," she said, regarding my flat belly. "My husband, too. We brought Julio up properly." She looked up at the domed roof draped in tangled jasmine.

I said nothing. She'd get no apology from me.

Then she took my hand and squeezed firmly. "But I'm happy now, to know that my son will live on in this child. Will you still stay with me during your pregnancy?"

I squeezed her hand back in confirmation.

Before Mama left, I told her I was pregnant. She remained quiet and toyed with the handle of her purse before sliding it farther up her forearm.

"Are you angry?" I asked.

She cleared her throat. "I wish you had told me sooner. But I understand, given everything . . ." She looked past me toward the waiting car.

I put my arms around her and squeezed. "I'm not going to fight any more bulls."

Her expression remained solemn. "That's your decision," she said. Again, she cleared her throat. "You asked for my blessing once and I withheld it. I'm sorry for that. I'll support you in whatever you decide to do."

Up until Christmas, which I spent at the hacienda, I believed fervently I'd never enter the bullring again, as I'd told Mama. I refused to accept Maestro's telephone calls, which grew more frequent with each passing day. But after the fierce grief expended itself and the new year arrived, my thoughts came into a more orderly focus. On his deathbed, Julio had told me he'd have canceled a year of contracts to be able to come to my corrida in Plaza México, the jeweled bullring I'd been aspiring to since I first set foot on the sand. He was a professional and would be disappointed in, if not outright despise, my resignation.

When Maestro next called, I agreed to return home. Carmen's presence in the house had always been comforting, but made me anxious now. I loved her like a sister, but I was keeping terrible information from her that would change her life. Her calf-eyed sympathy for my loss crushed my heart. I always stiffened when she asked if there was something, anything, she could do to ease my grief, because I knew I would not be able to help with hers, if she learned the truth.

I took to reading in my bedroom. I used the flimsiest excuses to avoid eating with the family. When I did join them, I ate hurriedly and avoided conversation with Maestro entirely, as it felt artificial now. I loaded Carmen with excessive praise for her cooking, trying to heal wounds she didn't know she had. During our training sessions at the ring, I followed Maestro's orders as if I were an automaton, while a film reel of him walking through the streets of Nuevo Laredo with the flamenco dancer to her hotel spooled across my mind.

One evening, Carmen appeared in my room with a copy of the latest *Vogue*. I was cutting up my two lavender hats into small pieces and tossing them into the garbage pail. She set the magazine on the nightstand.

"Chiquita, what's wrong?" She sighed. "It hurts that you won't take me into your confidence. You do not play with the children, either. Fermin says you're also distracted at the bullring." Her eyes locked on mine, woman to woman. "Please tell me how I can help you."

I rose slowly and closed the door. I took her hand and led her to the bed and asked her to sit.

My voice trembled. "It's about your husband."

Her jaw slackened, but she didn't speak. I looked at the wall and took a deliberate breath.

"I've wanted to tell you for a long time but I've been afraid."

"Is he sick?" She laid her hands on my wrists.

"I saw—I saw him with another woman," I managed. "I'm sorry Carmen, but I felt you should know."

She let go of my wrists. The measured tick of my bedside clock grew loud in the silence, so loud it seemed to rebuke me.

"Fermin does this," she said. "I know he has other women." Her voice was curiously small, like a young girl, uncertain. "He has two other children. I found out by accident, years ago. His bank called about a problem and I examined the checks and accounts."

"He beats you, and now this," I said, growing angry. "Why don't you do something?"

"What can I do, chiquita?" She lifted up her hands, palms out. They were red from years of washing dishes and scrubbing floors. "He's never hurt me badly and provides very well for us. I have my children to raise and I could not provide for them if I were alone. Here, they live comfortably."

"Do you love him?"

"Not like before." She rose, still shaking her head. "But I don't hate him, either. I accept that he's a man. Men do this."

After she left, I lay in bed thinking about the similarity between Mama's and Carmen's circumstances. Both had been caught in the same trap. Mama gave up work she'd enjoyed, had stayed at home to be a loyal wife and raise me, but my father failed to keep his end of the agreement. Carmen stayed at home as a loyal wife, too. Would Julio have been one of these men if he'd lived? In my heart, I didn't believe so.

36

"KATHLEEN, WE NEED TO TALK ABOUT PLAZA MÉXICO AND WHAT happens after it," Maestro said, after the day's training session ended.

In one week, we'd travel to Mexico City for the corrida. I forced myself to look him in the eye.

"After the fight, we'll walk around the bullring, basking in the people's adoration. Mexico will respect us forever."

I looked across the bullring and said nothing.

"But afterward . . ." He sighed heavily. "It's very sad El Cabrito's gone, but we must be realistic. He was the only matador who agreed to be your godfather and welcome you to the rank of *matador de toros* at your *alternativa*. That won't happen now. Remember how hard it was to find someone to sponsor you to the union?"

I etched an arc in the sand with the tip of my shoe. To my right, a young apprentice who looked no older than fifteen caped a mechanical bull operated by his trainer. He was as eager as I'd been when I'd first trained here.

"It's not such a bad thing," Maestro said.

"That Julio died?"

"That you can't take the *alternativa*." He smiled. "But you can continue as an apprentice and make lots of money. The fees will double after your fight in Mexico City. We'll fight in the same bullrings and command the same fees as the most famous matadors. You just won't be one yourself." Maestro winked like we were best buddies. "And as I've said, that's not important. You'll still be adored and respected—and very rich."

Maestro had been a *matador de toros*, but was now, according to what Julio told me, terrified of the larger bulls. His feet danced faster than chattering teeth in front of them. He gave ground. As I looked at him, standing in his grubby overalls with his arms crossed, a thought dropped into its slot like the last piece of a complicated jigsaw puzzle. Maestro was talking about himself when he mentioned my appearance in Plaza México. This was all about him. He didn't care about me.

Patricio sprinted out of the *callejón* toward us. His face was bright red. "Fermin, come quickly."

"Can't you see I'm dealing with my pupil?"

"We're past that stage," I said immediately. "I'm no longer a pupil."

"It's the men," Patricio said.

"What about them?" Maestro asked.

"Luís and Agustín and one of the picadors have quit." Patricio turned to me. "They asked me to send their apologies to you, but they said Fermin must pay for everything he's done to them and now's the time."

Maestro charged toward the *callejón*.

When I reached the horse patio, Maestro was lying on the cobblestones near the exit. Blood rushed from his nose and he had a large bump on his forehead. I was happy to see he'd gotten the whuppin' he deserved, but anxious also. I no longer had a cuadrilla.

"Bastards," he said, wiping his nose with the back of his hand. "Luís is the brain behind this. I'll see he never works again."

Patricio caught my eyes and shrugged. He and I both knew that after word got around about how Maestro had cheated his men, they'd easily find work.

"I'll show them," Maestro continued. "Picadors are easy to find and I'll find two banderilleros by Wednesday."

He went to work after that and, as he'd said, it proved easy to replace the picador. Finding a good banderillero was more of a challenge. By Thursday, he still hadn't found anyone. When I asked, he snapped, "I'm working on it. You tend to your own work."

The following morning, he left during our training session and returned half an hour later with someone. About five-nine, like Maestro, slender, and deeply tanned with almond-shaped eyes, I recognized him immediately. He was the man I'd seen Maestro talking to in the *callejón* back when I'd been squaring my bull in Reynosa, when I'd gotten distracted and the bull's horns had shredded my jacket and grazed me.

"This is Bernardo," Maestro said.

"Fermin has told me how good you are," Bernardo said politely. "I'm pleased to meet you."

A massive feeling of dread came over me. He spoke fast, but I remembered the accent vividly. I'd never heard one like it until *that* night. The dread catapulted into fear and I took a step away from the men.

"Bernardo's going to serve as our banderillero."

I heard what Maestro said, but the words made no sense. I looked at him as if he were someone I'd never seen before.

"I know how important this corrida is and will not let you down, Señorita Boyd."

Did he think I didn't know who he was? Or did he not even recognize me? Summoning every morsel of composure, I looked at Maestro and said, "I need to speak to you."

"Let me see Bernardo out, first."

The man bowed slightly and I watched them cross the sand until they merged in a blur. A wave of nausea came over me. I bent over and vomited. Scalding bile set my throat on fire. When there was nothing more to jettison, I eased down, exhausted, on the sand. After I felt well enough, I went to the passageway to wait for Maestro.

"That man," I said, as he walked toward me. "I saw you with him in Reynosa. You told me he lived in Spain."

Maestro looked puzzled for a moment and then said, "Ah yes, I remember. But he returned to Mexico over two years ago. He lives in Reynosa now."

"I won't have him in my cuadrilla."

"You have no choice. Luís has been busy spreading gossip. No one else with Bernardo's talent will agree to come to Mexico City."

"You *must* find someone else."

"Bernardo's a friend."

"He *raped* me."

Maestro's expression froze, but only for a moment. "You're mistaken," he said. "Bernardo's married with four children. He'd never do that."

"It's him." My mouth was parched. My tongue felt like it had swollen to twice its size. "I recognize his strange accent. It's partly Spanish. That's why it confused me."

Maestro shook his head. "You're not a native speaker. It's easy to be confused."

"It's *him*."

Maestro swept back his oily bangs. "Let's not be hasty, Kathleen. This happened a long time ago. You're strong; you overcame it."

"I should go to the police."

"Why? Even if he did this to you, there's still no witness. You couldn't even remember his face. The police will say it's your word against his." He shrugged. "You're also a foreigner."

"Can't you place the banderillas in the bulls yourself?"

His eyes bulged. "I don't go to the Plaza México as a banderillero. I go as your manager and trainer."

I started shaking. I couldn't control my body. "I'm not going."

"The contract's signed. You're the main draw to fill the seats. If you don't fight, the impresario will sue. You'll be ruined."

I thought about what Sally had once said to me about professionals, how we couldn't choose when good or bad things happened to us. Julio had said the same.

"You're not thinking straight." Maestro laid both hands on my shoulders and squeezed. "Plaza México's what we've been working toward. After your appearance, you'll be famous throughout Mexico. Millions of people will love you and pay good money to see you." He smiled broadly. "Are you going to give all that up because of something that happened long ago, something from which you've recovered? I've always had faith in you. That's why I took you on." He paused, then added, "This isn't just about you. What about *me*? I've spent all my time and effort training you to dominate the bulls. I've made you into what you are today."

My mind threatened to explode. It all made horrid sense. Maestro cared about the money. He cared about domination. I was just his tool. He used me to dominate the bulls. I was dominating them for him. He'd trained me to be like him. This was why he demanded I make the passes exactly as he insisted. This was why he hated the flashy pass Julio had loved and taught me. This was the reason he demanded I use his sword. The sword he'd given me had been a gift to himself.

"Do you understand now, Kathleen?" he asked.

I forced a smile. "Completely, Maestro."

37

THE TRUMPET BLARED AND I QUICKLY DRANK THE LAST OF THE water and handed the glass down to Patricio. I hadn't anticipated the start of another bout of nausea just as I was about to enter the Plaza México, sandwiched between the two other apprentices appearing with me in the corrida. In the last week I'd suffered four bouts, two of which had resulted in dashes to the bathroom to be sick.

Both apprentices looked up at me sourly, as if they'd somehow telegraphed their thoughts to each other through my horse's massive chest. They were pissed. My presence threatened to diminish their sense of entitlement to both visibility and the crowd's adulation. First, I was making my debut into the ring on a pure white stallion. I'd been lukewarm about the stunt initially, but now relished it as a sort of prequel to the history I intended to make in this infamous bullring. Then, instead of folding my cape in the crook of my arm, as I always did, I'd slung it over my shoulders and draped the end over the horse's back, like Joan of Arc riding into battle. I'd also styled my hair in a chignon adorned with a huge scarlet rose. Maestro had demanded I plait my hair and exhibit the cloak in the traditional way, had even screamed at me in front of the other apprentices about it, but I'd refused.

Every seat in the forty-three-thousand-seat arena was filled. The rumble of spirited conversation emanating from the terraces was like distant thunder. As I exited the gate behind the costumed constables and started across the sand toward the judge's box, the band stopped playing the traditional Paso Doble and the crowd fell abruptly silent at the spectacle of their Texan Goddess on a blindingly white stallion. But they recovered quickly and began applauding and whistling. It felt now like a swarm of insects crawled beneath my scalp. Every part of me tingled and shivered, the ebb and flow threatening to make me faint and topple off the horse.

Only six years old and brutalist in its architectural style, the ring's wooden barrier fence had been freshly painted red. Behind the fence was the narrow passageway where the managers, agents, ring servants, media, and members of cuadrilla stood to watch the fight, then the ring of expensive shade seats, five rows deep, and finally, scores of gray concrete tiers rising precipitously toward the cotton-clouded sky, where four buzzards rode high in the air currents.

The previous evening, I'd stood outside the bullring with Sally, who'd agreed to come and help me after I told her about the hiring of Bernardo. We'd admired the plinthed sculptures of matadors sparring with bulls placed around the outer perimeter and the breathtaking herd of muscled, dangerous bulls following a rancher atop his rearing horse suspended above the main entrance gate.

My stallion genuflected in front of the judge on my command, a gentle tug on the reins and a slight kick on his right side. Any astonishment from the judge that I had ridden into the ring in such an unorthodox manner was masked by an impassive face.

I cantered over to the horse patio entrance, where I dismounted and handed over my mount to a waiting stable hand. Thirty-five minutes later, when my turn to fight came, I walked across the sand toward the red *toril* gate. I stopped when I got within twenty feet of it, knelt, and gripped my cape, holding it with both hands under my chin.

A moment later, I heard rapid footsteps behind me. Peering over my shoulder, I saw it was Maestro, as I'd anticipated. He was dressed in his emerald green suit of lights. He'd never before worn the suit during my performances.

"What the hell are you doing, Kathleen?" Maestro asked.

"*Faroles*," I said, referring to a flashy pass where the cape is flipped over and around the head as the bull charges by.

"But the team hasn't tested the bull. You don't even know which side he favors."

"Leave the ring," I said.

"Do *veronicas* like I've taught you."

The trumpet blared. A ring servant began to swing open the toril gate.

"Leave me to my bull, *Fermin*."

Maestro's jaws slackened. I turned away to stare into the black tunnel, but couldn't see the bull. Three seconds passed. Then, suddenly, a gray-and-white body burst out of the darkness. The bull was magnificent. Beautifully muscled in the front quarters, he was larger than any bull I'd ever fought. I couldn't believe a four-year-old could be this size. His hump was as big as a five-year-old's, at least, and he possessed a set of straight, white horns that gleamed in the sunlight. The sign above the *toril* gate stated his name was Emperador. He skidded to a stop, looked around the arena, and then took three strides toward me.

"This bull looks mature," I shouted, glancing over my shoulder at Maestro. He was backing away rapidly, his splayed hands held out in front of him like shields.

"Haven't you always wanted to be treated equal to a matador?" he said. "I picked him so we will prove you're as good as them."

I flicked my cape to attract the bull's attention. Maestro reversed faster and slipped into the passageway. Emperador's hot eyes pierced me.

Instinctively, I laid my hand on my belly and patted it twice. What I was about to do was very dangerous, but Julio was watching over us—the baby and me—and I was determined no harm would come to our child. Before, I hadn't cared whether the child was a boy or girl, but now I hoped for a son. With his birth, my darling Julio would never be dead.

"Hey, *toro*, hahahahaha," I hollered, to incite a charge. "Hahaaaaa, *toro*."

The bull pawed the sand, but didn't move.

"*Toro*, haaaahaaahahahaha."

He started toward me like an airplane thundering down a runway. Closer and closer he came, head lowering to the same level as my chest in preparation to spear and obliterate his enemy. Thick wads of saliva flew like quicksilver from his mouth. When Emperador was just about two feet away, I swung the cape over my head from the left side to the right. The end of the cape ballooned and the bull's enormous head and then his body followed, as he tried to hook the cloth, the acrid smell of his breath filling my nostrils. His left horn passed just inches from my eye, far closer than I'd intended. The crowd groaned with relief. I remained on my knees and executed the *farole* pass again, as the huge creature thundered again within a foot of my face.

The crowd grew delirious. The brass band played dianas. But there would be no prizes for me at the end of this fight. This time, I would not walk around the bullring to soak up the adulation.

After climbing back to my feet and performing three sets of *veron-icas*, ending each series with the *rebolera* pass Julio had taught me instead of making the *media-veronica* that Maestro required, I left the ring to allow first the picadors and then the rapist Bernardo to do their work. I'd had to accept Bernardo in my cuadrilla if my plan was to work, but it was bitter knowing he'd never be punished for the evil he'd done to me. How many other women throughout Mexico, throughout America, throughout the world, had to endure this kind of torturous acceptance? Having Sally helped me deal with the rage I felt, and I simply refused to acknowledge the barbarian's presence. I'd warned Maestro earlier that I did not want to see the man's face until he was ready to perform his work in the bullring.

"You pull *no* more cheap stunts like that," Maestro said, handing the longest pair of flame red-and-yellow barbs to the monster. Bernardo slipped out of the passageway and took his position behind the wooden shield, waiting until the second picador finished lancing the bull.

As I watched the rapist walk toward Emperador, I whispered a prayer to the Virgin that she'd cause him to make a mistake and he'd be gored, that his death would be slow and bloody.

"Do exactly what I say in the third act and the people will love us," Maestro said.

"They love me already, Fermin."

Like before, his mouth fell open. He shook the other two pairs of barbs in the air. "You've no permission to call me by my name. Don't get ideas above your station because of where you are. You're here only to make perfect art with the bull."

"If I fail, my shame is your shame," I replied. "Isn't that right, Fermin?"

He didn't reply. Crow's-feet at the outer corners of his eyes deepened as his face became a mask of anger. I was certain he'd have struck me if he could have gotten away with it.

"I can't bear to watch that monster," I said, and walked away.

He couldn't follow, as he had to pass the remaining pairs of banderillas over the fence to the rapist when he needed them. Quickly, I met with Sally, and we exited the passageway and sprinted to the women's lavatories. It stank of stale urine and large flies buzzed noisily as they zoomed by my head. All the cubicles were occupied. Sally took my carefully folded new suit out of a canvas bag I normally used to hold extra capes.

Hurriedly, I pulled off my riding boots, shucked my old jacket and pants, and put on the new Andalusian suit. I'd had the waist made one inch wider in case my stomach grew, which luckily hadn't been necessary. The jacket of the *traje corto* was much stiffer, but fit snugly. Even in the low light oozing in from two overhead windows, the suit winked and sparkled. My old tailor had balked at the alterations and had agreed to do them only when he saw the determination in my eyes.

"I don't know why male matadors don't wear something comfortable like this when they fight instead of those tight pants and pink stockings," Sally noted as she walked around me, fussing over the jacket. She tucked in loose strands of my hair and readjusted the clip attached to the scarlet rose. "You look beautiful. They'll eat you up."

A mother and her child entered the lavatory. When they saw me, the woman clasped her hand over her mouth. After I'd signed her program, Sally and I raced back to the *callejón* just as Bernardo was returning from placing the last barbs into the bull's withers. When Maestro saw me, his head whipped back and then he reached out quickly to grab the top of the wooden barrier fence to stop himself dropping to the ground.

"Have you gone mad?" he said. "You can't wear that. Only matadors wear the *traje de luces*."

"It's not a suit of lights," I corrected him. "This is still a *traje corto*."

Either disbelieving what he saw or desperate to find truth in my words, his eyes roamed my body again, taking in the hundreds of winking black sequins and twin golden embroidered stripes sewn on the outside of my pants legs and bolero jacket. Elaborate flowers made of golden thread were also embroidered on the sleeves and back of the jacket. Before he could pitch a full hissy fit, I left the passageway, slipped through the opening in the wooden shield, and entered the ring as the trumpet sounded to start the final *tercio*. I met the rapist on his way back to Maestro.

"I hope my performance pleased you," he said.

I met his smug gaze. "I wanted the bull to kill you."

His face turned white.

"Don't expect payment for this," I continued coldly. Seeing his confusion, I prodded him, "Don't you remember me from Los Pinos?"

A look of crazed panic crossed his face, and then he started running toward the *callejón*. That would have to be my justice.

I closed my eyes briefly and banished all thoughts of him. Ignoring tradition, I didn't approach the judge to request permission to kill the bull. Instead, I walked up to Emperador, jiggling the muleta as I drew nearer.

The crowd whistled, applauded, and screamed. They didn't care that I wore sequins.

"*Hermosa, mi gringa dorada,*" hollered a silver-haired gentleman seated off to my right. "*Cásate conmigo.*"

"No, not him," an American man called in response. "Marry me! I'm Texan, like you."

My handsome bull was like silk. He charged in straight lines, like a bullet when he passed by my body. I started, as is traditional, by holding the muleta elongated by the sword in my right hand, executing three series of *derechazos* that required me to precisely time the movement of the muleta, not moving it so fast the bull would go for my legs or so slow Emperador would step on the cloth, and ending each with *media-veronicas* that fixed the bull in place like a statue. Knowing I had just ten minutes to irretrievably win the crowd's heart, I switched the muleta to my left hand and commenced a series of *naturales*.

With each pass, I brought the bull closer and closer to my body until the breath expelled from his nostrils was as loud as I remembered the engine of Don Raúl's airplane when we'd sped along the grass strip at his ranch. Emperador and I merged, his massive bulk twisting around my waist, as I performed first one pass and then another in the opposite direction in such rapid succession that he completed a full circle around my body. The crowd screamed deliriously.

The feel of Emperador's course, wiry hair against my chest was at once exhilarating and terrifying. I gave him his exit and he raced ten yards away, turned, and came to a stop.

"It's time," Sally hollered from the passageway.

I'd asked her to warn me five minutes before it was time to kill the bull or risk getting a warning blare of the trumpet. Ending the series of passes with a *remate* that temporarily fixed the bull, I went quickly to the fence, where Sally handed me Maestro's old sword.

"You're magnificent," Maestro said, clearly having forgiven my insubordination.

"Come, Maestro," I said, the deference necessary to coax him out nearly making me choke.

"Why?"

"Listen to them." I looked slowly around the stadium. "You're my teacher. Come out and greet the people properly."

He wasn't sure how to react to the unorthodox request and looked quickly up and down the passageway. The bull unfroze and trotted over to a spot in front of the *toril* gate, his *querencia*.

"Hurry, or they'll blow the trumpet."

In an instant, he was beside me. I took his hand and walked up to the judge's box where I bowed. Maestro bowed, too. The judge waved a white handkerchief, giving permission to kill the bull.

When I got twenty feet from the bull, who still stood rigid, watching us, I let go of Maestro's hand and waved at the crowd, turning in a slow, full circle.

"Wave, Maestro. They know now that you're the matador who trained their Texan Goddess."

I took a step away from Maestro and lifted both my arms slowly toward him as if offering him up to the crowd. A roar surged from the audience and they rose off their seats. Maestro walked in a small circle, waving madly, with a huge smile on his face.

"This is what you've wanted, isn't it?" I said over the roar of the crowd.

He was so caught up in the adulation he didn't hear me, just continued to wheel in a tight circle and wave. His smile nauseated me. I went to him and quickly placed the sword and furled muleta in his hands.

"The bull's waiting for you," I told him.

Maestro's body stiffened.

"You've taught me everything and deserve your due," I said insistently. "Finish Emperador. He's my gift to you."

I began walking away. Unsure what was taking place, the roar and applause weakened.

Maestro scuttled up behind me. "Don't make a spectacle of yourself. The bull's yours to kill."

"I've gifted him to you. Just like you gifted your sword to me. Look how tired he is. He's panting and hasn't moved. I've taken the fight out of him. Go see to him."

"I don't want to."

The crowd was quiet now. A trumpet blared in the silence. I was now officially warned. I stopped and turned quickly to Maestro.

"Are you afraid?" I asked.

His chest expanded like a puffer fish and his eyes flashed with rage. "How can you say such a stupid thing?"

"Julio fired you because you're a coward. Take your sword and prove to me—to Mexico City—that you don't give ground."

The crowd began to boo and toss their shoes into the bullring. How fickle they were—one moment they worshipped and the next despised. Maestro grabbed the muleta and sword and took three steps toward the bull, but stopped abruptly and turned back.

"This is a big misunderstanding," he said. "You and I have come too far. We'll talk after the corrida. I'll even consider a small drop in my percentage." His eyebrows lifted. "What do you say?"

"Kill Emperador."

"It's your professional duty to finish it off," he said, and tossed the muleta on the sand. "Not mine."

The judge and his assistants were on their feet now.

"I order you to kill your bull," Maestro said, his voice rising. "You risk disgracing us, if you don't."

"I take no more orders from you."

"You'd be nothing without me," he replied.

"El Cabrito was right." I shook my head slowly. The jeers grew louder. "How can you stand in this bullring dressed in a matador's suit? You've got no right to wear gold trim anymore. You're a coward."

"You ungrateful bitch! Americans can't be trusted. I should have known their women are the same."

"You're a coward who cheats on his wife and beats her."

His head snapped back.

"You told me you're like my father," I said. "It's true. My father betrayed my mother, just like you have Carmen."

"That is not your business."

"You're weak and yellow, and the whole of Mexico knows it now." I took the sword from his hands. "You're fired."

Turning in a full circle with the sword raised in the air, I acknowledged the spectators, who'd stopped booing and were curious again. I shuffled toward Emperador, still in his safety zone, his gray tongue dangling out of the side of his mouth because he'd lost so much blood and was mad with thirst. He stood with his front hoofs together, which meant the death-notch was fully open. A huge shiver rocked his muscular body as I came to a stop within ten feet of him.

I raised my sword to sight. He shivered again. I looked deep into the bull's dark eyes and knew instantly what he was thinking. We were the same, Emperador and I. This was his moment of truth, too. He was terrified, in the exact way I'd been terrified the night I was raped. Adrenaline may have stopped him from experiencing great physical pain, but terror was equally excruciating. Emperador stood exhausted in his safe place, not because of any comforting smell or because he'd first emerged into the ring from the *toril* gate, like the journalists, matadors, and aficionados said. My heart jolted and then began to pound urgently. My lovely bull stood in his *querencia* because he was terrified of me; he felt safe only in this one place. Julio had been my safe place and now he was gone forever. I had no *querencia* anymore. But I needed to go on. I had to, to honor him.

I dropped the sword and muleta on the sand. I'd fought to become a professional matador, fought to make art with bulls, fought to win the adulation of the crowd and journalists. But, in a rush, I realized that none of it was important. Soon I would have Julio's child to raise, an art I would practice as perfectly as the art I was leaving.

Breaking every rule of safety, I turned around from the bull and walked away. The people started to boo and hiss. But they had it entirely wrong. I was not abandoning everything I'd worked and sacrificed for out of repulsive fear like Fermin. I was not retreating like he had. I was advancing. I was advancing to find a new *querencia* for my and Julio's child.

The trumpet blew shrilly to indicate I'd contravened the official rules, a crime under Mexican law. Several men raced into the ring and engaged the bull so he wouldn't charge and gore me. Moments later, two constables in their feathery plumed hats arrived and seized me by the arms. They marched me roughly across the sand and up the wooden steps to the judge's box.

"You must kill your bull," the judge said. "That's the law."

"Spare Emperador, Your Excellency," I said. "He's brave and beautiful. Wave your green handkerchief and spare him."

His narrow, brown-purple lips pulled tight and he flicked his gaze to the constable on my left. "Take her to the jail."

The guard didn't speak as he led me out to the grubby reception with its low ceiling, battered furniture, and naked lightbulbs. I'd been incarcerated in the tiny, dank cell at the police station for four hours with only feeble scratching sounds within the wall and a black, long-legged spider and her hundreds of tiny offspring for company. When I emerged, Sally was waiting on a long wooden bench opposite the reception counter.

"Where'd you get the bail money?" I asked, as we negotiated past people in the narrow hallway. It smelled as foul as the gymnasium at the Los Pinos bullring.

"Yankee friends come through when you're in a bind," she said.

Outside on the street, the sun blinded me. I stopped and closed my eyes tightly, and when I opened them again, life unfurled before me as it always did. Men, women, and children strolled past us. Diners checked menus posted in restaurant windows. Church bells pealed. Buses picked up waiting passengers. Taxis and cars honked in irritation. It was as if nothing illegal had happened in their beloved bullring.

Sally peered ahead for a moment. "Do you remember Garza?" She laughed. "That time we fled from the bullring and ran along the streets. We were frightened the police would chase after us."

"I was naive then. I didn't understand anything about the world of the bulls."

Sally turned to me. "Come to New York. You can have the baby there."

I rubbed my belly in delicate circles. "Julio would want his mother to know her grandchild," I said. "Maybe I can come later on."

When I took away my hand, she placed hers where mine had been and rubbed gently, too. We looked at each other and laughed. New lives were beginning: the life of my and Julio's child, and my own. I grasped Sally's hand and we started to run. People gave ground as we charged down the street. We charged in the fierce Mexican sun.

acknowledgments

THANKS TO MARGARET O'CONNOR OF INNISFREE LITERARY and editor Katie McGuire, and all the other folks at Pegasus Books who worked diligently to help make this book a reality. To Terin Miller for his generous advice about the world of bullfighting. To Patricia McCormick—the first professional female bullfighter in North America—whose life was the inspiration to write this novel. To Ernest Hemingway for his copious writings on the subject. To Jeanne Denault and Marie Lamba from my writer's group, as well as Chris Bauer, David Jarret, John Wirebach, and Russ Allen. Thanks, too, to my family and friends for their encouragement. To my mother and late father for raising me to become what I am. And last but by no means least, to Larry Caban for his love and support.